Born Under a Lucky Moon

Born Under a Lucky Moon

DANA PRECIOUS

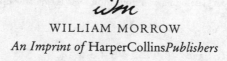

WILLIAM MORROW
An Imprint of HarperCollins*Publishers*

BORN UNDER A LUCKY MOON. Copyright © 2011 by Dana Precious. All rights reserved. Printed in the United States of America. No part of this book may be used or
reproduced in any manner whatsoever without written permission except in the case
of brief quotations embodied in critical articles and reviews. For information address
HarperCollins Publishers, 10 East 53rd Street, New York, NY 10022.

HarperCollins books may be purchased for educational, business, or sales promo-
tional use. For information please write: Special Markets Department, HarperCollins
Publishers, 10 East 53rd Street, New York, NY 10022.

FIRST EDITION

Designed by Diahann Sturge

Library of Congress Cataloging-in-Publication Data is available upon request.

ISBN 978-0-06-187687-5

11 12 13 14 15   OV/RRD   10 9 8 7 6 5 4 3 2 1

Dedicated to
Gus and Martin Gueulette
and
Sylvia Precious

Acknowledgments

With love for
Ralph Precious, Randy Precious,
Kristina Martinez-Precious, Lisa Precious,
Lori Precious, and Julie Precious

In appreciation of
Carrie Feron, my amazing editor at William Morrow,
Nancy Yost, my literary agent at Nancy Yost Literary Agency,
who believed in me,
and Jane Cavolina, who helped to show me the way

Many thanks and deep appreciation to the people who advised or helped me in getting to the next step, in the many steps, leading to this novel:

Betsy Amster, Esther Aronson, Rich Barber, Tom Biggs, Todd Brock, Dick Buckley, Shannon Buckley-Newell, Julie Curtis, Steve Erickson, Jill Green, Dani Kollin, Cheryl Lodinger, Jessica Rich, Jeffrey Stewart, Steve Stone, and Anna Termine

Born Under
a
Lucky Moon

Prologue

*A*ll roads in my hometown lead to water. I used to think they were all dead ends.

It is a four-block-wide bit of land with one main road, Ruddiman, running its length. From this road, every other road marches off in strict perpendicular fashion to stop abruptly at Muskegon Lake or, on the other side, Bear Lake. Ruddiman does get a good running start before it hits Lake Michigan a few miles down.

I grew up at the end of one of these roads. Almost everyone I knew lived at the end of one of these roads. I was always ping-ponging between points, hoping that I would not be stopped short by a body of water.

Evan, my brother, was the first one of us to leave the house and its surrounding lakes. He moved one half mile across Bear Lake where the roads sweep all the way north to the Upper Peninsula, Canada, and beyond.

My three sisters, Elizabeth, Sammie, and Lucy, found themselves on the West Coast. Like salmon swimming upstream by sheer instinct, they are still blinking, I think, wondering how they arrived in such a place so far from home.

With equal lack of thought or planning I took a path that ultimately led me across the Causeway to Chicago, and then west to Los Angeles. There, people spoke only of New York and Los Angeles and waved a vague hand at all of those square states in between. They referred to the Great Lakes as though they were mud holes George Washington could pitch a silver dollar across. When I moved to L.A. and people asked where I was from—because no one is really from L.A.—I would hold up my right hand like I was being sworn in. I would point to my hand, which all Michiganders know as the shape of our state.

"I'm from here," I'd say, indicating a place on the side of my hand just above the Headline and below the Line of the Children. I quickly learned to stop doing this after people looked at me as though I might rub off.

I moved to L.A. simply because Elizabeth and Sammie were already there and it didn't occur to me that I could move some-where else on my own. Beautiful Elizabeth had moved to L.A. to help plan a national political event. The spotlight always found Elizabeth, and suddenly she was appearing in the gossip pages looking polished and confident on the arm of this or that politician or movie star. I flipped through the magazines—how wondrous that someone to whom I was actually related was in them.

Elizabeth's behavior bemused my parents. My dad is a county administrator in Muskegon, which is a nonpartisan job. He spent his life riding the political fence so that he would continue to have support from both parties on the county commission. Without it, he would be flat ass out of a job. The process exhausted him though and he learned to fully hate politics. I think it ticked Dad off that Elizabeth went blindly into one political party.

It would have annoyed my parents even more if they had realized she had really moved to L.A. to chase a much older man with whom she had fallen—sincerely but briefly—in love.

My sister Sammie had followed Elizabeth to escape marriage to a nice Polish-Italian guy who had aspirations of being the foreman at the Howmet factory. She didn't have anything against factory work. Sammie just longed for something different. She could have just as easily wound up in New York or Prague or Tokyo. She went where the wind blew her. Her real name is Stephanie, but when Lucy was learning to talk she couldn't say that so she called her Sesame. When I was learning to talk I couldn't say Sesame so I called her Sammie. Sammie once climbed Mount Kilimanjaro all by herself. Well, not entirely by herself—there were guides and other intrepid tourists with her.

When Lucy and I were born, one after the other, Mom and Dad basically threw us on the pile of other kids. They had started out strong with the discipline and guidance of Evan, but that started to wane as each new baby appeared. Mom said she and Dad got more relaxed about being parents, but personally I think they were just tired. So we grew up with a kind of loving, benign neglect. Lucy, however, longed for more structure. She eventually ran off and joined the army, searching for adventure matched with firm regulations.

Then there's me. I'm not sure how I can describe myself. It's like the way you never see yourself in a mirror the way other people see you. You see exactly opposite. I think I'm the slower, steadier type. Unlike Elizabeth, I never figured the world would hand me anything on an abalone caviar spoon. And unlike Sammie, I was too pragmatic and fearful not to try and control my destiny. So I worked hard and stumbled my way out of a tiny midwestern town and up a corporate ladder by sheer instinct, luck, and hard work.

Growing up in my family was a free-for-all. We weren't delinquents, although if we had been kids of a different kind, we might have wound up that way. All five of us managed to find our place in the world. But while we lived together, life was chaos mixed with unexpected complications. We attracted drama as surely as lightning will find the lone tree in a field.

This is just one story of my family. It starts with a long-planned wedding on a Saturday, followed by a surprise wedding on Sunday. It ends with a murder and a sex scandal.

Like every relationship in every family, this story doesn't reside in the black and white of right and wrong. It resides in the gray area called love.

ART I

The Proposal
2006

The Weddings
1986

One

January 2006

*J*eannie, there's a problem," my assistant, Caitlin, said calmly. "She won't come out of her trailer." The photographer and I jerked our heads up from studying the lighting on the test shots. The "she" was the star of the movie. The photographer looked at me. We both knew this one was my problem, not his. He got paid fifty thousand dollars a day just to snap photos, not deal with unreasonable, egotistical, or just plain psychotic movie stars. That was my job. I'm an executive at a major film studio, Oxford Pictures, and I handle the advertising. This means I head up teams of people to create the movie trailers, television spots, and posters.

I was in the middle of a photo shoot for Oxford Pictures' *Heaven Is in the Wind.* It was a dog of a film and we all knew it. I could just see the review headlines now: "It blows." But that didn't matter. Opening weekend of a picture is the marketing executive's responsibility. After that, it stands or stumbles on its own merits. But an audience initially goes to a film based on the advertising and publicity. So while I didn't make the films, it was my job to sell them to an unsuspecting public.

Right now, I was attempting to get photos of the damn star, Nikki Strong, so we could create a poster. And, as usual, Nikki Strong was not cooperating.

"Okay, where's her publicist?" I asked Caitlin. Although we spoke in quiet tones, it was a calm neither one of us felt. It had taken months just to nail down a date for this photo shoot, then another month to get the star to agree to a photographer, all while the studio pressed me to make it happen.

"She's at two o'clock and bearing down on you," Caitlin said in my ear. "And you have the director of *TechnoCat* on hold on line one, the producer of *Sheer Panic* on line two, your iPhone just beeped with some emails from the studio, and a messenger delivered a bunch of paperwork you have to sign and return ASAP." I nodded, feeling that tightening in my stomach that happens when it seems that I can only keep up if I run at a dead sprint all day and all night. I have that feeling pretty much all the time.

"Oh, and your sister Sammie called and wants you to call back as soon as you can," Caitlin called over her shoulder as she whisked away to check on the special catering that had been ordered for Nikki—no carbs, no fats, no pepper, salt, cheddar cheese, or brown M&M's.

The publicist stormed up to me and thrust a bottle in my face. "Where is it? I demand to know why you don't have the Belgian water that Nikki drinks. I won't let her come out of that trailer until she has it! No Nikki, no shoot!" I looked this ranting woman straight in the eye. This shoot day was costing about $125,000. No matter how much I had to beg, squeeze, cajole, or threaten people, it had to happen. A publicist, on the other hand, is hired by the star to handle things like appearances on Jay Leno or in

People. They spin the press when "their star" is caught doing something like mating with a donkey. (*He was only* petting *it. Don't believe the photos. Did I tell you how much of a humanitarian he is? Every cent he makes goes to the ASPCA.)*

They are also responsible for working with the likes of me on photo shoots. Most of the publicists are pretty nice, but this one was on the verge of being fired by Nikki Strong, her meal ticket. The gossip was all over town and, worse, all over the industry blogs. I took the bottle and studied the label. Then I looked at my clipboard, which had the list of the star's "needs" for the shoot. This very publicist had emailed it to me personally. I had checked and double-checked it. "There is no mention of Belgian water on your list," I said in my sweetest voice.

Caitlin came up behind me. "Perhaps if you tell me where I can buy it I can send someone for it."

"You moron! You buy it in Belgium. You would have had to ship it here two days ago via FedEx." Desperation had crept into the nasty tone of her voice. She snatched the clipboard out of my hands and studied the list. The water wasn't mentioned.

Caitlin's face didn't register the name-calling. She just whispered, "We've lost an hour between this water thing and the makeup artist being late. That means you have to kill two shots. Want me to talk to the art director about it?" I gave an imperceptible nod without turning from the frantic publicist and Caitlin glided away. The publicist sagged on the Philippe Starck couch and leaned against the purple wall. She knew the water wasn't on the list. I sat beside her. "Let's work this thing out. How many bottles do you have with you?"

"Just this one," she croaked. "Nikki said she wouldn't come out unless there are twelve." Ah, I thought. There's the truth. The publicist had said that she wouldn't let Nikki come out, but it was really Nikki being unreasonable. The publicist had made a little power play so it would look like she was in charge, but nope.

Now, I could have marched up to Nikki's trailer and nicely explained that we didn't have the water and asked her if perhaps another water would do for her. But that's not the way it works. The trick is never to let the talent have an excuse not to show up on set. If I admitted that we didn't have the water, I would be at the mercy of the pampered star. You might expect Nikki to be reasonable and say, "Of course. Don't be silly. I'll drink tap water and be right out there on set in a jiffy." But chances were pretty good that she would really say, "This is unacceptable! I'm taking these scented candles and that case of Cristal champagne and this cute makeup man and going home!" Then the studio would be out all the money we had spent on the shoot. But, more importantly, I wouldn't have the photos for the poster. While Oxford Pictures will forgive a cost overrun, it will never forgive the movie advertising being late.

I looked at the bottle shape. It looked like a bottle of Evian except for the label. I signaled Caitlin to get the ad agency art director. He bounced up to me with a smile that quickly faded when he saw the publicist's face.

"Do you have a computer and printer here?" I asked him.

"Yeah," he said warily.

"What about a scanner?"

"No, but I could get one here in ten minutes."

"All right, this is what you are going to do," I said. "Gently, and I do mean gently, peel this label off the bottle. Then scan it and print out twelve copies." The art director nodded. I turned to Caitlin but she had already anticipated me.

"I'll get twelve identical bottles," she said and walked off. She called over her shoulder, "I told the director of *TechnoCat* you would call back but he had a hissy fit. He's still on hold. The producer of *Sheer Panic* said he'll phone back in an hour. Oh, and that guy who stars in *Jet Fuel* left you a message."

I felt my colon twist again. There was never enough time to take care of everyone. I felt like a kindergarten teacher. No parent cares that you have twelve other kids to deal with besides their precious Jane or Johnny. And no film director or producer wants to know you're handling any other movie than their own.

The art director reaching for the Belgian water bottle brought me back to the here and now. I hung on to it fast. "Can you give us just one sec?" I asked the art director. He moved out of earshot.

"Here's the deal," I told the publicist as I patted her hand. "You're going to have to do one thing that you're going to hate before any of that bottle-making can happen."

She lifted an eyebrow.

"You're going to apologize to Caitlin for calling her a moron."

"Who's Caitlin?"

I couldn't believe it. Caitlin had been speaking to this publicist on the phone fifteen times a day for months. "She's my assistant."

"I'm not apologizing to an *assistant*."

What a bitch! I stared at her. Then I called her bluff. I handed her back the bottle, stood up, and walked away. I thought she wasn't going to do it. Nobody in Hollywood apologizes for anything. You will never hear the words "I'm sorry" because this indicates fault, and nobody is ever at fault in Hollywood. I had taken four steps before I heard, "Okay, I'll do it."

Caitlin was on the other side of the room talking urgently to a caterer. I assumed she was telling them to get the bottles. Catching her eye, I motioned for her to come over. The publicist didn't even look up as she breathed, "I apologize for calling you a moron."

"I accept your apology," Caitlin said promptly, then turned on her heel and went back to the caterer. I patted the publicist's hand again. Then I handed off the bottle to the art director and ran to pick up line one.

"Do you realize you have kept me waiting for almost four minutes?" a familiar nasal voice rang in my ear.

"I'm so sorry," I said, trying not to pant from running, "I was in the bathroom." That's a pretty fail-safe answer because nobody can dispute it and nobody particularly wants details.

"I want to talk to you again about the marketing strategy for *TechnoCat*. I don't understand why the studio thinks we should downplay Cat's mother dying of cancer. It's a timely issue. People will flock to see that."

I had serious doubts that anyone would flock to see a movie about cancer on the Fourth of July weekend, or on any other weekend. But I couldn't say that. "Well, Stripe"—I shook my head to myself every time I had to say his absurd name—"this is a film with big special effects, huge action, a love story, and it's based on the most beloved newspaper comic strip of our time. The cancer is just a minuscule portion of the story."

"But it's pivotal. It's what gives TechnoCat her strength and angst. We have to portray that!"

"But we're targeting our primary advertising to people from the ages of thirteen to thirty-four. There are more exciting ways to drive them to a theater than to talk about cancer." I held the phone to my ear with my shoulder while the art director handed me the phony water labels. I looked at them and nodded and the art director darted off.

I tuned back in to the voice in my ear. "I'm not stopping until I get the trailer I want! And the trailer I want focuses on cancer. I'm calling the president of marketing *and* the chairman of the studio and telling them you are being uncooperative!" The phone slammed in my ear. Be my guest, Stripe, I thought. The studio knew that *TechnoCat* had to open to at least sixty million dollars to make its money back. They would not support the cancer approach to marketing.

But I also knew that they wouldn't directly tell him that. No, I knew I was going to be told to cut a cancer-ridden trailer so that boundless amounts of money could be spent on research. This research would prove what the studio knew all along: that not too many people would race to see a movie about cancer. But it deflected a confrontation with a valuable director and the director could then blame the appropriate party: the audience.

I sighed but was happy to see twelve Belgian-labeled bottles, filled with Evian water, sitting proudly on the catering table. Caitlin was in charge of making sure nobody, but nobody, touched the bottles except for Miss Nikki Strong. I checked my watch. Only seventeen minutes had elapsed. Not bad.

I reviewed the photo shoot list I had meticulously planned out over the past week. It had every detail of the day listed down to the minute. Shot one: Headshots (happy) 10:00 a.m. Shot two: Headshots (sad) 10:15 a.m. And on and on. After confirming we hadn't lost one of the crucial poses, I finally took a break. All we could do now was wait for the star to come on set. Caitlin sat down next to me and checked her BlackBerry.

"Hey." She nudged me while looking at an email. "Looks like Katsu got that promotion." I barely looked up from my own emails. Katsu Tanaka was another creative advertising executive at Oxford Pictures. He was a few ranks below me and worked on the smaller-budgeted films. I didn't pay him much attention.

"Yeah, he's been bucking for senior vice president for a while now. I heard it was finally going to happen."

"He didn't get SVP, Jeannie," Caitlin said. "This press release says he got executive vice president."

"What?" I snatched her BlackBerry to see for myself. No way had Katsu skipped up two levels to EVP. That was unheard of. Furthermore, it meant he was now my equal. I studied the press release. How the hell had this happened? It wasn't like Katsu had done anything spectacular for the studio—which meant he had formed allies in high places who were helping him with a meteoric rise. Working at a studio is a lot like playing chess. Most everyone is a player and trying to maneuver into a better position. I realized with a sinking feeling that somehow I hadn't noticed a few crucial moves.

Before I could dwell on the situation, Nikki finally arrived on set. She blew air kisses on either side of the photographer's face and ignored the studio people. I saw her eyes narrow and move to the water. She was making sure that we had jumped through the proper hoops for her. After all, she was the third most powerful female star in America, wasn't she?

"Would you like some water, Miss Strong?" Caitlin inquired.

"No water today. I want a Diet Coke with two cubes of ice," Nikki sniffed, and tossed her famous golden ringlets. I looked over at the catering table, where Diet Pepsi bottles were neatly lined up, and sighed.

The shoot finally ended around eight o'clock that evening. Since it was a Saturday, it had ended fairly early. After thanking the star for actually doing her job, I bolted out the door.

I was having dinner with Aidan tonight, and he had told me it was for something special. He was making me a gourmet dinner. He's a great cook. I'm a lousy cook but a good eater, so it works out. At red lights I texted furiously, trying to get more information on Katsu's promotion. But those who texted back seemed every bit as surprised as I was.

When I finally arrived at Aidan's house he was already in full force, pulling something that smelled really fattening out of the oven. I just love a man in oven mitts. I hugged him and asked what I could do to help.

"Stay out of my way," he said and waved me off to the couch as he handed me a glass of wine. "It's a Chateau Margaux 1966 so make an effort to appreciate it." Aidan knew that my tastes ran to bologna, Miracle Whip, and potato chip sandwiches. He'd been trying to educate me, but it's hard to rehabilitate a midwestern girl.

"I'm making a pork tenderloin roast stuffed with figs, rosemary potatoes, and grilled asparagus," Aidan shouted from the kitchen. "Sorry, no chocolate soufflé tonight. I got stuck in a production meeting and was late getting home."

I leaned back and felt all the tingling tensions of the day begin to ease away. I decided that, for tonight anyway, I was not going to worry one bit about Katsu Tanaka and firmly put him out of my mind.

The table was set with white linen, candles, and china I didn't even know Aidan had. Red roses were in a crystal vase. I couldn't imagine what was going on to prompt such an elaborate dinner. "What are we celebrating?" I asked.

Aidan set the loaded plates down on the table. "You're just going to have to wait until after dinner." When we were finished with the food I thought I had it figured out.

"Did your new movie get green-lit by the studio? Is that the reason for this great dinner?"

"No."

"It's not?" I asked. Why else would he go to all this trouble? Aidan pulled a small box out of his jacket pocket. He held it in both hands and took a deep breath. So did I.

Aidan looked into my eyes. "Jeannie, will you do me the honor of marrying me?"

I stared at him. My normal tendency would have been to say yes so I wouldn't hurt his feelings. But I'd already answered one proposal that way and my first marriage had turned out to be a disaster. I'd been seeing Aidan for two years and I was madly in love with him and, I was pretty sure, he with me. But I knew all too well how things could change.

"I . . . uh . . ."

"That's very eloquent, Jeannie. Is that a yes or a no?" Aidan smiled at me.

"Can I think about it?"

He sat back and looked at me. "You have to say yes. I rented china and everything." When I started laughing, he joined in. Then he said, "Honey, I love you. I know it didn't work out for you before with Walker, but it's no reason not to try again."

I said, "My work schedule already finished off one marriage. I don't want that to happen again." I was in pain for him and myself. I stared at my empty, dirty plate.

"I have a similar schedule myself, in case you hadn't noticed. That's all right; we mesh that way. We're both high-speed, high-pressure kind of people and we like that. It gets the adrenaline running."

"Work is only a part of it," I said haltingly. "It's sort of about my family."

"You don't think they'd like me?" Aidan grinned. "How would you know? It's been two years and they've never even met me.

I can force them to like me, you know. I can be very charming when I want to be."

"Oh, they would like you in a heartbeat. It's just that, well, they're kind of unusual."

"What is it? Someone in your family chopped up his wife into small pieces and was sent up the river?"

"No," I sighed. "That was our next-door neighbor."

Aidan sat back at that. "So what is it?"

"My family isn't like your family. Your family seems to have everything under control at all times." I pushed a strand of hair out of my eyes. "But stuff just *happens* to my family. I think of it as really funny but apparently other people don't. Like Walker, or most of the other spouses in my family. A lot of them are ex-spouses now. My family seems to be very trying on the people we love."

"Give me an example."

I looked at him long and hard. "I'll give you one story. But you should be warned that there are lots more."

He topped off my wine and then his. "I'm ready.

Two

Sunday, June 22, 1986

om, phone for you. It's Elizabeth," I called from around the kitchen door. Then I left the phone on the counter and sat back down in my official place for the wedding shower. I was the ribbon keeper. The ribbons were not-so-carefully entwined on a paper-plate bouquet. Anna opened the next package and appropriately cooed at the toaster.

"Williams-Sonoma! Exactly what we wanted!" She beamed at Teeni, who was balancing a mimosa on her knee. That about wrapped up the present opening. Thank God, because Anna had broken fourteen ribbons, by my careful count—which by bridal-shower superstition means fourteen kids, and I just didn't know how my brother, Evan, would feel about that. Sammie was refilling champagne. Mom had managed to convince Sammie not to wear her skintight, peg-leg jeans and ripped zebra-striped shirt with the safety pins all over it. But there wasn't a lot Mom could do about Sammie's pink spiked hair. Sammie crossed her eyes at me when she walked by. All we had to do was get through the toilet-paper wedding dress contest and we were free.

Mom had returned. "Jeannie, help me with the cake in the kitchen, please." She stepped by me so fast I dropped the ribbon plate. I bent to sort it out. "Now, please." I looked up past her knit dress, which clung untidily to her hips. This was not about cake. Oh God. It was Elizabeth. Now what? The psychic healer thing? That biotechnic religion of hers? Car broke down again? There were so many possibilities it boggled the mind. Sammie followed, sensing drama, and she, Mom, and I sat at the kitchen table in family-conference mode.

"It's Lucy," Mom started.

"No, it was Elizabeth on the—" I interrupted.

"It's about Lucy." Mom paused and took a long pull of her cigarette. She'd been smoking for about her whole life. She swore it had never hurt any of us. She ignored the secondhand smoke warnings, but it's probably the reason all five of us kids are so nearsighted.

"Lucy's eloped."

"Don't you have to run away from home to do that?" I asked. Of course, she already had, I suppose. Mom continued with what she knew of the story. She was usually at her finest in a crisis. A born doer. If it was only a small problem, she needed to blow it up into something worthy of her skills. If she only had a little bit of the story, she would darkly fill in the details with her worst imaginings. If Elizabeth didn't answer her phone in L.A. for a day or two, then Mom's assumption was that she'd been killed in the big car pileup outside of San Diego that she'd heard about on the Channel Thirteen local news. No matter that Elizabeth had never mentioned going to San Diego or had never even been there. Mom would fret so sincerely that soon you would be right there with her in the fret-zone. Then Elizabeth—or whoever the current object of attention was—would randomly call, only to be scolded for worrying her half to death. But give Mom a great big, full-on, real-life problem, and she'd be the epitome of grace under pressure.

Apparently Elizabeth had driven to Monterey to visit Lucy. While she was in Lucy's barracks, she realized she had forgotten to bring any underwear with her. So, like any good sister who is desperate for undergarments, she started rooting around through Lucy's locker and found the marriage certificate.

"Is she sure it's real? You know, not like a fake one you would get at Six Flags?" I asked. Mom paused to give me a look.

"So there it is. She's eloped."

So far Sammie hadn't said anything. Staring out the picture window she seemed fixated on a speedboat blaring by on Bear Lake.

"I give. To who and why?" I finally asked.

"His name is Chuck. That's all Elizabeth saw." Mom got up to knock her cigarette ash into the ashtray on the counter. Then she cupped one hand under the other elbow. Cigarette held aloft, she mused, "Chuck? On a marriage license? Maybe his real name is Charles."

Several giggling women came into the kitchen with dirty cups and saucers. Teeni had spilled red wine on herself. She really should have stuck to the mimosas. They were much easier to clean up. Mom went to the fridge for soda water, grabbed the Morton's salt, and began fussing over the stain. She's the consummate hostess. Years of practice, I guess.

Anna, my sister-in-law-to-be, came in with more dirty plates.

"Honey, you're the guest of honor. Put those down right now," Mom chirped from her stain-fixing crouch.

"Six days until the wedding," Anna twittered. "I can hardly believe it after all these years."

Us either, I thought. The way we figured it, she had finally worn Evan down like water smoothes a stone. Anna's mother stroked her hair and spoke quietly in her ear in French. She was probably saying something mean about us. Like about how Sammie had joked around during the wedding shower about the word "nuptials" and how erotic sounding it was. And it is. "Nuuuup" is up, then "tiiials" is down. *Nuuuptiiials, nuuuptiiials.* Up down, up down. It sounds like humping in the backseat of a Chevelle. Mom had looked disapproving, but I could tell she wanted to laugh. Instead she had just put her hand firmly on Sammie's knee and gave her a look. She had perfected this method in church. If any of us were acting up, she couldn't exactly yell at us down the pew. She just put her hand on the nearest knee and we had to pass it down until it got to the right person. It usually worked.

Later, Mom and Anna were saying good-bye to the guests out in the front hallway. Sammie and I watched the women in the kitchen trickle out. Then Sammie pushed her punked-out, pink-streaked hair out of her eyes. "At least we can thank Elizabeth for getting us out of that T.P. wedding dress game." She stared out the picture window. "But why would Lucy elope?"

"Why does she do anything?" Lucy is two years older than me. Last year, she came home from Western Michigan University to announce blithely she had joined the army. She told our parents they had said she could leave if she didn't like it. Later, I realized Lucy knew you couldn't just up and leave. She was far too smart not to have asked those questions. She was just hoping Mom and Dad didn't know, to give them some hope. But of course they did know. After finding out she had already signed all of the papers, they just hugged her and said they supported her decision.

But later, when Lucy was gone, Mom sat at the kitchen table staring at her coffee and asked, "What kind of girl joins the army?" I knew what she was thinking. In her mind, the army was for people with no other prospects—not for girls who wore Kelly green sweaters with their initials embroidered on them in pink. First and middle initial on either side of a large last initial.

Dad read the paper in the adjoining TV room, trying to veer away from the storm that was my mother "in mode," as we called it. "Couldn't it at least have been the Air Force?" he grunted. For reasons unknown to any of us, Dad had always had a thing for planes.

Dad tended not to say a lot. He viewed his four daughters with equal vigor and love, but we belonged to our mother. Evan was his son, and his son was his. I once asked him why he started talking to us more when we got older. He said that we weren't that interesting until we were eighteen. Then he went to smoke a Tareyton and sit in his half-finished gazebo down by the lake.

"Call her. See if she says anything," I demanded from my place at the table. It had been my place since I graduated from my high chair.

"I talked to her last night and she didn't say anything, so why would she now?"

"Because now we have info, and we're nosy."

I sat tracing the familiar brown laminate of the kitchen table with its roosters painted in the four corners. I'd sat at this table next to Lucy forever. She'd pinch me or whisper mean things. Once she told me that she was going to tell her best friend, Terri, to tell her little brother, Jason, that I didn't get my period until I was sixteen and that I was frigid. It wasn't something to make the boys come running. Unless maybe they figured you couldn't get pregnant.

There's a semi-tacky sign hanging above our back door. It has dorky flowers painted on it and says PEOPLE NEED LOVING THE MOST WHEN THEY DESERVE IT THE LEAST. I thought it was true. So I never really blamed her for her torment. It wasn't Lucy's fault that she had been born into a stick-thin, size-zero family. Not that she was fat. Far from it. She was actually quite tiny herself. But she never saw her thighs that way. If bulimia or anorexia had been popular then, she would have had it. She never focused on her amazing dark hair and big blue eyes. She only saw her faults. I thought I had it all figured out about the real reason she joined the army: enforced exercise. She figured she'd be working out six hours a day. She'd be doing push-ups, running, the works. But in my mind, Lucy screwed up. She scored too high on the entrance exams. Before she knew it, she was at the Defense Language Institute in Monterey, California, sitting on her butt learning to speak Russian. Sure, she had gone to boot camp at Fort Dix, but even after the ten-mile marches and everything, Lucy said she didn't lose any weight. Apparently, army food is on the starchy side. And now she'd eloped.

Mom stuck her head through the kitchen door long enough to say that we were wanted in the hallway. Sammie and I dutifully lined up at the front door, hugged everyone good-bye, and thanked them for coming. Mom stared at Teeni's backside wobbling its way down the front walk. "Think we should have taken her keys and driven her home?"

"Cripes, it's only four blocks, in broad daylight." Sammie shut the door firmly. "How much trouble could she get into?"

We resumed our places in the kitchen. But I popped up from my chair a moment later and headed for the cupboard below the kitchen sink. Grabbing the Ajax, I sprinkled the blue stuff over the kitchen counter, wet a sponge, and went to work.

"It's clean already," Mom said.

"Not completely." I rubbed vigorously.

"We won't have any grout left if you keep on like that." Since she sounded halfhearted I continued scrubbing.

"What did Lucy tell Elizabeth?" Sammie asked.

"Elizabeth didn't ask her," Mom said, pursing her lips. My family will happily snoop through everything, but we draw the line at letting the others know we've invaded their privacy.

Dad, thinking it was safe to return to the house now that all the women had gone, came in from the backyard.

"Harold, are the sprinklers fixed yet?" Mom asked.

He sighed deeply and went back outside.

Satisfied with my cleaning, I put my equipment away, poured a cup of coffee, and sat down.

"You don't even like that stuff. You're just putting on," Sammie said over her shoulder as she microwaved tea.

"Am not," I retorted eloquently. I had started drinking coffee at college. It seemed a grown-up thing to do, and doused with enough sugar and milk, it was actually okay. I had just come home from my sophomore year at Michigan State. My three sisters had gone to Western Michigan University, which was half the reason I went to State. The other half was that my dad went there. Many years later, he told me that he didn't care for MSU and wished I'd gone to the University of Michigan instead. I didn't have the grades for U of M but he still could have mentioned it. Why don't people ever say what they think at the right time? It sure would save a lot of time and trouble.

Mom stood at the window and watched Dad dutifully tinkering with a sprinkler head. A small geyser of water shot up, narrowly missing him but catching our dog, Buddy, right in the face. He sputtered away while Dad poured coffee from his always-present thermos and pondered the situation.

"Elizabeth told me that Lucy said she intended to bring a boy home with her for Evan's wedding," Mom said, resuming the conversation from the one going on in her head.

"Where are we going to put them?" I was concerned because I was usually the one to wind up on the couch if all the beds were spoken for.

I looked at Elizabeth's schedule and agenda on the fridge door. As much as we all made fun of her hyperorganization (7:30 p.m. dinner, 9:00 p.m. family fun time), we did grudgingly use it.

"It says here that Lucy and I have the pink room, Grandma has the guest room, Sammie has the dessert room, Elizabeth and Ron are staying at Evan's in the Jimi Hendrix room, and Jean-Paul, Anna's brother, has their back room." We pondered all of the various options open to us. Chuck could stay on the couch. But no, he was a guest, and furthermore, he was married to Lucy even if we weren't supposed to know about it. Chuck and Lucy could sleep in the pink room and I would take the couch, since Sammie's room only had a twin bed, and I really didn't want to share the double bed with Grandma. She had issues with flatulence. That satisfied everyone, until Dad came back in and heard about the plans for Lucy and Chuck. "No daughter of mine has ever slept under my roof with a man she isn't married to."

"That you know of," Sammie snickered.

Dad sighed again, and scooped Maxwell House into the Mr. Coffee.

"But Lucy *is* married," I countered.

"She hasn't told us she's married. Therefore, she still is not married," Dad announced. Mom was smoking frantically now.

And so went the conversation, like so many conversations before. I finally went out for a walk, up the tree-lined streets I'd walked for almost two decades, past the Worthingtons' house, past the Keenes' house, past the silent grade school, middle school, and high school in one. It was almost ten thirty at night when I pushed open the chain-link gate, went into the playground, and rocked idly on a swing. Why hadn't Lucy called me? She didn't call that often, but if any of us were lonely or in trouble the word usually flew through the family grapevine. I hung on to the chains and swung my head far back. The streetlight was shining through the trees above my head. When I was younger, I would lie down in a silent intersection of the road and stare at the leaves above me. I marveled at how many different colors of green there were. Gray greens, lime greens, black greens. It seemed impossible that anyone could capture all those colors.

I sat up and looked at the darkened windows of the high school. When I was a sophomore and Lucy was a senior, she and all but one of the varsity cheerleading squad were suspended for drinking. The one who got off was the girl who had ratted them out. She had been miffed because she hadn't been invited to drink beer with them in the cold, windswept parking lot at Lake Michigan.

I was on the junior varsity squad, which got called up to go to the semifinals with the varsity basketball team. Lucy cried for days. I would hear her sniffling as she lay on her side of our bed. When I asked her if she wanted to talk, she kicked my legs with her heels. She was a senior—this would have been her last game to cheer. That Friday, I dutifully came to school in my cheerleading uniform. My blue and gold pleated skirt was made as short as possible by rolling the waistband. As we cheered through the afternoon pep assembly, the varsity basketball players watched dolefully. They were going to the semifinals without their hot-babe varsity squad, and they were not happy about it. Lucy's face was blank as she sat in the bleachers watching.

"In between the calm lake waters, scenes we call our own . . ."

I sang the alma mater, hand over heart. That afternoon, I stood waiting with my pom-poms to get on the pep bus. The sky was March gray, and I shivered with the wind against my bare legs. The bus driver, Wes, jokingly asked me if I was coming.

"No," I told him, "I'm not coming."

I walked away before he could respond. He waited a minute for me to change my mind and then pulled away. The other JV cheerleaders were mad at me for days.

"We couldn't do any of our mounts," they whined. "Lindsey was too heavy to get on top."

Back then, I couldn't have begun to explain why I stayed home. But now, I stared up through the leaves again and remembered Lucy holding my hair back when I got drunk on Stroh's beer and was on my hands and knees puking into the toilet. She wiped my face, forced me to brush my teeth, and didn't tell Mom and Dad. Like with every family, there were thousands of kindnesses mixed with the pain. Maybe pain is just easier to remember, or sticks harder. Kindness gets a bad rap that way. Family first, I thought. So why hadn't she called now?

When I got home, the house was dark. Instead of going to the pink room, I crawled into bed with Sammie, who was currently in the guest room. I poked her in the side. I knew she had to be awake.

"What'd they decide?"

Sammie turned over. "I don't know. Mom cried for a while. She doesn't understand her daughter sometimes."

"Which one?" I whispered, and we laughed quietly in the darkness. We talked softly deep into the night as we had so many nights before.

Three

Wednesday, June 25, 1986

$\mathcal{J}$ could feel the chaos downstairs as soon as I opened
my eyes the next morning.

"Uh-oh," Sammie said.

A vacuum roared into life and there was a clatter of dishes
and water. I went downstairs to find Roxie on a stepladder taking
down the crystals from the chandelier my mom had salvaged
from a garage sale. She waved her dust rag at me. "Your mom's in
the backyard. She said to send you out."

I hadn't brushed my hair and I was wearing my nighttime uniform of boxers and tank top, but I went outside anyway. Mom
was pointing in various directions and stepping off measurements
on the ground as Dad looked on.

"And the tent will go here," she finished. "Jeannie, good, you're
up. Get some clothes on. We have to go to Steketee's."

"God, Mom, can't I have some coffee first?" This was too much
of a launch into the day for me.

"You don't like that stuff anyway, and we have to get to Steke-tee's."

"What for?" I pushed my hair back, hoping nobody would walk by.

"We've got to get Lucy registered."

I began to have the feeling I usually got when Dad told us he got a job in Egypt or Botswana, and we would all be leaving soon, and I would be going to school in Switzerland—half excitement and half trepidation. These things usually petered out after a few months and we never went anywhere, except for the time he moved us to Somalia. But there was a coup six months later and the Americans got kicked out so we came back to Muskegon.

Sammie wandered out.

"Sammie, you have to go get the invitations," Mom told her.

Sammie stopped short by the rock birdbath. Mom waved the hand with the cigarette in it. "We're giving Lucy a wedding. I don't want her looking back in twenty years and wishing for the white wedding with flowers she never had."

"Couldn't we just wait for her *next* wedding?" Sammie moaned.

"When exactly is this blessed event to be?" I sat down on a lawn chair and started playing with Buddy's ears. I stopped when a flea jumped on me.

"Sunday, the day after Evan's."

I could see how Mom had worked this out. Everybody would be home for Evan's wedding anyway. Elizabeth was flying in from L.A., Sammie was already here from L.A., and Grandma was coming from Houston.

"How does Lucy feel about all of this?" Sammie ventured, knowing full well that Mom hadn't told her.

"It will be a surprise," Mom said.

"That seems like kind of a drastic surprise, Mom, even for us," I said.

"I tried calling her. But apparently they are off doing drills or maneuvers or some type of thing and she can't be reached."

"They do drills even at a language school?" I asked.

Mom shrugged. "It's still the army."

Dad and I went back into the house. Roxie warned us about messing up her clean floors.

"How are we going to pull off another wedding by Sunday?" I whined.

Dad gestured out the sliding doors to Mom. "That's how."

There was a flurry of allocating cars and errands and the synchronizing of watches. Sammie was to go get the invitations printed. We wrote down the language on a napkin but got stumped pretty fast.

Mr. and Mrs. Harold Thompson
invite you to the wedding
of their daughter Lucy Caroline
to . . . Chuck.

We didn't know his last name. After a few tries we came up with:

Mr. and Mrs. Harold Thompson
cordially invite you to the wedding
of their daughter Lucy Caroline
Sunday, June 29, 12 p.m.
St. Peter's Episcopal Church
RSVP by tomorrow
616-555-3024

Chuck didn't know it yet, but he was about to learn that men take a backseat in the Thompson family race car. Sammie went downtown to the printer with strict instructions to wait while the invitations were printed. Dad was told to call Evan and have him and Anna come over at one o'clock to receive the news. Mom and I went to Steketee's, where we were faced with an alarming amount of CorningWare and Pfaltzgraff in the housewares department.

"Can't we at least go to Grand Rapids to register her?" I said while fingering a cheesy flowered tea towel.

"If we don't have time to go to Grand Rapids to register her, how would anyone else have time to go there to buy anything?" Mom countered with perfect reason.

Mrs. Roly Poly waited on us. At least, that's what Sammie and I called her. She went to our church, and she and her husband sang in the choir.

"Your hair looks lovely today," Mom began. Her gray curls stuck tight to her head and didn't look different than they did any other day to me. I could tell Mom wished it wasn't Roly Poly waiting on us. "I need to register my daughter for her wedding."

"Oh, Anna registered here long ago," Roly Poly beamed.

"No, my daughter. Not my daughter-in-law."

"How exciting for you! Another wedding! When is it?"

"Sunday."

Roly Poly eyed my stomach suspiciously.

"No, not me . . ." I said.

"We'll just look around for a bit," Mom interrupted. She dragged me over behind the Mixmasters. "It might be easier if we didn't tell Mrs. Carpenter much. I haven't called Father Whippet yet and I don't want him hearing about the wedding from her first."

I cast a nervous glance back at Roly Poly. She was pretending to price faux Hummel figurines while she watched us. I was starting to feel like Mom and I were involved in a conspiracy. Finally, we selected a pretty Lenox pattern with a thin gold rim. I thought Lucy would like it. I'd at least saved her from the Pfaltzgraff stoneware mugs and plates, which I thought were ugly.

When we got home, Evan and Dad were out staring at the sprinklers like they might start working by themselves. Anna was in the kitchen on the phone and barely nodded at us when we walked in. I could hear that she was trying to change the reservations for their honeymoon trip to Jamaica. From the look on her face it didn't seem like she was getting very far.

"Yes, from Sunday to Monday," she said, then listened, and continued, "I know it's very short notice. We'd have to do what? Stop in Miami and Cancun? How much more?" The look on her face was thunderous. "Okay, put it on hold and I'll call back."

She hung up the phone and sagged against the counter. Mom went up to try and hug her but she brushed her off. She was trying to hold back tears, but she had that waver in her voice. "As if there weren't enough pressure trying to have a wedding for three hundred people! Do you know what you're putting me through?" Anna stomped her foot, which I'd never seen anyone do in real life. "This is about the bridesmaids, isn't it, Rose?"

Mom and I eyed each other.

"You're still mad that I didn't invite your daughters to be in my wedding! This is some twisted way of getting back at me!"

"There are easier ways of getting back at you other than marrying off Lucy," I volunteered.

Mom looked at me as though she wished she'd only had four kids, and then she turned to Anna. "Honey, of course not. Don't be silly. You're absolutely right. We are putting too much pressure on you and it's your big day. If you can't change the reservations for your honeymoon, then that's just fine. You head on out on Sunday and don't worry about Lucy's wedding."

Anna regarded her through watery eyes. "Really?"

"Really." Mom tried to hug Anna again, but she was already dialing the travel agent. She stretched the phone cord so that she could go through the door to the dining room for privacy.

"She does have a point," Mom said. "It is her weekend and her wedding. Maybe we should call this off." She turned to the stove to light a cigarette. "But I *was* a little ticked off about the bridesmaid thing." Anna had not asked any of us girls to be in the wedding because she thought if she had one of us she would have to have all four. And since there were already eight bridesmaids, she would have had to uninvite four of her friends or up the number to twelve. We accepted it and told Evan we would throw extra rice at him to make up for it.

I followed Mom out to the living room, where Evan and Dad were smoking. She stood by the couch and gave her son a sad look. It did seem like we were shoving Evan aside. This was his wedding and we were supposed to be focused on him. As usual, one of the girls had managed to upstage him. Mom was hoping he would offer up a sign that everything was all right. Sure enough, Evan stood up, walked over to Mom, and hugged her.

"I may have blown this one," Mom sniffled.

"You've done better things," Evan said and rocked her back and forth. "But Dad and I talked it over with Anna. She'll be fine."

"I should call it off. We can, you know. Lucy doesn't even know about it yet."

"Lucy deserves a nice wedding, too," Evan said. "But I'd better go get Anna before she melts down again." He left to go find her.

When the phone rang, I gladly left the room to answer it. Unfortunately, it was Father Whippet. It took me a while to convince him that it wasn't me who was getting married. I told him it was Lucy, but he couldn't remember which kid she was even though he had baptized and confirmed every one of us. Finally, I reminded him that Lucy was the one who as a junior usher forgot to pass the plate to half the church and who had, along with Kim Barnett, broken into the wine cabinet. Then he remembered.

I went ahead and explained what had happened and made the plans for the Sunday wedding. Apparently, it had to happen after the 10 a.m. service and before the 1 p.m. Linen Guild meeting. He couldn't do it in the afternoon because he was in a foursome of golf. So Lucy's wedding was set for noon sharp. Which was a good thing, I thought, because that was what was on the invitations. Father Whippet said he would have to meet the happy couple on Friday to give his blessing. Normally, they would have had to go through six weeks of marriage counseling in order to ensure their lifelong happiness together, but he was willing to waive that since Chuck was an Episcopalian. Or so I told him when he asked.

"An Episcopalian? I'm sure he is. No. Yes. I'm positive. Absolutely." I got off the phone and wondered what the penalty for lying to a minister was. When I went back into the living room to tell Mom and Dad about my conversation with Father Whippet, I volunteered that Roly Poly had gone straight to the Man. "How did you know the wedding had to be at noon?" I asked Mom.

"Oh, because he plays golf in the afternoon, and that only left the time between the 10 a.m. service and the 1 p.m. Linen Guild meeting."

Dad grumbled, "Christ, after all the money I've given to the church, he can't rearrange his golf outing so we can have the wedding at a decent time? I mean, these people will barely have

recovered from Evan's wedding. You know how they all drink."
He settled back in his chair. "Well, maybe that means our bar bill
will be smaller than Anna's parents'."

Sammie came in holding a cardboard box. "Boy, what's wrong
with Anna? I just asked her if we could borrow her invitation list
and she burst into tears."

Mom winced. "Oh God, Sammie, she's still getting used to the
fact that there's going to be another wedding."

"Yeah, but I don't want to have to go through the phone book
for the same zillion addresses. She already has them. What's the
big deal?" Sammie dropped the box on the table and took out an
invitation. They looked nice, I thought.

"Sammie, these look like an invitation to a funeral!" Mom said
as she looked at the black type on white stock.

"What's wrong? They look official."

"Where are the pink paper and roses we talked about?" Mom
sat down and rubbed her forehead.

"This is all they could do in the time frame—which was rather
short, if you remember," Sammie sniffed.

Sammie and I spent the afternoon addressing and licking en-
velopes. We pretty much copied Anna's guest list, which we had
lifted from her purse before she and Evan left. I paused at one I
had just finished addressing. "What about Jeff Petty?"

"What *about* Jeff Petty? I wish Elizabeth would get home so
she could help with this mess. She started it all."

"Technically, Lucy started it. She just doesn't know it. But
anyway, Jeff."

"Lucy and Jeff broke up months and months ago," Sammie
said.

"Should we invite him to her wedding? Don't you think that
would be a little weird after they dated for four years?"

Sammie didn't answer me. Elizabeth would be home in a few hours. I could consult with her then. She had Emily Post memorized backward and forward. When Mom had called her about the additional wedding this coming weekend, Elizabeth had about had a heart attack. She kept saying it just "wasn't done."

Mom had replied that it *must* be able to be done because, after all, we were doing it.

Four

January 2006

I paused in my story and looked over to see if I had put the love of my life to sleep yet. "Well?" I asked.

"Well, what?"

"Aren't you sorry that you asked me to marry you?"

"Your family sounds more entertaining than ominous."

"Just wait," I replied. Yawning, I got up and wandered into the kitchen, where I spied my iPhone. "Do you mind if I check emails?" I called over my shoulder.

"It's after midnight, and it's the night I asked you to marry me. Sure, you can check emails," Aidan said good-naturedly.

I scrolled through the twenty new emails, and I promptly wished I hadn't. A prominent star, who shall go by only the initials F.U.—appropriately, I might add—had sent an email bitching about the billing block in the movie poster for *Sheer Panic*. The billing block is that list of tiny little names at the bottom of every poster. Nobody much cares about it except for the people whose names are in it. Ms. F.U. had sent me the message at 11:12 p.m.

The last time I had seen this person, she was having a pedicure in her home. In order for me to show the art for the poster, the star insisted I kneel down next to the pedicurist so that the art could be seen from "the proper angle."

"My head looks too small for my body," the star had proclaimed.

"But that's your head," I carefully protested from my prostrate position at her feet.

"No, it's not. You stripped a hideously small and out-of-proportion head onto the body from another shot."

I knew this star well. We weren't buddies having each other over for dinner parties or anything, but I knew her neurotic behavior. She was a diva in every sense of the word. Aging, but still a diva. I knew she obsessed over every detail down to the way her fingernails looked on a poster. We had had to reshoot her hands already, at a cost of fifty thousand dollars, because she didn't like the manicure.

When I suggested that we could just fix the way her nails looked on the computer, she had regarded me as though I had toads springing out of my mouth. Funny, she didn't feel that way when it came to getting her wrinkles retouched.

Before any meeting with her, I obsessively made sure I knew every detail about anything that could possibly come up. This was not a head strip. It was a single body and head from one photograph. I said to Ms. F.U., "I have the original photograph right here. See, it's not a head strip. Therefore, your head is in proportion."

She looked casually at the photograph. "So you retouched this photograph to look like an original so you could cover up your mistake?" Did she actually think I had the time or the inclination to do such a thing?

"I . . . it actually is your . . ." I was stammering now. I do that sometimes when I am faced with an all-out lack of reason, courtesy, or just plain damn common sense in my profession. I stammer often. "It is your head. On your body. In one complete photo," I finally managed.

"I don't believe you. I demand you make my head bigger."

The pedicurist cast me a sideways look, and I knew she was thinking about all the jokes you could make in reply to that statement.

Don't get me wrong. I love my job. God knows I had come a long way from being a receptionist in an ad agency but it sure can be trying on some days. My job is twenty percent development of creative materials and eighty percent psychology to sell the movies, and that's just to the studio, the filmmakers, and the talent—all of whom have a say.

Every day has a fevered energy. Almost everyone on the advertising side of films works on twenty-four-hour adrenaline surges. People don't realize what goes in to making the film trailers and the TV spots and the posters. You deal with the talents' vanities, the filmmakers' egos, and the studios' pressure to open a film. The ad agencies struggle to "break the back" of the campaign while hopefully you, the studio marketing exec, are guiding them all correctly. I listen to research and my own gut instinct on how to reach an audience, and I've been proven correct more times than not.

But in the meantime everybody is squabbling the entire time to get his or her own way—me included. I've always thought that growing up in my particular family prepared me for a lot of that. What it hadn't prepared me for was the politics. I was lousy at studio politics. Since my brain didn't think in particularly devious patterns I assumed others operated the same way. I figured if you worked hard and did a good job that was about it. After all, that was how I had risen up through the ranks. But Katsu's promotion was one more example of my being clueless about such things.

Glancing back at Ms. F.U.'s email, I decided it could wait. Since she hadn't called me on my cell phone I knew that the situation wasn't urgent. I would solve the billing block problem by basically passing it off to our legal department. I just had to get an art direc- tor to design the damn billing block. It was not my responsibility to determine which screenwriter out of the forty screenwriters who had rewritten the script was going to get the credit for the illustrious work.

I scrolled through the other emails. Elizabeth had sent one. Opening it, I smiled. It was a photo of my nineteen-year-old niece accompanied by an invitation to a ballet performance she was dancing in at UCLA. Quickly, I replied, "Yep, I'll be there," and hit SEND.

When I put down the phone Aidan was getting ready for bed, and I joined him. He yawned, "Don't forget we have brunch to- morrow with my mom and stepdad at the Hotel Bel-Air." I had, in fact, forgotten all about it.

We both brushed our teeth and climbed into bed. We each had our side and each knew that he spooned me first, then we flipped and I spooned him. The rituals were all there. For all the world like an old married couple. Before we fell asleep I stroked his back and whispered in his ear, "Aidan?"

"Mmm?"

"Thank you for asking me to marry you."

He reached around, patted my bottom, and fell asleep. I how- ever watched the shadows on the wall for a good long time before my eyes finally closed.

The next day was, as usual, bright and sunny. We woke up on the late side and had to scramble to get dressed. I had brought clothes and makeup with me. I usually bring one decent outfit with me in case something comes up—like a brunch with parents. After driving up Stone Canyon we pulled in to the valet in front of the hotel. Leaving Aidan's Mercedes behind we strolled into the restaurant. Aidan's mom, Charlotte, was already seated. A bottle of champagne sat on the table. She held a mimosa in one manicured hand and stretched the other one out toward us. "Aidan! Love! I'm so happy to see you." She beamed at him. Then she turned toward me and smiled. "Jeannie, it's so nice to see you, too. Aidan says you've been very busy at work." Was it my imagination or was she noticing my ringless left hand? Maybe she was just wondering if not wearing nail polish was the "in" thing right now.

I kissed her cheek and sat down. Charlotte was dressed in a taupe knit pantsuit that showed off, even at her age, a damn good body. I knew she did Pilates three times a week and had a personal trainer in another two days a week. While envying her dedication I soothed myself that if I didn't have to work I'd go to the gym too. Maybe.

I spotted Sam, Aidan's stepfather, across the restaurant. Even though he was retired it was clear he was still working the room. He stopped by almost every table to say hello. Sam had been the chairman of a major film studio for decades. While I had heard the stories about how he had been both loathed and feared at the studio, I had never seen that side of him.

Striding over he gave me the biggest hug he could while I was still half rising out of my chair. "There's our girl!" He beamed. Straightening up, he grabbed at a waiter who was walking by carrying a full tray of food. "How 'bout a Bloody Mary, my good man?" The waiter recovered his balance, nodded his head, and moved on. Sam took his seat next to me.

"So?" He looked across the table at Aidan and winked. A silence followed.

Then Aidan cleared his throat. "Yeah, so, Sam. What's up in your world?" Sam sat back in his chair. Then he looked at me. The bottle of Dom Pérignon on the table took on a new meaning. They were expecting this to be a celebration of our engagement. Quiet fell over the table again and I took an overly long time getting my napkin arranged in my lap.

"Well," Charlotte said to break the awkwardness. But she couldn't think of anything to say after that, and when no one jumped in to fill the void, she busied herself with the roll on her bread plate. I snuck a sideways glance at Aidan but he was pretending to study the menu. My napkin became fascinating to me again.

Sam was the first to recover. But even with my eyes cast downward, I felt his long stare before he finally switched the subject. "So, Jeannie, the grapevine tells me that Katsu what's-his-name got promoted to EVP."

My spine stiffened. Word sure had whipped through town. Any major move in a studio could cause a domino effect. One person's promotion might very well mean another's demise so gossip was usually gleeful and rampant.

"He's coming on fast behind you. What do you suppose that means for you at Oxford?" Sam said as he tinkled his empty Bloody Mary glass at the waiter.

"There's always plenty of films to work on," I snapped. My voice sounded downright petulant even to my own ears.

"Well, I'm sure the powers-that-be let you know all about it, to be sure you were on board." Sam crunched the celery he had pulled out of his glass. Something told me that Sam damn well knew already that they hadn't.

Aidan squeezed my hand under the table. I hadn't told him of this development yet but he understood the possible implications. He also knew that Sam reveled in industry chatter. Sam might be his stepfather but he could also be a blowhard jerk—especially if he thought I might have just wounded his stepson.

Attempting to get off the subject of Oxford Pictures, I cast around for small talk. "You know, I think this is only the second time in my life I've had eggs Benedict." I willed my voice to be pleasant.

Charlotte sat back. "Really, Jeannie? I think Aidan was having this by the time he could talk."

"Wow, you must be a really good cook," I said, relieved we had moved the conversation to safe ground. I imagined a civilized table where people calmly sat while eating a decadent breakfast. My mom usually tried futilely to shove scrambled eggs at us as we were all trying to get out the door to school.

"Yep, Mom cooked it for me every morning." Aidan smiled at Charlotte as he took a bite of toast. Charlotte laughed and clearly there was a joke here I was missing.

Charlotte turned to me. "I've never cooked a meal in my life. If it weren't for restaurants and our personal chef I'm pretty sure Aidan would have starved. I was just never home enough to do things like cook. I was at work every morning by 7 a.m."

I thought about Aidan's life growing up. I mean, who wouldn't like a life where you could order up what you wanted and then have it served to you in your own house? When brunch was over we all strolled down by the little lake and watched the swans glide by. Then we hugged Charlotte and Sam good-bye.

On our way home I asked Aidan, "Why didn't you call them this morning and tell them what was going on? They thought they were going to be celebrating our engagement." I felt my cheeks reddening at the memory of the champagne on the table.

"I didn't think they would remember I was going to ask you last night!" Aidan downshifted hard. No one else in Los Angeles drove a stick shift because it was too difficult with traffic. But Aidan said it got out his stress. As we flew around the curves of Stone Canyon it was apparent he was getting out a fair amount. As we neared Sunset Boulevard the car slowed and I could tell Aidan was calming down.

"I want to hear more of your story," he said.

"We just left your elegant family. Why would I want to keep telling you about my crazy, messed-up one?"

"Because I want to know," he said quietly and patted my hand.

Five

Thursday, June 26, 1986

The night before, Dad had picked up Elizabeth and Ron from the airport. Elizabeth had not readily accepted that her layout of bedroom plans had changed. "But there is a schedule!" She stood in front of the refrigerator with her arms crossed. Mom sorted her out while Ron got into an argument with Dad about politics.

"It's apparent you don't have a full understanding of the real issues at hand." Ron slouched comfortably in Dad's favorite armchair and pushed his jet-black curls out of his eyes. Dad muttered something under his breath that sounded a whole lot like a swear word and escaped back to the gazebo.

"Honey, there is a whole lot more to do than argue about bedrooms. Why don't you check outside and see if the tent will be okay?" Happier now to be in organization mode, Elizabeth flipped on the backyard lights and went outside to see how the rest of us had gone awry. Finally, she and Ron borrowed Mom's white Cadillac and drove over to Evan's house, where they were staying.

Mom woke Sammie and me up early to begin hand-delivering the invitations. Then we were to go to the florist and choose flowers. "Pink. Not black," Mom said sternly to Sammie.

"God, make one little mistake and you'll never hear the end of it," Sammie yawned.

After breakfast, Sammie and I were getting ready to go when we realized we didn't have a car. Elizabeth had taken the Caddie the night before to Evan's house and Dad had already disappeared with the Oldsmobile.

"Damn it, Elizabeth won't be up for hours," Sammie said. "She'll never bring the car back."

"So take your bikes," Mom said, wholly unperturbed by our predicament.

"You've gotta be kidding me," I said. "I think my bike is my Schwinn from the seventh grade." I was not about to be seen on that decrepit piece of shit.

"And I don't have a bike," Sammie said.

"Use Lucy's."

I remembered Lucy's bike. One year she had desperately wanted a bike for her birthday. I knew she was hoping for a Fuji. She had the whole thing scoped out. All of her friends had Fujis from the Bicycle Rack downtown. They could get to the Four Corners in record time to hang out and do nothing. And they would do it in that ultra-casual cool way—with no hands.

When her birthday came, Mom and Dad did get her a ten-speed, but it was a Huffy from J. C. Penney. It was white with black tape on the ram's-horn handlebars. She tried really hard not to look disappointed, but it was from *Penney's,* for God's sake. She only rode it a couple of times and I think that was only so Mom and Dad's feelings wouldn't be hurt. My birthday was a month later, and since Lucy had wanted a bike, of course, so did

I. My parents, knowing they had made a mistake with Lucy, had given me a green metallic-flake Schwinn ten-speed. Not a Fuji, but definitely not a Huffy. I never forgot the look on Lucy's face. Or the look on my parents' faces when they looked at Lucy.

"Or take the truck," Mom said absentmindedly.

"Oh God. That's worse." I flopped into a kitchen chair.

But Mom gave me the eye like she was at the end of her rope. We were taking the truck. My dad had bought the secondhand truck in his handyman phase. It had a red door, which wouldn't have been so bad if the rest of the truck was red as well. Over the years, as it got more and more broken down, Dad had tried to fix it up. When Mom had said it would look better painted, he hit it with white spray paint. She should have said *professionally* painted. Semantics can be important around here.

Someone knocked on the back door and I went to answer. It was Walker, my boyfriend. He had on a wrinkled blue-and-white-striped button-down shirt worn untucked over a fraying pair of khaki shorts. With his black hair and brown eyes, he was easily the most handsome man I had ever met. Towering over me, he gave me a hug. "It's going to be eighty degrees today. Grab your swimsuit. We'll get some sandwiches and hit the beach," he said.

Looking over my shoulder I saw that Sammie had heard him. "No way, Walker. We have to deliver invitations to Lucy's wedding, and I'm not doing it by myself."

Walker eyed me questioningly. I inwardly cursed Sammie. I hadn't broken the news to Walker yet about Lucy's wedding. Opening the door wider, I swept my hand toward the kitchen to usher him in. Walker helped himself to a Coke from the refrigerator, then looked in the freezer for ice. "So Lucy is getting married, huh?" he said.

Before Sammie or I could answer, he said under his breath,

"Why is it that no one in this house refills the ice trays?" He pulled out six empty ice trays, carried them to the sink, filled them, and returned them to the freezer. He flopped into a kitchen chair and picked up one of the invitations. Then he read it. "It's *this* Sunday?"

"Yeah, um, that's just kind of how it worked out," I muttered.

"So who's the guy?"

"His name is Chuck. We don't know anything else about him except that he's in the army, too," I said as I started stacking the invitations.

"If he's in combat training, then that at least will prepare him for your family, especially Lucy," Walker snickered.

I wasn't in the mood to hear how nuts my family was. I changed the subject. "I know you want me to go to the beach but I can't today. We have too much to do."

Walker softened. "Okay, sorry. I guess I shouldn't be too surprised by anything Lucy does after, you know . . ."

I did know. He meant Lucy suddenly dropping out of school to join the military. It was something that was hard for a Princeton undergrad to understand. "I'll just go to the beach myself," he continued. "Plenty of other people will be there to hang around with. If you think you can get away later, just let me know." He gave me another hug, kissed the top of my head, and left.

Sammie divvied up the invitations and handed me half. "Okay, let's get started."

Shaking my head, I took her stack from her and sat down at the table. "If we don't organize them we'll be driving back and forth all over town." Methodically, I arranged them by street and street number. "See, now we just start at the east end of town and make our way west down Ruddiman, then back up Mills Street, and you get the idea."

Sammie and I took the truck, lurching and screeching up and down the streets delivering the invitations. We really could have just walked. The truck, however, allowed us to hide more easily. If we were lucky, we could just stick the envelope into the mailbox out by the road unseen. But a couple of people caught us.

"Yes, Mrs. Petty, that's right. Lucy's getting married," I stammered on the Pettys' front walk. I backed up as she started to open the envelope, but she was quicker than me.

I was almost trotting back to the truck when she called after me, "Honey, *this* Sunday?"

"Yes! Sure hope you can come."

"But . . ."

I had already slammed the truck door. Let Mom handle the phone calls. Sammie didn't have a much better time on her side of the street. We finally made it home, exhausted from outrunning the questions. Elizabeth and Mom were upstairs. They yelled for us to come up and help them.

"Jeannie, you are going to be the maid of honor," Mom started out.

"Why me?"

"You know you're the one Lucy would choose if we let her know about this."

"Why can't Terri Worthington do it?"

"Because Terri Worthington is not family and it would be too hard to explain anyway." Mom reached into the closet and pulled out a dress.

"Oh God. Not that." It was Sammie's high school prom dress. It was about eight years old and made out of silky polyester stuff with big red roses printed all over it.

"You'll look lovely in it." Mom was smoothing the fabric and holding the dress out to inspect it.

"Let's just hope everyone is still drunk from Evan's wedding the night before," I sighed.

"What is Lucy going to wear?" Sammie asked.

"I'm not sure yet." Mom pursed her lips.

"Why don't you call the June Wedding?" I asked. It seemed logical, as it was the one and only bridal shop in town.

"I already did. Nothing is available in her size, and it's obviously too late to order one."

It wasn't like we had an old wedding dress in the closet. Elizabeth volunteered hers, but it was in California. Not to mention that Elizabeth is about five inches taller than Lucy. Sammie had ceremonially burned her wedding dress in a Weber grill. I remember we had all barely flown back from her California wedding before she divorced the guy. Apparently he made some remarks about how she should get her family under control and that was that.

"What about Anna's wedding dress?" I asked. We all stared at each other. They were about the same size, but this might be pushing things a bit too far with Anna.

"It's not like she's going to need it after Saturday night," I added in defense of my idea.

"So we track her and Evan to their hotel room on their wedding night, wait outside, then knock and ask if they're undressed yet? That seems very not right," Elizabeth said.

"So who's going to ask her?" Sammie asked. Nobody volunteered for this duty.

"I guess I'll call her mother first," Mom finally said. She turned and went downstairs.

"Does anyone else think this is crazy?" Elizabeth asked. Sammie and I didn't even bother answering.

I went out into the hallway and opened the hall closet. As I figured, it was jam-packed with towels, blankets, old curling irons, squashed boxes of tampons, and my brother's free weights. On tippy toes I reached up and began pulling the mess from the top shelf. Blankets cascaded on my head and fell to the floor.

"No way, Jeannie!" Elizabeth rapped out behind me. "Mom will kill you if she sees this mess!"

"Just this one shelf," I pleaded. "It will only take a second."

Elizabeth simply glared at me until I reluctantly gathered up the blankets, climbed up using the bottom shelf, and shoved the whole pile back onto the top shelf.

Deprived of cleaning, my normal method of calming myself, I went downstairs. The caterers were spreading out brochures in the kitchen. Dad had the sprinkler heads apart on the kitchen table and grumbled that they were getting his parts all out of order. Mom was pointing to various photos of food while she spoke on the phone. "Yes, Helen, I know this may be difficult for Anna, and you should absolutely not ask her if you aren't comfortable with it." There was a long pause before Mom said, "That's a good idea; think it over and let me know. We'll come up with some other idea in the meantime." She hung up. "This is some fine welcome for Anna into our family."

"Do you want cheese balls or the crudités?" the caterer asked.

"Crudités. Where else could we get a dress? Jeannie, get the phone book."

"Chicken, fish, or steak?"

"Chicken and steak. We should give them a choice, right, Harold? I'm so worried about Anna. I should call Helen right back and tell her not to bring it up. That poor child, we are just running roughshod over her."

"Palate-cleansing sorbet?" the caterer continued.

"Yes, but lime."

I paged through the Yellow Pages and found something. "Here's a store that sells costumes. They list wedding dresses," I said.

"Give them a call right now. Lucy is a size six."

The caterer thrust another photo in Mom's face. "Now for the wedding cake, you can have either marble or white with, I assume, white frosting."

"Marble with white frosting. Harold, aren't we supposed to put a sixpence in the cake or something? Or is that in her shoe? Isn't there some English family tradition we're supposed to follow?"

"Yeah, post banns in the church six months before the wedding. But it's a little late for that."

"They've got a dress," I said to Mom with my hand over the mouthpiece.

"What's it look like?"

"It's white, high-necked, full skirt."

"Perfect. We'll take it."

"But it's a size ten and it has fake blood all over it."

Mom shook her head and I hung up the phone. She finished up with the caterer while Dad and I went outside. The sun was setting over Bear Lake and the water carried its red reflection. For once the lake was quiet, without speedboats and water-skiers. A lone Butterfly sailboat was making its way home. Dad and I sat for a long time without speaking. We could do that, while everybody else seemed to make endless chatter. When it was almost too dark to see him, he said, "I hope she's happy." His voice cracked just the littlest bit. I nodded in the darkness and we rocked on the porch, swatting at mosquitoes, until the streetlights came on.

Six

Friday, June 27, 1986, 10:00 a.m.

*T*he day started with an airport run. Dad does these because he can get out of the house for some length of time
and into the quiet of the car. One time I was talking to
him about the life expectancy of men versus women and told him
that statistics show that men die off a lot earlier. Dad said they
probably did it to get away from the women.

That morning, he took off in the Oldsmobile for the hour trip
to Grand Rapids to get Grandma, who was landing at 11 a.m. We
were a bit worried about her flying by herself. Last time, she got
lost making her connection in Chicago and didn't show up for
about four hours. She told us that she became disoriented by the
hallway of neon lights between United terminals B and C and just
kept going back and forth.

Lucy and Chuck were coming in to Muskegon at noon, and
Sammie, Mom, and I were going to get them. Elizabeth, after much
cajoling, had returned the Caddie. Of course it fell to me to drive
her back over to Evan's house and drop her off. It was Sammie's

idea to make the signs and buy the confetti. I went up to Keefe's Pharmacy and bought a bottle of Korbel sparkling wine. The lady at the counter didn't card me but she did say, "Hi, Sammie." When I got back, I called Evan to see if he wanted to go, too.

"Nah. I've got to go pick up my tuxedo. Plus, I don't want to be around when Lucy sees what you all have in store for her. She might just turn right around and get back on the plane. Let me know what the guy is like. God knows what he'll think of us."

"Okay. See you tonight at the rehearsal dinner. I wouldn't come by here today if I were you. Dad has the crew coming to put up the tent. And the new crisis is that Pete from next door told Dad we have big gopher holes, so he's trying to figure out what to do about that." Elizabeth and Ron were going to the beach, as Ron had announced that without Vitamin D from the sun he would become depressed. More likely he didn't know what to do without a tanning booth nearby.

Muskegon County International Airport is composed of one runway and one small building. The only planes that came in there were twin-prop deals. All bags were off-loaded from the plane and you picked them up right on the tarmac. Lord knows where the "International" part of its name came from. They must have counted the fact that you could make connections in Chicago or Detroit to exotic destinations like Canada. The runway was set among cornfields, and the farmers kicked up such a fuss when the airport went in that the county commission didn't have the heart to take the land away from them completely. In August, the planes had to change their schedules to accommodate the machinery and the workers harvesting the corn near the runway.

We positioned ourselves at the chain-link fence just off the tarmac. I saw the plane first. It emerged from the clouds, then disappeared into them again, as if it were scared to show itself. It finally descended and touched down. Sammie handed me a sign and started to uncork the champagne.

"I'm not so sure this is a good idea," Mom said as she held the fence as though it might fall down.

I put my arm around her. "We can stop if you want."

"I want all my kids to be happy. I want them to marry good people and lead good lives. And I want to do right by Lucy. I need to do right by my little Velvet."

The plane rolled to a stop in front of us. The props were starting to slow down.

"You're doing this because you love her, right?" I asked.

Mom nodded mutely. I could see that she was thinking hard. Then there was a discernible straightening of her back and her chin came up. "Okay, girls, let's welcome Lucy and Chuck home."

The door opened, and Lucy was the fourth one to step out. I had never seen her in uniform before, much less her dress uniform. I thought she looked pretty snappy. I held up the sign as Lucy looked over at us. She stopped in mid-step. Her smile came and went like a flickering lightbulb as she read it, WELCOME HOME, MR. AND MRS. CHUCK. Sammie popped the champagne and whooped as it sprayed over the fence. A few other people waiting next to us smiled and clapped, not knowing what they were clapping for. Lucy turned and said something to the man behind her. He looked over at us but his face was hidden by the shadow of his hat. She came down the steps with, we assumed, Chuck, but she didn't come over to us at the fence. Instead, she headed straight for the arrivals door. I was holding Mom's hand and it went limp. When Lucy was almost at the door, she turned and gave the briefest of waves. Mom took her hand out of mine and clutched the handles of her purse.

Sammie stared at the door Lucy had gone into. "There's not

another plane leaving for California right now, is there? She might be buying a ticket."

Then the door leading from the terminal to our side of the fence opened and Lucy stepped out. She might have stayed right there, but people poured through the door behind her, forcing her toward us. Chuck was struggling with a piece of pull-luggage that didn't want to be pulled. Mom covered the space between her and Lucy and cupped Lucy's face in her hands. "Welcome home, sweetheart." She touched her forehead to the brim of Lucy's army hat and smiled at her daughter.

"Did I . . . are you . . . I mean . . . omigod." Lucy didn't seem able to put a sentence together. She blinked at the signs as though she had just learned the English language and was unsure of her reading ability. Sammie shook the champagne again and it sprayed across Chuck, but he didn't seem to mind. He shook our hands and called Mom "ma'am."

"Aren't you embarrassed for yourselves?" Lucy finally managed to say as she wiped champagne off her chin.

Sammie just threw confetti on her. "It would take a hell of a lot more than this to embarrass us." Chuck lugged the baggage to the car and we all squished in. Mom drove, with Lucy in the front. Sammie, Chuck, and I sat in the back. I craned my head back so I could see the sky and trees fly by the back window. A flock of seagulls took off overhead in a single arcing motion. I thought about the fact that a bunch of larks is called an exaltation. That made me smile. Somebody way back when had had a sense of joy when naming them.

Lucy sat erect in the front seat. Her dark hair was pinned up under her hat. Mom studied her profile at the stoplight. "So, honey, you're married," she said, half question and half statement.

"Yes," Lucy said, but didn't look at her.

We drove in silence for a few miles. Mom tried valiantly with Chuck. "Where are you from originally, Chuck?"

"I'm from Needles, California, ma'am."

None of us knew anything about Needles, and that kind of killed the conversation for a while. "And your parents?" Mom struggled. I'm not sure what the question meant, but I was interested in Chuck's answer.

"Jackie and John Tanner, ma'am."

Ah, now we had a last name: Tanner. What kind of name was that? We were from the land of the Worthingtons and Prescotts or maybe the occasional Van Owen.

"And do they know about your, ah, recent marriage?"

"No, ma'am. Only Lucy's friend Fudgie knew about it."

Lucy slunk down a bit in her seat, her hat over her eyes.

"Fudgie Shaw?" Sammie asked, perplexed.

"Yeah, Fudgie Shaw," Lucy answered.

How the hell did Fudgie Shaw know about it? Fudgie had been a good friend of hers in high school, but he certainly wouldn't be the first person Lucy would call.

"Oh, Lord, I don't think we invited the Shaws," Mom fretted. "Jeannie, check the guest list when we get home. Lucy, do Fudgie's parents know about this?"

"I don't know. I asked him not to tell anyone. Which he apparently already has." Lucy scowled. "And a guest list for what?"

Silence fell over the car again. It was one of those moments when you've been going hell-for-leather to solve a problem and think everybody else is up to speed, only to realize how completely wrong you are. The three of us in the know pondered the answer. Chuck was looking increasingly uncomfortable between Sammie and me. I tried to lean up against the car door to give him more room. Mom took a drag of her cigarette.

"Can you put that thing out? It's really bad for you, in case you didn't know. And it's really bad for us, if you care," Lucy stated flatly.

Mom rolled down the window and flicked the butt out. Since she gave no response, I knew she was still thinking.

"Lucy, your father and I have always wanted the very best for you. We were startled to learn of your marriage. But we wanted you to have happy memories, shared with your family, memories that you could always look back on. So we're giving you a beautiful white wedding on Sunday. It's because we love you, honey."

Lucy didn't look like someone who had just found out how loved she was. Her blue eyes seemed bigger than normal and her mouth was slightly open. "This Sunday?"

"Yes, sweetheart. But if it's not what you want we don't have to do it. It's nothing that can't be undone."

"Except for the invitations being out. But I suppose we could just call everybody," Sammie muttered.

"Everybody?"

"Just all of your high school friends and their parents. And your old teachers, people like that," Mom said.

Lucy was ramrod stiff in her seat, speechless for the first time since I'd known her.

"When did you find out that we were married?" Chuck asked.

"On Sunday. We've been working on the wedding ever since. It will be beautiful." I could tell Mom desperately wanted a smoke.

"Why didn't you call me?" Lucy demanded. "You know, pick up a phone and communicate with me and *ask* if it was okay for you to marry me off!"

"I tried to, honey. I did. But you were out on maneuvers."

"Drills," Lucy corrected her sharply.

"I picked out your patterns, Lucy. They're really pretty. And I'm going to be your maid of honor," I volunteered.

"Is everyone coming?"

"Pretty much everybody said yes," Mom said. "We just, uh, have to stop by the church so Father Whippet can meet Chuck." We drove the rest of the way to the church in silence.

When we pulled up, the foreboding finger of some religious figure was pointing down at all of us threatening hell and damnation if we were bad. A sculptor aptly named Mr. Love had made it for the church. He'd been married so many times it was hard to keep track. Once when I came home, I ran into an acquaintance of mine. I jokingly said that I hadn't been home for so long that I had no idea who Mr. Love was married to now. With a frown she told me that the man was currently married to her mother. Sometimes it's hard to keep up.

But that was the beauty of being an Episcopalian instead of a Catholic. I call Episcopalianism "Catholic Lite." We have all of the pomp with none of the consequences. We can get divorced, our ministers can get married and have sex, and birth control isn't a sin.

Mom prepped Chuck in the church hallway, telling him, "Don't lie, but you're an Episcopalian."

"Episca-what?" Chuck looked confused, but before Mom could answer, Father Whippet came out into the hall from his office and smiled, showing us his crooked yellow teeth. He gave me the creeps. Father Whippet shook hands with Chuck and then gestured for us to enter his office. He took a seat behind his enormous desk.

"Lucy, this is a very happy day for me." Father Whippet beamed at me. I flicked my head toward the right sister and Father Whippet redirected his gaze. "As I'm sure you know, we usually take our couples through several weeks of marriage counseling in order to prep them for what is in store for them. But since this is an unusual situation and as you are both Episcopalians"—he now beamed at Chuck—"we'll do this in an hour. Lucy, I've known you since you were a baby and I've always found you to have good judgment."

Sammie nudged me from her place next to me on the settee. "Senility is so sad," she whispered. I managed to turn my laugh into a cough.

Father Whippet continued. "So you've known, uh"—he looked down at a piece of paper—"uh, Chuck, long enough to know you want to spend the rest of your life with him?"

"I've known him for seven weeks." Lucy looked straight at Father Whippet.

"Well, uuuum, but you love each other deeply?" Father Whippet was beginning to have the same desperate tone my mother had had in the car.

"Sure." Chuck shrugged.

At that point Father Whippet gave Mom the eye, and Sammie, Mom, and I found ourselves back out in the hallway. Lord knows what he was going to say to the happy couple. Mom paced while Sammie and I sat on the wooden bench outside his office. "She didn't look happy," Mom fretted.

"She looks how she normally looks," Sammie said as she tried to adjust her back against the slats. This same conversation took a few different forms while we waited. Eventually, Lucy and Chuck emerged from the office looking slightly dazed.

"He said it was okay," Lucy announced. "Since we're already married by a judge it doesn't really matter."

The drive from St. Peter's in downtown Muskegon over the Causeway to North Muskegon only takes about five minutes. We passed the Rupp Plant, which was situated just off the Causeway on the edge of Muskegon Lake. When I was little, it spewed nasty black stuff from its stacks out over the road, the marshes, the lakes, and our town. When it started killing the Canadian geese, the good people of North Muskegon starting calling for an environmental rehab. They weren't that worried about the geese, but they were damn sure worried about their property values. Now the plant had a two-hundred-foot smokestack so the wind could catch the black spew and spread it more generously on our neighbors.

Figuring that hitting the house and seeing the limp tent lying in the backyard might be a bit much for Lucy, Mom pulled in to Main Street, a restaurant three blocks from our house. Chuck hadn't said a word since we had left the church. Granted, men did not tend to speak much around the Thompson females, because it meant jumping into the fast-moving current of our words. Seated at the table, Mom, Sammie, and I looked expectantly at Chuck. He looked expectantly back at us. Lucy fiddled with her fork and kept checking the door to see if anyone she knew was coming in.

"So, Chuck, do you study Russian as well?" Mom asked politely. I could tell she was wondering when he was going to take his hat off.

"No, ma'am."

"Are you an officer?" It was a good question, but none of us knew what that meant anyway. He could have told us he was Field Marshall Rommel and we would have nodded our heads politely until we could check with Dad.

But his answer again was "No, ma'am."

Then he did it. He made the fatal mistake. The one thing that sealed his fate in my mother's eyes. She would deny it, but I knew better. It was a small gesture, but my mother had not spent her life trying to better herself for no reason. Chuck's Coke was sitting in front of his plate. Leaving his hands resting at his sides, he leaned forward and fumbled for his straw with his mouth. I watched Mom lean slightly back from the table. Her eyes were glued to Chuck's lips as he slurped his Coke, his hands dangling uselessly. And that was that. He was not "our people."

None of us dared to look at Lucy, who surely must have noticed. Chuck, clueless to the awkward silence, volunteered, "I'm a private first class, ma'am, in B Five-Three Company." This sounded vaguely like a Boy Scout troop. I wondered if their oath was similar to the Girl Scout oath. Once, on a Girl Scout camping trip, I had been asked to lead the pledge. I practiced hard the night before, lying in my Raggedy Ann sleeping bag in my tent. The next day, we all stood in a circle around the flagpole. The troop leader looked at me expectantly. And—I forgot. Absolutely could not remember the first words to save my life. I recited them silently to myself for reassurance, "On my honor, I will try to serve God and my country . . ."

"Jeannie." Mom was talking to me.

"Huh?"

"Chuck just said he's a runner."

"Oh." What was I supposed to say? That I was a runner in high school? Did this mean we had a deep connection?

"I run long distance for the army."

"Why? Is it training for combat or something?"

"No. It's for medals. Competition between units." He stuck a fist in the air and belted out, "Hoorah B Company!" The lunch crowd paused and stared in our direction to see what was going on.

"Chuck, sweetie, maybe not in here," Lucy said. She turned to us. "He's very good. He's won almost every event. It's a big deal in the army."

Sammie was surprisingly silent through all of this. Looking at her, I saw something like worry, mixed with compassion, on her face. She reached across the table and squeezed Lucy's hand. "It's nice to have you home." They exchanged long smiles. Lucy knew exactly what we were all thinking. "Now give me your hat. It'll look great on me."

Lucy took off her hat and handed it to her. "I have to have it back. It's against regulations for a civilian to wear it."

"If I see a general I promise to hide," Sammie assured her. We finished the "biggest sourdough sandwiches on the coast of Lake Michigan" and drove the last few blocks home. As Mom had feared, Dad was out back with a gigantic tent sprawled on the ground. He got up and wiped his hands on his plaid pants before shaking hands with Chuck. He gave Lucy a big hug.

"Chuck, I sure could use some help out here. The crew left the tent and said they'd be back, but that was hours ago. On top of that, I've got a gopher problem. But Pete next door said this would take care of them." He held out a handful of M-80s, which anybody north or south of Tennessee could tell you are big old firecrackers. The kind that blow mailboxes off their posts. The kind they run commercials about around the Fourth of July, showing kids with bandaged eyes and hands. We left Chuck out back with Dad so they could bond over explosives and went into the kitchen. Lucy sighed and sat down at the table. Mom hugged her and stroked her hair. "My little Velvet." However, it said PRIVATE THOMPSON on her name tag, which Sammie asked if she could have for an art project. Lucy took it off and handed it to her.

"Where is everybody?" she finally asked.

"Dad said Grandma is upstairs napping and Elizabeth will be over in a bit. Evan is getting ready for the rehearsal dinner. Which is"—Mom checked her watch—"Lord, in just a few hours. Do you know what you're wearing?" she asked.

"Yes. I just need to shower."

Thank God Elizabeth isn't here yet, I thought. She had the shower schedule with her and I didn't know if we could handle that just yet. Although the house was fairly big, for some reason we had only one full bathroom. When we were growing up, all five of us women would squeeze into the bathroom at once, four of us doing our makeup and blow-drying our hair and doing our business while one of us showered. Then we would bitch at the person who was showering because she was fogging up the mirror. I don't recall Dad or Evan ever actually getting their turn in the bathroom, although I'm sure they must have, as they didn't pee out by the garage. I hoped.

We all prayed for a second bathroom, but Mom enlarged the kitchen instead. It had been a "one-butt kitchen," she said—which was a problem when you had seven butts.

We heard the first explosion go off. Mom lit a cigarette. I went over to the sliders to see what was going on. The first explosion seemed to be successful. Chuck and Dad were peering down at a decent-sized hole.

"That'll fix them," Dad crowed. "Or at least scare them over to the Longs' yard." Dad didn't like the Longs. Mr. Long always complained about our dog, Buddy, peeing on his lawn. All of their kids played flute or violin in the school orchestra, and the entire family was high-strung and always on some vitamin regimen. When they started selling Amway products, Dad wrote them off for good.

The second explosion erupted. Chuck and Dad gleefully raced over to inspect the damage. A trickle of water started overflowing the hole. Dad was scratching his balding head when a geyser shot up in the air—not just some mini Old Faithful, but a thundering-straight-up-in-the-air-for-twenty-feet geyser.

"Shit. I hit the water main." Dad trudged off to the side of the house to switch off the main. The geyser slowed down and became more like an open fire hydrant in New York in August. Then it died completely. "Is it off?" he shouted from around the corner.

"Yup, Mr. Thompson. It's done," Chuck shouted back.

The third explosion took them by surprise as Dad was rounding the corner of the house. They both leapt back about ten feet. Smoke began to rise from the pile of dead leaves under the stairs that led down to the dock. Mom had been bugging Dad since last fall to rake them out. Then we saw flames. They weren't huge, only licking about a foot in the air.

"Get the hose!" Dad screamed.

I turned from the sliding doors back to my Mom, Sammie, and Lucy. "Is anybody else interested in this?"

The doorbell rang, and Mom went to answer the door.

Chuck ran around the corner of the house and reappeared on the other side. "Where is it?" he asked.

"It's . . . shit. It's right here." It was on the lawn where Dad had left it while fixing the water sprinklers. He raced for the faucet and cranked the handle. Nothing.

"Oh shit. No water. Rose!"

Mom was by now, thankfully, not in the house. I ran out front and listened to her try to explain to Mrs. Petty why the love of her son's life was marrying another man a mere nine months after they had broken up. Mrs. Petty tearfully said that it shouldn't matter that Jeff had dumped Lucy for another girl. The other girl hadn't worked out, so why couldn't Lucy and Jeff get back together? They still had those Christmas ornaments with their names painted on them from the high school Christmas dance, after all. I decided that Mom was much too occupied to deal with our house being on fire and ran back to the kitchen.

Through the open sliding doors, I could see Dad trying unsuccessfully to stomp out the fire with his shoe. "Chuck, get a bucket!" he finally yelled.

Chuck ran into the kitchen, looking dazed and panicked. "Bucket?"

Sammie calmly opened a cupboard door and handed him a saucepan.

"Is that it?" Chuck looked at the saucepan as if he had never seen one.

"That's it," Sammie said, and closed the cupboard door. Even if we did have a bucket we would never find it. It's not like there was a special place in the garage marked BUCKETS, for God's sake. Chuck ran back out to the backyard. Dad pointed down the hill at Bear Lake. Chuck ran around the fire burning up the dock stairs and nearly fell down the hill trying to get to the lake. He scooped a pan of water and ran back up the hill. By that time, Dad had put out the fire with what was left of the coffee in his thermos and the water out of Buddy's bowl. As he stood surveying the damage, Chuck poured his 1.5 quarts of water onto the smoldering ashes.

"Guess I'll need to rebuild these stairs by tomorrow, huh?" Dad said, and went into the house to make a new pot of coffee and ponder the situation. The backyard was left with a bedraggled tent, three large holes in the lawn, and charred dock stairs. The top section of the stairs rolled over and fell down the hill later that night.

Chuck came in, stuck his face under the kitchen faucet, and tried to gulp water that wasn't coming. Crossing to the fridge, he found an old bottle of lemonade and gulped it down. I was sure he'd have stomach cramps later. Who knew how long that lemonade had been in there? Then he wiped his face with his sleeve, sat down, and began tracing the roosters on the kitchen table. I knew how he felt. He'd get used to it.

"Chuck?"

It was Jeff Petty. Sammie and I exchanged a look that meant "uh-oh."

Chuck looked up, and Jeff extended his hand. "Hi, I'm, um, a good friend of Lucy's. I thought maybe you'd like to meet some of the guys. We're playing flag football down at the high school field. Do you want to come?"

I thought this was a pretty damn nice gesture on Jeff's part and Chuck didn't seem to recognize his name. So there it was: he didn't know about Jeff Petty. He seemed glad to do something that would get him away from the house. Lucy had just come in from the front yard, where apparently she had been talking to Mom and Mrs. Petty. She seemed prepared for the situation in front of her.

"Can I go?" Chuck asked her.

"Sure, honey. Have a good time. Just be back by five because we have to get ready for our rehearsal dinner." Chuck looked blank.

"Mom decided to throw our rehearsal dinner at the same time as Evan's."

Oh God, now we were usurping Evan's rehearsal dinner, too. Forget about sending Evan over the edge into therapy; he was gonna hit bottom any second. Some psychiatrist was going to make a mint off him. Although I wasn't sure we even had a psychiatrist in Muskegon.

Chuck changed into some sweats, and I had to admit, he looked pretty good. He took off with Jeff in Jeff's Camaro to drive the five blocks to the field.

Mom went out to survey the damage in the backyard, and then she went to the phone and dialed Tom, the handyman who usually cleaned up after Dad. She must have expressed some urgency, because his pickup truck roared into our driveway moments later. Tom charged into the house, straight through the kitchen and family room, then out the sliding doors to the backyard. As I trailed after him, I wondered why he hadn't just gone around the side of the house. He had left dirty footprints everywhere on the carpet. Sammie looked at the footprints, then at me, expectantly. I was already getting the carpet cleaner and the vacuum out.

"Does that really make you feel calmer?" Sammie stood over me as I scrubbed away on my hands and knees.

"Yes."

"But why?"

"I don't know." I finished up with the vacuum, then went outside to see if there was any progress. Dad and Tom studied the second hole. "I have about seven or eight people who need to shower here within the next hour," Dad said.

"I'm gonna have to jerry-rig it." Tom took his cap off and scratched his head.

"Think it'll hold until the city crew can get here to fix it right?" Dad asked.

"Beats me." Tom got to work.

I don't know what he did, but about half an hour later he yelled at me to try the kitchen faucet. I turned the knob and water came out, which is what I yelled back to him.

"It's 4:00. You're supposed to be in the shower." Elizabeth had arrived. "And we have to figure out who is going in which car. Since it'll take us about ten minutes to get there, we should leave at 5:45 in case parking is bad."

"Someone has obviously lived in L.A. too long," I replied. All we had in Muskegon was parking.

Tom came in the back door while wiping his hands. "Okay, I think it'll hold together for at least a couple of hours."

Elizabeth whirled to face him. "What? What will hold together?"

"The—" he started.

I interrupted Tom. "Nothing. It's nothing."

Elizabeth eyed me. "Is this 'nothing' solved?"

"Yes."

That was good enough for Elizabeth. If she didn't have to come up with the solution, then she wasn't concerned about the problem. I went upstairs because being alone in the shower did not sound like a bad thing at the moment. The water pressure was a little low, but I still shaved my legs and worked the conditioner through my hair.

"Hey. Are you ever getting out of there?" Sammie called as she opened the bathroom door. "My turn is at 4:20." I heard her put the lid to the toilet seat down and sit on it.

"I thought I'd stay in here until everything was all over." I raised my voice over the sound of the water. "Or until your prom dress, now my maid of honor dress, disintegrates."

"Could be a long time. It's polyester. That stuff is built to last forever."

I shut off the shower and toweled down while Sammie shed her clothes. She hopped into the shower while I blew my hair dry.

"So. Chuck," she called from the shower.

That's all she said but I knew what she meant. I tried to clear the mirror with my hand but the shower steamed it back up. Blindly, I took the curling iron to my hair.

"Your bangs are sticking up," Sammie said as she got out of the shower.

Through a clean spot on the mirror, I saw that I had fried my bangs. They were now shriveled at the ends like when Mom would light a cigarette over the gas stove and catch her hair in the flame.

"Goddamn it! When you people all come home it's just chaos."

"Don't you yell at me!" Sammie was now shouting. Someone tried to open the door, but Sammie was directly in front of it, bent over toweling her hair. The door smacked her bare butt and she sprawled into me. I dropped the hot curling iron on my foot.

"Watch where you're going!" we both yelled.

With uncharacteristic calm Lucy walked in and took off her clothes. "It's 4:40 and it's my turn. And I know what you've been saying in here so just stop it."

"We haven't been saying anything. Really." Sammie looked at me.

We both knew this was Lucy's day. Actually it was Evan and Lucy's day, but Lucy was the only one in the bathroom. It was important not to upset her.

"Do you know that you're wearing Anna's wedding dress?" I asked politely.

Lucy turned slowly, one foot over the edge of the tub. "You've got to be kidding," she said. "Mom planned a surprise wedding and she doesn't even get me a dress?" She climbed into the shower.

"She tried, she really did."

"Anna doesn't mind me using hers?" Lucy peeked around the shower curtain and lifted an eyebrow.

"No. In the end she was quite cool about it," Sammie said while mascara-ing her lashes with her mouth slightly open.

"How was she in the beginning?"

"Not so cool. But she came around."

Lucy sighed. "Christ, it's her wedding weekend, after all. And Evan's. If I were them I'd be furious." Sammie and I looked at each other, and I switched the subject.

"You get to pick out your headgear-thingy tomorrow morning," I said helpfully. "We haven't found one yet. Mom made an appointment at the June Wedding."

"Why didn't she get me a dress there?" Lucy asked.

"Nothing in your size. Only size fourteens, the one-size-fits-all samples." I sat on the toilet seat fixing my hair. The cord from the curling iron stretched over the sink where Sammie was brushing her teeth. "Don't spit on that. It'll fry what's left of me."

There was silence from the shower for a while; then Lucy climbed out and all three of us crowded around the mirror trying to do our makeup. Lucy was au naturel, Sammie was in a towel that kept slipping off, and I had put on Dad's robe. Lucy looked at her reflection and handed the mascara wand to Sammie, who pushed Lucy down onto the toilet lid. Sammie studied Lucy's face.

"What are you wearing?"

"The green."

Sammie grabbed her eye shadows and started in on Lucy's face. She next applied powder and blush, and then added lipstick to Lucy's uncooperative mouth. When Sammie was finished, Lucy looked at her reflection in the hand mirror. "You always put too much on," she said to Sammie.

"You always put too little on," Sammie shot back.

When Sammie turned to the mirror to do her own makeup, I handed a tissue to Lucy, who promptly blotted her lips.

I stared at my own hair, which, being thin, had been subjected to a series of unfortunate perms, most recently a Toni home perm that left my semi-blond hair looking like I was in a constant state of fright.

Sammie grabbed Mom's Aquanet. "Close," she commanded.

I shut my eyes. She held my bangs down against my forehead and sprayed.

"Twenty minutes!" Elizabeth sing-songed a warning up the stairs.

"I hate it when she talks like that," I muttered.

"That nursery school teacher voice really annoys me, too," Lucy replied.

Elizabeth really wanted to be a news anchor. She'd have been good at it too, except she tried too hard and her voice sounded fakey. Elizabeth's hero growing up was Mary Tyler Moore. She even kind of looked like Mary Tyler Moore, with her tall, slender body and brunette hair. I could just hear her saying, "Oh, Mr. Graaaant!" and throwing her hat up into the air. When Elizabeth was eighteen, she had tried out for Miss Muskegon. She certainly had the beauty portion nailed. Confident and poised, she had strutted across the stage in a peach one-piece bathing suit—legs going from here to there. We clapped madly in the audience and, of course, she won the beauty segment of the contest.

Then she did her talent segment. For some reason, she had opted to dress as Sprout, the elf from the Jolly Green Giant TV commercials. Mom had gamely made her an elf outfit out of sparkly green material. We helped Elizabeth decorate a forty-gallon oil drum with tin foil so that it would look like a big can of peas. She did a skit, and maybe that wouldn't have been so bad, but she also decided to sing. Elizabeth can't sing. She came in third place overall. I thought she at least deserved second place, in front of that girl in a hoopskirt who recited something from *Gone with the Wind.*

I was shaken from my thoughts when Mom pushed her way into the bathroom. "Lucy, I don't want you to panic, but there's a problem with Chuck."

Oh God. She wasn't going to start in on Lucy right here in the bathroom, was she? Sammie and I would have edged for the door but there wasn't room to get around Mom.

"What's wrong?" Lucy asked. The hairbrush in her hand stopped mid-stroke.

"He's fine but there's been an accident."

"What happened?" she asked as she snatched Dad's robe off me and squeezed past all of us out the door. I grabbed one of Dad's long T-shirts from the back of the door, put it on, and ran after her and Mom.

Chuck was bent over in the front foyer holding on to his face. Jeff was awkwardly patting him on the back and looking at the air above Chuck's head. My first thought was that Mom wasn't going to be too happy about the blood streaming down on her Oriental rug.

Seven

January 2006

I hustled to get ready for work at Aidan's house on
Monday morning. Nine a.m. is the weekly meeting with
the entire Oxford marketing staff. When I kissed Aidan
good-bye he held me a bit longer as I made to pull away.

"Do you think you'll have an answer soon, Jeannie?" he said
into my hair.

"Sure. Soon," I said into his chest. Raising my head, I looked
into his eyes. "I promise." But my stomach was churning.

At 8:50 I entered the conference room and headed for the
coffee urn at the back of the room before taking my usual seat
near the head of the table. The highly polished cherry table had
room for about thirty people. More chairs lined the walls for those
who had not yet been ordained with a position at the table. Holding my Styrofoam cup and my notebook, I exchanged pleasant-
ries with people as I made my way forward.

Pulling back my chair, I stopped short. A notebook with a pen lying neatly on top was on the table directly in front of me. It practically had the word RESERVED printed on its cover. Flipping it open I saw Katsu Tanaka's name at the top. He wouldn't! Would he? He couldn't possibly think he could swipe my prime position at the table—just one seat from the head.

Seating was not a free-for-all. Some chairs had been occupied by the same butts for years. Sitting toward the head of the table, where the president of marketing ruled, indicated higher rank. People only moved up if someone died or got fired or if there was a direct coup in the works. Last week, Katsu was sitting along the wall.

I looked up to see some people watching me with interest. Hiding my anger, I grabbed the notebook and walked it down to the end, placing it in front of one of the few seats that had a history of rotating owners.

Nine a.m. and the meeting hadn't started yet. Tapping my pen in annoyance, I kept glancing toward the door for Rachael, the president of marketing, to enter. I hated it when meetings didn't start on time. At 9:05 Katsu strolled in. He was of Japanese descent but he was firmly Ivy League American. His jet-black hair was swept back with gel with a few pieces in front carefully arranged to stick straight up, and he draped his six-foot frame with only the latest designer suits from Barneys New York. I watched one person after another approach to offer congratulations. Stubbornly, I remained glued to my chair. Possession is nine-tenths of the law.

When Katsu glided toward me, I saw his eyes glance up and down the table, searching. His mouth twisted ever so slightly when he spotted his notebook down in the hinterlands. Without rising, I stuck my hand out at him.

"Congratulations, Katsu. Very impressive." I tried to sound sincere.

"Thanks, Jeannie. I'm looking forward to working more closely with you," he said graciously. Then he moved off toward the end of the table. I fumed inside.

Rachael finally entered and started the meeting with the announcement about Katsu. Applause followed. Was I imagining it or did her eyes narrow when she saw how far away Katsu was seated? With her steel gray hair and severe suits, Rachael made a lot of people nervous. I had always gotten along with her, though. Maybe I was just being paranoid. After all, what was the big deal? A guy got promoted. It didn't mean I was on the outs. I had opened billions of dollars' worth of movies. Rachael hadn't consulted me or even simply told me ahead of time but there could be a lot of reasons for that. I just didn't know what they were. Finally, after forty-five torturous minutes discussing the past weekend's box office, I was released.

Caitlin tried to follow me into my office with a stack of DVCAM tapes and notes but I waved her off. Shutting the door behind me, I took a deep breath. Then I noticed one of the framed photos of Aidan and me was hanging askew. Carefully I adjusted it, stepping back to make sure it was straight. Then I sat down at my desk with its two pens, call list, and typed-up list of notes of what needed to be done that day, neatly lined up side by side.

Opening my email, I noticed that Sammie had sent me another missive. Shit, I had forgotten to call her back. I left the email unopened so it would still appear as "new" when I got back to it.

An instant message popped up on my computer screen. Caitlin was letting me know Aidan was on the line. Before I could tell him what had occurred that morning, he said Warner Bros. had just called him. They wanted him to go to London immediately to check on a film that was going over budget.

Aidan is a well-known and trusted producer in studio circles. Every once in a while, when a studio had a film producer who "wasn't working out," they would call in Aidan to save the day. He sounded harried, so instead of telling him about Katsu, I told him I loved him and to travel safe.

In the two weeks that followed, we spoke on the phone every day and emailed constantly, but I missed him like crazy. He was under such pressure to straighten out the film's budget that I didn't have the heart to unload on him about Katsu's antics. But every night like clockwork, I woke up at 3 a.m. My head spun like a never-ending disc with the events jolting my life: Aidan and his proposal, Katsu and his pushiness.

Katsu continued to try and usurp my place at the conference table for the Monday and Wednesday meetings, forcing me to arrive earlier and earlier. Then he dropped thinly veiled criticisms in the meetings, saying that maybe my trailer test scores weren't as strong as everyone thought, or questioning whether it was a good idea to spend so much money on a particular song for the trailer. Finally, I walked into the executive dining room for lunch, only to see Katsu sitting at Ms. F.U.'s table. Unbelievably, he was even cozying up to the stars—*my* stars—to try and poach the films I was currently working on.

When I got back to the office I furiously punched in Aidan's number. He would know what to do. "Aidan, I—"

"I miss you too, lovebug. I can't wait to get home." Aidan's voice came from across the continent and the ocean.

"Yeah, Aidan, I have some things going on at work that I really need to talk—" My words came out in a flurry.

"That's how you respond to my saying I miss you?" Aidan sounded hurt.

"No, no, I'm sorry. It's just that I'm under a lot of pressure right now." I rubbed my eyes. This wasn't going right.

"Well, I'm under a fair amount of pressure too. But I still take time to tell you that I miss you. Is that so hard?"

Moving the two pens on my desk, I got them into even more perfect alignment. "I'm sorry. Can we start over?" I poured a glass of water from the bottle in my mini-fridge and added two Alka-Seltzers.

"Actually, I'm sorry to leave you this way but they just called me to the set. I'll talk to you later." He hung up without so much as a good-bye or an "I love you."

"Jeannie?" Caitlin poked her head into my office a few minutes later.

"What?" I fairly snarled at her. Caitlin furrowed her brow but didn't back out. It was pretty rare that I lost my temper. She entered and looked up at me.

"What are you doing?" she asked.

"What the hell does it look like I'm doing?"

"It looks like you are balancing in high heels on the back of your couch cleaning the windows with Windex. We have people who do that, you know."

"They do a terrible job." I tried to climb down but caught my shoe in the artfully placed afghan on the back of the couch. Windmilling the Windex and roll of paper towels, I fell into Caitlin's arms. As she is a fairly tall woman, at least I didn't take her down with me. She stood firm.

As we disentangled, she put me on my feet and regarded me. "Jeannie, how long have I worked for you?"

"I don't know. Maybe three years?"

"Five. So you'll excuse me when I tell you that you are acting weird."

"I've told you what Katsu's doing. He's making a move on my job." I slammed myself into my desk chair. I didn't mention Aidan's call. That was personal territory for me.

"Jeannie," Caitlin's voice was gentle, "you don't know that. Maybe he's simply trying hard to make a good impression because of his promotion. Why don't you just go to Rachael and ask her what's going on?"

"You don't *ask* what's going on in a film studio! You surmise. You ask semi-trusted sources what they know. You try not to act too desperate so they don't spread the word you are on the outs."

"Personally, I think you are making too much of this thing. Let it go and move on. You're valuable to the studio. Just look at your stats. You have no reason to be acting this way." Caitlin's voice was soothing but I was having none of it. When I didn't say anything she turned and left, shutting the door quietly. She couldn't understand why I was behaving the way I was. Frankly, *I* didn't know why I being such a freak.

I leaned back in my ergonomically correct Aeron office chair and stared at the white-tiled ceiling. Catching sight of the fire sprinklers, I involuntarily closed my eyes as the humiliating memory resurfaced of my first week working at Oxford Pictures. Nervous about making a good impression on my new colleagues, I had been dressing carefully and watching how everyone behaved to make sure I did the same things. I felt very much like I had been invited to a formal dinner party and didn't know which fork to use. Nevertheless, I had proudly invited Elizabeth to come see my wonderful new office. When she arrived she stalked around the office inspecting the furniture like she might buy it.

"Is this brand-new furniture?" She had arched an eyebrow at me.

"No." I was confused by the question. "Oxford has a big warehouse where you can pick out furniture that no one else is using."

"I thought as much." Elizabeth reached into her oversized purse and pulled out what looked like a dried bush. It dwarfed her hands. "This furniture has a lot of negative energy attached to it from its previous users—employees who were probably fired. You need to smudge the office with sage to drive away this bad energy."

I didn't know what "smudging" meant, but I did know that Elizabeth should not be lighting a dried bush and making a fiery torch out of it in my shiny new corporate office. She began waving the torch around over her head. "You put the flame out and then the smoke will take care of the negative stuff in here." That's when she waved the flames a bit too near the ceiling. The fire sprinklers had come on, drenching both of us, the furniture, TV monitor, and computer. Alarms had squalled through the entire building and hundreds of people had been evacuated to the parking lot. So much for being inconspicuous during my first few weeks at Oxford Pictures. At the time, I had tried to console myself that at least the sprinklers had gone off only in my office and not on the entire floor.

I was lucky I hadn't been escorted off the studio lot right then and there. But by the time the security guards and firemen had piled into my office, Elizabeth had crammed the evidence of the burned and now dripping sage bush into her purse. We lamely explained that the sprinklers had suddenly started by themselves for no reason at all. I don't think they quite bought the story of a malfunction but no one had questioned me further. After all these years I still hadn't let any of my family back in my office.

Shifting my eyes from the ceiling and the offending fire sprinklers, I buried myself at the office for the next eight hours. When Aidan still hadn't called me back, I finally texted him that I loved him and that I was sorry. I got a text back almost immediately. He loved me too, things were wrapping up, and he would be home in two days.

As promised, Aidan came to my house two nights later straight off the plane. "Will you marry me yet?" he asked as I opened the front door.

"No, not yet." I threw myself at him.

He smiled at me, then stepped in and dropped his bag. "Woman, you are an exasperation." We were both too happy to see each other to pursue the subject of marriage though.

Aidan took a quick shower while I chopped up veggies for dinner. He had just come back into the kitchen when a cell phone rang. We both sighed and looked at each other. Both of our phones were programmed with the same ring tone. Which one of us was going to have a work emergency now? Aidan fumbled in the pockets of his cargo pants while I grabbed mine from its special pocket in my purse. Aidan won, or lost, as the case may be. "This is Aidan," he answered formally. Then he relaxed. "Oh yeah, hi. What's up?"

I took out eggs to make us an omelet, my only specialty. He lifted an eyebrow at me and shook his head at the omelet. With the phone balanced between his ear and shoulder, he pulled garlic and tomatoes from the fridge.

That's when my cell phone rang, too. I checked caller ID and saw it was Caitlin.

"Hi," I answered.

"Jeannie, your sister Sammie called me," Caitlin said.

"Called *you*?" I couldn't imagine Sammie calling my assistant.

"Yeah, I guess you gave her my number in case of an emergency. Anyhow, she said she's called a bunch of times and sent emails but you haven't responded. She wanted to make sure you were okay."

"Oh, well . . . all right. I'll call her back." I clenched my eyes closed and gave an inward groan as I leaned against the refrigerator. I was in big trouble. I suddenly remembered Sammie's emails and phone messages that I kept thinking I would get back to.

"Jeannie, one last thing. She said you missed your nephew's tenth birthday party last week. That's why she was originally calling—to invite you."

"Um, okay. Thanks, Caitlin." I slowly pressed END on my cell phone. Oh no. I hadn't missed yet another family event, had I? It appeared I had. Worse, I had let down my nephew. Months ago I had promised him I would be there. I'd have to call Sammie and my nephew, apologize, and face the music. But I sure wasn't going to do that now, just when Aidan had walked in the door. I looked over at him where he stood by the chopping block.

He was still dicing tomatoes with his phone pressed between his ear and shoulder. "Uh-huh. Uh-huh. Mm-hmm, you too. Okay, bye."

He bent to take out a saucepan. "That was Montana."

Montana was Aidan's business partner. She had been a much more intimate partner of his years ago. They had broken up but remained civil and eventually teamed up to form a production company. Aidan insisted it was only business and I believed him. He had an innate ability to remain friendly with his past girlfriends.

Since they were generally friendly to me, I didn't bother mustering up any jealousy. Not that I would have anyhow. Jealousy is a useless emotion. If you get jealous of your boyfriend when he's just innocently talking to a woman at a party, you're ruining both of your good times. And if he's actively trying to make you jealous, he's not *worth* your time. Not that I didn't mind getting in a good dig once in a while. When I heard that Aidan's partner's name was Montana, I had mused, "If parents are going to name their kid after a state, why don't they ever pick states like Wisconsin? They could call her Connie for short. Or Whisky. And you never hear of anyone named Idaho. Of course, it's probably because when they would introduce themselves, the response would be 'Idaho? No, *you* da 'ho!'"

"So what's up?" I now asked. It wasn't like Montana to call him at night.

"One of us has to go to Australia to deal with a problem film. She said she would go since I just got back from London." Aidan and Montana never went to a film set together since that would have defeated the purpose of having a partner. They could get more work done if they split it up.

"Why did you do that 'Mm-hmm, you too' thing?"

"What are you talking about?" Aidan turned from the stove.

"Men say, 'Mm-hmm, you too' when someone has just said they love them but they can't say it back right then." I said I wasn't jealous. I didn't say I was stupid.

"Jeannie, that's ridiculous. I don't even remember what Montana and I were talking about right then, but she certainly wasn't telling me that she loves me." Seeing Aidan's wounded look, I relaxed.

"So who called you while I was talking to Montana?" Aidan said, switching the subject.

"Caitlin. Just a work thing." I looked down and fiddled with my dinner.

We finished the night the way we always do: dinner, coffee, *Law and Order* on TV, then bed. Our wonderfully predictable routine. Except this time Aidan turned to face me in bed. "I want to hear more."

"More what?" I yawned.

"More of your story."

"It's late," I said as I pulled the pillow over my head.

"Then think of it as a bedtime story." Aidan pulled the pillow back off my head and smiled.

Eight

Friday, June 27, 1986, 5:43 p.m.

With Chuck bleeding profusely, Mom went into nurse mode. She pulled Chuck into the kitchen, pushed him into a chair, forced his head back, and gently pried his fingers away from his face. Blood was flowing down his chin onto his T-shirt.

"I brought these along." Jeff held out his dirty hand, in which lay two teeth.

"Omigod, Chuck, honey!" Lucy was rubbing the top of Chuck's head frantically. I could've bet that wasn't making him feel a lot better. Mom first stanched the blood flow with the hem of Chuck's shirt. Then she grabbed her first aid kit from under the sink and pushed white gauze up into his mouth.

I ran to the phone and called Dr. Jones, our dentist. After I quickly explained the situation he agreed to go back in to work and open up his office.

"What did you do to him?" Lucy turned on Jeff.

"I didn't do anything," Jeff said. He was looking for something to do with his hands. After sliding them up and down his jeans he settled for putting them in his pockets. "Chuck stiff-armed Greg in the throat when Greg was about to get his flag. So Greg tackled him, and Chuck fell on a sprinkler head."

The blood was starting to slow down when Elizabeth walked in. "Okay, everyone! Two-minute warning." Then she stopped and analyzed the situation. "Doctor's office?" She looked at Mom, who nodded. "Lucy, you take the car to—" She turned to Mom. "What kind of doctor?"

"A dentist. Dr. Jones."

"Jeannie, call Dr. Jones," Elizabeth barked.

"Already done," I said.

Elizabeth nodded and continued. "So, white Caddie to Dr. Jones's office. Or Jeff, can you take them?"

Jeff shuffled his feet.

"Okay, that's a no. So. White Caddie goes with Lucy and Chuck. When you're stitched up or whatever, meet us at the Century Club. I'll call Evan and have him pick up Mom and Dad. Sammie and Jeannie, we'll go in the Oldsmobile. If we all leave now, there's a chance we might be on time." Elizabeth whisked out of the room. She was nothing if not efficient. We followed her orders. She was a TV commercial producer in L.A., and man, she knew how to produce. She was used to problems on set like, "The props have been misrouted to Taiwan and we shoot in an hour. The props person is crying in the corner and downing Vicodin. Unless we find a fifteenth-century coat of armor for a horse we'll lose the shoot day and three hundred thousand dollars." Our family had probably prepared her pretty well for her job, too, come to think of it.

Everyone hustled out the door with the exception of Mom and

Dad, who were waiting for Evan and Ron. We drove the six minutes across the Causeway Bridge and arrived at the Century Club. Predictably, we got Doris Day parking at the curb, right in front of the oversized doors.

The Century Club had been a formidable men's club in its day. The lumber barons of Muskegon, and later the auto parts barons, would gather in the drawing rooms to smoke cigars and sip scotch and sodas. The club began to decline in the seventies and most of the older men blamed it on the admittance of women.

Elizabeth strode in as though she were storming the citadel, with Sammie and me meekly following. I split off from them to go check the place cards. Elizabeth called over her shoulder, "Jeannie, go check the place cards." Before I could tell her I was already doing just that, she disappeared with the social director to go over the menu my mom had already gone over.

Sammie gave a cursory glance at the cards, moving her own from next to Anna to next to Evan. I went through them more carefully, comparing the cards to the seating chart Mom and I had worked out earlier in the day. Sammie stopped at Lucy's and Chuck's place cards. They were not at the head table but at a table next to Mom and Dad. Mom, after much thought, had decided not to torment Evan and Anna more than necessary and had made sure they had the place of honor to themselves.

"This just doesn't seem right. Did anybody consult with Elizabeth on the protocol for this?" Sammie asked.

"There is no protocol for two weddings in the same family on the same weekend when one of them is a surprise. Mom had to go without a safety net on this one."

Elizabeth motioned to me from the doorway. I walked over. "They say they need a check right now for the caterer."

"Tell them to wait until Mom gets here."

"They can't. The caterer needs to leave and he won't leave the food without a check."

"Where's your checkbook? If I write a check it'll bounce."

"I don't have one."

"You don't have one?" I have a bad habit of repeating people when I'm sure they can't be saying what they're saying.

"I'm not a signatory on our checking account," she hissed. "Ron just gives me cash when I ask." I stared at my sister, the one who wore her hair in a French chignon, who hobnobbed with celebrities, who had started her own company just a few years out of college.

"You'll have to ask Sammie."

"Will you ask her? And please don't tell her that I don't have a checkbook."

I went back over to Sammie. "Got a check? Caterer needs it. Mom'll pay you back." Sammie rummaged in her purse and wrote out the check, which I ran back and gave to Elizabeth.

"You didn't tell her?" Elizabeth asked anxiously.

I shook my head as Elizabeth took a deep breath, then calmly took the check to the back. The big doors opened and Anna, her parents, and her two brothers stepped in. Since I was standing directly in front of them I couldn't do anything else but play hostess in my mother's absence.

"Welcome. Hi. How are you?" I grasped each of their hands and did the European air kiss on both sides thing. Evan had taught me that the year before when he saw that I would become confused and pull away from them as they were still in mid-head-bob mode, their lips searching uselessly in the air.

"Where is everybody?" Anna asked a bit too brightly. She'd been with Evan long enough to know his family.

"There was a little accident."

Her eyes narrowed, waiting.

"But everything is fine and they'll be here soon." I deftly pawned the family off on Sammie and made an excuse to go get a waiter. Instead, I went to the powder room and waited it out on a chaise lounge with my Laura Ashley floral skirt folded under me, until I heard new voices. My parents had arrived and were introducing my grandmother to Anna's family. I had completely forgotten about her in all of the commotion. I went out.

"Hi, Grandma, how was your trip?" I bent down to give her a hug. I was only five feet four, but Grandma was about three feet tall. At least she seemed that way. I watched her lips move soundlessly. "It was good, huh?" Her lips moved again. None of us ever had a clue what she was saying. She had lived alone for so many years that she seemed to have lost her voice. She said everything in an inaudible whisper. It made me want to turn up her volume control. Usually, after a few days with us, her projection got better, probably in sheer self-defense against the noise that surrounded her. I took a shot at what she had just said. "So you didn't get lost in the United terminal this time?" She shook her head vigorously.

We smiled at each other in that way grandkids and grandparents do when they haven't seen each other in two years and have no idea of what to say.

Grandma had lived in the same house in Houston for more than forty-five years. It was about four hundred square feet with a chain-link fence around it. She waged a continuous if losing battle against the cockroaches, and that was the central topic of conversation with her. I myself have a morbid fear of cockroaches. While they may be a fact of life in Houston, they weren't something I wanted to know too much about. Over the years,

Grandma's neighborhood had declined, and her neighbors were now mostly crack dealers mixed in with the few elderly people who, like Grandma, were still there. Last time I visited, my rental car was stolen.

My grandmother was the seventh out of seven kids. She grew up in West Texas, about six miles outside of Leuders, population 182, about an hour's drive from Abilene. They lived in a small farmhouse on 161 acres of farmland on which they raised cotton. Her family had a bit of money until her father fell ill. He cut himself shaving one day in 1915. He ignored it and went out to tend to the mules and check the crops. The cut became infected, and bright red streaks traveled up the side of his face. His wife cleaned it but it didn't check the infection. A week later, he collapsed in the kitchen. His wife and his youngest son, Fred, dragged his two-hundred-pound body across the floor and lifted him into bed. It was the only time in his life he had been in bed at 7 a.m. He struggled to breathe the white-hot Texan air. His wife lay a cool cloth across his head and spoke quietly to Fred, who was eight years old. The rest of the kids were far out on the farm with the two mules bringing in the cotton.

"Fred, you are going to have to run as fast as you can into town. You have to catch the train and take it into Stamford and bring the doctor back. Hurry!" She hugged him and sent him out. She stood on the porch and watched him running across the cotton fields. The one dirt road to town wound circuitously through several other farms and would have taken three times as long to travel.

She watched the smoke from the train on the horizon. The train, known as the Doodlebug, came through twice a week. Fred saw it, too. He and the train were both converging on the town from different directions. Fred tried to leap over the cotton rows but he wasn't tall enough. The stiff cotton boles scratched and slapped at his face as he pushed through them. A shoe came off but Fred did not stop. He would later mourn the loss of that shoe when he had to wear a mismatched pair for two years. He ran, afraid to stop, afraid of not accomplishing his task, afraid of letting his family down, afraid for his father. The father who lifted huge bales of cotton with ease and played the fiddle at night. The heat hovered at a hundred degrees and sweat poured off his small body. At times, the cotton was so high he couldn't see anything but the endless rows in front of him, the faultless blue sky above him, and the smoke of a train that was moving too fast. He sprinted four miles over cotton fields, ditches, and cattle guards; he squirmed under the barbed-wire fences, cutting his shirt in long strips down his back. About a mile from the depot he realized he wouldn't catch the train. It was almost in town, and it waited for only ten minutes before leaving. He tripped and fell and picked himself back up and kept going. Tears were streaming down his face as he willed the train to wait. He shouted, "Stop! Don't go!" His small voice barely pierced the heat that hung in waves across the fields. Fred saw the train begin to pull away and changed his course, trying to get ahead of it. But he could not move that fast. He scrabbled up the gravel incline to the tracks and watched the train move away from him. "Stop, please, please, stop!" he screamed as the whistle blew. Then he sat down in the middle of the tracks and cried.

His father died that night. The doctor told them later that it was a simple case of blood poisoning. If he had gotten help in time he would have been all right. He didn't think to tell the family that "in time" meant several days before Fred's journey into town to catch the train.

I met my great-uncle Fred more than seventy years later, sitting on the front porch of the VFW hall in Leuders. He told me that after his father died, my great-grandmother hung on for a few more years through sheer determination. Not too many men wanted to do business with a woman, and those who did cheated her. Eventually the family scattered. Some, like Fred, married young and became migrant workers traveling between Leuders, Texas, and Roswell, New Mexico, picking cotton. Another sister, Velma, married a Southern Baptist preacher named Billy Bozman and traveled the South doing tent revivals. A few others took to drink and catfish hunting on the East Fork of the Brazos River. My own grandmother tenant-farmed cotton for years until she got her big break and was hired as a waitress at the Rice Hotel in Houston.

I am named after my great-grandmother. My mother constantly reminds me, "We are from a long line of strong woman," and I am proud of that.

I regarded my grandma. She wore the gray dress my mother had bought for her. I knew she was only wearing it to shut my mother up. She and Mom didn't see eye to eye about much. "So, nice trip, huh?" I said again needlessly. Being a Southern Baptist, she didn't drink, so I brought her a glass of water. Her lips moved again and I bent down close. "What? Can you repeat that, Grandma?"

"Pearl?" she asked.

I realized she was asking where my other grandmother was. I said, "She's fine; she just couldn't make the trip." That was true enough. Dad's mother was currently taking a little trip in her own head. Her senility had gotten worse over the past couple of years and finally, much to Dad's chagrin, she had to be placed in a nursing home. Dad had wanted her to be in a home nearby, but his brother had insisted she stay in Michigan City, Indiana, near him. I didn't explain all this to Grandma.

Anna walked up and pointedly asked me where Walker, my

boyfriend, was. I gave my stock answer that Walker had something important to do with his parents. This wasn't true and most people in the room knew it. Walker avoided contact with my family. He thought it was like walking under a ladder. Something bad was bound to happen. For a while he tried to have me meet him outside my house on the sidewalk so he wouldn't have to come in. But I would wind up waiting for him on the curb for fifteen minutes at a time so I put a stop to that.

We all sat or stood in the library waiting for Lucy and Chuck to show up. There were the long silences of people who don't know each other that well and have run out of small talk. Mom struggled valiantly to keep conversation going until Dad announced we should go ahead and sit down for dinner. The group moved to the next room.

I was the last out of the library and, glancing through the window, saw Lucy and Chuck standing outside. Chuck's back was to me but I could see Lucy stroking his face. His head was down and his shoulders were shaking. Then he grabbed Lucy and hugged her close. I stood there for a long moment watching that hug, then, not wanting to be caught at the door again, I turned and entered the dining room. My place card had been moved. Looking around I saw I was seated next to Anna.

Lucy and Chuck had come in and now stood in the doorway like deer in the headlights. What little conversation was going on stopped cold. For a split second, no one moved or said anything. For Evan, it might have been because he hadn't laid eyes on Lucy for six months. For me, I'm ashamed to say, it was because I was staring at Chuck the way you might stare at a traffic accident. Chuck was wearing a mouth guard like a football player's. But bigger. Metal headgear was strapped around the back of his head holding it in place. His eyes were fastened on the floor.

Anna abruptly swept from her place of honor at the head table, nearly upsetting me in my chair, and moved toward the doorway. I thought she would brush by them and collapse in the ladies' room, sobbing, on the chaise lounge I had earlier vacated. Instead, she kissed Chuck on both cheeks, ignoring the headgear. Then she took Lucy by the shoulders and smiled at her. "Welcome home. Evan and I are so pleased that we can share this wedding weekend."

Lucy melted into her arms and Anna swayed her back and forth. I glanced over at my mother, whose face was visibly losing its wrinkles. Mom called her wrinkles her "badges of honor," but I think she could have lived without the badges from the past few days.

Anna pulled Lucy and Chuck into the room and seated them next to her and Evan. I moved over to Mom and Dad's table to accommodate them. After that, there was only the clinking of glasses and laughter.

Nine

Saturday, June 28, 1986, 7:32 a.m.

The hammering woke me, and I rose blearily from the couch to yell at somebody. It was Tom, the handyman, pounding new boards into the dock stairs. When I reached the kitchen, Dad was already at the table reading the paper. He passed me a cream horn and a cup of coffee. I had a particular weakness for cream horns from Meijer Thrifty Acres. Dad always remembered to pick them up for me when he went out there for hardware or fertilizer or new white T-shirts when we girls had taken all of his. We sat together and read *The Muskegon Chronicle*. As usual, I turned to the crimes section to see what kids had been busted trying to get someone to buy them a six-pack of Stroh's. Then I read the anniversaries, weddings, and engagement section. In our town, people having their twenty-fifth wedding anniversary always looked seventy years old in their pictures, although most of them were probably only about forty-five.

At eight o'clock, Dad got up and let Buddy out to go do his business. Then he switched on the small TV on the kitchen counter.

He turned it to the local station broadcast out of Muskegon Community College. The signature music for *The Michigan Bass and Buck Show* came on. The opening titles cut to Evan, who stood in a kitchen set drinking black tea. He looked like he needed it, too.

"Jeez, Evan usually at least shaves before the show," Dad said.

Evan had on his red flannel shirt, jeans, and beat-up Docksiders. He put on an apron while he talked. "It looks like the Caddis Hatch has started right on time and it may be a blue-ribbon year for fly fisherman. For the uninitiated, the Caddis Hatch is more commonly called the Mayfly Hatch. It's named for the big-bodied insect with the"—Evan searched for the word—"the gossamer wings. It's like catnip for trout." Evan took a trout out of a Styrofoam cooler. It flopped in his hands as he gutted it from rectum to gill and pulled out the inside mess. He grabbed a little fleshy organ and cut it open. "See, the stomach of this little fifteen-incher is completely full of Mayflies. So you may want to consider tying a larger-bodied fly with a hint of blue showing."

Dad stretched. He liked the cooking parts of the show but didn't care much about fishing. "For trout, this is a perfect moment in time," Evan continued. "They are feeding at the calm edge of life's riffling waters. For once, they do not need to work because the currents of fate sweep along the river and bring what they wish—the Mayfly. Or the Caddis, if you will, for the purists out there. They are not eating because they are hungry; they are eating because they can have exactly what they want and as much as they want. It's that golden jewel of a time when everything is as it should be. We should all be so lucky as to have a moment as satisfying and full as that."

Evan moved to the microwave. He heated up water for his Yogi tea. He'd been into that for a few years now. Dad and I watched Evan watch the timer on the microwave count down, then open the door, remove the cup, and dunk his tea bag in and out. He stroked his face and worked his jaw in that way men do when they are tired and need a shave. "Right after the commercial break, we'll talk about smoking trout with beer."

"He sure is comfortable on television. I don't even think he combed his hair," I said to Dad. I was envious of my brother's casualness about it all. The phone rang and I got up to answer it.

"Hi, Jeannie? Are you up?"

"Yeah, hi, Walker. How did it go last night?" I didn't have to ask what my boyfriend had been doing. Every fly fisherman in Michigan knew that, if the temperature was right, the Caddis Hatch occurred the last week in June. No fisherman would be anywhere but on the river that week.

He launched in. "I was up on the Little Manistee River last night. Roger went with me. We fished until about 4 a.m. Damned if my headlamp didn't go out just as I had a little fourteen-inch beauty on the line. Lost him. Then Roger threw his line full of air knots and by that time we had to hike out. Roger had to be to work by eight anyway." I could hear the disapproval in Walker's voice. Air knots in a fishing line were for amateurs.

Fly-fishing for Walker was not a sport. It was a religion that, for him, only honorable men who were throwbacks to honorable times could correctly practice. He once said that he belonged to the church of the Great Outdoors. That was probably true because he wasn't much of a Protestant. Every year most fishermen here kept complex log books of date, river temperature, air temperature, water depth, type of fly hatch—the fly to be tied in order to correctly fool the trout—and, most important, how all of this affected the trouts' appetite. Each fishing hole on the river was given a name or the name was passed down from generation to generation of fishermen. There was the Come Back, named, not particularly cleverly, for the place where most fishermen turned around to come back home. And there was the Beaver Hole. Contrary to what this might sound like, it was famous for a time when Walker's father was fishing and a beaver tore his trout right off the line. There was also the Wop Hole, named for a sarcastic and funny Italian boy whom Walker had brought home from Princeton and tried to teach to fish. The Italian boy had named the hole himself after he had fallen into it, had water fill his waders, and nearly drowned in three feet of water. He finally made his way to the riverbank and sat there cursing the Wop Hole. I always chided Walker when he referred to the Wop Hole in front of people who did not know the story. I feared he would be taken for a redneck at Princeton.

Fly-fishing in Michigan is a bit like surfing in California. Prize locations are ferociously guarded, locals only. Some fishermen have been fishing after the same fish in the same hole for years. Folklore abounds about these fish—their own personal Moby Dicks. Walker had read and memorized every topographical map for most of Lower Michigan. He could find his way around on a river in complete darkness just from his memory. People will travel from Grosse Pointe or Royal Oak to fish in the prime stretches of the Little Manistee, the Sable, or the Muskegon rivers. They show up in their brand-new Orvis vests with their shiny fly boxes and their unscratched Ford Explorers. They get stuck in the two-tracks leading to the rivers—a two-track being the tire tracks worn through a field after repeated use. Then they bother local fishermen to drive out to the highway and call them tow trucks. Walker called all of these people "Teds." For some reason several of them one particular summer had the name Ted, and the derisive term stuck. Now most local fishermen used it and we all knew what they meant.

Walker had begged off the rehearsal dinner. Now he was call-ing about the wedding.

"You can't miss Evan's wedding," I begged him. "Please don't miss Evan's wedding."

"No one will even notice. Your family is so damn chaotic they'll think I'm there. Come on, Jeannie. You know the Hatch only lasts a couple of days. This is important."

"But Evan will be hurt."

"No, he won't. I was just watching his show. He gets it."

"He gets the metaphoric part of it. He hates to fish. He doesn't like the smell of wet waders."

I put down the phone and thought, This is important, too. This is something that doesn't even happen a couple of days a year. It only happens once, at least with any luck. Walker had been making noises about our getting married. I made a mental note that it would have to be in the dead of winter. Of course, that was grouse-hunting season, but it wasn't as dependent on the weather. As usual, I let Walker off the hook, so to speak.

My family made him nervous. Being a highly disciplined sort, he did not view my family as a vibrant force but as a disorganized mess that needed cleaning up.

Dad looked up. I slumped back into my chair and he stroked my head and smiled. "Come on, pumpkin. Today is one day you should be smiling."

When I continued to pout, he sang my favorite song. He'd done that since I was little. *"You are my sunshine, my only sun-shine . . ."* I begged him to stop, but he wouldn't until I laughed with him. *"You make me happy when skies are gray . . ."*

Lucy wandered in and headed to the fridge for a Tab. She was the only person I knew who still drank Tab. She probably kept several people at a Tab factory employed.

"You guys have any aspirin? Chuck didn't sleep so well last night and I couldn't find any in the medicine cabinet. Mom finally gave him some whiskey to cut the throbbing."

Dad got up and went over to the cupboard where he kept paint and wire and hammers and stuff and reached way into the back and fished out a bottle. "My own private stash," he explained. Lucy shook some tablets out and wandered back out of the kitchen rubbing her eyes.

"Didn't Dr. Jones give him a prescription for something stronger?" I asked.

"And when would I have gone to the pharmacy between last night and this morning?" she groused.

"Don't forget, you and I have to go get your headpiece today," I shouted after her. She mumbled something from the hallway and disappeared.

"Close your eyes," Dad said.

"Ah, come on, Dad. I'm not going to steal your aspirin."

"Close 'em."

Dutifully, I shut my eyes as Dad found a new hiding place for his aspirin. In our big family, we all jealously guarded what we had. If we really wanted to keep something for ourselves, we hid it. When Mom came home from grocery shopping, the Cokes disappeared, immediately hidden. The Little Debbie snack cakes followed. Years later, we found forgotten Cokes hidden in the backyard and down the laundry chute.

Tom knocked on the sliders and then came in. Behind him were three other handymen I did not know. And even if I did know them, I certainly wasn't going to stand there in my usual sleepwear in front of them. They ignored me, though, reached for coffee cups, filled up, and sat down with Dad as though they all lived there. I started for the door when one of them took my section of newspaper.

"Evan's show on yet?" one of them inquired.

"Started a few minutes ago," Dad replied. I went upstairs and tiptoed into Sammie's room, where my clothes were. I put on a pair of jeans and a T-shirt as quietly as possible, but Sammie bitched at me to keep it down.

"What time is it?" she asked as I was leaving.

"About noon," I lied. Let her figure it out after she was up. Mom was in the shower, but I went in anyway to brush my teeth. Lucy came in, peed, then flipped the lid down and sat on it. She rubbed her face in her hands.

"Is that Lucy?" Mom asked from behind the shower curtain.

"Yes," Lucy said.

"Is Chuck better?"

"How did you know, Mom?" I asked.

"Oh, about 1 a.m. I heard Lucy get up, so I got up to see if I could help."

Moms are truly amazing, I thought. Here I had slept through several people traipsing through the living room—currently my bedroom—to get to the kitchen, and Mom had woken up from the other side of the house. Moms must have built-in radar for problems in the middle of the night. Or maybe she honed that radar when Sammie used to sneak back out of the house after she had come in for her curfew. She never had that problem with Lucy. Lucy was the only one of us who would come home early. Her friends would drop her off at the front door and honk as they sped away. Lucy just got sleepy around ten and that was that. Mom often said that if all of us had been like Lucy, she would have had years more sleep under her belt.

The doorbell rang.

"First the phone and now the doorbell. You'd think it was mid-afternoon. Doesn't anybody have any manners around here?" Lucy stuck in her contacts while she griped.

I waited to see if Dad would get the door. When the bell rang again, I went downstairs and stopped dead when I saw the cop's hat through the window. I opened the door a crack. Officer Carson had Buddy by his collar. Buddy didn't even bother to fight. He sat complacently on the stairs.

"Hi, Officer Carson. Buddy was out again, huh?"

"Jeannie, this is the third time we've found your dog wandering around off the leash."

"So if I tied a leash to his collar he could roam around by himself?"

Officer Carson latched his thumbs in his belt. He did not see the humor in my words and didn't appreciate the insult to his authority. "This dog could be a danger to others!" Buddy lazily raised a leg and began licking his genitals vigorously. "I could haul you and your family into court right now. I have photos." He drew several Polaroids from his shirt pocket. There, in glorious color, was Buddy sitting in a leaf pile, peeing on a tree, and sniffing another dog's butt.

"But these were taken right there." I pointed to our sidewalk and the curb beyond.

"Your property line ends at the sidewalk."

Sensing things were getting out of hand, I decided to appease him. "Okay, Officer. I totally understand the situation. We're real sorry and I'll make sure it doesn't happen again."

Officer Carson settled down. He let go of Buddy's collar and I dragged the dog inside. "Thanks, Jeannie. I knew I could rely on you." He tipped his hat and left.

Sammie came rushing down the stairs, brushing her hair. I followed her into the kitchen and joined the crowd at the table while Sammie made toast, the extent of her culinary skills.

"Who was at the door?" Dad asked.

"Marv Carson. He said we're all going to dog jail."

"Oh, for cripes sake. Was Buddy out again?"

"Dad! You let him out yourself—I saw you!"

Dad raised the paper but I could see him smiling behind it.

"Now it's my damn responsibility to make sure Buddy doesn't roam around."

"Don't swear," Dad answered me, already having lost interest in the conversation.

"Goddamn it, Jeannie! It's 8:15 in the friggin' a.m.!" Sammie had just caught sight of the stove clock. "What kind of a jerk lies and says it's noon when it's really 8:15? That is just immature."

"If I have to be up dealing with dogs and workmen and aspirin and fishing schedules, then why shouldn't you be? I didn't get the choice of having a room to myself. Everyone just assumes that since I'm the youngest I won't mind the couch. Maybe I mind!"

We glowered at each other. Sammie flung toast at my head. The workmen got to their feet and ambled back outside.

"Well, I never." Mom entered the kitchen. "You girls should be ashamed of yourselves talking to each other that way. Just when everyone is home and it's been so pleasant. Now kiss and make up."

Oh God. Not that. Ever since we were little kids Mom would make us kiss and make up. We had abandoned the actual kissing part when we were about six years old and it was pretty much a figure of speech now. But we still had to apologize and hug each other. We'd been through the drill so often that Sammie and I just eyed each other, then awkwardly hugged.

"Sorry."

"Yeah, sorry, too."

Sammie smacked me on the butt and went to make more toast.

Evan's wedding started at 6 p.m. Elizabeth had given us strict instructions to get the headpiece and then be home by 3 p.m. When Lucy and I finally got to the June Wedding to buy the bridal headpiece it was almost one o'clock. June descended on us immediately, moving her girth through the narrow aisle. We had known June for years, and I had particularly admired her polka dancing at various weddings held at the Polish Falcon Hall.

June beamed at us. "Lucy dear! This is so exciting for you. Mrs. Petty called me to tell me all about it. I'm so glad that you didn't marry her awful son, Jeff, but don't tell her I said that." She barely stopped to breathe. "Are you pregnant, dear? Would you like to sit down?"

"No, no, I don't need to sit down. And no, I'm not pregnant."

June looked disappointed. "Oh dear, well, I'm sure you have plenty of time. Tell me about your wedding dress first."

Lucy looked at me and I looked back at her. "I have no idea what it looks like," Lucy said. Neither one of us had thought to ask Anna to see her dress.

June's smile faded. "No dress! Your mother assured me she would find you a dress." She looked like she would cry at Lucy's predicament.

"No. There's a dress. We just don't know what it looks like." Lucy was waving her hands and starting to talk very fast. "We'll just look around if you don't mind."

June hesitated, as if she were leaving two lambs out in an open storm, then said, "If you have any questions, I'm right here," before walking away.

I tried on a headpiece with a full-length veil that would have taken two flower girls to hold up. I turned this way and that in the mirror and thought I looked a bit like Princess Diana at her wedding. Lucy rejected everything I showed her. She didn't seem very into the whole thing. Finally, in exasperation, I told her we had five minutes before we had to head home. Lucy grabbed a headpiece off the rack and went to pay June without even trying it on.

Ten minutes later, we were home and back into the frenzy of the shower schedule and car arrangements.

I walked into my parents' bedroom to steal some nylons from my mom. Chuck didn't see me come in. He was sitting on the bed talking on the phone and gazing out the window. "The whole thing has just gone too far." Pause. "I love you, too. I am so sorry about this. Yeah, I'll call you tomorrow. Okay, good-bye." He started when he saw me. "How long have you been there?"

"I just walked in. Sorry, I didn't mean to disturb you." I fumbled through Mom's lingerie drawer and extracted a pair of nylons. I stuck my hand inside each leg, spread the material, and counted how many runs were in them. These weren't so bad. I asked him how his mouth was.

"Better. The pain is gone but I'll have to wear this for a few weeks." He knocked lightly on his headgear. "Otherwise I'll lose the teeth."

"Oh. Right. You don't want to lose your teeth." I shut the door behind me, feeling a bit desperate. Who had Chuck been talking to on the phone? As I rolled each nylon leg down to the toe and struggled into them, I pondered the situation. It must have been his mom or his dad. The alternatives didn't appeal to me.

At Elizabeth's two-minute warning call, I went downstairs to find that I was the last one ready. My grandma, mom, sisters, and I lined up for the requisite photos. Every major occasion demanded the same photo. The backdrop was always the fireplace. We have umpteen shots of proms and graduations taken in the same place. As usual, Dad kept fiddling with the timer on the camera until Mom yelled at him that we were going to be late. Chuck waited patiently, sitting on the edge of a chair behind Dad. When we were done, Lucy said, "Dad, would you take a shot of me and Chuck?"

Mom stopped dead. We had left out a family member. I could tell she was mortified by her faux pas. Growing up, she had been made to feel unwelcome in many social situations. She didn't have the right clothes or the right whatever. It was a big thing with her that we kids always treated everyone as equals. And here she had gone and forgotten Chuck.

Dad recovered first and pushed Chuck forward. "We were just saving the best for last." Then Lucy and Chuck were immortalized in front of the fireplace.

Evan and Anna were getting married at St. Francis De Sales, a Catholic church across town. Evan, who was fairly apathetic about religion, got up in arms for some reason about being married by a Catholic priest. Finally, after much discussion, Father Whippet had been invited to participate in the ceremony. When we arrived at the church, Father Whippet's wife, Miriam, was at the door.

"It's about time you got here." She pointed at Dad. "Evan wants to talk to you. He's in one of the back rooms." Dad brushed by the bridesmaids, walked down the side aisle, and disappeared into the sacristy, where Evan and his groomsmen were. Miriam turned to my mother. "Cold feet," she said in a stage whisper. We bunched up in a group trying not to get in the way as guest after guest arrived and was seated. As family, we were supposed to be escorted down the aisle by groomsmen and seated at the front, but they hadn't asked for us yet. Mom smiled at each arrival. She grabbed my arm and leaned over.

"Go see what's holding up your father," she whispered, then straightened to continue greeting guests.

I followed the path Dad had taken and entered the darkness of the hallway behind the altar. Door after door faced me. I made my way through the barely lit hall and tried each door. They were locked, but eventually one gave in my hand. I stuck my head inside only to see Father Whippet standing much too close to a woman whose back was to me. I ducked my head back out and hoped they hadn't seen me. I found Evan and Dad behind the next door. "What's going on?" I asked Dad. "Mom's getting antsy." I shut up when I saw his face.

"Where is she?"

"Up front in the vestibule."

He walked ahead of me and I hopped to keep up. Dad was already talking to Mom when I got there. They had pulled away from the crowd.

"I don't know. We'll just have to sit down and see what happens," was all I could make out. Sammie looked at me and I gave her a wide-eyed shrug.

Elizabeth looked at her watch. "It's twenty past six." Ron shuffled in his Gucci loafers. Grandma stood patiently to one side, as if waiting for something to happen was the story of her life. Since it didn't seem that anyone was coming to seat us, we decided to go ahead and seat ourselves.

St. Francis De Sales was not a small church. It was a large modern one. The regular congregation numbered in the thousands, unlike our church, St. Peter's, which held only a couple hundred. They had sectioned off pews, delineated with red velvet ropes, for the wedding. As the nine of us walked down the aisle, every head turned to look at us. Our steps on the stone floor rang up to the rafters, five stories above us. For some reason the pew reserved for our family held only six. Lucy and Chuck and I had to go back up the aisle and search for seats. We looked like rejected family members, but everyone got a good look at Chuck. Most of them had burned up the phone wires that day discussing the latest Thompson folly. We split up and had better luck. I wound up on the bride's side with people I didn't know. Thankfully.

When the music began, signaling the start of the ceremony, I strained to see the altar. There was no Evan and there were no groomsmen. There was no Father Whippet, either. The brides-maids were starting to come down the aisle, all eight of them in peach taffeta. As they reached the altar, one after another looked around, bewildered. Then a trumpet blew and Anna appeared at the door on her father's arm. Smiling left and right, left and right, she didn't notice that there was no one to meet her at the altar. I would have given anything to be sitting in my family's pew right then.

The woman next to me exclaimed, "Where is the groom?"

In the meantime, Anna reached the altar and looked around like she wasn't sure what was missing. Then she stood still. The music stopped. The bridesmaids smiled frozen smiles as they gamely held their bouquets at their waists. Anna threw a glance back at Mom and Dad, as if they had stashed Evan somewhere. I could see Anna's mom, Helen, glare at my mom across the aisle. Finally, they all couldn't keep up the pretense anymore and gathered in an untidy group on the steps of the altar. The guests watched them avidly. This was certainly more interesting than most weddings.

Then Evan came striding out from the wings, his groomsmen

trailing behind him. They were all talking among themselves and gesturing. It was not the most orderly entrance I've ever seen. Father Whippet flapped along behind them while he adjusted his robes. Everyone sort of crowded into place while Father Whippet fought to get through the bridal party to the altar. Evan took Anna's hands, gave her a quick smile, and they turned toward the minister. Helen glared again at Mom, then tipped her nose in the air and back to the action at the altar. Mom kept her attention fixed on the bride and groom, pretending not to notice. Sammie, however, shot Helen the finger. From behind, I could only see Mom, head poised, still looking straight ahead, reach up and push Sammie's hand down and out of sight. I was so anxious to hear what had transpired in the back room I barely paid attention to the ceremony.

Ten

March 2006

Sammie was furious with me. Missing my nephew's tenth birthday had blown up into something larger than I expected. We had a roof-raising phone call in which she unloaded about years of my perceived slights. Apparently I had missed or been late for one too many family events.

"Remember how we all flew home to Michigan to surprise Mom and Dad for their anniversary, but you 'couldn't make it' at the last second?" Sammie had snapped.

"I was stuck in Paris! The international team at Oxford Pictures scheduled an emergency meeting about global film piracy just when I supposed to leave for Michigan! Isn't that a pretty good reason?" I retorted.

Sammie snorted in response. And like Sammie, I knew deep down that, no, it wasn't a pretty good reason. It didn't matter that I *had* finally shown up. I had shown up about thirty hours too late.

Sammie had ended the call by hanging up on me. After storming around my house and kicking the ottoman several times, I took the only course available to me: I called Mom. Sobbing, I told her about the fight Sammie and I had. As usual, she listened patiently. Finally, after I had blathered out the whole story about how unfair Sammie was being, I stopped, exhausted. Mom's silence let me know she was weighing her words. Eventually she said, "Sweetheart, you know that Sammie loves you . . ."

"I knooowwww," I interrupted to sob some more, "but she's being so meeeaaann."

"Maybe you should look at the whole picture, what Sammie is really trying to say to you."

My eyes narrowed on my end of the phone line. "Sammie already called you, didn't she?" Damn it, Sammie had gotten to Mom first. I shouldn't have spent so much time kicking the ottoman.

"Well, yes, she did, honey. She's just as upset as you are. I think she's just worried that your job is consuming you. We're very proud that you are so successful, but . . ." Mom paused.

"But what?" I rubbed my arm under my nose and was rewarded with a long string of snot. I stumbled to the bathroom to find some toilet paper to clean myself up as I heard my mom take a deep breath.

"But you take this job too seriously. Surely nothing could be so important that you wouldn't have time for your family," Mom said carefully. "Or is it Aidan? Is it that Aidan doesn't want to see any of us?"

"No, no," I stammered. "That's not it." While I didn't want Aidan to meet my family, I did talk to my mom at length about him: what a great guy he was, how he put up with me, all of which, I'm sure, just left poor Mom all the more perplexed about why I kept him hidden from the family. It would have hurt all of their feelings too much if I had told them I thought they would scare him away.

After I hung up the phone I miserably ordered a large pepperoni pizza, then sat on the couch and ate the whole thing. My family didn't understand my life. I had to be perfect. Especially now, with Katsu constantly questioning every move I made at work. It was like having a terrier nip at my heels everywhere I went.

The consequences were too big if I wasn't perfect. One screwup or misspoken word and months of work on a trailer or poster would be down the drain. I was proud of my track record, but it took hours of work and preparation. Plus, I felt the pressure even more now to win the approval of my boss. Last week I had made an uncharacteristic mistake on how much had been spent to date on a campaign. Katsu had jumped all over it. He was so persistent that even Rachael had given him the eye to shut up. That, at least, had made me feel better. What part of *seniority* did Katsu not understand? I wondered. He could at least pretend to have respect for the work I had done. But many twenty- or thirty-somethings had risen to president or chairman in film studios. And it wasn't because they were such nice people.

In the meantime, Sammie and I still hadn't made up yet, and it gnawed at me, around the edges of my brain. It now was one more thing to wake me up in the middle of the night.

That night, I had carved out time with Aidan to go see his family. The irony was not lost on me. Aidan picked me up at my house and, as had become our ritual when we had a moment alone, I continued my story. Over the weeks, a little bit would be told over dinner, more would be told in bed. Or, like now, on the way to dinner with Aidan's father and stepmother.

At a stoplight I paused in the tale of growing up in my disastrous family.

"God, in my family we just get married, and then we just get divorced. Simple," Aidan commented.

"Wow, there's a ringing endorsement for marrying you." I shifted deeper into his car's leather seat. "And nothing is ever simple. Even if it looks simple, it usually isn't. There are always complications brewing under the surface."

"Not in my book. I think it's the inherent difference between men and women. Men accept things the way they are and women analyze them."

We were going to his dad and stepmom's house in Holmby Hills. It was a thirty-minute drive from my house and a world away. I stared at the houses we passed. Rather, I should rightfully call them mansions. My family's house could easily fit inside most of their garages. Each one was gorgeous, but because Los Angeles grew in such a haphazard manner, each one was a different style. An English Tudor might be next to a Spanish Mediterranean that might be next to a starkly modern house. It's sort of like Disneyland for very rich people.

While I lived in a much less desirable neighborhood, I loved my little house. It was on Maple Street in Santa Monica. Tree-lined and kid friendly, it was one of the few streets that hadn't had its original homes from the nineteen twenties knocked down in favor of an expressionless apartment building. My house, built in 1927, was Spanish style with arched doorways, wide wood floors, and glass doorknobs. I'd furnished it with cushy, oversized down chairs and a sofa covered in a soft, green floral pattern. Aidan had commented when he saw it that it was a far cry from the severe modern furniture I kept in my office. I felt like I could let down my guard in this house. The only problem was that it was a long drive to Aidan's house, in the San Fernando Valley.

We pulled in to the circular driveway and parked between Aidan's stepmom's BMW and his dad's Mercedes. Careful not to scratch the Mercedes when I opened my car door, I reflected that in Michigan, if any one of those cars had appeared in a driveway, the neighbors would be talking snidely for years. When I was growing up, you simply didn't buy a foreign car if you lived in the state that Henry Ford had built.

Aidan's dad lived in a Spanish-style home, and the great wooden front door burst open, spilling out two kids. Max and Audrey raced, shrieking, across the courtyard separating the house from the driveway. These were Aidan's half-brother and -sister, ten-year-old twins who, from the way they were climbing on Aidan, clearly adored him. Aidan hoisted Max over his shoulder while Audrey, more shyly, came over and took my hand. We all went to meet Jim, Aidan's dad, who stood in the open doorway.

Aidan deposited Max on the step and bear-hugged his father. Jim then took my hand and kissed my cheek. We entered the foyer with its original eighteenth-century Mexican chandelier and I heard Janet call from the kitchen, "Jim, are they here?" A petite blonde hurried through a door, wiping her hands on a dishcloth. Janet hugged both of us and led us to the living room. While Jim opened a bottle of wine at the wet bar on one side of the room, Aidan and I sat on the couch. "I still can't get over your view," I said as I gazed out at the city lights sparkling far below.

"I'm a lucky man and I know it." Jim smiled as he handed me my wine. "I'm going to go help Janet in the kitchen, but I'll be back in a second." As he left the living room I heard him shout into the TV room, "You kids better not be playing video games! You have homework to do."

I stood up to look at the photos sitting framed in the floor-to-ceiling bookcase. The first one I came to was actually a framed piece of paper. It was the patent for Jim's invention, the thing that allowed him all this luxury. Several years before, I knew, Jim had invented a simple device now used in hospitals the world over. He had retired and now spent most of his time either with his family or serving on various corporate boards.

I moved on to the next frame. "Is this you?" I teased Aidan. I held a grainy, discolored photo of Aidan taken when he was about five years old. It showed him trying to drink out of the garden hose. A smallish white house stood behind him. Aidan took the photo from me and regarded it. "Where was this taken?" I asked.

"At home. This is where we lived right before my parents split up. My dad wasn't making much money then. He was still completing his residency."

A thought struck me. "What about what your mom said? That you had a personal chef and all that stuff?"

"That was just a little bit later. When Mom married Sam. Until then, my dad made meals for me because, as Mom said, she didn't know how to cook. Actually, my life became pretty schizophrenic. I alternated weeks living with my mom or my dad. So one week I'd be living in a mansion with a chauffeur to drive me to school. The next week I'd be living in a small house with a babysitter who looked after me." Aidan put the photo gently back into its place. "Max and Audrey are pretty lucky kids."

I regarded his profile. He was still looking at the picture, but his expression was unreadable. Aidan strolled over to fiddle with the audio system, and I went to see if I could help Janet.

The kitchen could easily have been a commercial kitchen in a restaurant, except it was a lot more luxurious. Janet waved a fork at me and said I could set the table. I went to the cupboard where I knew plates were kept and started, with my load, toward the dining room.

"Oh no, honey. Let's just eat in here. It's much more cozy," Janet called after me. So I returned to set the plates and silverware on the granite island in the middle of the room and sat down on a stool. Soon all of us were eating good old steak, mashed potatoes, and peas. Max and Audrey pouted and refused to eat their peas, but Janet was having none of it. Finally she scooped the peas up with a spoon and deposited them in the center of their mashed potatoes. "There, now it's a bird's nest. See, the peas are the eggs and the potatoes are the nest," she announced. Max and Audrey dubiously looked at it but started eating.

"I haven't heard that in years," I said. "My mom used to do that with us, too."

"How are your parents, Jeannie?" Jim asked as he opened another bottle of wine. "We don't hear much about them."

I shifted on my stool. "They're fine, thanks."

"When are they finally going to come out here? We'd love to meet them," Janet said.

"I'm not really sure," I hedged. "They don't like to travel much."

Aidan stared at me. "I thought you said they went to China last year for a vacation."

"Um, yeah." Now I felt like an idiot. "Well, now that I think about it, they came to see me and my sisters about two years ago."

Aidan slowly put down his fork and knife. "We were dating two years ago. I didn't know they were in town."

I could feel the air slowly getting sucked out of the room and saw the glance that Jim and Janet threw each other. Too brightly, I said, "We had just started dating. You know, it would have been too soon to introduce you." I was hoping that Aidan didn't remember that our third date was to the twins' eighth birthday party.

Aidan dropped the subject, but I could still feel his eyes on me as I ate. Finally, we said our good-byes and headed to my house. When we got there I checked my cell phone for messages. I had one from Caitlin. She said that Ian McMann, the male lead in *Heaven Is in the Wind,* had gone to see a movie and his name was mispronounced in the trailer for his upcoming film. His publicist, Franklin Gold, had called in a huff. I called Caitlin immediately.

"It's not possible." I shut my eyes. "We sent the trailer to Franklin for approval."

"I know, I was on the phone line when you talked to Mr. Gold, remember? He said the trailer was approved."

"Get him on the phone."

Caitlin promptly patched him through. "This is unacceptable!" Franklin ranted. "Ian is furious! My client's name is pronounced 'AYE-an,' not 'EE-an.' What are you going to do to make this better?"

I squinched my eyes together tightly. It would cost a lot of money to reprint and reship a new trailer. Aidan sensed this was going to take a while and started checking his own messages. I watched Aidan write down some messages. Then he dialed a number. "Hello, Montana?" I didn't hear more because Franklin was still ranting at me.

"Franklin, you approved this trailer. This is not the studio's responsibility," I stated flatly.

"I never saw this trailer." Franklin's voice was cold. I heard Caitlin's quick intake of breath on the line.

I ignored his lie. "He has been 'EE-an' in every movie he has ever been in. I have all of those other movie trailers in my office. Are you saying he just now realized that everyone was pronouncing his name incorrectly?" I was thinking it wouldn't be the first time a star had suddenly decided to change his or her name to make it sound "cooler."

"Oxford Pictures wants my star for their next picture. I'll pull the deal right now. I have the chairman's number right here. No new trailer, no Ian," Franklin pronounced. He had trumped my move. It didn't really matter who was right or wrong. He had four aces up his sleeve and he knew it. I didn't give a rat's behind if he called the chairman, but the outcome was going to be the same. The studio would cave in to keep the deal.

I hung up. "I can't believe I have to have these conversations this late at night."

Aidan took me by the shoulders. "You look tired. Can you back off a little bit? Just for a while? Maybe we could take a trip together."

"Look, you know as well as I do that I can't back off. There's always some fire burning." I stretched. "So is something up with your work too? I heard you call Montana."

"Um, no. I was just passing along a message." Aidan suddenly seemed very interested in figuring out the TV remote control. I looked at him for a long minute. He was acting strangely. "Is everything okay?" I pressed.

"To be honest, I'm feeling really uncomfortable about a situation." Aidan rubbed his face. "Montana is seeing a married guy. I know his wife very well. I said I wouldn't say anything to her. But for some reason this guy left a message asking me to tell Montana where to meet him next."

I was incredulous. "That's so . . . so . . . wrong in every way. Why are they using you as a go-between?"

"Maybe this guy's wife checks his cell bill for odd phone numbers."

"Sounds like she has a reason to," I spat out.

"Yeah, I know. It's a bad situation. I'm going to have to tell Montana to leave me out of it."

"Why does Montana need to see a married man, anyway?" She was five feet ten, had strawberry-blond hair, weighed about fourteen pounds, and was smart as a whip. In short, the girl other girls loved to hate.

"I don't know, Jeannie." Aidan sighed. He picked up his car keys.

"Where are you going?"

"You have work to handle, and I want to sleep in my own bed tonight." He kissed me good-bye and shut the door quietly behind him. I knew I should go after him, but I had promised Franklin I would telephone back with an answer. I called the guy who prints our trailers. Despite the hour, he picked up on the second ring. He listened and said he'd call me back. Four minutes later, my phone rang. I was told that about three hundred out of a total of ten thousand trailers had not yet printed. I figured out that we could change the pronunciation of the star's name on the three hundred at minimal cost. Then I called Franklin back to tell him that the trailer could be changed for some theaters—the ones that counted to celebrities, like the Promenade in Santa Monica and the Lincoln Center Theater in Manhattan.

"And get one to the Carmike Cinemas in Des Moines, Iowa," Franklin demanded. "That's where his parents live."

I rubbed my forehead. "Okay." Franklin Gold gets to save face by telling his client that he had knocked some heads around at the studio. I don't create a big problem for the studio with this star and his next picture. We'd played the game so that we could both win. But looking around my Aidan-less house, I wasn't so sure that I had won anything at all. I took two Tylenol PMs in the hopes of staving off insomnia. They didn't work. At 3 a.m. thoughts about my failures with my family, Aidan, and work spun in my head in a never-ending chant.

By now I knew that getting back to sleep was hopeless. I got out of bed, showered, and dressed and was at the office at five in the morning. There I carefully retyped my daily notes in a new and improved format until it was a decent time to start making business calls.

Eleven

Saturday, June 28, 1986, 7:15 p.m.

*E*van and Anna swept down the aisle in wedded triumph. I had to wait to leave until the church emptied from front pew to back pew. I made my way through the crowd until I spotted Sammie's leopard-print hat.

"What happened?" I whispered in her ear once I got close enough.

"I don't know. Dad won't say."

I looked over at Dad, who was in the receiving line next to Evan. He was still shaking one hand after another. "Why not?"

Sammie shook her head and I left her to see what Mom knew. I tried talking to her but ended up next to her in the line and started shaking hands, too. "Yes, they were beautiful, weren't they? See you at the reception? Oh, you're Anna's roommate from college's mother? How nice."

During a break in the action, I snuck away. Elizabeth and Ron pushed through the crowd in the church foyer and asked if I was ready to go with them to the reception.

"Yeah. Do you know what happened to Evan?"

Elizabeth looked blank. "Did something happen?"

I stared at her. "He was half an hour late to his own wedding. Didn't you notice?"

"Of course I noticed. I called the country club to tell them to delay dinner."

I walked away from my sister wondering how she could be from our family. She didn't wonder why Evan was late, and she had called the country club, even though it wasn't our party; it was Anna's parents' party. I considered myself organized but Elizabeth took it to a whole new level.

At the reception our family's table was in front, and everyone else was already seated. There was a pink place card for Walker next to mine. I stared at the empty setting and its accompanying chair. Mom reached over and touched my hand. "Honey, he might show up."

"No, it's perfectly okay. Now we have somewhere to put the coats and purses."

The DJ announced the bride and groom's dance during the salad course. Anna and Evan got up and slowly twirled around the floor to "Summer Wind." Then the DJ launched into "Celebration" and asked the family and bridal party to join them on the floor. Our table emptied, and I sat by myself, hoping nobody was looking at me. Sammie had grabbed an old friend and dragged him out to the dance floor so I didn't even have her to commiserate with.

I pretended to wave to people across the room but eventually realized I couldn't continue that charade and got up from the table. I swiped a glass of wine from a passing tray and went out onto the eighteenth green. The grass was spongy and the air had a moist smell. I lay down on the green in the dark.

This was where Walker and I had had our first date a few years back, on the Fourth of July. I didn't know how to golf and he teased me all day. My score was 122 for nine holes. Then I had turned somersaults all the way down the hill leading to the fourteenth hole. We had laughed, and then we watched the fireworks when darkness finally came. It doesn't get dark in Michigan until about 10:00 or 10:30 in the summer. I missed my 11:30 curfew and had to clean out six closets to avoid being grounded.

I stared at the stars above my head. It was a beautiful night to be humiliated.

Lucy stood above me. "Mom sent me out to find you."

"How come?"

"Because she figured I knew all the places around here to hide."

"Good point."

Lucy stretched her hands out. I leaned forward to grab them and jumped to my feet. "The fact that your boyfriend didn't show up isn't all that bad."

We started walking back to the porch. "It's not?"

"Hell no. Take it from me, worse things than this will happen to you."

"That's a comfort."

She put her arm around my shoulder. As we entered the room, Evan was tapping the side of his wineglass with his spoon. The room quieted down and everyone looked at him expectantly. He lifted his glass to his bride and said, "I now know a perfect moment of joy. And it is because of you." Anna's eyes welled up, and, to the many tappings of spoons on glasses, she got up and kissed him. Elizabeth, Sammie, Lucy, and I applauded from our table.

Sammie muttered under her breath, "God almighty, it's a long life. I hope he gets more than one perfect moment of joy out of it."

"Stop being cynical," Elizabeth chided.

"Start being cynical," Sammie retorted.

"Can both of you shut up and let me enjoy this?" Lucy threw down her napkin. It was one of those times I knew well. Either a big fight was going to break out or somebody would back down. The three of them glowered at each other. They knew they couldn't have a catfight right here at Evan's wedding. They only had a few options open to them. Somebody could stomp away in anger. Somebody could start crying. Or they could realize what damn fools they were being. We had been through this so many times. Like knowing the punch line to every joke, we knew the eventual outcome of every scenario and, for the most part, skipped the drama and went straight to the inevitable ending. Sammie sputtered with laughter. Elizabeth, Lucy, and I joined her.

Sammie raised her glass to us and said, "To Evan and Anna. Let's hope that growing up together will be easier for them than it was for us. And that they have as much laughter as we've had." We nodded our heads in agreement and clinked glasses.

Chuck and Ron walked up. "What's so funny?"

"Nothing you are going to understand for years to come," I said. Chuck looked perplexed and said he was going to the bar to join the kamikaze shot challenge. Anna and Evan got up from the bridal table to do the ceremonial wedding bouquet and garter belt toss. At the DJ's urging that "all single women report to the dance floor," Sammie and I got up to stand amid the milling women only because we didn't want to embarrass Evan. Anna's throw went way right. The crowd of women launched themselves in that direction. Sammie and I didn't move and were suddenly conspicuously by ourselves on one side of the dance floor.

"Who thinks up these dumb traditions?" Sammie asked me.

I shook my head and we returned to our table as Evan threw the garter. His best friend, Phil, caught it and kissed his girlfriend, Patty.

Mom and Dad were up at the head table beaming at Evan and Anna, who were now making motions to leave the reception. "Who's going over to the Holiday Inn tonight to get Anna's wedding dress?" Elizabeth asked.

"Dad is," I said.

"You're kidding me, right?" Lucy moaned. "This is so embarrassing."

"Hi, Lucy, haven't seen you since the big day." It was Fudgie Shaw. Lucy leapt up and hugged him.

"Why are you here?"

"I'm not. I'm over at the bar with Jeff and some of the guys." Fudgie patted his pockets. "I have something I wanted to give you." He finally located what he was looking for and handed it to Lucy.

She looked at it impassively, then put it in her purse. "Thanks, Fudgie. It meant a lot to me to have someone from home there."

Fudgie turned to walk back to the bar. Lucy called to his back, "Fudgie?"

He walked back. "Yeah?"

"Why did you tell them?"

"Tell who?"

"Whoever you told about Chuck's and my elopement told my parents. That wasn't cool. You promised me."

"I didn't, Lucy. I thought you did." Fudgie had the flustered look of someone who is innocent but feels guilty for being accused of something.

Jeff Petty was hollering for Fudgie to come back to the bar. "Jesus. That guy has class, huh? I gotta go stop him from doing more shots. Lucy, we'll talk more." We watched him swing through the crowd, grab Jeff in a manly-man sports-type of bear hug, and move him back into the more private reaches of the bar.

Lucy turned back to the table and to three faces staring at her. She stared back. "It wasn't Fudgie who blabbed."

Elizabeth was the first to try to bolt. "Excuse me. That waiter is serving from the wrong side. I should—"

"No way." Sammie grabbed her arm and made her sit again.

"You?" Lucy looked at Elizabeth incredulously. "How did you know?" Elizabeth explained the whole thing in fits and starts.

"Couldn't you have asked me? I mean, for Christ's sake, we went to dinner that night. You could have asked me."

"It seemed too personal."

"Too *personal*? More personal than having an entire wedding thrown for you without your knowledge? More personal than *that*?"

Sammie rubbed Lucy's arm. "Come on, Lucy. We love you. That's what this whole thing is about." The Lucy from ten months earlier would have made a righteous scene, but something about her now seemed more grown up. This Lucy didn't launch into histrionics but rather just sat quietly and watched Mom and Dad dancing to "String of Pearls." Dad spun Mom out neatly and she tucked back in. They laughed at a minor misstep. Lucy looked back at us and gave us the big goofy smile she always did when she was feeling silly.

"I'm loved."

"Despite everything, yeah." Sammie grinned.

"Hey, what did Fudgie give you?" I asked. I felt safe enough to direct attention to myself now. The ammo seemed to be put away for the moment.

"I'd rather not talk about it right now," Lucy said, gathering up her purse. "Are you all ready to go?"

We went to collect Chuck and Ron. Chuck was dribbling kamikazes out the side of his mouth guard.

I handed him a straw. "Try this."

Ron was drinking a Hennessey XO, sitting by himself on the other side of the bar. That'll run up the bar tab for Anna's parents, I thought. Jeff was staring hard at Lucy. She ignored him and quietly asked Chuck to get up and escort her home. But he was leaning across the bar trying to get the bartender's attention.

Jeff stood in front of Lucy and me. "So this is what you brought home?" He jerked his head in Chuck's direction.

"Leave it alone, Jeff." Fudgie was on his feet and pulling on Jeff's arm.

"You bring home this jarhead? I tried to be nice to him, but he's a loser."

"Jeff, I am at my brother's wedding and you do not want to start this right now. Do not embarrass me or yourself in front of my parents and everyone we know," Lucy said evenly.

"I knew all along you weren't worth anything, and they should know, too." Jeff was starting to yell and Fudgie tried to pull him away.

Lucy stood frozen in silence.

Fudgie yanked Jeff away to a corner and spoke to him in low, intense tones.

Chuck didn't seem to know what was going on. He came up to Lucy and threw a drunken arm around her shoulders. "Ready to go, sweet pants?" She turned away with Chuck and walked out.

I strode up to Jeff and jammed my finger in his chest. "You asshole. First of all, a jarhead is a marine, not an army soldier. And second of all, Lucy is learning Russian at the best language school in America and is proudly serving her country. What did you ever do? Besides getting a DUI last month and taking three years to get through a two-year school?" At least, that's what I said to him in my head when I thought it through later. All I managed to get out at the time was, "You asshole."

We guided Chuck and Ron outside to the cars. Ron was fine, but Chuck was like a drunken Slinky. "You're really pretty," he slurred in my ear as I struggled to hold him up. "Is your boyfriend taking care of you?"

I managed to get the car door open and dumped him inside. "Do you want to drive, Lucy?" I called over to the other side of the car. I was worried she would be shaken up by the exchange inside, but she just seemed sad, not angry.

"Yeah, I'll follow you so I don't get lost."

I smiled as I climbed into the other car with Sammie, Elizabeth, and Ron. Lucy and I had driven these roads together for years, and there weren't that many places to get lost unless you were trying to get lost. There wasn't much to do when we were growing up. In the evenings, we would drive the three miles to Lake Michigan and hang out in the beach parking lots waiting for friends, who also didn't have much to do, to show up. We would raise the hatchbacks or lower the tailgates and let music pour out from the stereos. It's also where we kept the coolers with the beer or the sloe gin fizzes. I shuddered now at the thought of either drink. There were lots of long, slow summer nights when we drove the back roads just to pretend we were going somewhere, but we always wound up at the beach parking lot. We were a Bruce Springsteen song personified. Barefoot girls drinking warm beer on the hood of a car. I hummed under my breath. Mostly I had watched the water. The blue waves of Lake Michigan rolled up on sugar-sand beaches. The sand was so fine that an industrial company had come years before and mined off most of the dunes to make glass.

Like Walker knew his rivers, I knew this lake. I knew the cold smell of the lake mixed with the diesel exhaust of boats. I knew the perfect time for swimming was late July, when the water was sixty-nine degrees and the sun was beating down. I knew that when the sky turned green, a storm was coming in from Wisconsin across the massive lake. Spitting fireworks and rolling thunder, the storm would kick up whitecaps and boats would head into the channel. When the sun finally went down, the Connies—the State Park Conservation Officers—would come to kick everyone out and close the gates. After that, when someone could get a keg, we would all meet out on Fenner's two-track. We would build a bonfire and pump the keg and drink beer out of red Solo plastic cups. Kids just leaned against the wagon circle of cars trying to look cool.

Lucy and I had driven every road hundreds, maybe thousands, of times together. She drove by herself in faraway states all the time now, but when she was home, she was certain she would get lost.

Twelve

Sunday, June 29, 1986, 1:00 a.m.

*T*he exchange at the country club bar didn't seem to bother Lucy as much as it did me. When we got home she said she was going to bed and went inside. Ron waited in the car to go over to Evan's house. Out by the curb Elizabeth asked me if I thought Lucy was going to be all right.

"I don't think she needed that tonight," I said.

"Check on her later, okay?" Elizabeth twisted the handles on her purse, a sure sign she was worried about one of us. She looked up at the house and hesitated like she might rush in to save Lucy. Ron honked the horn. "Make sure she's up by seven. The wedding's at noon." Elizabeth had a way of breaking things down to their most elemental. What is the problem? How do we solve it? It was her way of having some control and logic in a family that had little of either. As she got in the car I heard her chide Ron, "Keep it down. You'll wake the neighbors."

I stopped to take off my white heels on the way up the front walk. Through the front window I could see Sammie maneuvering Chuck to the couch. I went inside and Sammie followed me to the kitchen.

"Can you make some coffee?" Sammie asked. "We'd better get him sobered up before he goes to bed."

"Why were you so pissy about Evan's toast to Anna?"

Sammie sat down at the table and played with a spoon. "Evan's special. He's the most sensitive of all of us. His whole life he's gotten run roughshod over by us girls because he's so much quieter than us. I don't want to think that his wife would do the same thing to him. I mean, how many guys like Japanese art and Yogi tea and still like to go out to some duck blind or deer camp with the guys? He's unique."

"I didn't know he liked Japanese art."

"You should talk to him more often."

Buddy was following me around like I had bacon in my pocket. "Sammie, would you take Buddy out?"

"Nope. I didn't make the deal with the cops."

I got Buddy's leash out of the closet and opened the front door. Before I could snap it on his collar, Buddy had blown by me and out the door. I followed after him into the darkness. He pummeled through the bushes into the Longs' yard, and then I heard him turn and crash down the steep hill to Bear Lake. God! He was going to make me chase him in my skirt and hose. I hadn't bothered to put my shoes back on because I had only planned to walk about ten feet. I could now hear Buddy racing along the beach. I made my way across the yard to the back of the house, avoiding the big tent. Gingerly, I tried out the new dock stairs that led down to the lake. They seemed solid enough. The lights Dad had put in along the stairs weren't working, though. Like Dad, Tom the handyman couldn't fix one thing without messing up another. I gripped the railing and felt for each step with my toes. My eyes were starting to adjust to the darkness and there were a few stars out to help me. My feet finally touched the beach grass. Ah jeez, now I had sand inside my nylons, which is just a bizarre feeling. I looked down the beach and thought I could see Buddy's black silhouette moving around about fifty yards away.

"Buddy!" I hissed.

Nothing. I couldn't yell too loud at 1:30 in the morning, and Buddy wouldn't have paid attention anyway. As I turned to go back up the stairs without him, I caught sight of someone sitting in our speedboat.

"Who is that?" I said sharply, feeling that tingly feeling of fear and adrenaline.

"Shhh. It's just me. Lucy."

I walked across the beach and halfway out on the dock. "I thought you went to bed."

"I wanted to be by myself for a while."

"Oh." I wasn't sure if I should leave or not. "Can I be with you while you're being by yourself?"

Lucy's dress was tucked up under her feet. She was seated on the back of the boat facing the water. "Sure."

I stepped onto the gunwale and made my way next to my sister.

"What are you doing down here?" she asked.

"Chasing Buddy."

We sat in silence. Every once in a while, a bluegill or a sunfish broke the surface to feed.

"Do you want to talk?" I nudged my shoulder into hers.

"No."

"Why did you get married?"

"I just said I didn't want to talk." She flipped a stone into the lake.

"Do you want me to leave?"

"No."

There were a few lights on the other side of the lake a half mile away. Evan's house was directly across from my parents' house. We watched the lights click off. Elizabeth and Ron had gone to bed.

"Why do you suppose Elizabeth married him?" Lucy asked.

"I don't know. He doesn't say much, he wears Gucci shoes, he brags about how expensive his cars are, and he says he was raised in Manhattan but he speaks with a New Jersey accent. Maybe because he's not like anybody around here?"

"I married Chuck because I had to."

"Are you pregnant?"

"No. He was about to be shipped overseas and the only way to stop that is to be married to someone stateside. At least it delays the process."

"You've only known him seven weeks. You must really love him."

"He's in love with someone else."

I was starting to wonder if I had had a few more drinks than I thought. Or maybe I hadn't had enough. A slight breeze came up on the lake and I wrapped my arms around myself.

"If you're cold, there's a beach towel over there." Lucy indicated the captain's chair. I got it and Lucy took one end and I took the other end and we huddled inside it together.

"Why did you marry him if he was in love with someone else?"

Lucy sighed. "He's in love with some girl from Illinois. He was shipping out in two days and she couldn't get there in time. She said her car broke down and she didn't have enough money for a plane ticket. So I married him as a favor."

"Why didn't he go to her?"

"You can't just go AWOL. It's not like cutting class."

I didn't know what to say to this and looked down the beach to see if I could see Buddy. I couldn't. He had probably made his way back up to the house by now and was scratching to be let in. He tore up the screen door every summer.

I could sort of see why Lucy would marry Chuck as a favor. Dad always said, "Take a chance. If you ever have a chance to do something different in this life, do it." Our family was also big on helping out. Walker called it our "hostess gene." If someone had car trouble, I'd lend him or her my car even if I barely knew the person. Marrying Chuck combined two of the things Lucy did well.

"Why did you bring him home?"

"After we got married," Lucy went on, "we started sleeping together. We planned to get the whole thing annulled. I just brought him home because I'm dating him."

I pondered the idea of dating someone after you had married him.

"Lucy, you have to tell Mom and Dad. You can't go through with the wedding tomorrow."

Lucy pulled the towel closer around her shoulders. "How can I do that? All my life they tried to do the right thing for me, and it always made them feel bad when it didn't work out. I went to college and they paid all that money and then I dropped out. Now they're spending all this money on a wedding for me."

"This is not about money. Why would you go through with this?"

Lucy dropped her chin into her knees. "I can't look like a loser to every single person I grew up with."

"They don't have to live with Chuck. You do."

"Maybe I love him."

"Do you?"

"I don't know. Sometimes I think I do."

Lucy unwrapped herself and got up to leave. Her motion upset the boat and her purse and shoes started to go over the side. I made a valiant grab and wound up with one shoe and the purse. We watched the other shoe disappear under the water.

Lucy sighed. "Now I don't have a mate." Then she tossed the other shoe in after its partner.

We trudged back up to the darkened house. Chuck was snoring on the couch, my bed. I followed Lucy upstairs and we both climbed into her bed. Lucy lay on her side, turned away from me.

"Lucy, are you awake?"

"No."

"What did Fudgie Shaw give you?"

"Hush up."

I snuggled up to her so her back wouldn't be unprotected and we both fell asleep.

Thirteen

March 2006

"What do you mean you can't come?" Aidan was incredulous. He had a right to be. Tonight was the premiere of one of his movies. It was being held in Westwood with klieg lights, red carpet, paparazzi—the works.

Earlier, in the bathroom at work, I had changed into a decent dress and fixed my makeup. Walking out the front doors, my cell phone rang. It was Elizabeth. "I just wanted to tell you where to park tonight."

I stopped looking for my car keys in my purse. Alarm bells went off in my head. "Parking?"

"Right, for Madison's ballet performance."

Ballet? I had no idea what she was talking about. Cautiously I said, "Can you remind me about this?"

Elizabeth spoke in a controlled tone. "Don't tell me that you're blowing this off."

"No, no, of course not." I stood in the middle of the parking lot, phone to ear, and fake-smiled at some colleagues walking by. "I just can't remember the address."

Elizabeth's voice became friendlier. As she reeled off the information I suddenly remembered. I had responded yes to the invitation by email. Then I had forgotten to write it down. Two places I absolutely had to be tonight meant one big problem.

I tuned back in to Elizabeth. "Be sure to get there early because Madison is in the second and fourth numbers. Your ticket is at will-call. Unless Aidan is coming? Then I can get one more ticket. Do we finally get to meet the mysterious Aidan?"

"Uh, no. Um, Aidan is out of town right now." I cringed at my lie. Then I listened to Elizabeth rattle off parking instructions. After promising I would be there early, I had called Aidan.

"Jeannie, you've known about this movie premiere for months. This is a huge moment for me. I'd like you there by my side, you know, like someone who loves me? My girlfriend?" The hurt and anger in his voice were more than evident.

"I'm sorry. It's just . . ." I trailed off. I couldn't explain about Madison's ballet performance. Up until now, I'd been able to keep Aidan, Elizabeth, and Sammie apart by some creative maneuvering. Fortunately, the rest of my family lived a couple thousand miles away. But Westwood and the UCLA campus are literally a few short blocks apart. Aidan might want to go meet Madison and Elizabeth after his movie premiere.

"It's just . . . an emergency at work," I finally finished.

"I don't believe this. Can't Caitlin handle it?" I heard Aidan up-shifting his car furiously.

"Take it easy, Aidan. I love you and I want you to get there in one piece." I hit the remote control to unlock my car. "Okay, I'll be there. I promise."

I sat in my car and leaned my forehead against the steering

wheel. What the hell was I going to do? Miss the ballet, and my family might disown me. Miss the movie premiere, and my boyfriend might break up with me. I finally pulled out of the parking lot and commanded myself to think.

Could I pull off both? The two events were about half a mile from each other. The movie premiere started at 7:30. The ballet started at 8:00. But premieres never started on time. You had to wait for the stars to run the gauntlet of press outside before the lights could go down. I quickly calculated: lights out at 7:50, opening credits would roll and be done by 7:55. I had to stay for the credits because the audience would cheer for the names of people they knew, and I needed to be there when Aidan's name appeared.

Could I then hoof it to the performance by 8:00? Unlikely. I tapped the wheel while waiting at a red light. I'd have to at least try. Looking down I regarded my strappy Jimmy Choo shoes. They were perfect for a movie premiere but not so great for running.

After circling the area twice, I gave up and pulled my car into the only parking lot with empty spaces, exactly as Elizabeth had predicted it would be. The lot was halfway between the premiere and the ballet performance. My car was going to be of no help, as I had expected.

Hurrying up the street, even in my angst, I still marveled as I always did at the elaborate display of neon on the art deco theater. The title of Aidan's movie was splashed in three-foot-tall letters on the marquee. I searched the crowd and found him almost immediately. He was waiting for me at the entry to the red carpet and he broke into a broad smile at the sight of me.

"You made it," he said as we hugged. Taking my arm he led me down the red carpet cordoned off by velvet ropes. To one side was a long line of paparazzi and on the other side were publicists from the studio who directed Aidan to the various photographers and video crews

I respectfully stepped back when Aidan was being interviewed. The shot the magazines would want to publish was one of Aidan with a glitzy star next to him. During one of these moments I furtively pulled my left sleeve back to catch a glimpse of my watch.

"Don't do that!" a publicist whizzing by with a clipboard snapped at me. "Someone will take a photo and run a caption saying, 'Is this movie over yet?'"

Already 7:38 and we weren't even seated yet.

At an agonizingly slow pace, Aidan made his way down the long line of media waiting to speak to him. I had gone on ahead and was waiting in the theater lobby making nervous chit-chat with business acquaintances. It was 7:47. I peeked out the door. Aidan still had more people waiting to interview him. I had to take drastic measures. I marched back up the red carpet against the flow of traffic.

"Aidan." I tugged on his sleeve. He turned from the cameras and smiled, but his eyes said, "What the hell are you doing?" "Aidan, they need you to come in and get seated right away. They're running behind schedule."

Aidan bent down and spoke low in my ear. "But I haven't spoken to *Access Hollywood* yet. I can't ditch that."

"Yes, yes, you can. The publicist was very firm. She asked me to come get you." I was pulling on his elbow now.

Aidan pulled back, hissing, "I *can't!*"

I yanked his arm harder. "There's a problem. They need to turn the lights down *now* and roll the film."

Aidan yanked back. "I have to finish up here!"

The cameras now were focused on us for a different reason. It appeared we were engaging in a minor lover's spat. We both realized it at the same time and stopped to plaster smiles on for the press. Our faces read, "Don't mind us, we're just one happy couple." Aidan put his hand at the small of my back and propelled me rather forcefully into the theater. An usher showed us to our seats, which had been cordoned off by masking tape. A piece of paper with our names handwritten on it was taped to each of our seats.

We slid into our seats at 7:59. Thankfully, it was lights out at 8:02. Credits were done by 8:08. "Aidan, I have to go to the bathroom." I was already climbing over him to get to the aisle.

"Can't you wait a few minutes? The opening scene is so good."

"I know, I know. That scene is great. But I'm not feeling real well." I was already past him and hurrying up the aisle. Once I cleared the doors, I bolted through the now-empty lobby and out to the sidewalk. The camera vans were packing up and leaving. One was just pulling away from the curb when I pounded on the driver's door. The driver stopped suddenly, clearly startled.

"Hey, can you give me a ride just up the street? Please?" I tried not to sound too desperate.

"Are you anybody we can interview?" the driver asked. Everyone is looking for an angle in L.A.

"No, I'm a nobody. But I need a ride. Please?" Now my desperation was showing.

He shrugged. "Okay, hop in." Someone slid the large door on the side of the van back and I crawled in and crouched among the cables coiled on the floor. We got lucky and caught the green lights and two minutes later I was racing up the sidewalk to the performing arts center where Madison was dancing. After snatching my ticket from the hands of the woman at the will-call ticket booth, I ran for the doors to the auditorium. An usher blocked my way.

"Sorry, miss. But the doors are closed. No one is allowed in until intermission."

"But I have to!" I protested while trying to dart around him. He stepped into my path, blocking me.

"The ballet has started. You'll have to wait."

"But this is a matter of life and death!" I heard myself blurt out. Oh my God, what was I saying? But it was too late to take it back. Anyway, it was kind of true because Elizabeth would kill me if I didn't show up.

The usher's demeanor changed. "What happened?" He looked like he was ready to sit down and listen raptly to every gory detail.

"Um, car accident. Yes, there was a car accident. I need to let my sister know."

"Was it bad?" The usher didn't know when to quit.

"Yes, very bad. It just happened up the street." Now why did I have to say that?

"Did anyone call an ambulance?" The usher was pulling out his cell phone now.

"I have to get in there, okay?" I pleaded.

This time the usher didn't try and stop me when I reached for the doors. It took me a while to find my seat next to Elizabeth in the near dark. Of course, she would have to be seated in the middle of a row. I climbed over several irritated patrons, none of whom were shy about hissing their displeasure at me. Finally I settled into my seat.

"You're late," Elizabeth said, staring straight ahead at the stage.

"Traffic. Sorry," I muttered. After a few moments, Elizabeth reached over and squeezed my hand. I was forgiven. Onstage Madison danced with confidence. She looked just like Elizabeth at that age: willowy and gorgeous. Relaxing for a moment, I enjoyed watching her. She really was good. After she danced into the wings, I peered at my watch. It was 8:33. Somehow I made it through the next performance until Madison reappeared onstage. As her part neared its end, I started edging my butt to the front of my seat preparing for a fast getaway. The moment she finished I was on the move.

"Madison was amazing, Elizabeth. Truly great." I had stood up and was now wedging myself between Elizabeth's knees and the seat in front of her.

"Where are you going?" Elizabeth was incredulous.

"I have a problem at work. I'll call you later." The same patrons who were mad at me on my way into the row now acted ready for civil disobedience on my way out. I hightailed it away from their angry comments and up the aisle. Fortunately the usher was nowhere to be seen in the lobby and I pushed my way out the doors and to the sidewalk.

This time there was no helpful car to ferry me back to the premiere. I trotted as fast as my high heels would let me go. It was 9:12. I had been gone for over an hour. My heels made a harsh clack-clack noise as they banged against the concrete at a pace they weren't made for. Sweat was forming at the small of my back and I was breathing hard. I really needed to try to do more cardio.

Up ahead of me I could make out flashing lights. A cop car was angled across the street blocking traffic. It didn't alarm me because it's not that unusual a sight in a big city. As I jogged past the cop car I saw an ambulance parked in the middle of the street.

Damn! The sidewalk inexplicably ended on this side of the road. I was going to have to cross over to pick it up on the other side, which meant jaywalking. Crossing anywhere but at a designated crosswalk is a big no-no in California, and I didn't want the cops to see me.

I stealthily maneuvered around the ambulance and heard a cop bitching that some moron had called in a phony report about a car accident with injuries. As I darted behind the ambulance, it started to back up. The next thing I knew I was skinning my hands and knees along the pavement. I must have hit my head, too, because when I opened my eyes a paramedic was already kneeling down next to me, and I was still sprawled out on the street.

"Shit! Lady, are you all right?" He was taking my pulse. "I didn't even see you behind me. You came out of nowhere."

"I came from my niece's ballet performance." I heard my words as if they were echoing somewhere far away in the universe.

Groggily I sat up and took inventory. The ambulance had sharply bumped me, but nothing seemed to be broken. Ruefully I looked at my stockings, torn from knee to ankle. One of my shoes had also lost a heel.

The paramedic insisted on treating me. After leading me by the arm to the rear of the ambulance, he sat me down on the wide bumper with its raised no-skid metal protrusions. Rectangular hash marks were going to be embedded in my ass for days, I deliriously thought.

He examined my knees, then motioned that I needed to take off my ruined nylons. So there, in the middle of a major thoroughfare, with a crowd beginning to gather, I reached up under my dress, yanked at the top of my tummy-control pantyhose, and wiggled out of them. The paramedic then picked gravel out of my wounds and shone a flashlight in my eyes. The cops took my statement even though I said it wasn't necessary. They were probably more worried about a lawsuit than they were about me.

Finally, with large, white gauze bandages taped to both knees, one hand, and my cheek, I set off for the premiere again. Barefoot and bare-legged, I staggered into the theater lobby at 10:22. Part of me wondered if I had shaved my legs that morning but then reasoned that the last thing anyone would notice was my hairy legs.

Trying not to be seen, I skimmed close to the wall and scanned the crowd for Aidan. A few people I knew asked if I was all right. But most cut a large swath around me. In L.A. being uncool is considered a contagious and dangerous disease. And right now, I was clearly looking uncool. Still looking for Aidan, I bumped into something large. Looking up I saw, damn it, that it was Katsu. He was looking at me quizzically while keeping his iPhone pressed to his ear. He raised an eyebrow at my appearance. Mumbling something unintelligible, I moved around him. After a few steps I couldn't resist turning around to see if he was still gawking. He wasn't. His iPhone was lifted out in front of his face as he pressed a button on the screen. That bastard! He had taken my photo!

Gritting my teeth, I waded through the crowd. Finally, I caught Aidan's eye and waved above the heads of the people crowded around him. His return look was not pleasant. I moved over to cower by the concession stand for a while instead of facing him.

Minutes later I saw him push through the throng and stride toward me. Once he got a better look at me his step at first faltered. Then he practically ran to me.

"Honey! I was so worried when you didn't come back. You're hurt! Are you all right?" He swept me into a hug. Guiltily I pulled back and hung my head. Aidan held me by the shoulders and looked me up and down. "What happened?"

"I got hit by an ambulance." My head hung even lower.

"An ambulance?" Aidan wrinkled his brow. "What were you doing outside?"

"I . . ." Good question. What *was* I doing outside?

"I wasn't feeling well so I went outside for some fresh air," I lied. Now I knew for sure I was going straight to hell.

After a few more questions to make sure I was, in fact, all right, Aidan escorted me to my car. "You're positive you can make it home?" he asked, peering into the driver's-side window.

"I'm sure." Blessedly, Aidan had to attend the after-premiere party; otherwise I knew he would have insisted on coming with me. I just wanted to get home, get into my comfy bed, and pull the covers over my head. Which is exactly what I did.

The next morning I was awoken by two phone calls. The first was from Elizabeth. "Aidan is out of town? Then can you explain to me why there's a photo in *Variety* this morning of him attending his movie premiere in Westwood last night? That's why you left so suddenly last night! Damn it, Jeannie, you have got to get over this thing with the family!" A dial tone then suddenly rang in my ear.

I had just pulled the covers back over my head when the phone rang again. "So you were at your niece's ballet performance at UCLA last night, huh?" Aidan's voice was apoplectic.

"How did you know?" I asked weakly.

"I subscribe to an electronic news service, Jeannie. It emails me any article with a name in it that I'm interested in. You appeared today in the *Los Angeles Times* as a pedestrian who was involved in an accident with an ambulance. You gave a statement to the police."

"But I got hit by an ambulance trying to get back to the premiere," I protested.

"Let's hope it knocked some sense into you!" For the second time in five minutes a dial tone buzzed in my head.

My iPhone dinged softly, signaling a new email had come in. Out of habit, I checked it. Instantly, I was horrified to see a photo of myself looking like a crazed, bandaged escapee from the psych ward. The email was sent to the general address for all studio employees. The sender was no one I knew and it was a good bet that it was a fake address anyway. But I sure knew who had sent it. I burrowed deeper under the covers, then pulled the pillow over my blanketed head for good measure.

I hate the new age of instant media.

Fourteen

Sunday, June 29, 1986, 7:30 a.m.

I cannot, *cannot*, believe you are not up yet!" Elizabeth stood over us like a prison warden. "Get out of bed and into that shower, Lucy. Jeannie, go check Anna's dress to see if she spilled anything on it. Dad has it downstairs."

By the time I got to the kitchen, I had already pushed through the flower delivery people, the caterers, and the guys who were dropping off the rental china. The couch was vacant.

"Where's Chuck?" I asked.

Dad shrugged as he signed a check for the flowers.

The dress was lying over a chair. I went through all its folds carefully but found no stains. I gathered the dress up to carry it to Lucy's room.

"Did you have to wait outside their hotel door long last night for the dress?" I grinned at my father.

"Actually, it was embarrassing how fast it came out," he grumbled.

"Good for Evan," Sammie said, buttering her toast at the counter. Mom came in and turned on the water to fill a vase. A shriek from upstairs let us know that the water temperature had suddenly risen in the shower.

Sammie bit into her toast. "The entire town is buzzing about us. If this family ever moves out of town, no one will have anything to talk about."

"I'd rather be talked about than ignored." Mom sniffed and walked out. But I heard her mutter under her breath, "Small-minded people." Then she called to me over her shoulder, "Jeannie, take the dress upstairs and bring your grandmother down."

Grandma was waiting at the top of the stairs. I dumped the dress on Lucy's bed, came back, took her arm, and came down with her, step by shuffling step. Since there was no room in the kitchen with the flowers and china piled everywhere, I deposited Grandma in the living room.

"Coffee, Grandma?"

"Do you have any Dr Pepper?"

I was pretty sure there was no Dr Pepper anywhere in the state of Michigan. Finding a Dr Pepper here was like trying to find a Vernors soda pop in Texas—not going to happen. But I said I would go look and left her waiting patiently, like a toy dog that had to be moved from place to place.

Instead, I went back upstairs to shower and don Sammie's prom dress. I looked at myself in the mirror. The red rose pattern made me look like a small couch. How could she possibly have worn such an atrocity to the prom? I wondered. But remembering her boyfriend's prom wear—a rust red tuxedo with a ruffled shirt tipped with red—I figured it must have been a style that went in and out in a blink. Mom came into the bathroom, felt the top of the hot roller box, and, satisfied, started rolling her hair up. Sammie applied Lucy's makeup in her room.

"Has anyone seen Chuck?" Lucy called out.

"No," Dad yelled from downstairs.

"He couldn't have gotten far. It's a small town; somebody will spot him," I shouted from the bathroom.

"You're not helping her nerves." Mom balanced a cigarette on the edge of the sink. She was wearing her pink, fluffy robe and was putting the last curler in her hair. "I thought you were going to help her pick out her wedding veil."

"I did."

"Jeannie, Lucy bought a white cowboy hat."

It seemed I had been lax in my duties. Fortunately, a wail echoed in the hallway, interrupting this conversation. Mom and I hurried across the hall to Lucy's room.

"What's wrong?"

Lucy was standing in front of the dresser mirror holding up the strapless wedding dress. Mom pushed her way past Sammie.

Lucy looked at her with tears streaming down her face. "This is what's wrong!" She let go of the dress, which promptly sagged to her waist. Lucy stood there with her bee-sting breasts exposed.

"Now, honey, I'm sure we can fix this with some, um, safety pins. It'll be fine." Mom hoisted up the dress and surveyed it from the back. Dozens of little buttons marched down the back and Mom looked perplexed about where to tuck a seam real fast.

"Don't you have a strapless padded bra?" she finally asked.

"I didn't bring it! And *why* didn't I bring my strapless padded bra? Gee, is it because I didn't know I was getting *married*?" Lucy dissolved again.

"I had just finished her mascara, too," Sammie said.

"I have a strapless bra," I volunteered.

"Go get it," Mom said. Somehow, a mouthful of pins had materialized. I went and searched through my drawer, found it, and brought it back. Lucy slid the dress back down to her waist and put on the bra. We all stared into the mirror. The bra was not padded since I was better endowed than Lucy, to put it politely. The stiff cups stood out like empty vessels. Lucy flung herself away from us and threw herself facedown on the bed.

"It's almost ten o'clock," Elizabeth said as she entered the room.

"Not now, Elizabeth." Mom was stroking Lucy's hair.

"But—"

"Not now, Elizabeth," Mom said sternly, giving her one last chance to shut up. Elizabeth looked at the faces around her and took it.

Mom got up, left the room, and came back with a box of tissues. Lucy sat up and eyed her warily. "No way."

"I can only pin the dress so far."

"Absolutely not."

"It will look fine. No one will know." Mom pulled about twenty tissues out of the box and handed them to me. I dutifully balled them up and stuffed the right cup. Mom took the left, while Lucy held her arms out to her sides and stared up at the ceiling, slowly shaking her head. After much of the box was emptied, we spun Lucy around to the mirror.

"Voilà!" Mom said. "You look beautiful."

She did look good. The lace bodice of the top was filled out and Lucy appeared to be stacked. She touched the bodice gingerly. "Think it'll stay up?"

"Yes," Mom said with probably more conviction than she felt. "Now wipe your eyes. Sammie, fix her makeup."

Mom and I rushed back to the bathroom, where Mom frantically pulled rollers out of her hair. I leaned in below her for mirror space and put my eye shadow on.

A voice called out from the bottom of the stairs. "Mr. and Mrs. Thompson! North Muskegon Police here!"

"Uh-oh, are they here about Chuck?" I looked at Mom.

Lucy stuck her head out the door of the bedroom. "Is it Chuck?"

"No, honey, I'm sure it's not. Just keep getting ready. Jeannie, come with me." Mom trotted down the stairs with half of her rollers still in.

The cop stood by the door ramrod straight. "Sorry to walk in but no one answered my knock."

"Is Chuck all right?" Mom asked.

"Who's Chuck?"

Mom looked him up and down. "Marv Carson, what in God's name would make you walk into our house, shout up the stairs, and scare us half to death?"

Marv shifted a bit. "I have your dog, Buddy, in the squad car. I picked him up two blocks down, heading toward your house."

"Thank you. That's very considerate. Could you bring him in?" Mom sounded testy even though her words were polite.

"You don't understand. Your dog is under arrest and I'm taking him to the pound. He'll have to stay there for five days for observation and you'll have to pay a two-hundred-and-fifty-dollar fine."

Mom was already brushing by him. She stormed out the door, down the front path, and strode up to the cop car in front of the house.

Marv was trotting to keep up with her. "Mrs. Thompson! You can't do this."

Mom turned to him all aquiver in her pink robe with her half head of curlers bouncing. "Marv Carson! I have been through a week that you could never imagine. I have a daughter upstairs crying exactly one hour before her wedding because her breasts are too small. I have a son-in-law-to-be that we can't find. And you tell me I can't take my dog? Watch me!" Mom threw open the back door of the squad car and grabbed Buddy's collar. Buddy was out of the car so fast he didn't know what cyclone had hit him. Mom marched him back up the walk and into the house and slammed the door behind her. I stood helplessly on the walk. When Marv Carson looked like he was about to appeal to the good citizen in me, I bolted for the door, closed it behind me, and locked it. Then I dropped to the floor below the window for good measure.

"Did you find me a Dr Pepper?" Grandma asked.

"Not yet," I said as I lifted a corner of the curtain to see if the cop had left yet.

"I would have thought Chuck would be back by now with a bottle," Grandma said from the living room.

"Where is he?" I asked her.

"He was going running this morning so I asked him to find me some Dr Pepper. It's not like your mother would bother having any in the house for me."

I hoisted myself up. "Grandma, I'm sure Mom didn't mean to forget your Dr Pepper. It's just been a little crazy around here. I don't think anyone has even remembered to feed the dog."

"Are you comparing me to Buddy?" she asked.

I silently wished Grandma would go back to low volume. Just then, Chuck slammed in through the back door carrying a six-pack of Dr Pepper and a round tin of Kodiak chewing tobacco. He had on a pair of red running shorts and his shoes. Sweat shone on his lean body. Bounding into the living room, Chuck flopped down next to Grandma and gallantly opened a can. It promptly fizzed up and squirted all over the place. Chuck put his mouth to it and sucked up the excess, then handed the can to Grandma.

She nodded her thanks. Chuck pulled his white mouth guard out and rubbed the strings of saliva and Dr Pepper on his forearm. "Sorry it took me so long but I had to run nearly ten miles over to someplace called Twin Lake to find any Dr Pepper." Bouncing back up, he took the stairs two at a time. I stared at spilled soda pop on the carpet and then the sweat outline that his back and legs had made on my mother's prize antique couch.

It had been decided that Chuck would wear his dress uniform. This was mainly because Evan's wedding had wiped out most of the tuxes at Le Tux Shop. Plus, no one trusted any of Evan's groomsmen to get a tux back on time without major dry cleaning needs. Lucy, I think, was pleased that Chuck was wearing his army uniform. It represented her new life and she was far more comfortable with it than the life she had lived here for twenty years.

Elizabeth was outside completely coiffed, put together, and perfect, directing where the tables were to be set up under the tent. Ron was sitting near her in the same clothes he had worn the night before, reading the paper and drinking coffee. It was 11:20, so I scrammed out of her way. As I went upstairs to finish my makeup, I heard her belt out like a drill sergeant, "Ten minutes until we leave!"

"Did one of you girls take my black bow tie?" Dad shouted from deep in his closet. There was a pause as we all considered.

"I think I have it," Sammie said as she ran from the bathroom to her room holding a towel in front of her. I went in behind her, watched her root around in a bottom drawer, held my hand out to receive the tie, and took it back to Dad.

"I don't even want to know why she had it," he said. He fumbled with it and Mom went to help him. Chuck was now showered, dressed, and sitting downstairs with Grandma. At 11:30,

Elizabeth finally could not restrain herself. "It's time. Right now. And I do mean right now. Everyone down those stairs and into the cars." For once we all listened and assembled in the hall foyer.

"Oh, Harold, just look at these two." Mom looked at Lucy and Chuck with tears in her eyes. I wasn't sure if they were tears of happiness or what. "Let's get a picture."

"There is no time. Period," Elizabeth barked.

I looked at Lucy as we trooped down the walk. She had her white cowboy hat on with her frilly lace dress. She looked kind of like a Dallas debutante.

Dad opened the car doors, and I heard Lucy say to Chuck, "Spit out the chewing tobacco."

"This mouth guard thing holds it in real good."

Lucy gave up and threw herself into the car with Chuck, piling up the white tulle and satin behind her. We got to the church at 11:58. Father Whippet ran out to meet us. He practically pulled all of us from the car. "Everyone is seated. I took care of that. Jeannie, you just have to walk down the aisle when I point at you from the altar. Step, smile. Step, smile. Harold, you've been through this before with Elizabeth and Sammie so just same thing, different daughter." He pointed at Chuck. "Come with me; I'll place you. Relax, everyone, and good luck."

Chuck went with Father Whippet, while the rest of my family raced to the front pew. Lucy, Dad, and I waited in the entry hall before walking down the aisle. Lucy gripped her bouquet and turned to look through the open doors at the backs of the hundreds of people waiting for her.

Dad walked up behind her and put his hands on her shoulders. "Sweetheart. You don't have to do anything you don't want to do. Your mother and I can call the whole thing off right now. We will always love you no matter what."

"I know," Lucy said. "But what if I'm not sure and I call it off? What if I was meant to go through with it? If I call it off now it means that Chuck and I are done."

"Do what's in your heart, honey."

I could see Father Whippet point at me. People were turning in their pews in anticipation of the processional. I stood in the open doors in full view, holding my bouquet. I glued a smile on my face. Lucy and Dad were still talking, and I was throwing frantic looks sideways at them. Was I supposed to step, smile, or not? I missed the music cue and people were starting to murmur. Father Whippet gave a hand signal to the organist and she played the last few measures over. Father Whippet pointed at me again.

I gave up and marched over to where Dad and Lucy were conferring. "Do I go or not?"

Dad kissed Lucy's forehead and tilted up her chin. He raised his eyebrows and smiled. Lucy nodded. Dad gave me a head jerk and I resumed my place in the open doors. Father Whippet seemed downright happy to see me reappear, and he signaled to the organist, who had been treading musical water. I step-smiled down the aisle and took my place to the left of Father Whippet. Chuck was waiting on the right. While Lucy and Dad walked solemnly down the aisle I looked at the pew that held my family and studied their faces. Mom, who had been married for thirty happy and some unhappy years, looked beatific. Sammie, who was divorced, watched Lucy with a beaming smile. Elizabeth and Ron stood apart, not touching. Grandma was looking for something in her purse. A few rows behind my family, I saw Walker and his family. Walker and his dad looked tired. They probably hadn't even been to bed. When the trout are biting they'll go all night.

Dad delivered Lucy to Chuck, who shook his hand. Then Lucy, Chuck, and I turned toward Father Whippet. He held the book of prayer high above his head. "We are gathered here today . . ." Father Whippet began the marriage ceremony. He droned on.

Dad had only asked that the ceremony include communion. It was important to him that the entire family had the body and blood of Christ together. Father Whippet began the Nicene Creed, again lifting the prayer book above his head. "God from God, Light from Light . . ."

It was then that Lucy started to cry. Mascara was running down her face again, ruining Sammie's makeup job. I wasn't sure what my role was as maid of honor. Clearly Lucy wasn't happy, but since she had her back to the church Mom and Dad didn't know yet. Was I supposed to save her by pushing her off into the wings? She was really beginning to get going in earnest now, not quiet little girly sniffles but the kind you get when you're alone in your bedroom and you're hiccupping and snorting and your nose is running down your chin. Father Whippet's microphone was now picking up the sound and echoing it around the church. Oh God. I looked back at Mom. She was halfway out of her seat but Dad pulled her back down.

Father Whippet kept right on going like nothing was happening. "Do you"—he checked his notes—"Chuck, take Lucy . . ."

Lucy's sobs carried around the church again. People were beginning to either titter or look concerned. I knew right then we needed something badly. Kleenex. I signaled to Mom and she started rooting through her purse. She always had some balled-up piece of tissue among the Jujubes and loose tobacco. But how was I supposed to get it? March down the aisle to Mom's pew, pick up a used tissue, and deliver it to Lucy?

I did know where there was a mother lode of tissue. I reached over and dug into the top of Lucy's dress. The videographer, seeing my hand in Lucy's bra, woke up and went in for a closeup. The look I gave him made him back off. I grabbed a ball of tissue and handed it to her. She wiped her tears and stared straight ahead. Chuck was nervously clicking his mouth guard like it was dentures and the sound also reverberated throughout the church. I pulled another tissue out of the bra and handed it to my sister. She reached in for a third herself. Father Whippet had finished with Chuck and turned to Lucy. "Do you, Lucy—" he said, and then he stopped.

His jaw fell open and he dropped his notes. Lucy's strapless dress, having lost the support of the tissue-stuffed bra, had given up its battle to stay in place. Her left titty was exposed for God and country to see. The videographer got interested again. I stepped straight in front of Lucy to block his view, grabbed the dress front and back, and yanked it up mightily. The dress stayed in place, and I kept my hand on Lucy's back so I could tell if it was going to make a break for it again. Father Whippet had busied himself by getting on his hands and knees to gather his papers.

"It's okay, Father Whippet. She's covered," I whispered down to him.

He got to his feet, brushed at his pants, and carried on with the next part of the service. Fortunately for him, and us, the singer took over and we had a few minutes to get ourselves together. "Ave Mariaaa . . ." she warbled.

I looked back at the assembled guests. I had known most of them my whole life. We had ridden bikes together, learned to drive together, argued and laughed with each other, and just about all of us had dated each other. In some cases, we knew each other's parents almost as well as we knew our own. And I could tell you, I was grateful for my own. The Prescotts were sitting in the pew where my family normally sat. It was halfway back in the church. Not too close and not too far, which is pretty much our relationship with God.

It was the pew where I had passed out cold on Easter Sunday in seventh grade. Everyone thought it was because of too much candy. While I liked a good marshmallow chick as much as the next person, that's not what it was. I had passed out from guilt.

It had started with a book I found buried in Sammie's closet. A very dirty book. Then I had discovered my "joy button." Every time I did it, I swore to God that I would never do it again. But of course, I did. That's when I started hearing the radio ads on WTRU, the local AM station. *"VeeeDeee is for everybody, not just for a few,"* the singer warbled away about the dangers of venereal disease. I had no idea what it was, but I was certain I had it. Otherwise, why would the ads have started just then? It was clearly a dire warning. I had to tell someone. After a few agonizing days, I cornered my mom while she was watching *Jeopardy*.

"Mom, can we speak alone?" I asked solemnly.

We walked back to my bedroom and sat on my bed. My mother looked at me with some amount of terror in her eyes.

"What is it, honey?"

I blurted out, "I have venereal disease."

She regarded me, sitting on my pink bedspread clutching my stuffed kitty.

"Sweetheart, now be very honest with me. Are you sexually active?"

I hung my head. "Yes."

"With who?"

What did she mean with who? "With myself."

To her credit, she didn't laugh. But I could see the tension leave her face.

"Why in the world would you think you had venereal disease?"

I told her everything. The book. The ads. God striking me down.

"Where would Sammie get a book like that?" she mused. I couldn't believe it. She was missing the whole point.

Then she came back to the issue at hand. "What you are doing is perfectly natural. Unless you are doing it too much."

I wondered what too much was but didn't ask.

"You don't have venereal disease, sweetheart. You can't give it to yourself." She went on for a bit more about boys and a book called *Our Bodies, Ourselves* and then told me that I should absolutely wait until I was married. Then she went back to watch Final Jeopardy. I was relieved I didn't have venereal disease, but the fact remained that God must be pretty damn pissed off at me.

That Easter Sunday didn't start out so bad. I was wearing Lucy's navy blue dress with cherries all over it, and I had on my very first pair of nylons. L'eggs, tan-colored with a reinforced toe. It was my first time in church since my talk with Mom, and I was determined to make it up to God. We were sitting in our usual pew and I was squished between Sammie and Lucy. The prayer for forgiveness began, and I prayed as hard as I could. "We have done those things which we ought not to have done," Father Whippet intoned, and I chanted right along with him. Then everything started to go red and black in front of my eyes.

"Sammie, I don't feel good."

"You're not getting out of church that easily."

That's when I passed out. People later told me that I hit my head so hard on the back of the pew that the noise stopped the service, and that Dad had reached over Mom, Evan, and Sammie to grab my arm and drag me over all their bodies out into the aisle. Then he got me out of the church. Not carrying me like Scarlett

O'Hara, which might have been somewhat graceful, but dragging me, facedown, by my arms. I came to on the church steps. My nylons were torn at the knees. Dad lit a cigarette and looked at me with concern.

I knew right then and there what I had to do. Or not do. I didn't masturbate again for the next five years.

I tuned back in to the service. Father Whippet was just wrapping up with Lucy and Chuck.

"Ladies and gentlemen, I am proud to present Mr. and Mrs. Chuck Tanner."

Lucy and Chuck turned around to face the crowd. They all clapped wildly until they took in what was really being presented to them: Lucy, with her mascara-stained face, clutching the top of her dress, and Chuck, with his massive white mouth guard. The clapping faltered as the bride and groom both feebly waved to everyone. I raced to get Lucy's wedding train out from under her feet and spread it out nicely behind her. Then they walked back down the aisle with me trailing behind.

"Where are the cars?" Mom asked, blinking in the sun.

"After we dropped you off we parked across the way." Dad pointed. "They're just across the Sears parking lot." He looked around for Evan to help him but then remembered he was jetting to his honeymoon. "The other ones can help me get them. Um, Ron and um, um . . ."

"Chuck," Sammie volunteered the name.

"Right, Chuck."

Lucy walked up. "Let's just walk over there. It'll be easier."

We straggled in our wedding finery across the dirty parking lot. We had to wait while a Ford truck backed up to the service entrance to load a refrigerator. I lifted Lucy's train and put it over my shoulder.

"Oh, Harold, we should have had a car for them right there at the church," Mom fretted while the wind blew her hair.

"To go less than a hundred yards?"

"It's just not very . . . ceremonial." Mom would continue to fret about this for the rest of the summer. The reception itself was comparatively uneventful. The guests entered our backyard and headed straight for the bar Dad had set up. But true to Dad's prediction, people were still feeling pretty hungover from Evan's wedding and most drank the mimosas. The tent rippled nicely in the wind. Mom eyed the poles. "It is going to stay up, isn't it, Harold?"

"Absolutely," Dad replied. Then he chucked me under the chin. "The question is for how long?"

"Harold! That is not funny!" Mom strode away to corral the photographer.

Dad grinned at me. "Good thing she doesn't know I forgot to pick up the dog poop in the yard."

I edged away from him. I envisioned myself in my couch dress stooping among the guests and picking up Buddy's leavings.

"I'm only kidding. Can't anyone in this family take a joke?" Dad muttered and lit a Tareyton. Guests crowded around the buffet tables that lined two sides of the tent. Then they trickled out to the little white tables set up on the lawn. The only ones that day who ripped through the bar were Kim Barnett, Lucy's cohort in the communion wine caper, and Teeni Patterson.

"Do you need a ride home, Teeni?" I asked politely.

"Oh no, honey. A Bloody Mary is actually just vitamins." She waved the drink at me while crunching on the celery stick. What about six Bloody Marys? I wondered.

The men in the crowd started calling for the flinging of the garter. The chant got louder and seemed downright raucous for this hour on a Sunday afternoon. I saw my mom and Elizabeth whispering and knew what they were talking about. We sure as hell didn't have a garter hanging around the house. That kind of thing is for people who actually take time to plan their weddings. Lucy shrugged at Chuck and an awkward silence fell over the crowd.

I had an idea and ran into the house. Scrambling through Dad's junk drawer I actually found what I was looking for. Running back outside I pressed it into Chuck's hand. "Throw this." Chuck looked at it and shrugged. Then, taking careful aim, he snapped the extra-wide rubber band into the crowd. It caught Jeff Petty in the neck pretty good. It obviously stung. Jeff's face reddened. But what the hell was he going to do? Chuck grinned at him as best he could with that thing in his mouth. Jeff smiled gamely and, rubbing his neck, went to slide the rubber band up Terri Worthington's leg, as she had caught the bouquet. He did the stupid little dance with the "garter," running it higher and higher up her leg. Then he went too far. He had pushed it far enough up her thigh for everyone to see the gigantic rip in her nylons. Terri gasped. People tittered. I saw the light glint off the stockings and knew she had done a pretty decent job with the clear nail polish to keep it from running farther down her leg.

"Omigod, did they get that on video?" Terri shrieked and ran into the house, followed by several concerned girlfriends. Jeff stood awkwardly in the middle of the tent until Mom walked over to him and gave him a half hug. "That was very nice, Jeff. You should be looking around at all the girls. After all, since you caught the garter, you're next to be married."

She eased him out of the center of attention and over to the bar. He looked at his savior with relief. Mom walked away from him shaking her head while Jeff downed a glass of champagne.

Mercifully, the guests didn't stay long. There was only one incident, when Mrs. Long stepped into a gopher hole and twisted her ankle. But since she lived next door and she said she had an ACE bandage there, we were okay on that count. The family flopped in the living room while Lucy and Chuck opened their gifts. I was rubbing my feet when Lucy held up the white Lenox plate I had selected for her. "What's this? Couldn't you have registered me for some Pfaltzgraff? At least that's useful."

PART II

The Pressure Cooker
2006

The Worst Summer Ever
1986

Fifteen

April 2006

After much pleading and apologizing on my part, Aidan finally forgave me for the debacle on the night of his premiere. I told him that I blamed the pressures at work for making such a dumb decision. Once he saw the email that Katsu had undoubtedly sent out to the entire studio, he started to understand what I had been going through.

"But why is he doing this?" Aidan wondered aloud. "They do need the two of you. You've been bitching for years that you have too many movies. And he's already at the executive vice president level, so what is it he wants?"

Neither of us could answer the question.

Elizabeth was a different story. I thought she would be more understanding about the night of Madison's ballet performance. After all, her own marriage had flamed out years earlier and a big reason was that her husband was too nervous around our family. It had proven to be an enormous stress between them.

I had finally broken down and told Elizabeth that I thought

Aidan would be scared off much like my first husband, Walker, had been. Certainly, I had thought, she could see my point.

Instead she had surprised me by stating coldly, "Aidan, I presume, is a big boy. If he can't handle a couple of crazy relatives, then *que sera, sera* and all that. But you, Jeannie, you can't keep treating us like this."

This time she didn't hang up the phone on me in anger. We managed to say our good-byes politely if stiffly. Neither of us had been in touch since then.

Now Aidan and I slouched in theater seats with our heads together. "Pass the popcorn. You're hogging it." Aidan poked me with his elbow.

"You're the one who snarfed down all the Sno-Caps."

"You don't even like Sno-Caps."

"Yeah, but it's the princip—"

"Shhh!" came an admonition from a few rows in front of us.

My face grew hot and I slumped down even further in my seat. "What are you doing?" Aidan whispered down at me.

"I'm so embarrassed. I forgot I was in a movie theater," I said, almost inaudibly. I hated being rude. I poked my head up to see whom I had offended. A middle-aged woman two rows ahead of us was still turned around, glaring at us.

"I'm so sorry," I called to her softly.

"Shut up!" was her response. Then my cell phone rang from somewhere in the depths of my purse. I had forgotten to turn it to vibrate.

The woman was now pointing me out to her friends and shaking her head. I grabbed my bag and stumbled over Aidan and out into the lobby. By the time I got to my phone it had stopped ringing and the message icon was flashing.

Aidan joined me on the bench. "Are you always that nice to people?" he asked, referring to the woman inside the theater.

"No. Only to strangers."

"You should have told her to go fuck herself."

"Aidan! I'm from the Midwest. People in the Midwest are actually nice. Just like people in New York are actually jerks and people in L.A. are actually liars. It's a regional thing."

"You are nice to a fault, though. You never tell anyone no and you hardly ever say what you really think except if it's about work. No wonder your insides are all twisted up."

That was true. Some people hold their stress in their backs. Me, it's in my gut. I could win the Olympics if they had an event in constipation.

"You're probably right," I said, "but it's nothing that several years of therapy shouldn't be able to knock out of me."

"You would never make time for therapy. You never make time for anything except work and"—he smiled and tossed popcorn up in the air and tried to catch it in his mouth—"me." He missed the kernel and laughed.

Yes, I worked. And worked and worked. Now, with Katsu analyzing my every move, I worked even more. I had dragged myself home last night—or should I say this morning—at 4 a.m. It wasn't frivolous. A trailer was in trouble and had to be up on screens in just a few weeks. Normally I might have stayed at the ad agency with the unfortunate editor until midnight, then gone home while he still slaved away; I would console myself that, if he was lucky, he could grab a few hours of sleep in the morning, while I had to be at the studio. But now I was in the habit of staying to the bitter end.

I started putting in these kinds of hours when I was married to

Walker. It felt like everyone at the studio relied on me, and Walker didn't seem like he needed me that much.

Aidan lived pretty much the same life I did, except that his long workdays came in spurts. Then he had several weeks off before the next crisis. But it seemed like every time I worked on a movie, the studio heads would solemnly call me into their offices and inform me, "If this movie doesn't open, this studio may have to close its doors."

So I would arrive at eight in the morning and leave anywhere from nine at night on a good day to midnight on a not-so-good day. And I worked on anywhere from twelve to twenty films at a time. Several times I would have just arrived home only to receive a frantic phone call from a producer or studio head. They had a new idea for a TV spot, and could they see it first thing in the morning? And when they said jump, I jumped. It never occurred to me to say no. I would call in the ad agency people—I had their home and cell numbers memorized—and we would work all night.

Walker, on the other hand, had had a nine-to-five job as an engineer. He used to say that we were like two gears. I was running at high speed and he was running at low speed and we could never mesh. He also said he hadn't bargained for this. While he was at Princeton, he was the one who was going to make it big. I was a lowly art student who couldn't seem to get my act together. He expected it to be the pattern our lives would take after we married, too. I would stay home and raise babies and figure out new ways to make zucchini bread. He hadn't planned on my making more money or working more hours than he did.

He thought I would always be the same girl who hadn't questioned him when he informed me that the order of priorities in his life was: 1. Fishing, 2. Sailing, 3. Work, and 4. Me. (Later, when

Walker acquired a dog, I moved into fifth place.) We were drink-ing Long Island Iced Teas at a crowded Princeton watering hole at the time.

I had looked at him and laughed, thinking it was a good joke, because who would really say such a thing? Unfortunately, he meant it. Maybe somewhere deep down I did know that, but didn't think enough of myself to consider the issue in an in-depth way. After all, he had been the valedictorian at the private school Cranbrook, then Mr. Princeton, and he had a bright, shining future. I just had that damn book *What Color Is Your Parachute?*

I looked at the phone number of the call I'd missed. It was my boss—at eleven o'clock on a Saturday night.

"Why do your work crises only happen at night when I'm with you?" Aidan asked.

"They don't. They happen every minute of the day and night." I listened to the message and, as I had feared, Rachael, the presi-dent of marketing, was calling to give me a heads-up on a brewing storm. I turned to Aidan. "There's a problem with the *TechnoCat* trailer. The director saw it play in front of an audience tonight and says that they 'didn't feel the emotion.' He wants it revised im-mediately, as in now."

"I thought that trailer did extremely well in research testing."

"It did. It was through the roof. I saw it myself in a theater and the audience was cheering." My cell phone rang again. I hesitated when I saw the caller ID. "Hello?"

"You've ruined it! You've ruined my movie!"

I held the phone slightly away from my ear. "Stripe, the trailer is getting cheers. People are throwing popcorn in the air and bang-ing on their seats. You don't get a reaction like that very often."

"That's just it. They are cheering. *TechnoCat* is a movie about internal struggle and angst and finding the courage to fight evil.

The audience should be embracing the film's profound intensity. This could be my Academy Award picture and you are ruining it."

Academy Award picture? Profound intensity? Was this guy on crack? It was a summer blockbuster complete with B-level stars and lots of special effects and explosions. This wasn't a Civil War period picture with A-level stars practicing their accents and dying on-screen. *That* was Academy material.

Oxford Pictures had everything riding on *TechnoCat*. It was our one and only big summer movie, and it was opening on the coveted Fourth of July weekend. Film production was already topping $175 million, and everyone was stressed. *Entertainment Weekly* predicted disaster, making snide remarks about the special effects and calling it *TechnoDog*. *Access Hollywood* had taken to doing nightly reports on the cost overruns of the film along with updates on the affair between Stripe and the film's young starlet. This would have been all right except that Stripe was separated from a big-time executive at a rival studio. So his soon-to-be ex-wife wanted this film to fail and was feeding *Access Hollywood* every negative tidbit she could think of. I knew that the Oxford publicity department was working overtime to control the bad press.

"Stripe," I said in an even tone, "if you recall we did create the trailer you are talking about. The research showed that people wouldn't go see the movie based on that trailer."

Stripe continued his rant. "You just didn't do it right! I want this trailer re-edited and this time with the emotion of Cat's mother dying of cancer! I think you are losing your touch. I saw that nutty photo of you from Aidan's film premiere!"

I gasped. The gall of the man. Enough was enough. Time to find my inner rudeness.

"I'm sorry, you're breaking up. I can't hear you anymore. Hello? Hello?" I said into the phone, then tapped END.

"Bad reception?" Aidan asked as he opened the car door for me.

"No. Stripe just said I was losing my touch and mentioned that photo. My saying I had bad reception was the new me being confrontational." I leaned back in my seat and rubbed my eyes. They were always red because I usually forgot to take out my contacts.

"We're going to have to work on your definition of confrontational," Aidan observed.

He put the key in the ignition. "Come on, I'll drive you home so you can get to your meeting Monday. And look, I understand that you're going to be running your ass off from now until the Fourth of July. But Jeannie, you are going to have to slow down long enough to talk about this marriage thing soon. I'm not getting any younger and I really would like to start a family. A family with you." He was staring out through the windshield. Then he shook his head sadly. "God, I sound like some of my old girlfriends. Now I know how they felt."

I felt a cold prickle of fear run up my scalp. Aidan wouldn't leave me over the marriage proposal, would he? I mean, it wasn't like I didn't love him. Why couldn't everything just stay the way it had been six months ago? The space between our car seats suddenly felt like a million miles. "I finally talked to my dad about all this," Aidan continued. "He said that when I found the right girl, it would be obvious to both her and me."

"Of course he'd say that," I snapped. "He has the perfect wife, the perfect kids, and the perfect life."

Aidan turned and looked at me for a very long time. Finally he said, "He didn't always have the perfect family." He looked at his watch. "I'm going to go pick up Montana from the airport now. She's coming in from Prague tonight."

"Can't she take a cab?" I was glad to switch the subject but wasn't sure I was glad it got switched to Montana.

"The guy she was seeing broke up with her. Said she was too needy. So she's been crying on my shoulder. I keep telling her there is some nice unattached guy out there for her. But she says that the good ones are taken, so it's easier for her to steal someone else's guy."

As long as it isn't *my* guy, I thought, staring out my own window. Finally I said, "Tell you what. I'll ride with you to the airport. We can both pick up Montana. That'll give me a chance to give you another chapter of my story."

"You want to ride with me all the way out to the airport? That's not really necessary," Aidan said as he put the car in gear.

Oh yes, it is, I thought as I fastened my seat belt.

Sixteen

July 1986

I carried the plates the way I was taught: one on my left forearm and the other two in my hands. "Fried perch sandwich," I said, and put one in front of Evan, "and a junior BLT burger, medium," I said as I set another down in front of Dad, "with a side of fries," and the last dish went between them. "Need another Coke or anything?" They shook their heads and I went back to the kitchen.

The Bear Lake Tavern was located on the Bear Lake Channel, which connects Bear Lake to Muskegon Lake. From Muskegon Lake you could head out to Lake Michigan if you had a boat, and everybody around here had one. It was like having a car in this part of the world. The Bear Lake Tavern was built in the early 1900s and hadn't changed a lot since then. It was a roundish one-story building painted brown with red trim. The windows faced the docks, which were usually crowded. The lunch crowds were huge during the summer. The boats at the dock usually delivered hordes of Teds along with the locals. Inside, there was a dark wooden bar with a beer cooler, also trimmed in red, built into the wall behind it. Every other wall was covered with photographs of famous North Muskegon sports figures: the State Championship football team from 1918, the BLT "Brew Crew" softball team from 1975, a guy from NMHS who played briefly for the Detroit Lions proudly posing with a football. All were hanging alongside the many Michigan State University or University of Michigan pennants. One long wooden table ran down the middle of the room with other tables surrounding it. My friends and I had spent many a night at the long table laughing and gossiping. When we all went off to college we brought our new friends back with us to share the experience. I'm not sure they got much out of it; it was a tradition that came from spending your whole life in the town.

Sometime in the nineteen seventies, Tommy Loyse had bought the place. He tried to turn it into a restaurant and not a tavern, in his mind making it respectable for parents to bring their kids there to eat. But every family I knew was already doing that. Tommy had renamed the place the Bear Lake Inn. It was painted on the sign, but it never took. To the locals, it would always be the BLT, or the "Blit." We didn't just go for the Stroh's. The Blit had the best damn burgers in the world. I mean that, really. Rumor was that it was because of the grill—that in almost one hundred years, the grill had never once been cleaned, and all that grease gave the burgers their distinctive flavor. Now that I worked there, I knew that was not true. But for whatever reason, the BLT burger and fries was about the best-tasting meal I'd ever had. The fried perch sandwich was a close runner-up.

The Blit was packed, and I was running my ass off. Evan hollered "Ketchup?" at me, and I tossed it to him from about six feet away. He snagged it with one hand.

"Miss, can we please order now?"

I turned my attention to a blond Ted. He was wearing a yellow Izod shirt with a light blue Polo button-down shirt over it—both collars up, of course—khaki shorts, and the requisite Docksiders, all brand new. I took his order for the French Dip sandwich, an order that confirmed the fact that he was not from around there. Who would order the French Dip? I turned to his friend, then stopped and smiled. I hadn't seen Fudgie Shaw since Lucy and Chuck's wedding. "Hey, Fudgie."

"Hey yourself. How's Lucy doing?"

"Good. Mom talks to her more than I do, but I got a letter. Said she's studying twelve hours a day to pass her Russian finals. Her graduation from the Defense Language Institute is in about a month."

"What's Chuck doing?"

I was a bit fuzzier on Chuck. Lucy didn't seem to talk about him a lot to Mom. "I think he's finishing up, too. His two-year stint is about over." I didn't mention that Lucy had called Mom crying one night and told her that Chuck had been getting into fights on base and that he kept getting tossed into whatever prison the army had reserved for such offenses.

The bell in the kitchen rang, which meant that food was up and ready to be served. I moved away from Fudgie's table after taking his order. "Hey, come see me soon. I have a question for you. It's about Lucy."

Fudgie waved and said, "I'll stop by tonight," as I ran back through the saloon doors to the kitchen. My shift was over around 4:30, when the lunch crowds had left and the dinner crowds hadn't started yet.

Evan came back to give me a ride home, not that he really needed to. It was only about a mile walk, but he knew I'd be dead tired, because I'd worked a double shift. I'd gotten a call at 6 a.m.

that morning from Tommy saying he didn't have anyone to cover the breakfast crowd. Two of the waitresses had called in sick. More like they had called in "beach," I thought, when I saw how sunny it was outside. Tommy knew I was the only one who wouldn't hesitate to come in when it wasn't my shift. He also knew that I could handle the entire restaurant by myself. He said it was like watching a perfect zone defense or something, the way I worked. I just got this rhythm going along with laser focus and somehow, handling twelve tables plus the dockside orders, I would not miss a beat.

I put fifty cents in the jukebox and watched the Violent Femmes slide into play. Evan and I sat in the now near-empty restaurant, both of us drinking coffee, since the Blit had no idea what Yogi tea was. *"Let me go ooonnn, like a blister in the sun,"* hissed over the speakers.

"Do you have to play such a head-thumping song right now?" Evan poured a good amount of sugar into his coffee.

"What's your show going to be about tomorrow?" I asked to change the subject.

"I'm not sure yet. The walleye are running pretty good right now in Lake Michigan. Nothing better than smoked walleye. And the blueberries are coming in, too, so maybe I'll do the segment out at Blaine's Blueberry Farm."

"Could you get Mrs. Blaine to bake a blueberry pie for the show?"

"Nope. Already tried. I wanted to do a piece comparing Michigan blueberries to the poem 'Raisin in the Sun,' but she's camera shy. Plus she said she doesn't like my show."

"How come?"

"She says I get too philosophical. Said if people want that they can watch Phil Donahue or something. She says if it's a cooking show, then it should just be a cooking show."

"Huh."

"Yeah, huh." Evan grimaced at the coffee.

I heard coins drop into the jukebox at the back. The opening strains of a song poured out.

"Oh no," we both said.

There had to be someone from the Upper Peninsula hanging out in the Blit. Nobody else would ever play that song. The upper and lower peninsulas of Michigan generated a rivalry like crosstown high school sports teams. We, from the Lower Peninsula, called them You-pers—this, not so cleverly, from a slurring of the initials U.P. They in turn called us Trolls because we lived under the bridge—the Mackinac Bridge that is, and please don't pronounce the last c of Mackinac. It's pronounced "Mack-in-aw." The good folks of the Upper Peninsula petitioned every now and again so they could secede and become their own state, which of course they wanted to name Superior State. They said it was because of their proximity to Lake Superior. But everyone knew it was really a slap at us Trolls. It'll never happen, though. Fifty-one stars on the flag would just be awkward.

But to play that song. And so early in the day. Usually it didn't get played until about eleven at night when everyone was in their cups. Gordon Lightfoot had written it. It was about a shipwreck that occurred in Lake Superior. One of those big freighters that moved cargo from the locks of Sault Ste. Marie into the Great Lakes had gotten caught in a storm.

What people don't realize is that the waters in the Great Lakes can become as ferocious as on any ocean. It's particularly dangerous during the fall months, when the winds whip the waters of the Lakes into a frenzy. This particular freighter, the speculation went, had gotten caught between two gigantic waves. The waves each could have been about thirty feet high, maybe higher. Enormous waves can occur much closer together in the Lakes than they can in the ocean. Further speculation was that the bow and the stern had each become balanced on the top of a wave. The freighter then split in the middle and went straight down, with all hands on board. No survivors. It was an incredibly sad event in our history. The song continued, ". . . *the wreck of the* Edmund Fitzgerald . . ."

For whatever reason, this song had become the anthem of the You-pers. I looked around and saw three guys sitting at the bar waving their beer mugs back and forth. One of them was wearing an IRON MOUNTAIN IS MAGNETIC T-shirt, so that sealed the deal.

You-pers.

"Let's go. I can't take one more verse of that song," Evan said as he grabbed his wallet and car keys. We wandered out of the Blit, and I threw some stale bread at the ducks waiting for their handout in the parking lot.

"Was that Fudgie Shaw who was in today?"

"Yeah, he's coming by tonight."

"I thought you were still dating Walker."

"I am." I poked him in the side and made him squirm away.

"What's Walker got against us, anyway? He hardly ever comes around. You'd think we were contagious," Evan said as he paused to light a cigarette.

"I don't really know. I think he thinks we're all disaster prone."

"What have we ever done to him?" Evan asked.

I thought for a moment. "Remember that time we took our rowboat out on Muskegon Lake? And instead of buying a new boat plug Dad stuck gum in the hole? When the gum softened up, the boat sank and you, me, and Walker had to swim about half a mile to get to shore. We all had to take turns clinging to the Styrofoam cooler because we forgot the life jackets in the car."

"Yeah, there's that," Evan mused. "He lost his dad's lure box, too. Must've taken his dad all winter to hand-tie all those flies."

"Two winters," I muttered. Walker never let me forget it. Evan got in the car and leaned across the seat to unlock my door. I slid in. "Anyhow, I wanted to ask Fudgie a question. When we were at your wedding he gave Lucy something. I wanted to know what it was."

"Nosy."

"Yep, and speaking of nosy, why were you late for your wedding?"

Evan and Anna had only just returned from their honeymoon and I hadn't had time to talk to him.

"I don't really want to say. It was about Father Whippet."

"What about him?" I prompted.

"Doesn't 'I don't really want to say' mean anything to you?"

"No."

"It was sort of like he had lost his robes. And we were helping him find them."

"Lost his robes? Like at the dry cleaner's or something?"

"No, not quite like that." He pulled up at the house. "Here you go."

"Thanks, Evan." I got out, slammed the door, and made my way up the walk. The back door was locked, but everyone in town knew that if you gave it a sharp bump with your hip it opened. Which is what I did now. I thought about my brother. Evan was a ship's captain and a food show TV host. He meandered around with a philosophy that life was meant to be lived. But the TV show only reflected one part of him. The other was dressed in starched whites with his captain's bars attached to his shoulders in very straight lines. He demanded a great deal from his crews and he got it. People just naturally loved Evan. He could read the Raytheon radar better than anybody, tell a story that would have you laughing so hard you would beg him to stop talking so you could catch your breath, tell from the waters when a storm was coming or the fish were running and at what depth. He knew that sometimes during a snowstorm the waters of Lake Michigan could turn the brilliant blue of the Caribbean. He taught me how to read a barometer and he knew how to steer by the stars with a sextant. Not many people knew how to do that anymore. He captained research vessels for the National Oceanic and Atmospheric Administration (the government can sometimes be too damn cutesy, as the acronym NOAA is pronounced "Noah"), and he captained party boats and private vessels.

He was commissioned to deliver a boat from Muskegon down to Fort Myers, Florida, once. Dad went with him. They crossed Lake Michigan to the Chicago River, then to the Mississippi, and then on down into the Gulf of Mexico. They had bikes with them and at every port they would ride around and talk to the locals, buy fruit from the roadside stands, and get a feel for the place. They were both pretty bummed out when they finally had to fly back home. Evan would tell tales of captains and their ships lost in the Great Lakes and of dead bodies floating up against the bow. He told stories of strange flying objects and of counting hundreds of shooting stars over Lake Michigan in late August.

And he tolerated me. He may have actually liked me. I'm nine years younger than my brother. Certainly when I was six and he was fifteen, we didn't have a lot in common. He moved in and out of the house like an apparition. But by the time I was nineteen and he was twenty-eight, we actually managed to carry on conversations.

Fudgie Shaw came over that evening. "Hi, Mrs. T," he said to

Mom, and gave her a hug. Then he opened the refrigerator. "No beer?" He looked at Mom.

"In the downstairs fridge," she said.

After Fudgie got his beer, we went out back and sat in the glider and looked at Bear Lake. Fudgie waved at Terri Worthington, who was out in her family's Chris-Craft. It was a wooden classic from the twenties that I had always loved. She squinted up at us with one hand over her eyes, then waved back and continued on, leaving a slow wake after her.

"How the hell did you come to be at Lucy's wedding? Her first one, I mean?" I cut to the chase.

Fudgie rocked the glider with one foot. "I was getting kind of burned out at U of M so I decided to hitchhike across the country. It was actually pretty easy getting rides. You wouldn't think that in this day and age. My mom flipped. She said I'd wind up murdered and in a ditch and would have to be identified by my dental records." He took a sip of beer. "Anyhow, so I'm pretty tired and really dirty and I had just gotten dropped off in San Francisco. I had stayed with people I knew across the country or their parents or their friends or whoever I could bum a night with. But I didn't know a soul in San Fran. Then I remembered Lucy was in Monterey. I hopped a bus and rode for an hour, then walked to the base. Helluva walk, I gotta tell you. Long way. I got there and asked for Lucy. She comes down with this guy who turns out to be Chuck. We do the usual 'Omigod, I can't believe you're here' and whatnot; then she tells me that they are on their way to the justice of the peace. Since I don't have anywhere to go she tells me to come along and I can be a witness. They needed one anyway. They were just going to pick somebody up at City Hall but Lucy said if I was there I might as well be it."

"Didn't you ask why? I mean, why she was getting married?"

"Oh sure. They were both laughing and hooting it up in the car. They told me that it was going to be a quickie wedding so that Chuck wouldn't be shipped out to Germany. Then they'd get it annulled when Chuck's girl showed up to do the real honors. The whole thing was pretty damn funny. That's why I was kind of shocked to see the whole deal happening back here. I guess they really fell in love, huh?"

"Um, yeah." I wasn't on solid ground here.

"Whatever happened to the chick Chuck was supposed to marry?"

"Lucy said she never showed up."

"That's weird. Do you suppose she really exists?"

I thought about Chuck's phone conversation in my parents' bedroom. "Yeah, I think she exists."

"We had a blast that night. Got them married and then we had a reception."

This startled me. They had a reception? Before I had a chance to imagine a small, intimate setting complete with a string quartet, Fudgie went on.

"We went to Chi-Chi's—you know, that Mexican chain. A bunch of their friends from the base showed up. We did tequila shots and danced around to the mariachi band."

I revised my initial thoughts. This reception sounded like fun, not like the usual WASPy thing we had around Muskegon—although the receptions that were held at the local Polish Falcon Hall were a lot of fun, complete with polka bands and dollar dances with the bride.

"Then this guy shows up dressed as Cupid. One of their friends had hired him. Cupid comes out and sings a song and then we got him drunk, too. It was a fun night."

I thought about how different this bride seemed from the sullen

Lucy I had grown up with. The Lucy I knew was one who had steadily waged war with every one of her high school teachers. The same teachers I would inherit two years later. When I arrived in their classes, they would look down at the attendance list and say, "Jeannie," long pause, "Thompson?" The long pause always tipped me off. They were already thinking how much they hated me. The French teacher, on the very first day of class, had seated me in the last row while the rest of the class occupied the first two rows. Since there were six rows in total, I spent a year staring at empty desks and the backs of everyone else's heads. In a school that was only composed of about ninety students per grade, it was hard to escape a teacher who hadn't had Lucy in class. It didn't make for a great four years. But I tried my best to be a model student and not bring any attention to myself.

The mosquitoes were starting up in earnest now. Fudgie and I slapped at them and I lit the citronella candle on the porch. It never helped, but we always used them.

"I wanted to ask you what you gave Lucy the night of Evan's wedding."

"A picture. One I took the night of the reception. I figured that that was what you wanted to know so I brought a copy with me." He pulled it out of his shirt pocket. I looked at it in the waning light. It was a photo of Lucy and Chuck holding up their marriage certificate and yukking it up pretty good. Lucy had on a blue ruffled shirt and her best Jordache jeans. Chuck was in a white T-shirt and a sombrero. Behind them was a man painted blue, sporting a skimpy Cupid outfit and pointing a stuffed satin bow and arrow at the smiling couple.

"She's wearing my shirt," I said. "I've been looking all over for it."

"How are they doing?" Fudgie asked. "Now that they're living together and all."

"They aren't. When they got back to base, the army didn't have anything available in married housing. So she's still in her barracks and he's still in his. But they're both getting discharged soon."

"Then what are they going to do?"

"Good question." I'd have to ask Mom whether she knew. Fudgie drained his beer and stood up. "I have to go back for my mom's birthday festivities. Tell Lucy I said hi when you talk to her." He strolled across the backyard to walk the three blocks to his parents' house.

"Bye. And thanks," I called after him.

He waved his hand in reply as he walked. I went back into the house to escape the mosquitoes. Dad was on the phone and rubbing his forehead. Mom was sitting at the table and watching him intently.

"Can't they find another place for her?" I heard Dad ask the person on the other end of the line.

"What's going on?" I asked Mom. "Is it Lucy?"

"Shush, I'm listening."

"But she's just not right in the head . . ." Dad continued

"Is it Elizabeth?" I asked Mom.

"No, now shush."

Dad talked for another few minutes, then hung up the phone. He and Mom regarded each other grimly.

"They say it will only be for two months," Dad said.

"Two months of what?" I demanded.

They both turned to me wearily. "It's Grandma Thompson. Her nursing home has been temporarily shut down for renovations to bring it up to code."

Grandma Thompson lived in Michigan City, Indiana, about three hundred miles south of us. She had refused many times to come up to Muskegon and live with us or in a local nursing home. She preferred to stay in the city she had grown up in and close to her other son, Robert, Dad's brother.

"Were you talking to Uncle Robert?"

Dad nodded. I asked, "Why doesn't she stay with him? She doesn't like us anyway."

"Jeannie, don't say such things." Mom sighed.

"But it's true!"

Grandma Thompson had always had a bug up her butt about our family. When Mom was pregnant with Lucy, she had given her a handbook on birth control. When Mom got pregnant with me, Grandma Thompson didn't speak to our family for five years. People often asked my mom if we were Catholic. She would just laugh and reply, "Not Catholic, just careless." Uncle Robert's family was correctly composed of one boy and one girl.

"Robert can't take her. He doesn't have an extra room." We all got coffee and sat down at the table. Dad started tracing the rooster in the corner.

"What about his kids' rooms?" I asked.

"He's turned one of them into a model train room and the other one into a sewing room."

"Hazel has never sewn a stitch in her life," Mom muttered.

"It's only for two months. Then she can return to the nursing home." Dad rotated his coffee cup on the table between his palms. Mom stood up and rubbed his back.

"Of course, Harold. She's your mother and we love her and we'll do everything to make her welcome here. When does she arrive?"

Dad looked at her miserably. "Tomorrow."

I left them to plan bedpans and wheelchairs and complicated prescription medicines. Later that night, I lay in bed and stared at the wall. As the others had gradually moved out of the house,

Lucy and I had finally gotten our own bedrooms. Hers was better. For one, it had heat. I'd wake up on winter mornings and see ice on the inside of my windows. Dad swore up and down that he had rearranged the ducts but nothing ever worked. Since Lucy had left, I slept in her room. Now I stared at her wallpaper. She had chosen white wallpaper with funny drawings of desserts all over it. Under each éclair or chocolate cake was written things like "No! No! No!"

Mom cracked open the door. "Are you asleep?"

"No." I sat up. She came and sat on the edge of the bed.

"Jeannie, having Grandma here will be fun."

"Uh-huh." I couldn't tell where this was going.

"She can tell you all kinds of family stories."

Like the one about Dad bringing Mom home for the first time to meet his parents? And Grandma taking Mom to see Dad's ex-girlfriend's house? She had told Mom that that was who Dad should have married. It didn't give her a lot of warm and fuzzy feelings toward Grandma. Mom should have gotten mad about that but she had just been sad and felt she could never live up to expectations. I decided not to bring up that particular family story right then.

"Sure, Mom. I'll listen to her."

"The thing is, you might be with her a lot."

I sat up straighter in bed. "What does that mean?"

"We can't leave her alone, honey. And I'm working now."

"But I work, too!"

"Only part-time. I'll talk to Tommy Loyse tomorrow about your hours so that you can be home during the day."

I wasn't sure which was more insulting, the fact that I was now de facto babysitter to my senile grandmother, or that my mother thought she had to call my boss for me like I was a ten-year-old. I decided not to argue right then and switched the subject. "What's Lucy going to do when she gets out of the army?"

Mom stroked my hair. "She's not sure. She's talking about finishing up her degree."

"That would be good. She only had a year left at Western."

"Oh, not Western. She wants to go to Michigan State. They have an advanced Russian language program."

That was news to me, but I wasn't exactly on an inside educational track at MSU. "What's Chuck going to do?"

"He said he's willing to come along. Said he doesn't have anything better to do."

"Wow. Well, I guess it's good that he supports Lucy."

Mom smiled and tapped my nose. "Get a good night's sleep; tomorrow is G-day. Grandma is coming."

She looked out the window at the trees and the street beyond. "Did you move the lawn furniture into the garage?"

"Yeah," I said wearily. It was a nightly ritual. A few years back we had discovered a lawn chair directly underneath Lucy's bedroom window. It had been dragged over there from its proper place about twenty feet away. Mom called the head of our neighborhood watch, Mr. Moorepark. We called him Mr. Moorebutt because of his large posterior. She informed him that we had a Peeping Tom and could he please keep a careful watch on the house. But the chair kept reappearing under the window, generally on the nights when one of us inadvertently forgot to close the blinds. Finally, my mom and I had hidden in the bushes one night, determined to catch the peeper. A figure had eventually appeared in the darkness. Mom clapped a hand over my mouth to keep me from yelling out a snide comment too early. The bushes were scratching my face and my knees were about to give out from crouching so long when the silhouette grabbed the chair and lugged it over to the window. Mom flicked on her flashlight and caught the culprit full in the face.

"Mr. Moorebutt!" she gasped. He blinked for a moment, either from trying to absorb the situation or at the crude reference to his behind.

"Mrs. Thompson, this isn't what it looks like. I was just testing out a theory about how difficult it is to move this chair. For instance, how strong a man would have to be."

Since the chair was made of lightweight aluminum and a four-year-old could have moved it, I didn't think this was much of an argument. Mom was torn. On the one hand, this was such a lame excuse that she had him dead to rights. On the other hand, he was a neighbor she'd have to see every day of her life. She decided to let it go. "If you're finished, then you should move along. Everything is okay here." We waited while he hustled back to the street and disappeared into the shadows. Now, every single night of the summer, Mom made me drag the chairs into the garage and back out again in the morning. Mr. Moorebutt continued as the head of the neighborhood watch, although Mom made it clear his services weren't needed at our house.

"Good night then, sunshine." Mom kissed my forehead and closed the door quietly behind her.

I woke up at 8:10 a.m. to the high-pitched whine of a buzz saw. I groaned into my pillow—now what? I pulled on a pair of sweatpants and went to the kitchen. Mom and Dad were already having coffee and watching Evan's show. Not that I could tell what Evan was saying because the buzz saw was so damn loud. I watched his mouth move silently while he demonstrated pouring a bottle of beer over wood chips. Ah, he was going with the smoked walleye segment after all. The trick was to soak wood chips in beer for about twenty-four hours, put the chips in the Weber Smokey Joe, and presto, smoked walleye.

The buzz saw whined down and then stopped. Tom bumped his hip on the locked back door and walked in. It was too early for me even to ask what they were all up to now. Tom got some coffee and the newspaper and we all watched Evan. He laid some fish on a grill. Then he put the cover on it and lit a cigarette. He sat on a picnic table smoking and regarding the grill. "Corn would be good with this I guess," Evan mused.

I could tell he was ad-libbing. His philosophical inspiration hadn't been with him much lately, he had complained to me privately. "But it would be better to wait until August when the corn is good and ready to be picked. In the meantime, some fried squash will do fine," Evan continued. We watched him stub out his cigarette on the ground, then pick up the butt and put it in his shirt pocket. "Have to be careful of the environment," he murmured. Then he wandered back into the kitchen TV set. The cameraman followed him. The camera bobbled up and down as we heard the cameraman sneeze.

"Bless you," Evan said as he picked up a yellow squash. He sliced it very thin, dipped it in water, and then rolled it in flour seasoned with salt and pepper. Then he threw it all into a pan and fried it in butter.

"That's my recipe"—Mom nodded proudly to Dad—"straight from West Texas. I told Evan I thought it would be good with walleye fish."

"Do you know how walleye got their name?" I asked Tom.

"Nope." His attention was on *The Muskegon Chronicle*.

"Did you know that Muskegon is actually a Native American word that means 'swamp'?"

"Like I give a sparrow's fart." Without taking his eyes off the paper, he reached for his coffee mug and took a sip.

I went back to watching Evan's show until a commercial came on. "So what's Tom making out there?" I asked Mom.

Mom explained, "Sometimes Grandma needs a wheelchair to get around so we had to make a plywood ramp for the back steps. She'll be arriving in a couple of hours. Dad is going to pick her up. Can you stay with her this afternoon?"

I knew it wasn't really a question. I would be staying in with my grandmother on a beautiful July afternoon.

"Come on, Mom. Walker was going to come by this afternoon."

"Then you can both stay with Grandma," Mom said and the case was closed.

"All right, but I'm still getting my hair done this morning." I had finally saved up enough tips from the Blit to try to repair my damaged hair.

"Then could you stop by the church and ask Father Whippet to come over? I'd like him to meet your grandmother."

Mom had apparently forgotten that there was a little invention called the telephone, but it wasn't worth arguing about. I drove to Alan's Beauty Shoppe and arrived to find a line of women waiting in front of me. They were seated reading *Redbook* and *Good Housekeeping* and the *Enquirer*. Alan was busily trying to shepherd a few women through their hair rinses while his assistant blow-dried another. I walked over to Alan, who had his hands deep in a shampoo.

"I have a ten o'clock, Alan. What's up with all this activity?" Usually I could stroll in without an appointment.

Alan rolled his eyes. "I have no idea, darling. You would have thought the word was out that they were discontinuing the blue rinse at midnight." He glanced down to make sure the woman he was shampooing had her ears covered in soap. "Can you come back in an hour? I'll have the ladies done by then."

This seemed doubtful to me, but I figured I'd run over to St. Peter's to talk to Father Whippet. I walked across the town park, skirting the World War II memorial, to get to the church. The Muskegon Seaway Festival was in a few days, and people were everywhere erecting booths and tents in the park. The festival usually had a couple of amusement park rides, an art fair, and, by far the most popular attraction, a beer tent. North Muskegon countered with an ice cream social up at the high school, followed by fireworks. Since these events were two of the few big things that happened in either town, they were well attended. The other big thing was the Polka Festival, which was a few weeks later.

I went in the side door of St. Peter's and down the corridor to Father Whippet's office. The outer office, where his secretary sat, was empty.

"Hello?" I called out. Nothing. I entered the office and knocked softly on the door leading directly to Father Whippet's inner sanctum. "Hello?" Again, nothing. His office hours were clearly posted and he was supposed to be there. I put my ear to the door and heard a gasping noise. I recoiled. He could be having a heart attack. One of my mother's relatives had died that way. He was in the bathroom, but they just thought he was having trouble doing his business. Nobody checked on him until another family member got anxious to pee.

I knocked again, but still just heard the same gasping noise. I jiggled the handle, but it was locked. Then I thought of my own family's door and I gave it a sharp knock with my hip. It bumped open. I moved inside the office, which was clearly empty. The lights were off, and only dim, filtered sunlight came through the lead-paned windows. The gasping noises had abated. I stood in the middle of the room not sure what to do.

He might have fallen behind the heavy antique desk. I moved around it but Father Whippet was not lying prostrate on the floor. I pulled the chair out from the desk and got down on my hands and knees to check the leg area. Maybe he had slipped down there. Nothing. I put my hands on the edge of the desk to hoist myself up, then I saw the papers on the desktop. They were drawings that could have put the *Kama Sutra* to shame. They were crudely drawn and involved poses that I didn't think were actually achievable between a man and a woman. I didn't get to see much more because at that moment Father Whippet opened another door that led to his office. I realized then, of course, that he had been in his private bathroom. He must be constipated to be making so much noise. He stood stock-still, staring at me with the papers in my hand, and I stood stock-still, staring at his secretary, who emerged from the bathroom, too.

Father Whippet took the offensive. "What are you doing in my office!"

If I'd had my wits about me, I would have retorted, "What are you doing with your secretary in the bathroom?" Instead I took a step back. "My grandmother is going to be staying with us for a few months. Mom wants you to come by to see her." I dropped the papers, edged toward the door, and bolted out.

I took a deep breath back out in the sunshine. It couldn't possibly have been what I thought. Father Whippet and his secretary having sex in the bathroom? It was too bizarre. I didn't know what to make of the drawings. I scuttled back across the park to the Beauty Shoppe. The overhead bell rang as I entered. Alan waved me to a chair and then flopped down in the one next to it. "What a morning. I've never seen anything like it."

"Me neither," I said heartily.

Alan reached over and picked up some of my hair. He let it fall again. "What demon gave you such a bad haircut?"

"You did, Alan," I said wearily.

He didn't flinch. "I must have had a good night the night before. This only happens when I haven't slept."

"Have you slept now?"

"Yes, and we'll make you look fab-o. But tell me I didn't do that to your bangs."

"No, that was me."

I was still thinking about Father Whippet. Mom always said I had an overactive imagination. Sammie even teased me, saying, "You are the biggest exaggerator in the whooole world." Clearly, I was just putting two and two together and coming up with seven. It was just too absurd to think that the good Father had something going on the side. I turned back to Alan.

"Why the run on the blue-hairs today in the salon?"

"They acted like schoolgirls, but"—he saddened—"not a bit of gossip. Every one of them just said she got in the mood to have her hair done. That, and something about Father Whippet and some kind of secret event."

When Alan finished my hair it looked marginally better than before. The color was back to a more-or-less blond color and he had trimmed the frizz off my bangs.

I was crossing the Causeway back to the house when I decided to pull over. I loved the Causeway. It crossed over the Muskegon River, connecting greater Muskegon to the tiny slip of land known as North Muskegon. The lanes going in either direction separated to go around a small island in the middle of the river. Then they rejoined on the other side.

The local VFW hall was in charge of the island's upkeep, and since the Fourth of July was upon us, lots of volunteers were busy getting ready. I watched the women as they bent over to plant the flagstaffs, their bottoms straining at their polyester pants. Every year, the entire perimeter was lined with two-foot-high American flags. Literally thousands of them fluttered in the sunshine as I looked out the driver's-side window and pondered my day.

So Father Whippet was having an affair with his secretary and had written some sort of sex ritual and a whole group of elderly women from the Linen Guild were involved. What could they be doing? Having sex orgies down in the basement where we have our bake sales and sell crocheted Christmas ornaments? Even my overactive imagination couldn't quite believe all that.

Three men in khaki army hats were standing by the main flag-pole. One of them—the one with the portable oxygen tank and red suspenders stretching over his belly—seemed to be in charge of unfolding the flag. My dad had taught me to fold an American flag when I was six years old. First, fold the stripes over the stars lengthwise, and then take one striped corner to the other side so you form a triangle of fabric. Continue with the triangle back and forth until you have a little flap of stars left. Then tuck the star flap into the crease. Never let it touch the ground. He taught me that when the flag has done its duty to the country, a good American honors it with a ceremonial burning. Never throw it in the trash. The men in khaki hats successfully snapped the flag onto its hooks and ran it up to the gold-painted American eagle at the top. Then they all smartly saluted. I looked over my shoulder to see if any cars were coming, then pulled back onto the road.

Dad was digging a hole down by the lake when I got home.

"Dad, have you noticed anything weird about Father Whippet lately?" I asked him.

He didn't even look up. "Weirder than what? His usual self?" He stopped digging and pondered the bottom of the hole he was standing in. "Do you see any water yet?"

"No," I said, looking five feet beyond him at Bear Lake. I decided not to ask the obvious. I tried to bring him back to the subject I was interested in.

"Hand me that hose, would you?"

I handed him a coil of black hose. "Okay, I give. What are you doing?"

"Digging a well."

He was about two feet below me and the sun glinted off the comb-over on top of his head. "The water pressure for the sprinklers is low. Somehow the pump just isn't pulling in the water."

"What's the difference if the water is coming from Bear Lake or if it's coming from a well five feet from Bear Lake?" I asked.

"I have a theory I'm working on"—he leaned on the shovel—"but it's a bit too early to see if it's going to pan out yet. Why don't you go up to the house and say hello to Grandma?"

I know when I'm being dismissed. I trudged up the stairs and went in the house through the sliding doors. Walker was sitting at the kitchen table with Grandma Thompson. A deck of cards was spread out in front of them. "You see here? Three nines together. That means you'll be taking a long trip." Grandma had her nose down close to the cards so she could see them.

"Hi, Walker." I kissed him on the cheek. "Hi, Grandma." I pecked her on the cheek, too. "What are you doing?"

"I'm reading his cards. What's it look like?" Grandma picked up the cards from the table. "I'll do you next, Elizabeth."

"Jeannie," I corrected.

Grandma tipped her head down and looked at me over her bifocals. "Oh, yes," she said, "the fifth one. What in the world were your parents thinking?"

They probably weren't thinking, I thought. I was conceived a few years after the Pill hit the market. Mom had said she was too busy with three little kids to get to the doctor for the prescription. That's when Lucy was born. Then Mom said that she got the birth control prescription but couldn't find the time to get to the pharmacy. That's when I was born. Dad got a vasectomy after that.

Dad came into the house and, after shaking hands with Walker, went to the TV room and settled down into his favorite red chair with a book.

Grandma tapped the deck. "Sit down. I'll give you a reading. What time were you born?"

"I don't know. Just a sec." I wandered out to the TV room. "Dad, what time was I born?"

He didn't hear me. He and I had something in common—we both read like madmen and used it as a way to tune out the chaos around us.

"Dad?"

"Huh?"

"What time was I born?"

He put his book down on his lap. "You were born at 6 p.m. I remember we couldn't find a babysitter for the other kids and—"

"That was Sammie."

"Are you sure? I thought that was you. Well, then you were born at 7 in the morning because the doctor had to get out of bed and he was late and your mother almost had you on the gurney out in the hallway."

"That was Lucy."

Dad sighed and picked up his book. "I don't know, Jeannie. Ask your mother."

"She's not here."

He peered at me over the latest Helen McGuinness mystery. He finally seemed to really be considering my question. "I remember now. You were the one when the headlights didn't work."

"Excuse me?"

"It was two o'clock in the morning. I left the other kids with a neighbor next door and got your mom into the car. But after a couple of miles the headlights on the car went out. We almost drove into a ditch. It scared your mom and me half to death. We stopped the car by the side of the road trying to figure out what to do. Your mom's contractions were coming fast. Then all of the sudden the moon came out from behind the clouds. It was a full moon and it lit the rest of the way to the hospital pretty as you please. You were born just a few minutes after we arrived and I remember your mom saying you were born under a lucky moon."

I did vaguely recall Mom mentioning something about a full moon so I figured this story must be my own. I went back into the kitchen.

Grandma shuffled the cards with a professional flair. I thought she probably would have loved Vegas. I could just see her with a little green visor telling the dealer, "Hit me." She laid out the cards row after row and studied them.

"You're going to die soon," she announced to me.

Walker reared back at the death pronouncement, but I just pulled out a chair and sat down.

"No, I'm not, Grandma. You say that every time," I said.

"Don't anger the spirits. I just tell you what they tell me." Grandma was getting huffy. She studied the cards again. "You may be right, though. It might not be you. But somebody close to you is definitely a goner. See, the ace of spades is upside down between the jack of diamonds and the queen of hearts, and the queen of diamonds is just below the ace. It's as clear as day." She tapped the cards with her index finger.

"Um, Jeannie? Do you want to go to the Whippi Dip for an ice cream? Or out to Lake Michigan or something?" Walker stood up, clearly ready to leave the nut house I call home.

"I can't. I have to stay here with Grandma. Why don't you just hang around with us? We can watch TV or something."

Walker rolled his eyes upward behind Grandma's back and shook his head. He came over and kissed the top of my head. I trailed after him out the back door and walked him to his car. "Do you really have to go? Come on, it won't be that bad. I just have to be here in case something happens."

"Jeannie, something *always* happens in this family."

"We prefer to think of it as excitement," I said stiffly.

"I'm sure your grandmother is very nice, but I don't want to stay inside and watch *As the World Turns* on a beautiful day. Or any other day for that matter. I'm gonna go sailing with John." Walker got into his Pinto and pulled away. He stuck his hand out the window and waved. I waved after him and turned to go back into the house. I broke into a jog when I heard the phone ringing.

I bumped through the back door and grabbed the phone in the hall.

"Hello," I gasped.

"Jeannie?"

"Yeah, hi, Sammie," I answered.

"Have you or Mom talked to Lucy lately?"

"I talked to her about two weeks ago and I think Mom talked

to her last Sunday. Why?" I fiddled with the tangled-up cord of the wall phone.

"I think something's wrong with her. She called me today and sounded really down. She wouldn't say what was going on, but she definitely sounded not so good."

I stretched the cord as far as it would go so I could look into the kitchen to make sure Grandma was all right. I couldn't see her. I went the other way into the dining room, but couldn't see her there either.

"Speaking of something wrong," I said, "have you talked to Evan? He seems a little off lately. His show just doesn't have that spark right now."

"People get creative blocks. Nothing to get worried about," Sammie said. "Anyway. Lucy. She did say that something was up with her and Chuck. I think she's going to try and come home soon."

I walked back to the kitchen as Grandma wandered back into view. I eyed her warily. She was removing her panties, which was the last stitch she had on.

"Sammie? I really have to go." Grandma's droopy rear end was facing me now. She walked over to the sliding glass door and pressed her body against it. I wondered how that looked from the other side and winced.

"Anyway, I wanted to give you guys a heads-up," Sammie said.

"Look, Sammie, Grandma is buck naked here in the kitchen and I have to go deal with that."

"Why didn't you say so?" Sammie said calmly. "Just let Mom and Dad know I called."

I hung up the phone and ran to Grandma, picking up her clothes from the floor as I went. "Grandma? Grandma? Are you okay? Why did you take off your clothes?"

"It's hot. The window is nice and cool."

I held her housecoat open for her but she darted away. I barely managed to stop her from opening the front door. "Grandma, no! You have to put your clothes on." I tried to wrestle one of her arms into the sleeve but didn't get very far. She had become a squirmy two-year-old who doesn't want to put on her shirt. She wiggled away and then stiffened her body so that I couldn't get the housecoat on her.

Thankfully, Mom arrived. She dropped her bag of groceries on the table and ran over. Grandma suddenly became compliant and allowed Mom to dress her. Darting her eyes over at me, Grandma whispered to Mom, "There's something wrong with that girl. She told me to take off all my clothes."

I went back into the hall and took the phone off the hook. Holding it by its cord, I let the receiver dangle. It began to spin, untangling its knotted cord. I watched it spin and spin until finally one thing in my life was all straightened out.

Seventeen

April 2006

I think you need to add emotion to the trailer," pronounced the young starlet of *TechnoCat*. She was picking at a salad that was about six hours old and was sitting in a plastic takeout box on her lap. Stripe, the director, nodded his agreement from his position next to her on the leather couch. He had obviously prepped her on what to say.

"Esperanza, don't you think that scene where your character's mother dies of cancer would be good?" Stripe asked her solemnly.

"Oh, yes! That's exactly what I was thinking." Esperanza gazed up at her ticket to the big time, her current lover, Stripe. "Thinking"? I rolled my eyes. This girl had ADD AIR HERE imprinted on her forehead. She had come to Hollywood with the name Susan Hammersmith but changed it to Esperanza Steele.

We were sitting in an edit bay working on the trailer. The director, star, and producers had all generously offered to come and "help" the editor and me. What could have been accomplished in a few hours had now become a marathon. The editor looked ready to drop but gamely plugged away. He wouldn't even have one change done before the group would decide it wouldn't work and request a different change. We were now on version 42. Guiltily I looked at my watch. It was 12:30 on a Saturday night. We still weren't getting anywhere.

"I'll see Katsu's trailer in the morning." Stripe yawned. "If he didn't nail it, then we're going to have to do a special shoot to create it from scratch."

I kept a polite smile on my face. Katsu's trailer? He was now working on *TechnoCat* too? This was news to me. As casually as I could manage I asked when Katsu had started working on the movie trailer.

"Oh, he came to me about two weeks ago." Stripe stretched and yawned again. "Said he had some great ideas about how to approach Cat's mother's cancer. I gave him the feature film and told him to run with it."

"Does Rachael know about this?" I was amazed at how nonchalant I managed to sound.

"Beats me."

Rachael had to know about it, I thought. An executive just couldn't wander off and spend money without someone's approval. Deflated and defeated, I sagged into the leather couch. After another hour, the director said we should all go home and "sleep on it." He made a point of thanking the editor but not me.

When I straggled into Aidan's bed, he flopped an arm across me and mumbled, "Rough night?" Then he fell asleep again. I felt the familiar tingling of tension through my body. Sleep wasn't going to come. I picked up my latest mystery paperback, turned on the itty-bitty night light, and read until my eyes finally started to close.

The first thing I did when I got up the next morning was to

check on the opening weekend box office grosses for *Sheer Panic*. Film studios fax them to the senior executives at their houses over the weekend. Mine would be sent to my house but Aidan was on the fax list from Warner Bros. Why most studios still used fax machines rather than email in this day and age was beyond me.

The movie had opened big—far bigger than research tracking would have indicated. This was a major victory for Oxford Pictures, not to mention that Ms. F.U. had to be over the moon. This was her biggest opening weekend since 1993. Glancing at my watch I saw it was only 7:15. It was still a bit early for Rachael to call me and other marketing people with the traditional congratulations. But the earlier the congratulatory phone call, the bigger the hit.

I had tried every trick in the book over the past two weeks with *Sheer Panic*, because it was *really* a bad movie that had *really* cost a lot of money to make. The studio had been looking to the advertising team to save it. When the bad reviews started rolling in, we carefully culled through the almost acceptable ones. They were from places like the *Sun City Sentinel* in Fairbanks, Alaska. So we did TV spots that said, in really big type, "Sensational!" and put the attribution for the *Sentinel* in tiny type.

My cell phone rang at 7:45. Rachael gushed on for a while about my great work.

But my happiness at the success was squelched almost immediately when Rachael said, "Jeannie, you've done an amazing job on this movie." I sensed a *but* was coming and I wasn't wrong. "But I spoke to Fiona Underwood this morning. While she appreciates your work, she would feel more comfortable working with Katsu on her next film."

Stunned, I didn't respond. I backed up until I felt the couch behind my knees and sat down heavily. Fiona—also known as

Ms. F.U.—didn't want me? I had *slaved* for that woman's film! Not to mention that it wasn't Ms. F.U.'s call to remove me. It was up to Rachael to decide who worked on what movie.

Not sure of my voice, I cleared my throat. "I've already hired an ad agency to get started on that film."

"Yes, so I'll expect you to turn over all materials to Katsu and give him a full briefing," Rachael responded abruptly. She wasn't the touchy-feely type, and I knew she just wanted to get off the phone.

"Okay," I said faintly. As I was pressing END on the cell phone I heard her say, "Again, Jeannie, really great job."

With my head in my hands I contemplated crying. Tears had never come easily to me, so while I choked out a few tortured gasps, my face remained dry. Aidan patted my back and kept asking me what was wrong. Without responding I crossed the living room, retying my bathrobe as I went. In the hallway I opened the overflowing linen closet and began pulling every single damn thing out. Methodically I began separating items to be refolded, washed, or thrown away. Piles of bed sheets, blankets, and towels grew around me. Aidan spent a while standing several feet away, sipping a cup of coffee and watching me.

An hour and a half later, I was finished. The closet was immaculate and sheets hummed in the dryer. Aidan had disappeared out into the garden long ago. I showered quickly and got dressed. In the kitchen I made some toast, then poured Aidan and myself some coffee and headed outside to find him.

He was watering the hillside that sloped away from his house. Seeing me, he shut off the hose and we sat at the small wrought iron café table on the patio. A yellow umbrella protected us from the strong sun. Aidan sipped his coffee as I told him of the latest treachery from Katsu. He didn't say anything for quite a while. When he did, it wasn't what I had expected.

"Jeannie, you've become obsessed. It's not healthy. You just opened a movie to big numbers, and all you can do is talk about Katsu."

"Don't you see?" I practically wailed. "It doesn't matter that I did a great job. Katsu and Rachael are playing some game and I don't get what it is."

"Yes, something is going on and most likely there is a bigger picture here. And we, two very smart film industry people, have not been able to figure out what that is. So it seems you have two choices: You can continue to have insomnia and drive yourself completely insane. Or you can just forget about it." Aidan looked at me steadily across the table.

I stared back at him. "This is my job we're talking about here. How exactly am I supposed to just forget about what Katsu is up to?" I beat a piece of toast into submission with a knife and a pat of butter.

"Be Zen, because what's going to happen is going to happen. You can't do anything about it. If you push back too hard instead of just going with the flow, you might guarantee losing your job. Look, maybe you'll have this job six months from now and maybe you won't. There's no doubt Katsu will keep trying to get under your skin. But what your quality of life is during those six months is up to you."

Frustrated, I pushed back from the table and walked out to the garden. Aidan didn't understand. I had worked too hard to just be "Zen" about the politics at work. Aidan quietly followed me out and began watering the rose garden. I sat down on a dry patch of grass and idly tried to pick weeds. I didn't really know which ones were weeds though, so I stopped. The nasty ones always looked so much like the good ones.

"Jeannie?"

"Huh?" I turned to Aidan. His back was to me while he swung the hose from side to side.

"We haven't talked about, you know, in quite a while."

"No, I guess not."

"Have you thought about it?"

I looked down at my coffee and dug my toes into the grass. He hadn't brought up this subject in a while and I was hoping he had forgotten about it.

"This isn't really a great time to talk about it."

Aidan just looked at me.

"You've seen the hours I've been working, Aidan. It's worse now than ever. How can we get married? It wouldn't be fair to you."

"Why do you never think that it's not fair to *you*?" I saw his back rise and fall as he sighed. "Jeannie, this is exactly what I'm talking about. Your quality of life sucks. You can't keep putting your personal life on hold for your work. You keep saying that we can't get married because of your family and your work and whatever else you can think of. I think that's just a convenient way to avoid what's really going on."

I looked down at my coffee again. How could I explain that at least work had always been there for me? So had my family in their own crazy way. Men, as a rule, hadn't. "Aidan, I love you. I can't live without you. I know you want to get married, but isn't simply being together enough for right now?"

Aidan watered the lemon tree without looking at me. "What if it's not, Jeannie? You're almost forty years old. If we want a family, then we don't have a lot of time to dwell on this. Have you ever considered what your life would be like without me?"

The truth was, I hadn't. As I sat there in the Southern California sun, I was ashamed of myself. Why had I been so inconsiderate of his feelings? Why had I blotted out the fact that Aidan, feeling rejected by me, might turn to a willing Montana? Still, the marriage proposal was a question I just couldn't bring myself to answer right now. My head felt too jumbled up.

I walked over to Aidan and rubbed his back. "I love you and, yes, I would love to marry you." Aidan turned, his face lit up. I continued, "But you still don't know everything about my family. So you can't make an informed decision. Walker was constantly embarrassed by my family. Other people were hurt in other ways by coming into contact with my family. I couldn't bear it if you felt the same way. Since we have a quiet morning, how about I continue the story?" Aidan turned abruptly and went into the house and I held my breath, thinking he had left in anger. But he reappeared with the coffee pot and filled up my mug.

"Okay, go."

Eighteen

July 1986

*I*t wasn't until later that night that I remembered to tell Mom and Dad about Sammie's phone call about Lucy.

"Lucy is coming home? Before her graduation at the language school?" Mom fretted. "Something has to be wrong." Dad stroked her head as she riffled through her address book for Lucy's phone number. That address book was a veritable log of our lives. As we moved from dorms to apartments to houses, the old address above would be crossed out and the new one added. I looked over Mom's shoulder at Lucy's list: her dorm at Western Michigan University, her barracks at Fort Dix, her brief sojourn at Fort Huachuca, and now her barracks at the Defense Language Institute. Mom dialed the number but didn't reach Lucy. The person who answered explained that this phone number was for a pay phone in the barracks hallway. She had no idea who Lucy was and, no, she wasn't going to go look.

"Why doesn't Lucy ever call us about stuff?" I complained. "It's like she's sneaking up on us all the time."

"Don't talk about your sister that way." Mom sighed. "All of you are the same way. If something is really wrong, you don't talk about it until you get home. Especially you, Jeannie. When you're away at college and I don't hear from you for a few weeks, I know you're struggling with something."

That was true. If something was bothering me I tended to retreat from my family. It was easier to avoid thinking about a problem that way. Mom had an uncanny knack for sensing your mood and prodding the problem out of you. Many times she had come up to my bedroom at night when I was just drifting off. Mindless of the sleeping lump that was one of my sisters next to me, she would sit on the side of the bed. "You'll feel better if you shake this thing out" was what she always said. Like our problems were a pile of crumpled-up laundry that just needed a good airing.

Most of the time she was right. She also knew that when any one of us was being particularly bratty or bitchy it was because something was eating at us. That's why she put so much stock in her wooden sign, PEOPLE NEED LOVING THE MOST WHEN THEY DESERVE IT THE LEAST. She repeated this mantra constantly during all the years of our arguing over the phone, throwing the nearest object at one another, and occasionally flat-out rolling-on-the-ground fighting. We never punched each other. We were far too girly for that. But we did indulge in a fair amount of hair pulling and scratching and waving our hands in front of each other's faces like we just might land a slap. Evan was immune to most of the arguments because he was older, because he was our brother and we loved him to distraction, and also because he didn't care about most of the things we fought about.

Twenty years later, my siblings and I are at the point where we know each other's buttons and don't bother to push them. Or, if one of us inadvertently does set another one off, the other party will eventually sigh and just say, "I know, I'm a pain in the ass on that front." Over the years, we've worn the rough edges off each other so that we are no longer like jagged shards of metal waiting to cut, but rather like smooth stones that rub and tumble against one another, polishing each of us to a high shine.

When I woke up the next morning, Grandma was sitting at my place at the table and Mom was already on the phone.

"Where's Dad?" I asked Grandma.

"He's already left. Poor man, he's wearing his suit and trying to act like he still has a job. He doesn't fool me, though."

I raised my eyebrows at Mom and she just shook her head at me with the receiver still at her ear. Eventually, she said good-bye and hung up the phone. "What's up with her?" I whispered to Mom, jerking my head toward Grandma.

"I have no idea. Your dad just went to work as usual." Mom gave me her wry smile that said, "Just go with it." "Anyhow, I was talking to your grandmother's doctor," she continued. Turning to Grandma, she put her own hand over my grandmother's wrinkled one. "We think that maybe your medication is too strong. The doctor is going to see what he can do."

Grandma nodded but didn't seem to be paying a lot of attention, instead staring out the window at the squirrel dangling off the bird feeder.

"Did you talk to Lucy this morning?" I asked.

"Yes. She's coming home as soon as she can get a leave. She didn't want to say what was wrong, but she definitely needs to talk about something. She said she could catch military planes across the country and eventually get here."

I yawned and stretched; then Mom said, "You'd better get dressed. Father Whippet will be here soon."

"Mom," I said slowly, "I saw something kind of strange at the church yesterday." I told her about the papers with sex acts drawn on them and Father Whippet and his secretary, Shirley, coming out of the bathroom together. Then I told her about the "secret" meeting at St. Peter's.

I waited for Mom to reprimand me for gossiping. I should have counted on her naturally suspicious mind. "Father Whippet has recently started a meeting group for women over the age of sixty," she mused, "but I'm not sure why they would all get their hair done just to needlepoint pew cushions. And at Evan's wedding . . ." She trailed off there. I waited for her to elaborate, but she didn't. We sipped coffee in silence until Mom started thinking out loud. "The old gals *have* been looking pretty good lately. Even that Sophie Mearston. She's lost weight and started dyeing her hair." Then she shook her head. "No, it's just not possible. This town is too small. If something were happening it would be all over the place and I haven't heard a word."

I went to get dressed thinking that if I were having an affair with snaggle-toothed Father Whippet I wouldn't be advertising it either. I came downstairs and almost tripped over Buddy.

"Did anyone take Buddy out yet?" I hollered into the kitchen. Mom came into the hallway and handed me the leash. Of course no one had walked the dog yet. Hey, it was only 11 a.m. He had probably been dancing around for hours. I clipped his leash on and he dragged me out the door and down the steps. Once he had relieved himself, we walked at a slightly more sedate pace. It was a sunny, humid day. Muskegon never got too hot because of what is called the "lake effect." The winds blew across Lake Michigan to cool us. We never got tornadoes, either. The theory was that they blew in over the lake, hit the sand dunes, bounced up and over us, and then landed in Kalamazoo. I'm not sure I believed that, but the fact remained that we hadn't had a tornado in my memory.

I walked down the tree-lined street enjoying the wind rustling the leaves above my head. Ahead of me, there was a group of kids playing street hockey. One of them was using a skateboard to hustle back and forth with his stick.

"Hey, no fair," I said good-naturedly. "You can outrun everyone." The kid stopped and I recognized him as the little brother of one of my friends.

"Can I borrow your dog?" he asked.

"What for?"

"So he can pull me around on my skateboard."

This seemed like a fair request, so I turned over the leash and went to sit on the curb. Buddy pulled the kid up and down the block while the other kids leaped and hollered next to them. Finally they pulled up next to me, Buddy panting, his mouth pulled back in a dog grin.

"Want a turn?" the kid asked.

I considered. It sure looked like fun, and nobody was around to see me doing such a childish thing.

"Okay." I got to my feet.

"Just hang on to the leash and try to stay on the skateboard," my munchkin instructor informed me. I got on the bright orange board and took Buddy's leash. The dog started out at a slow trot. Hey, this *is* pretty fun, I thought. We were just passing the Worthingtons' house when Buddy spotted a squirrel in the street. He took off like a rocket. Our speed was building at an alarming rate. The skateboard was vibrating violently under my sneakers.

"Let go of the leash!" the kids yelled after me.

My wrist was firmly looped through the leash and I couldn't

get my hand out. The squirrel decided staying on the street wasn't the best course of action. It veered up the curb and across the sidewalk. Buddy followed him, and that was the last thing I remembered.

I woke up sprawled on the grass between the curb and the sidewalk. Little heads came into focus above me. "Hey, lady, are you alive?" one of them asked. "We called nine-one-one for you. Somebody will be here soon."

Bright blue stars were pinging in front of my eyes. I idly thought, Wow, you really do see stars.

"Why did you put your hand through the loop on the leash?" the little kid said reproachfully. "You're not supposed to do that."

That would have been a good tip to give me *before* I got on the skateboard.

"You hit that curb going about a hundred miles an hour, and boy, did you fly."

Marv Carson arrived with his siren blaring. He took one look at me sprawled in the grass and sighed. "You okay?" he asked, leaning out of the driver's-side window.

I sat up and rubbed my head. "Yeah, I think so. My knees are pretty skinned up."

Marv opened the car door, got out, and extended a hand to me. I hauled myself up with it. "Why is it I always find the Thompson girls knocked out cold on the street?"

I wobbled to the car. "Oh, come on. It's been a good ten years since that happened."

Marv let me in the front and then pushed Buddy into the back. "Maybe. But it doesn't seem to happen to any other family. You never see the Keene girls flattened out like road kill."

The last such incident had started with clothes and a crush. It was Sammie. In a town that boasted only J. C. Penney and Sears, it was hard to find clothes to express your individuality, so Sammie took to embroidering her faded Levi's with elaborate, colorful stitching. Every girl in town copied her style. Finally, a clothing boutique called JayJay's opened up downtown and Sammie was first in line to get a job there. She took most of her payment in clothing. All this was to win over a cute senior nicknamed Poodle because of his bushy hair. Sammie would sashay around the high school twitching her tiny butt and enjoying the fact that her platform shoes made her five feet five instead of five feet tall. Poodle never seemed to notice her, not even when she batted her blue-mascara'd eyelashes at him. She was a lowly sophomore and he was an almighty senior. Sammie's best friends, Diana and Jenny, tried to tell Sammie she was acting like an infatuated idiot. Even practical Elizabeth, who was also a senior, warned Sammie that the guy just wasn't interested. Nothing sank in. Sammie was in love.

One fine spring day she was walking home from school. She knew that Poodle would soon be taking the same route home in his Trans Am. She heard a car behind her and concentrated on trying to swish her nonexistent hips. Unfortunately, what happened next still makes Sammie blush to this day. Just as Poodle was passing her and she raised her hand to give a casual wave, her baby blue suede platform shoe caught in the hem of her gigantic elephant bell-bottoms. She flipped forward and hit her head on the curb. She woke up with her notebooks scattered around her, to find a concerned Marv Carson standing above her. Poodle had never even slowed down. We would have liked to think that he hadn't seen the incident, but we knew better. He was just as embarrassed as Sammie at her graceless exhibition.

Marv started toward my house. "That dog is dangerous," he said as he pulled into the driveway. "You okay to make it inside?"

"Yeah." I grabbed the door handle.

"I'm pleased you had Buddy on a leash."

"That leash almost killed me," I said as I pulled Buddy out of the backseat.

Mom, Father Whippet, and Grandma were sitting in the living room holding cups and saucers. The only time I saw a saucer in our house was when we had company. I waved but they all just stared at me.

"Jeannie, what on earth happened to you?" Mom gasped.

I looked down at myself. My knees were bleeding, my shorts were ripped, and there was grass in my hair.

"Nothing, why?" I fled up the stairs and sat on the toilet seat. I picked the gravel out of my knees and applied Bactine and bandages.

"Jeannie? Jeannie? Come down and say hello to Father Whippet," Mom called from the bottom of the stairs. I rolled my eyes up at the bathroom ceiling. I changed into jeans and a clean shirt and made my way into the living room.

"Hi." I gave a brief wave to the good Father, who was sitting on Mom's uncomfortable Eastlake chair. He lifted his coffee cup to me in response. The four of us fell into a strained silence.

"More coffee?" Mom offered.

"No, thank you," Father Whippet demurred. He probably wanted this torment to end as soon as possible, too.

"Do you find me attractive?" Grandma piped up. Mom and I exchanged a startled look. Grandma had been paying more attention to our conversation this morning than we had thought. I noticed Grandma had unbuttoned a few too many buttons of her housecoat and was now displaying an alarming amount of long bosom. She squeezed her arm against the side of her breast to perk it up and leaned toward Father Whippet with a faint leer.

There was no right answer to that question. Buddy solved

Father Whippet's problem by wandering into the living room and puking at his feet.

"Oh Lord." Mom got to her feet. "Jeannie, get that dog outside."

I hauled Buddy by his collar to the back door and pushed him out. He meandered next door to the Longs' lawn. When I got back to the living room, Mom was scrubbing the carpet and apologizing to Father Whippet.

"Don't be silly." Father Whippet rose and put his coffee cup on the table. "I'll just see myself out, if you don't mind." He was clearly relieved that he could make his escape.

"How did he act?" I asked Mom after he departed.

"Just like he normally does," Mom said as she cleared the coffee cups.

"Ill at ease and kind of sanctimonious?"

"Jeannie, don't say unkind things about people," Mom said, opening the dishwasher. "We did get into a bit of an argument though. He probably thinks I'm an opinionated old lady."

Mom always imagined she was doing something wrong. If she had an opinion, she thought of it as an insult to any person who might have a differing point of view. She'd speak her mind but then worry it to death for the next week. Or the next decade. "Oh, they must think I'm just awful," she'd say. For a person who had so much iron resolve, it was odd how much she worried about what everybody thought of her. The flip side was that she realized when she was being a bit neurotic and then would say, "Well, I'd rather be talked about than ignored," lifting her chin defiantly in the air. I'd find it amusing if I hadn't inherited these exact same traits. So if Mom said she got into an argument with someone it most likely meant that she had offered a mild disagreement.

"I just don't agree with his stance on having women in the church," Mom continued.

I turned to her, startled. "Having women in the church?"

"Yes, as ministers."

"Oh. I thought you meant something else."

The innuendo drifted over Mom's head as she continued, "He doesn't think women have any place in the pulpit. Why, what if one of you girls had chosen that profession, only to be denied?"

Fat chance, I thought, but realizing that wasn't her point, I didn't interrupt.

"Women have as much right as men to minister to people. He says that it's in the Bible that men, not women, are the ones chosen to lead the church. Well, of course the Bible says that. Men wrote it. And God knows, Father Whippet's sermons are just a good excuse to sleep. I never have any idea of what he's talking about."

"You just told me not to say unkind things about people."

"You know what I mean." She paused at the sink and then giggled. "I just loved the look on his face when your grandmother asked if he thought she was attractive." She wiped the counter and then, clearly feeling like she had said something not nice, added, "Of course, your grandmother in her day was just beautiful. You look just like her."

"Could you tell her to stop telling me that either I'm going to die soon or somebody close to me is going to die soon? It's getting kind of disconcerting."

Mom turned to me. "Is she doing her readings again? I think she's going overboard on that stuff. But she really can be uncanny about her predictions."

"That's not real comforting, Mom," I said. "It's getting late and I have to go to work pretty soon. Are you going to be okay here with Grandma?" I asked.

Mom said, "Sure." I went upstairs for my third clothing change of the day. My work uniform consisted of a Bear Lake Inn T-shirt and a jeans skirt. Jeans were acceptable, too. Pretty much any attire was acceptable. As long as you had on the logo-imprinted T-shirt, you were okay.

Dad and Evan were in the kitchen when I came back down. They had something spread out on the kitchen table and were reading instructions.

"Evan, can you give me a ride to work?"

"Yeah, as soon as we're done here."

I sat down to watch them. It was yet another "squirrel-proof" bird feeder. Every year it was the same thing. Dad had tried bird feeders on slippery poles, hung from tree branches with a barbed wire hanger, every damn thing in the world, and always with the same result. The squirrels managed to get to the feeder and eat every bit of seed meant for the birds. Dad waged a steady and losing war against them.

"Why do you even care if the squirrels eat the seed?" I asked.

"It's the point of the thing," Dad said around his cigarette. "It's called a bird feeder. If I wanted a squirrel feeder, I'd buy one of those." He held up the house-shaped feeder. "And this one is going to work. See here? There's a perch for the birds. But the clever part is that it's actually a lever. If a fat squirrel sits on it, it pushes it down and triggers a Plexiglas piece that comes down and covers the seed."

I pushed on the perch and the Plexiglas smacked down from under the roof and sealed off the seed. Still, I regarded it doubtfully.

Dad and Evan went outside and mounted it atop the waiting pole. Then they sat back in lawn chairs and waited for an unsuspecting squirrel.

"Evan, it's almost four o'clock. I don't have time for you to wait to fool a squirrel. Can I get a ride now?"

Evan grudgingly got up and I followed him out to his car. "What's your show about this week?" I asked.

"I'm not sure yet." He turned onto Ruddiman Drive and headed for the Blit.

"Your show seems kind of flat lately. Is something wrong?"

"Yeah. Anna is making noises about moving to Florida and some other stuff is bothering me."

Why in the world would Anna want to move to Florida? I decided not to ask.

"Thanks, Evan," I said as we pulled up in front of the Blit. "Damn it, I forgot Buddy. He was over at the Longs. Would you check on him?"

"Nope. He knows his way home." Evan grinned and gunned out of the parking lot.

In the summertime the Blit was always packed. There were a lot of to-go orders from boaters who would pick up their dinner and a six-pack of beer and head out to Muskegon Lake. It was common for friends to meet out there and tie their boats to each other. There could be as many as ten or twelve boats hooked together like a giant floating raft. It was kind of a progressive picnic. Each boat would have a different featured drink and food and people would clamber in and out of each other's cabins. Someone usually cranked up a stereo and everyone danced until the boats were rocking. I knew that was where most of my friends would be that night. Walker had already called to say that he'd be on the Worthingtons' boat if I got off work early. I looked at the packed room. There was no way that was going to happen.

One of the bad things about a small town is that everyone

knows your name. And they were using it liberally that night. "Jeannie! Over here! Jeannie, can I get another Stroh's? Jeannie, this burger has mayo. I said no mayo."

I ran outside to deliver an order to a boat at the BLT's private dock. Music was playing somewhere in the distance. The way sound traveled over water, it sounded like the stereo speakers were in the parking lot instead of two miles away across Muskegon Lake.

Tommy hollered at me from behind the bar. "Jeannie, phone for you." The restaurant phone was popular. If you couldn't be found at home the next call would be to the Blit. Chances were good that you would be there. When I went behind the bar to take the receiver, he grumbled, "Keep it quick. We're swamped."

"Hello?"

I heard sobbing.

"Lucy?"

There was a muffled "Noo" from the other end.

"Sammie?"

"It's Elizabeth."

"Elizabeth, are you okay?" I asked, even though it was obvious she wasn't. I put a finger in my other ear to hear her better over the din.

"Ron sold my car today."

I relaxed. This wasn't life threatening.

"Why are you crying?"

"He didn't tell me he was going to sell it!" she wailed. "He did it because he didn't have the money to make our mortgage payment."

Tommy made motions for me to hurry it up. None of what Elizabeth was telling me made any sense anyhow. She made good money and Ron was a therapist, which, I assumed, meant he did well.

"Elizabeth, I know you feel really bad right now, but I can't keep talking at work."

Elizabeth sniffled, "Oh God, I'm sorry. It's the Fourth of July. You must be just jammed."

I looked around nervously at the eight tables waiting for me to take their order. "Yeah, it's really busy. Why don't you call Mom and talk to her?"

"I can't. She would think so badly of Ron."

I didn't volunteer that we *all* thought badly of Ron. "I've got to go, Elizabeth."

She hung up the phone and I went back to my irritated customers. I had been on the phone for less than three minutes, but you'd have thought I'd kept them waiting an hour. Chris Prescott made a snide remark about how slow I was. I leaned down close to his ear so his mom couldn't hear. "You say one more word and I'm going to tell your mother how her car *really* wound up on the tennis courts the day after the prom."

He had the good grace to look embarrassed. "Sorry, Jeannie."

I cheerfully chucked him on the back of his head and went into the kitchen.

The Blit finally cleared out around 10:30. Everyone was either getting on their boats or driving up to Custer Park to watch the fireworks over Muskegon Lake. I finished up my work and was just getting ready to walk home when Walker arrived.

I was surprised. "I thought you were out on the Worthingtons' boat."

"I was, but they dropped me off at our dock at home. I grabbed the car because I figured you could use a ride home."

"Thanks for coming," I said, although I really didn't mind the walk. I had never had a reason to feel unsafe in this town. Walking through the silent, dark streets was comforting to me. We sat down and shared a coffee while the sounds of exploding fireworks echoed outside.

Inside, the jukebox thumped the Romantics. *"What I like about you, you hold me tight, tell me I'm the only one . . ."* echoed around the tavern while Walker told me about the Sea Scout sailing race he had been in that day.

Walker sipped his coffee. "I'm sorry I haven't been around much lately, but with sailing during the day and fishing at night, it's been hard to get together. Plus, you're so busy with work and now your grandma."

I accepted his apology and sat back. We had known each other since we were five years old. Walker's parents had sent him to the exclusive boarding school Cranbrook, near Detroit, so the kids in our town only saw Walker during the summers. I had never even thought of dating him. He was far too handsome and smart for me. I tended to date guys who didn't have a lot going for them. I figured that way I would look better by comparison. We started dating just before we both left for college. Difficult, since MSU and Princeton were seven hundred miles apart.

"Do you have your purse?" Walker asked.

"Yeah. Let me go tell Tommy I'm leaving."

Tommy waved his bar rag at us in a good-bye and called out to Walker, "Tell your parents I said hello."

Walker said he would, and we took off into the warm night. I put my hand out of the window and let it surf the breeze. The radio was blaring Tom Petty's "American Girl," and we sang at the top of our lungs the whole way home. *"She was . . . an American girl . . ."*

"You want to come in?" I asked in the driveway.

He looked up at the house, where every light was on. Through the kitchen window we could see Mom pouring a cup of coffee. "No," he said slowly. Then he leaned over and kissed me. "My dad and I are leaving at midnight to go fishing."

Thunder rolled through the air as I made my way up the walk. It had been so hot it would be good to get a storm, I thought. Mom, Dad, Grandma, Evan, and Anna were drinking coffee at the kitchen table when I walked in. "Are you guys talking about Elizabeth?"

"No, why? What's wrong with Elizabeth?" Mom's radar went up.

"Nothing. I just . . . Well, what *are* you guys talking about?"

"Florida," Anna said.

"Nice state. Oranges, alligators, and retirement homes. Oh, and Disney World."

"What are you, the tourism board?" Evan made a face at me.

"No one appreciates me," I sighed. "Someday you'll all be sorry you weren't nicer to me." I got a cup of coffee and sat down to listen to them debate the pros and cons of Florida.

Apparently, Anna's parents were moving down there and wanted their daughter close to them. Mom and Dad were, as usual, being supportive of whatever Evan and Anna felt was right for them. They didn't believe much in forcing their opinions on us. Their theory was that if, say, you were going to marry someone and they said that they were against it, and then you married that person, there would always be bad feelings. Better that you made the mistake and they could say later, "We saw this coming, honey." It wasn't an "I told you so"; it was more like an "I could've told you so but that wouldn't have been right." Only once in a great while could you force them to say what they really thought. So they were now saying that Florida might really have good opportunities for Evan and Anna. But even I could tell they didn't really mean it.

Grandma suddenly weighed in. "It's so damn hot down in Florida. I hated it—all those old people clicking their dentures and gumming tapioca pudding."

I stared at her. To my knowledge, she had never gotten farther south than Indianapolis. Mom and Dad exchanged a look that told me there was a story to be told. Anna stood up and put her purse over her shoulder. Evan got the hint. When they went out the door, Buddy came in.

"Has that dog been out since this afternoon?" I was incredulous. "Didn't you guys wonder where he was?"

"I saw him over at the Keenes' earlier today when I took a walk," Dad volunteered.

"You didn't call him home?"

"Nah, he seemed like he had important business with their poodle." He turned to Mom. "What's that poodle's name again?"

"Snickers," Mom replied.

"Right, Snickers. So I gave him a pat and went on. Buddy knows where he lives."

Mom helped Grandma to her feet and they went slowly up the stairs. I could hear her gently urging the elderly woman, "That's it, Pearl, just another step. Almost there."

"What gives with Grandma?" I asked my dad. "You never told me she lived in Florida."

"It was a long time ago, Jeannie."

"Was it before Grandpa died?"

For a long minute I only heard the crickets outside.

"Yes. Your grandmother had a . . . a little problem."

I waited. I didn't want to interrupt a rare discussion of my father's childhood. Dad finally went on. "She ran away from home.

I was about thirteen years old. She had spent years taking care of her own mother, who died of cancer. She went over the edge at the funeral and eventually took off with another man. We didn't know where she was for a couple of years."

A couple of *years*? I tried to imagine Mom running off when I was thirteen and not reappearing until I was fifteen or sixteen. I couldn't picture it. Mom would never leave us. I thought about poor Dad. Uncle Robert was eight years older than him, so he was undoubtedly out of the house by the time this occurred.

"My father and I looked everywhere for her," Dad mused. "We went to Chicago, we went to Detroit, but we never could find her. Then one day she was just there when I got home from school. She never talked about it to me, but she told my father that she had lived with that man in Naples, Florida, for a few months, and then he had deserted her. She got a job in a nursing home and wound up doing exactly what she was trying to escape: taking care of elderly people and watching them die."

Dad never spoke about stuff like this. Mom came back downstairs and gently rubbed his balding head. I went over and hugged my father, who had always, always been there for me. I told my parents that I loved them, as I did every night, and I went to bed.

Nineteen

July 1986

*M*om was shaking me. "Jeannie, Jeannie, wake up."

I opened my eyes and sat straight up in bed. Both Mom and Dad were standing above me. My mother's hazel eyes were full of tears. Dad was holding her and rocking her back and forth.

"What is it?" I whispered. "What happened?"

My mother turned and buried her face in Dad's chest. He wrapped his arms around her and laid his head on top of hers.

"It's Lucy, honey," Dad said. "Her plane went down this morning. There aren't any survivors." His voice broke and he sat on the edge of my bed and sobbed and shook until he scared me. He put his face in his hands while Mom clutched herself. For a moment, we were a still life in the gray light, me holding the covers with both hands, Dad hunched over his knees, and Mom staring out the window.

I looked at Lucy's cheerleading photo stuck into the frame of the mirror. This wasn't possible. Bad things always threatened my family but they never really happened. "Now come on, why would you think such a thing?" I spoke in the tones of someone who thinks others are overreacting and I could make it better if I pretend it's not really so bad.

"Her name is on the passenger list." Mom's voice was a distant shell of itself. "Can you get up? We need you."

The TV was tuned to the local news. I silently joined my parents and we watched the report. A military plane out of Marquette, Michigan, en route to Grand Rapids, had been struck by lightning. The pilot managed to get off a mayday and then the plane had disappeared from the radar somewhere over Lake Michigan. Twenty-eight servicemen and -women were on board and presumed dead. We watched the news helicopter footage of bits of green metal floating in the giant expanse of slate blue water.

"Are you sure she was on the plane?" My voice wavered.

Dad sat next to me on the couch and held me. "We called the TV station as soon as we heard the news. They gave us the number for the army. They told us she was a passenger."

"Maybe it's a mistake! The army could've made a mistake!" I was becoming hysterical. Mom sat straight upright with her hands folded in her lap, staring vacantly out into the backyard. Dad held me even tighter.

"Do you want me to call anyone?" I asked through my tears.

Mom didn't respond. Neither did Dad. We just watched the footage of the radar screen with its circular green arm sweeping and a tiny green blip that represented my sister's life. Then the blip was gone. The bottom of the screen read BREAKING NEWS.

I asked again, "Do you want me to call anyone?"

Dad didn't have words. He looked at Mom. She shook her head.

They hadn't begun to absorb this yet. They certainly couldn't find the words to tell my brother and sisters or Chuck. The longer they put off telling anyone, the less real it would be. I tried to make them drink coffee but the mugs just sat beside them. Finally, I ran upstairs and got dressed. I took my sister's photo from the frame of the mirror, lay down on the unmade bed, and tried to make myself cry, but I just couldn't. All of this just didn't seem possible.

"Jeannie! Where are you?" I heard Mom's hysterical voice from below.

"I'm here, Mom. I'm right here." I ran to the top of the stairs and looked down to where she was clutching the banister. She was swaying like she was about to faint and I ran down the stairs two at a time to catch her. Instead, she grabbed on to me and said, "Don't go out of my sight." With my arms around her, I led her gently back to the living room and turned off the television set.

"The army said they would send someone to see us," Dad said dully.

We all sat in silence. After a while, I said, "I'm driving to the lake."

Mom burst into tears and begged me not to leave her. Dad soothed her by wrapping his arms around her again and he nodded at me to go. He knew I needed the solace of the lake. Appropriately, the rain had not let up from last night's storm. I ran to the car and drove down Ruddiman Drive, past the Bear Lake Tavern, past Bay Mills Harbor, and into the state park to Lake Michigan. I pulled over on the side of the road, where the beach grass was whipping in the wind and the lake was kicking up whitecaps fifty feet away. I watched the rain slide down the windshield in long gray teardrops. Somewhere out there in all that vastness of water was Lucy. I closed my eyes. How could my beloved lake have done this to me? To her? Or maybe I should be happy that it had happened here and not in some strange state.

Maybe the lake had cushioned her and the other twenty-seven people, opening its welcoming arms to them.

I stared out of the driver's window, willing myself away from Lake Michigan. On the other side of the road was the Sugarbowl. With the exception of the Sleeping Bear Dunes farther north, the Sugarbowl was one of the few gigantic sand dunes left. During winter, a few hardy souls would drag toboggans or inner tubes to the top. The climb, particularly in deep snow, could take more than an hour. Lucy had done it just before she ran off to the army. The white world blurring by her, she had missed a turn and gone over a twenty-foot cliff. When her friends helped her into the house, Lucy was hypothermic and bruised on her arms, legs, and tailbone. Mom insisted on taking her to the hospital for X-rays. The doctor said it was pretty miraculous that she hadn't been hurt more badly, particularly her spine. He'd seen a lot of less fortunate Sugarbowl sledders. That's the way things had always been in our family until now—a lot of near misses but no direct hits.

I pulled back onto the rain-slicked road and knew I had to go to Evan's house. When I arrived, I pounded on the door over and over. It was only 7:30 in the morning and they were still sound asleep. Finally, Evan opened the door. "Jesus Christ, stop making all that noise." He shuffled back inside, leaving the door open for me.

"Evan?"

He turned back to me. I wasn't wearing a coat and my shirt was soaked through. Water was running down my face and hair. He stood still where he was. He knew. He didn't know which one, but he knew it was one of us. He grabbed his coat and threw it on. He yelled to Anna to meet us at Mom and Dad's and tore out the door with me behind him.

"Evan, let me drive." I shoved him away from the driver's side. He pounded the roof of the car with a fist and started crying as

I poured out the story. When we got home he didn't even wait for me to stop before jumping out and running up the walkway. When I got into the house, Dad was holding Evan just like he had held Mom. Evan's glasses were askew from being pressed against Dad's shoulder and he reached blindly up and took them off. Dad continued to hold him tight.

"Okay, son, okay, okay," Dad said over and over.

Grandma was sitting at the table, silent for once. Mom was where I had left her.

Evan pulled back from Dad. "Did you call the Coast Guard?"

"No, Evan, the army said they were handling it."

"Screw that. The local Coast Guard will be in on the rescue for sure." Evan picked up the phone. He dialed the number from memory. "Stevie? It's Captain Evan Thompson." He paused and I knew what was being expressed on the other line. Evan listened and hung up the phone without saying good-bye.

He went to Dad and, mindful of Mom, kept his voice low. "They've located nine bodies so far. None of them are Lucy. Stevie Larson is on the rescue crew and he went to high school with her, so he's looking hard."

"All of those poor children," Mom moaned. "Their parents. Oh God."

The day dragged on. Anna came over and made food that no one ate. Every time the telephone rang, Evan would leap up to answer it. The passenger list hadn't been released to the public yet so he knew it would be the Coast Guard calling to give their colleague the latest news.

Around 4 p.m., Buddy started to bark, and I realized he had been silent all day. Sensing the tragedy, he had never even asked to be let out. The rain was still coming down hard. I opened the front door and saw that he was barking because a large black car had pulled up. It must be the army. I looked back over my shoulder at my parents. I wasn't sure they could take the finality of the news that was being brought to our door. Quietly I let myself out and waited on the top step of the porch. The back door of the Lincoln opened and a uniformed figure emerged. The figure turned back to the car and took a large duffel bag from the backseat, then started up our walk. The person's hat was down against the rain. I wondered why the car was pulling away. Were there other parents in our town to be informed?

Then Lucy lifted her head and waved at me. "Hey."

"Hey, yourself," I said faintly as Lucy came up the steps. She dropped the duffel at my feet and hugged me.

"Can you get this? My back is killing me." She left me standing on the porch and I heard her call out from inside the front door, "Hi, guys, I'm home and I'm starving. What a trip."

There was a momentary silence and then a roar of joyous commotion. I sagged down and onto the top step. Buddy licked my hand.

Lucy had missed her connecting flight. She was supposed to go from San Francisco to Dallas, Dallas to Atlanta, Atlanta to Marquette, Marquette to Grand Rapids. She got into Atlanta at about nine o'clock and the flight to Marquette didn't take off until midnight. She lay down on the airport floor, put her head on her duffel, and fell sound asleep. Lucy never could stay awake past ten o'clock.

Another near miss.

She had taken the next flights she could, then grabbed a ride home with the Longs, whom she happened to meet up with at the Grand Rapids airport. Evan was on the phone with the Coast

Guard when I walked back into the house. I could hear a whoop of happiness from the other end. He hung up and said, "Stevie Larson and the rest of the crew say welcome home."

"I'm glad we didn't call Elizabeth and Sammie," I said. "They would have been on a plane by now." Mom kept crushing Lucy in hugs. Lucy put up with it for a while and then finally shrugged her off.

"Mom! I'm alive," she said grouchily.

Dad was sitting across from her looking drained but relieved. He reached out and rubbed her hand. "We are just so happy to see you, Velvet."

"Why is it that every time I come home there's some big drama going on about me that I don't know anything about?" Lucy demanded.

I pushed her hat down over her eyes. She laughed and took it off. Then we watched a squirrel try out the new bird feeder. He went back and forth onto the perch several times. Off the perch, food available. On the perch, no food available. He continued trying to figure out this new complication for some time.

Grandma got out her deck of cards. "Want me to read you, Lucy?" she asked helpfully.

"No!" Mom and I said in unison.

"Your mother never did like me," Grandma huffed to me, as though Mom wasn't two feet away.

"You don't like her either," I volunteered. When Mom shot me a look that said, "Shut up," I knew everything was back to normal. Evan and Anna finally left. Much later, I woke up and watched the shadows of the trees play against the bedroom wall, where cupcakes and sundaes abounded. I looked over to where, in the darkness, Lucy's picture was back in its place on the mirror. Lucy had let me stay in her room so I wouldn't have to move all of my stuff. I got up and tiptoed down the hall and opened the door to the guest room. "Lucy?"

She rolled over sleepily. "What?"

"I've got sparklers."

She rolled back over and punched her pillow. "Go away."

"I've got Roman candles, too."

She sat up. "The jumbo kind?"

"Of course."

Lucy threw back the sheet and got out of bed. She grabbed a pair of shorts to go with her T-shirt nightie. Then we made our way out into the stillness of the night. The storm had passed over us by now but it had brought out the inevitable swarm of insects. "Damn mosquitoes," Lucy whispered, and slapped her legs. We felt our way quietly down the stairs to the beach. When our feet hit sand, we began the ritual. We took the Roman candles and stuck them in the sand, loosely forming a square.

"Ready?" I asked. In response, she scraped a match on a box and handed the little flame to me. Then she lit one for herself. On her nod, we bent to light them. Then we quickly lit the sparklers we each held in our hands. A piercing shriek split the night air as the first fireballs shot up and over Bear Lake. It was our signal to start. Lucy and I danced around and around the flaming candles, which shot off brightly colored comets at regular intervals. Matching arcs of color reflected on the dark water. We waved the sparklers and chanted, "Hail to the Fairy Gods! Hail to the Fairy Gods!" until the last pop came out of the rockets and the sparklers fizzled out. Then we collapsed on the beach, laughing.

"Wow, I'd forgotten all about that," Lucy said, out of breath.

"I know the Fourth of July was a couple of days ago, but it still seemed appropriate." Every Fourth of July since I was about five and she was seven, we had performed this ritual. We thought of it as a prayer, to whatever God might be listening, to grant us another good year. As we got older, we thought it was uncool. Somewhere along the line, the ritual died. Until tonight.

We lay on the sand watching for shooting stars but didn't see any. Finally, we walked back up to the house with our arms slung over each other's shoulders. We weren't very quiet with our giggling. Not that it mattered. We had probably woken up the entire town with the Roman candles. We went to our separate rooms and, finally, I could sleep.

Twenty

April 2006

*A*idan and I snuggled on the couch watching *Antiques Roadshow* to see who had hit it big with their grandmother's ugly vase. I was always amazed that some expert was inevitably there who instantly knew that the vase was from the tenth century, worth four thousand dollars, and made by a guy named Furtzenhaagen or whatever.

During a commercial break Aidan said, "Jeannie? I want to meet your family."

"Sure, all right." My eyes never left the television. There was a really good ad on for a film from a rival studio.

"Jeannie." Aidan shook my arm. "I mean it."

My attention shifted away from the TV. "Have you been listening to this crazy story I've been telling you?"

"Sure. You grew up in a zoo. So what?" Aidan gestured in impatience and somehow managed to knock over the glass of soda next to him on the low side table.

I leapt to my feet, went to the kitchen, and found the paper towels and 409. Coming back, I got to my knees beside the table. "Aidan," I said, while wiping away the soda, "I've already lost one husband partially because of my family. They do nutty things, and I do nutty things right along with them, and I can't bear to bring someone home who doesn't embrace that. It's just too painful." I sprayed the 409 on the table and wiped it down. Then I started scrubbing at the rug. "What if you can't deal with them either?" Bits of paper towel were now ground into the rug by my ferocious cleaning.

"Bring me home to Michigan and let's find out. Or start with Sammie and Elizabeth. They live right here in Los Angeles. You talk to them practically every day." Aidan had raised his voice because I had darted to the hallway closet to get the vacuum.

"Come on, Jeannie. It's time to get over this ridiculous fear."

I plugged in the vacuum, snapped it on, and started vacuuming under Aidan's feet. The paper towel bits were stubbornly clinging to the threads in the rug. You'd think with all that suction they would have let go by now. I pushed back and forth harder.

"Jeannie!" Aidan had raised his legs so I could get under them. "Jeannie!" I saw his lips move but the roar of the vacuum erased his words. "*Jeannie!*"

The vacuum went quiet. Aidan stood by the wall with the plug in his hand. "Leave it, Jeannie!"

"But I'm not done yet!"

"It's done." Aidan dropped the cord. Moments later I heard water running in the guest bathroom. When I got to bed, as I suspected, he wasn't there. He was in the guest room, leaving me the master bedroom. I knocked gently at the guest room door. When there was no answer, I leaned my forehead against it and closed my eyes. After a long while, I gave up and crawled under the covers of a bed that was much too large.

I had been awake for hours but when my cell phone rang I bolted up, scattering pillows. No one ever called quite this late unless something terrible had happened.

"What's wrong?" My voice sounded hysterical.

"I see you know about it already and you're upset too!" An equally hysterical voice came through the wire.

"What happened?"

"It's horrible! Just horrible!"

"What? Was there a car accident? Was anyone hurt?" My voice was rising.

"What car? I'm talking about my hair! Are you on drugs or something?" Esperanza fairly screamed at me.

I slumped over in relief that no family member was in jeopardy. "I was in bed."

"Are you home sick? Why are you sleeping in the afternoon?" The starlet's voice changed to sugar in half a heartbeat—not because she was concerned about me but because she figured she should feign concern about me.

"It's three forty-two in the morning here. You must be mixed up with the time change to Bali." I rubbed my eyes.

"Time change? What are you talking about?" she demanded.

"Bali is something like ten hours ahead of Los Angeles." This conversation was becoming too technical for me at this hour.

"It is?" She sounded surprised. "Is that why I was so tired when I got off the plane?"

"Yes." I pulled the covers over my head with my ear still pressed to my phone. "That would be why."

She began to prattle that Bali was beautiful and I really should try and come, but to stay at the Four Seasons because anywhere else was just so third-world, and then, why bother?

"Do you mind if we talk about this in a few hours?" I whispered.

"I can't. I have to get ready to go to dinner with the director. Have I told you about the director? He's fabulous."

I knew about the director. A famous womanizer. Seemed as though Esperanza had moved on to greener pastures than Stripe. I also knew I was going to have to get up. "Hold on," I said. I made my way out to the kitchen, where I scrambled for a pen and a piece of paper. I settled for the back of an old envelope. "Okay, tell me the problem with the hair."

She went on for ten minutes about how great the poster was but there was a "tiny little doohickey on the left, no the right, no the left, side of my hair—can it be removed?" she inquired. Practically sobbing, she said that it reminded her of her third grade class photo—a picture that she had never gotten over because her hair was sticking up and her classmates had teased her unmercifully. Now her hair was sticking up again and it brought back such bad memories that she was flying her therapist to Bali.

My head was in my hands. "Yes, it can be removed." I didn't even need to take notes for this one. "I'll send it to you for final approval in a day or so."

"That's okay. I trust you. Just fix it and go ahead and print it," Esperanza said now in a cheerful tone. Finally, I was able to extricate myself from the voluble star and make my way back to bed, turning off the lights as I went.

In the morning Aidan was already gone when I finally dragged myself from bed. No note, no kiss good-bye. Checking the clock, I saw that I had overslept. Shit, today of all days. I had a meeting with Rachael and Stripe to discuss the disastrous *TechnoCat* trailer. With no time for a shower, I stuck my hair in a ponytail, pulled on the clothes I could find the fastest, and flew out the door. I could do my makeup while I was stopped at red lights.

In the car, my cell phone rang and I pressed the button on the steering wheel to answer it hands free. It was Lucy. "I'm coming out to L.A. for a couple of days," she said. "You still have that extra bedroom, right?" My hands tightened on the steering wheel as Lucy's voice filled the car.

"That's not going to work out, Lucy. I'm going to be out of town."

"I haven't even told you when I'm coming yet," Lucy snipped. "And if you're out of town, you won't be using your house anyway."

Lucy had, for a long time, been a high-powered litigator at a major law firm in New York City. When her daughter was born, several years ago, she had given it up to be a part of a smaller company in Connecticut.

"My client doesn't have a lot of money, Jeannie. I'd like to save him a few dollars by not billing him for a hotel stay while I do the depositions for his case," Lucy continued. "I'll arrive on Sunday and will only stay for a couple of nights."

At a red light I grabbed my iPhone and checked my calendar. Aidan was going to be out of town Saturday through Wednesday.

"Sounds great." I was now sincere. I hadn't seen Lucy in a few years and it would be good to catch up with her in person— especially since I now realized Aidan would be in Vancouver at the time. Lucy said good-bye and I merged onto the freeway, my eyes glazing over in the perpetual traffic jam called the 405 South.

Ten miles and forty-five minutes later I arrived at the studio. Caitlin met me in the hallway outside my office, thrust a cup of coffee in my hand, and spun me around in the direction of Rachael's office. "You're late. Stripe is already in there with Rachael."

Balancing the coffee, I quickened my pace, all while disengaging my backpack and purse, then pushing them into Caitlin's arms. As I was reaching for Rachael's door, Caitlin said, "Jeannie, there's one more thing. You need to know that . . ."

I pushed through the door and didn't hear the rest. I should have waited. In Rachael's spacious office, seated in the plushy leather chairs, were Rachael, Stripe, and Katsu. They were just finishing laughing at something and turned to face me like I was an unwelcome interruption in their important day. Katsu, in his crisp Armani suit, looked me up and down and I became acutely aware of how I must look. Hair in a ponytail, jeans and white blouse, and oh God, had I forgotten to put on makeup in the car? I had. Lucy's call had distracted me. Taking a deep breath, I strode into the room with a lot more confidence than I felt and sat down in the fourth chair.

"I guess we can get started," Rachael said, "now that Jeannie has finally decided to grace us with her presence."

I fumed inwardly. I was ten minutes late. How many days had I shown up here at 8 a.m. after working until midnight? Rachael gestured to Katsu. "Katsu, we're looking forward to seeing the trailer you cut for *TechnoCat*. Jeannie has been having some problems with it, as you know."

I kept my face impassive but inwardly I was screaming, "Fuck you! I came up with a trailer that audiences loved. I did my job!" Aidan probably would have been proud of me, had I managed to say this aloud. Instead I finished up my silent ranting with another "Fuck you" for good measure.

Katsu stood and strode to insert the DVCAM into the deck beneath the giant monitor. As is custom, he stood to one side as the trailer played. I held my breath. Was it going to be any good? More importantly, was it going to be better than what I had done?

One minute into the trailer, I exhaled. Not only was the trailer not any good, it phenomenally sucked. Instead of feeling like a blockbuster movie, it felt like a small indie movie about a young girl crying over the death of her mother. There was no mention of superpowers or cool gadgets or big explosions. With a trailer like this, *TechnoCat* would open to about four cents at the box office. I was delighted but kept my face carefully expressionless. When it was over, Katsu came and sat back down. Then he and I looked at Rachael and Stripe. Rachael spoke first.

"Katsu, that was terrific. Really unusual thinking, which is what we need right now," Rachael said. Katsu couldn't quite hide his smile.

"I loved it," Stripe intoned solemnly. "I wouldn't change one frame." Katsu puffed up visibly.

Looking from one to the other I wondered, Are these people crazy? They have hundreds of millions of dollars on the line. I felt like I was in upside-down land.

Rachael stood and crossed the room to get herself some green tea. Her movements were slow and measured. When she returned I realized she had been buying time to think. Her words seemed carefully chosen. "This trailer is excellent. But, Stripe, I think we need your magic here." Stripe might have been surprised at this turn but he was an old Hollywood player. His face gave nothing up. "You had an idea for a special shoot. I think we should do that shoot, look at the trailer that comes out of it, then decide between that one and the one Katsu has just cut."

Stripe sat back in his chair. "Seems like a waste of money. We have a trailer right here that works."

"But it's such a brilliant idea." Rachael stroked him with her words, then stuck in the knife. "And we need to explore every possibility with a film that is costing the studio this much money." Ouch, I thought. She had just reminded Stripe about the cost over-runs he had incurred while making the film. I watched them swat the political ball back and forth like a fast-paced tennis match.

"Well, the marketing dollars are on your head," Stripe said in a jovial tone. "It's up to you if you want to spend money recklessly like that." He paused and seemed to consider for a moment, glancing at Katsu. Then he stood up and began gathering his things. "Sure, I'll do it. We'd better get cracking though. Katsu, you and I should meet today about getting this shoot together."

"Not Katsu," Rachael said evenly. "Jeannie will handle the pro-duction. Katsu has no experience with this kind of thing. Jeannie has handled plenty of special shoots."

Stripe gazed at her a moment too long. Then with a nod of his head he exited. Katsu said good-bye and strode out as well.

I stood in the middle of Rachael's office, not sure of what had just transpired.

"Rachael?"

"Yes?" She sat at her desk, studying the trade magazines and sipping her green tea.

"What the hell is going on around here?"

"I'll let you know when I know." She never looked up, not even as I quietly left her office.

Twenty-one

July 1986

*M*om immediately got down to business. "How do you want your eggs?" she asked Lucy.

Lucy popped the top on a Tab. "I don't want any eggs."

"So, tell me, what's wrong?" Mom demanded from the stove.

"Mooooommm." Lucy stretched it out into a two-syllable word. "I haven't even woken up yet."

Mom put a plate down in front of Lucy. "Here are your eggs."

"Does she not listen to me?" Lucy asked me.

Mom pointed a spatula at her. "Eat. Then we're going to shake this thing out."

"What 'thing'? You don't even know yet if there *is* a 'thing,'" Lucy complained.

"*Is* there a 'thing'?" I asked.

Lucy poked at her eggs. "Yes." Then she made a face and pushed the plate away. Mom watched her for a second. "I knew it." She sat down. "You're pregnant." She was careful not to show any expression until Lucy let her know how she should feel. Happy? Not happy?

Lucy looked up at her, and tears ran down her face. Ah. Not happy. "I just don't know how this could have happened," she wailed.

I opened my mouth to knock this easy ball out of the park, but Mom put her hand on my knee. Mom wisely didn't say anything until Lucy had spit out the story as fast as a chipmunk on speed: she and Chuck weren't getting along, but they got along once in a while, hence the baby, but she had been on birth control; she might have forgotten a couple of pills, but could you really get pregnant if you missed just a couple of pills, okay, it was two weeks worth of pills, but still, and she and Chuck fought a lot, but maybe everybody did, and if they lived together instead of apart maybe it would be easier. Lucy paused for breath and Mom patted her shoulder. Then Mom got up to get Lucy soda crackers and a can of flat Coke that was in the refrigerator. Lucy continued. What was she going to do with a baby? She wanted to go back to school and who could do that with a baby, but she knew that Mom went to school when she had a baby, but what was Chuck going to do for a job, and her whole life was over, and she was tired of everything being so hard. She stopped, made a twisted face, then raced out of the kitchen and threw up mightily in the bathroom.

Grandma came and took Lucy's place at the table. "I would like to get out of this house and go for a walk."

Mom took this as a good cue for me. "Jeannie, why don't you help your grandmother into her wheelchair and take her out for a while? Buddy, too," she said as an afterthought.

We heard Lucy retch again.

"Is that girl pregnant?" Grandma demanded. "Bad business, babies. Never could stand 'em. Lumpy lumps of flesh." I was glad

Dad wasn't around to hear this from his mother. My own mother was getting the wheelchair out of the hall closet and didn't hear her, which was a good thing, because Mom probably wouldn't have let this one go unanswered. I loaded Grandma into the chair and nearly lost her down the ramp.

"There's a brake on the left side," Grandma instructed over her shoulder. I pushed her down the street while Buddy pulled at his leash, trying to go any way but the way I was going. We strolled up to where volunteers were setting up tables and chairs in Custer Park for the ice cream social. It was starting later today, with a parade featuring the Shriners, the fire truck, and the high school band. Mrs. Mearston came over to say hello.

"Hi, Jeannie," she said, and then in that cooey voice people use with old people and dogs, she said, "And who might this be?" She knew Buddy, so I assumed she meant my grandmother. I introduced them, then continued wheeling Grandma through the park. After fifteen minutes I figured Mom had had enough alone time with Lucy so I took her home.

Lucy was curled up in Dad's red chair and Mom was on the phone. I helped Grandma out of her wheelchair and stuck her at the kitchen table with her deck of cards. She immediately began playing solitaire.

"What's going on?" I asked Lucy.

"She's making an appointment for me. She wants me to see a counselor so I can understand all my options."

"Did she say what she thinks you should do?"

Lucy looked at me wearily. "You know she would never do that. If I have it, she'll say I made the right decision, and if I *don't* have it, she'll say I made the right decision."

"If you knew that already, why did you come all the way home to talk it over?" I asked.

"Because she's the only one who knows exactly what to say to me."

Mom hung up the phone and told Lucy to get her coat. The counselor would see Lucy right then since she had to leave in a few days to get back to base. When they left, I was feeling a little lonely, so I decided to make brownies. I don't care if they come out of a box; I am proud of my brownies. Tom, the handyman, knocked on the back door just as I was pulling them out of the oven

"When did you suddenly start knocking?" I asked as I opened the door. He trailed in behind me.

"Seemed the polite thing to do, since you have company."

I was puzzled until I realized he meant Grandma.

"Your dad said he was leaving me a check, and there should be a big manila envelope here for me, too."

I looked on the counter but didn't see them. Searching in the mess of papers on top of the refrigerator I finally located both the check and the envelope. Eyeing the mound of letters and junk mail, I itched to organize it all. But I knew Mom and Dad would kill me if I changed their "system," as they called it. Climbing down from the chair that was my ladder, I handed the items to Tom. He peered into the empty Mr. Coffee, then looked at me, wounded.

"We're out," I explained. "Want a Coke?"

"Nah." He took off his John Deere hat and scratched his head. "But I'll take a brownie." He sat down at the table and I put the whole pan in front of him. He delicately cut out a piece and looked at me. "What? Do you live in a barn? Can a guy get a plate around here?"

I looked right back at him. "You know where they are." It's not like I was running a restaurant or something. This guy spent more time at our house than I did.

Tom went to the cupboard. When he sat back down, Grandma shuffled in and sat with him. "Did you bring these?" she asked him.

"No, Mrs. Thompson." Tom smiled. "Jeannie made them."

"They haven't had food in this house for days," Grandma insisted. She jerked her head at me. "Her father lost his job, you know."

Tom snapped his head around to me. "What? Jeannie, you didn't tell me!" He fingered the check in his hand like it could bounce right then and there. "You would have thought it would be in the paper, with your Dad being the county administrator and all. Do you have today's *Chronicle*?"

Oh, for crying out loud, I thought. Tom had the biggest mouth in town. Now this rumor would be all over the place. "Grandma!" I said sharply. "You know very well that Dad did not lose his job. Will you please stop saying things like that?"

Grandma leaned over and whispered loudly to Tom, "The kids are always the last to know."

Tom nodded conspiratorially, then got up and took another brownie with him. As he was heading out the door I asked, "What's in the envelope anyway?"

"Your parents' taxes."

"What are you doing with that?"

"It's time for them to file. I got them an extension in April, but they need to get these finished up now to avoid late penalties. Course, with your father losing his job and all, there may be complications."

I stared at our handyman, who apparently was also (hopefully) an accountant. "I didn't realize you were a jack of so many trades."

Tom stopped at the door. "I graduated first in my class in undergrad and grad school at Northwestern. But accounting is so damn boring. I just do it for the cash once in a while." He slammed the door behind him and I heard him pull the cord on the lawnmower. After a couple of tries, it came to life. I watched him run over half the marigolds while wheeling the mower to the lawn. He paused, looked back at the marigolds, shook his head, and began mowing.

I turned back to Grandma. "Why do you keep saying Dad lost his job?"

"There are some things adults don't tell children," she said. "They think you're too young to know."

I was wrapping up the rest of the brownies in Saran Wrap when I remembered Elizabeth's hysterical phone call to the Blit. That had been night before last. In the panic of thinking Lucy was dead, I had forgotten about her. I picked up the phone and dialed.

"Elizabeth?"

"Hi, Jeannie."

"Are you okay?"

"I don't know why you care. You didn't even call me back yesterday."

"We thought Lucy was dead, but it turned out she was all right. So we were busy, sorry."

I could feel Elizabeth's exasperation humming over the line. She said tartly, "I have a real life problem and Mom decided that one of us was dead again? She has got to stop imagining things."

"We had more evidence than usual so you can't blame Mom this time. But anyway, what's wrong?"

"I'm moving home."

I leaned against the wall and slid to the floor with the phone still to my ear. This was going to be a long call.

Elizabeth sobbed out her story. My liberated sister had agreed

to having only Ron's name on the checking account. She dutifully signed her name on the back of every paycheck she got and
turned it over to him. He took care of, or was supposed to take
care of, the bills. Today, a repo man had come to her door to re-
possess the car that had just been sold.

"Where was the money going?" I was bewildered.

"Who knows? There may also be a woman involved in all of
this somewhere."

I could hear the heaviness in her voice as she continued. "He
told me he was a therapist. But whenever I call his office, he's not
there. So I asked some people who work in offices on the same
floor if they ever see him. They didn't even know who he was. I
don't think he was working at all."

"Mom will be back soon. Do you want me to keep quiet or do
you want me to tell her you're coming home because Ron took
all of your money?"

After a long pause, Elizabeth said, "Tell her I'm coming home
because I'm pregnant." Then she hung up the phone. I got up
from the floor and put the phone back in its cradle. I could hear
the band warming up for the parade. It was almost noon. When
the firehouse blew its whistle, then the parade would start. It was
a source of consternation to most of the town that the firehouse
blew its whistle every single day at noon. It wasn't a pleasant
sound, like church bells. It was a horn that sounded like we were
being warned that the Japanese were flying in for a bombing raid
on North Muskegon. It went on for a full minute and had been
doing so since 1943. After Mr. Vanderman dropped dead unex-
pectedly at 12:01 one day, Mrs. Vanderman petitioned to stop the
infernal noise. But the city council voted her down because they
said that since he was raised in this town he should have been
used to, and therefore should have expected, the racket.

I suddenly realized Grandma wasn't anywhere in sight. I checked the sliding doors but they were closed.

"Grandma?" I called. There was no answer. I didn't think she could make it up the stairs by herself but maybe she had tried. I called up the stairs, but again there was no answer. She wasn't anywhere in the house. I went outside and tried to make myself heard over the lawnmower. "Hey, Tom!" Finally, he looked up and put a hand to his ear, and then he bent over and shut off the machine. Just then the noon whistle went off and we were both rendered speechless for the full minute. We stood with our fingers in our ears until it died away.

"Have you seen Grandma?" I asked.

"Nah, but I haven't really been looking. I meditate when I cut lawns. It's a Buddhist method that—"

I cut him off. "I'd love to know more, but I have to find Grandma." I ran back inside to double-check the house. She hadn't reappeared in the kitchen. As I was deciding where to look next, the phone rang.

"Jeannie, honey, this is Mrs. Mearston."

"Oh, hi, Mrs. Mearston."

"Honey, I just wanted to let you know I saw your grandmother wheeling up the street. She's headed for the ice cream social."

I didn't wait to hear any more. "Thanks, I'll run up and get her right now." I hung up quickly and ran out to the garage and grabbed the green Schwinn. I would have to wheel the bike and Grandma back. I pedaled up the street until I saw the crowd gathered for the parade. As I got closer, I noticed there was an opening in the crowd, like everyone was avoiding something. I got off the bike and put the kickstand down. Leaving it on the sidewalk, I trotted into the mass of people. I heard some shrieks and ran faster. I spotted Grandma in her wheelchair, all right. She was tearing through the crowd like a scythe in a field. I stopped cold. Mrs. Mearston had neglected to tell me that Grandma was bare-ass naked. I yelled for her to come back, but either she was ignoring me or couldn't hear me over the John Philip Sousa music the band was playing. Several people turned to me. "Is that your grandmother, Jeannie?" one asked.

"Yes," I said as I pushed on toward Grandma.

"She's trying to catch a cold," someone yelled after me, "but she's not running fast enough!"

Very funny. I saw an opening in the crowd and made a break through it. I was yelling her name now. "Pearl! Pearl! Come back here!" My face was bright red, and it wasn't from exertion. She looked over her shoulder and caught sight of me, but instead of stopping, she sped up. Grandma's wheelchair clipped a table ahead of me and knocked it over. Paper cups and lemonade went flying, and two little girls started crying. When their moms ran over to see what was wrong, the girls pointed at my grandmother. "That mean, naked lady knocked over our stand."

The red and white paper tablecloth from the stand was now entangled in the wheelchair. Grandma, seeing I was gaining on her, stood up and moved faster than I have ever seen her move. Boobs flopping, butt swaying, she ran toward the only open space, the street. If she kept going, she was in danger of being run over by the fire truck leading the parade. Forgetting my complete embarrassment, I darted and dodged through the crowd even faster. I had gone from thinking I would be teased unmercifully for the rest of my life to thinking I was going to be responsible for letting my grandmother get squashed by a fire truck.

"Please, someone stop her," I yelled out. A few men standing on the curb glanced over and saw the commotion. One of them jogged over and grabbed Grandma by the wrist. They struggled long enough for the fire truck to pass by without incident. But then Grandma twisted away from him and ran into the baton twirlers who were leading the band. She bumped into one short-skirted, tassel-booted, glittery girl, who dropped her baton. Like a trouper, the girl picked it up, glued her smile back on, and proceeded up the street. The rest of the parade parted to go around my grandmother, who was frozen in the middle of the street.

"Excuse me," I said to a group seated around a picnic table as I swept aside paper plates and plastic forks. "I need this." I pulled the paper tablecloth off and took it with me into the street and wrapped it around my grandma. She was shivering. Mindless of the band that was making its way around either side of us, I rocked her back and forth as I'd seen my father do to my mother. I lay my head on top of hers. "It's okay," I soothed. Someone had retrieved her wheelchair and, in a break in the parade, raced it out to us.

"Thank you," I murmured as I lowered my grandmother into her chair, careful to keep the tablecloth wrapped around her. With my head held high, I wheeled her to a side street and headed for home. When I opened the gate to push the wheelchair through, Tom came running to help me.

"Is she all right?" He looked down at her, concerned.

"I think so." I pushed my hair out of my eyes. "She's pretty shaken up and I'm not sure she knows where she is."

Tom took command and pushed her up the ramp. Then he lifted her, still wrapped in the tablecloth, out of the chair and carried her upstairs. I followed and, after gesturing to Tom to leave the bedroom, helped Grandma swing her legs up and into bed. I threw the tablecloth into the bathroom wastebasket. After making sure she was asleep, I went back outside. "Thanks, Tom," I said.

"No problem," he said. He took his hat off and rubbed his head while he looked out over the garden. "One day we all might be in that situation. I just hope my family is around to help out like yours."

I sat down cross-legged in the grass and plucked a dandelion puff that Tom had missed. "You don't think we're all crazy?"

"I didn't say you weren't all crazy. But I've never seen a family pull for each other so much. That doesn't seem like a bad thing to me."

"Sometimes I think it's actually a curse," I said, staring at the grass.

"Then think of it as a warm and comforting curse." Tom ruffled my hair and went to put the lawnmower away. I looked closely at the white spokes of the dandelion, then brushed its softness against my cheek—little seeds just waiting to land somewhere, plant their roots, and start growing on their own. I closed my eyes, blew on it, and made a wish. When I opened my eyes, the white seeds were floating around my head, catching the sun.

Twenty-two

April 2006

The next morning was spent with Stripe going over his special shoot concept. Stripe insisted that Katsu be in the room with us. "So we'll start the piece with a man entering the alley with a gun."

"Stripe, that's brilliant," Katsu solemnly intoned, "simply brilliant."

He said something to this effect after practically every word Stripe uttered. I kept quiet, took notes, and tried to figure out how we were going to shoot this within budget.

The afternoon was spent trying to persuade the star of *Jet Fuel*, Jeff Cross, to fly from New York to Los Angeles for an advertising photo shoot. Normally I would have done the shoot in New York, but the rest of the *Jet Fuel* cast—who also needed to be photographed—was still here in Los Angeles. Also, the concepts for the poster called for the talent to be shot on the fabulously expensive film sets that had been created here on the studio lot.

"I'm not coming," Jeff told me on the phone after he had slurped noisily through a straw. With my elbow on my desk I rubbed my forehead. This was the third phone call I'd had with him. And the answer was still the same. No. Jeff continued, "I haven't seen Stephanie in almost a month so I'm staying here with her in New York."

I didn't have to ask who Stephanie was. Jeff Cross and Stephanie Langer were a hot item and had become darlings of the press. Stephanie, in addition to being a well-known movie star, was the lead singer of a band that had shot to the top. The two of them had been nicknamed Jeffanie and they couldn't even go to Starbucks without attracting throngs of paparazzi.

"What if we fly Stephanie here with you? I'll put the two of you up in a suite at the Four Seasons," I begged.

There was a long pause. Then, "First class plane seats and spa treatments every day for the both of us," he announced. I perked up. This wasn't so bad. These were pretty typical demands. I quickly agreed and hung up. Then I juggled phone calls and meetings and reviewed tapes of trailers and TV spots that needed major revisions. All the while I waited for Aidan to call me. But no.

When I finally looked at my watch it was almost 9:30 at night. I decided Aidan and I needed to have a long talk.

When I entered Aidan's door a half hour later, I was startled to find him in the living room with two women. One of them happened to be the number one female star in America and the other was Montana. Aidan and I would have to put off our talk for another time.

"Hi," I stammered to Veronica Robison as I put down my backpack. "I'm Aidan's girlfriend, Jeannie."

Veronica took my proffered hand. "I'm Veronica. It's nice to finally meet you. Aidan talks about you all of the time." I couldn't take my eyes off her. She was every bit as beautiful in person as she was on-screen. Not only that, but she actually seemed like a normal human being. I became uncomfortably aware of my tangled hair and lack of makeup. By the end of a day, I pretty much looked like I had been through the wringer, as my mom would say. Montana looked elegant and confident as she lounged next to Aidan. She had a polite smile glued to her face that told me I had interrupted a pleasant evening.

Aidan asked me if I wanted a drink, but I shook my head. What I really wanted was to escape to the bedroom, quickly put some lipstick on, and lose ten pounds before I reappeared. "We were just discussing our next film," Aidan told me. I was pleased for him. He had been trying to land Veronica Robison for almost two years.

"Then we got on to the subject of babies," Veronica smiled.

"She saw the photos of my stepbrother and -sister and thought they were ours," Aidan explained.

"I would love to have a baby," Veronica said. "But I seem to keep doing movies one after another that involve either some nudity or stunts or both."

"Aidan loves kids," Montana cooed. This was true. Aidan made sure he spent time with Max and Audrey, his half-siblings. He'd taken them on ski trips and had hosted many a birthday party. He genuinely liked their company and I did too. They were fun, smart, and funny.

Having a baby still seemed like an abstract idea to me. But both of us could hear my biological clock ticking loud and clear. Since I was the last kid in my family, I had never really spent time around babies. I had never done any babysitting. Instead, I had worked at jobs like making twirly cones at the Whippi Dip.

"Yeah, I really want a couple of kids," Aidan said.

Montana looked at me pointedly. "Well then, honey, you'd better hurry." Bitch, I thought. Like I needed any reminders of my age.

"I'm trying to have a baby," Montana announced. I snapped to, fast. Whom, exactly, was she trying to have a baby *with*? Which is what Veronica asked her. "I don't really care. I just tell my latest and greatest that I'm on birth control. Men are so stupid; they really are such trusting creatures."

"What happens when the lucky man learns that you're pregnant?" I asked as politely as I could.

"I'll tell him the birth control failed. Then we'll discuss child support and that will be that." Was it my imagination, or was she staring straight at Aidan?

"You would do that to some poor guy?" My brain knew that I should let the subject go, but my mouth couldn't.

"Yeah. I'm raising it so what's the big deal?" Montana recrossed her long legs.

"I could never do that," Veronica said softly. "I couldn't imagine having a baby without the right person." She stood up and shook hands with Aidan. "I have to get going. But I look forward to working with you." She smiled at me and barely nodded her head at Montana. Aidan walked her to the door. Montana left soon after, kissing Aidan on the cheek, while barely acknowledging me. Clearly, she was pissed off that I had challenged her, particularly in front of Veronica. Aidan and I cleared away the dirty glasses.

"Congratulations on landing the one and only Veronica Robison," I said and kissed him as I passed by with my hands full.

Aidan yawned and stretched. "She really likes this script, so it looks like it will go into production soon. Probably shooting in Australia, but Montana is going to do the day-to-day production duties there. I'll handle things here in Los Angeles. But after tonight, I hope she can work with Veronica. I'm not sure the two of them will get along."

"Aidan?"

"Yeah?"

"Has Montana, you know . . ." I looked down in embarrassment. "Well, with all of this talk about wanting a baby, has she
come on to you lately?" When Aidan didn't respond right away, I
looked up. "Well, has she?"

"Sweetie, you know I love you."

"That's not an answer," I said.

He hugged me tightly. "I love you, I'm not in love with Montana, and that's that." I hugged him back, but I was thinking it still
wasn't an answer. Aidan as usual fell asleep the moment the lights
went out. Despite three Tylenol PMs my head spun its constant
chant: Lucy arrived in two days. What if Aidan found out Lucy
was in town? Did my good blue blouse come back from the dry
cleaner's? Why was Rachael throwing me under the bus at work?
I needed to call Sammie and apologize for our big fight. Not to
mention Elizabeth. My car had needed an oil change for seven
months. When was I going to do that? Why was Katsu trying to
get me fired? *Was* he trying to get me fired?

I turned over to look at the clock every twenty minutes until
finally, just past 3 a.m., my eyes closed for good.

The next morning Aidan packed his single carry-on bag with
military efficiency. With a kiss good-bye we parted ways. He was
off to Vancouver for production meetings and to check locations
on yet another film. Even though it was Saturday I headed for the
office. Lucy was coming the next day, and if I got enough done
today I could take some time off on Monday to be with her. She
had said her depositions didn't start until the afternoon.

At the office I plowed through emails that had piled up from
the week. Anything that wasn't urgent I saved for the weekends
or late at night. One had come in from Rachael late yesterday.

It asked when the final poster for *TechnoCat* would be ready to go up in theaters. Shit, I had forgotten to let our print production people know that the poster could go to print. The poster was late and we had all been on pins and needles trying to get the talent approval, which I had gotten days ago. I had simply forgotten about it. What was happening to me? It was like my brain was liquefying.

I went to the office kitchen to make microwave popcorn and try and calm down. Of course, the communal microwave was filthy. Why did people nuke spaghetti and then not clean up the red spatter? I spent fifteen minutes cleaning it out and then I scrubbed the countertop for good measure.

Returning to my office, I decided to not bring attention to my mistake. I replied to Rachael that it could be up in Los Angeles and New York in two days and the rest of the country within three.

Then I sent an urgent email to the ad agency and our print production people. All talent had approved, I typed, the poster numbered 43B Revised. Please push the final artwork and printing of this poster through at all speed.

After another couple of hours, I shut off the lights and headed to my house. First, I stopped by Gelson's to pick up groceries. Lucy would starve with what I kept in my house. After putting everything away in the fridge and cupboards I tackled the guest room. It was already immaculate, but I washed and dried all the sheets and pillowcases anyway. Then I put some yellow daffodils I had bought into a vase and placed it on the guest room nightstand.

Later, curled up with a book in my living room, I idly stared at a framed family photo circa 1982 that sat on the side table. I had really missed Lucy and realized I couldn't wait to see her. Of course, Lucy would want to see Elizabeth and Sammie while she was here, too. I hadn't quite figured out how to deal with that one. Obviously Lucy knew that my other two sisters were angry with me. Our whole family knows every detail of every argument within hours of its occurrence. My mom had been fielding phone calls about my behavior from both Elizabeth and Sammie for weeks now. I knew that because Evan told me. When I tried to tell him my side of the story, Evan had simply said to leave him out of it and let him know when it had blown over. Typical Evan. My dad hadn't said one word about it and probably wouldn't. He had learned a long time ago to stay out of the frothing waters of family drama.

I looked again at the photo of our seven smiling faces and really hoped Lucy's visit didn't turn into a disaster.

Twenty-three

July 1986

$\mathcal{M}$om and Lucy returned from the counselor a few hours after Grandma's naked adventure. I didn't have the heart to tell Mom right away that Grandma and I would probably be on the front page of *The Muskegon Chronicle* in the morning. Both she and Lucy looked worn out. They went into the family room and flopped down on the couch.

"So?" I asked.

"I'm five weeks gone." Lucy was holding a couch pillow to her chest.

I sat in Dad's red chair. "What are you going to do?"

Lucy dug her chin into the pillow. "Dunno."

"Does Chuck know?"

"Yeah." Lucy sighed. "He says it's my decision."

That was a pretty scaredy-cat attitude, I thought. I knew Mom was torn. She was pro-choice but often said that I, her fifth child, was her best argument against abortion. In her heart, she knew that Lucy and Chuck weren't a great match. Lucy was young and didn't have a lot of job prospects. Neither did Chuck. But Mom and Dad had been young with their first kid. I could practically see all this going round and round in her head. Finally, she said, "I'm going to get dinner started," and left for the kitchen.

It seemed like as good a time as any to tell her about my day. I followed her inside. "Mom"—I figured I'd start out slowly—"Tom picked up his check and your tax info today."

"Good," she said, clearly distracted.

"Grandma told Tom that Dad had been fired."

Mom looked up from the onion she was chopping. "She what? I don't know how she gets these things in her head. I'll have to talk to your father about what to do." She pulled out a pan and threw the onions into it.

"I think she doesn't really know what's going on most of the time." Then I told her the rest. "I think we owe the Wilson sisters for their lemonade stand," I finished. Mom didn't seem particularly surprised. But she was chopping tomatoes with a bit more force than necessary.

"Poor thing. She just gets so mixed up," Mom murmured. "Where is she now?"

"In bed. She was really tired," I said.

"I should think so." Mom stirred the tomatoes into the onions. She opened the pantry and took out some of her homemade tomato sauce. I cringed. It qualified as the worst on earth. "That's the last jar up here," Mom said. "I'll have to bring up more from the basement tomorrow." Rats. I thought that was the last jar, period. Every year, I had to ladle the damn stuff into the waiting Mason jars and make sure the rubber ring sealed tightly. Mom would go around behind me checking to make sure none of the lids had popped up, which would mean the jar had air in it and the sauce could go bad. She was always astounded at how bad

I was at getting a tight seal. Little did she know I was doing it on purpose, in self-defense.

"Are you talking about me?" Grandma wobbled in the doorway.

"Pearl! How did you get down the stairs?" Mom ran over to her and helped her to a chair.

"I'm not a complete invalid, you know." Grandma deliberately turned her face away from Mom. "These legs have a few more years in them."

"Mom, there's one more thing," I said.

"Lord, Jeannie! What else could possibly have happened today?"

"Elizabeth's pregnant." At Mom's open mouth, I quickly shot, "And she's moving home." No one had to respond, because Lucy tore through the kitchen right then on her way to the toilet. Her retching was the perfect punctuation to a perfect day.

The next day, Walker called at the crack of dawn. Not even Dad was up yet, and he wasn't happy about being woken up to get the phone. After yelling down the hall to tell me to pick it up, Dad went back to bed.

"Could you please wait to call until normal people are awake?" I groused. "You just got home from fishing, but the rest of us don't live on your schedule."

"Better check out this morning's *Chronicle*," he said. "Front page. Call me back after you read it." He hung up.

The paper was wedged between the screen door and the regular door. I was expecting a photo of my grandmother, but instead I saw an enormous headline that read, HAROLD THOMPSON OUT OF COUNTY JOB AFTER 18 YEARS? The article said that rumors were flying that Harold Thompson had either lost his job or was in imminent danger of losing it. Various county commissioners were quoted as saying that since everyone was talking about it, there must be a grain of truth. Nobody defended Dad. Small-town politics are like big-town politics. If someone senses you're down, they're not going to give you a hand up; they're going to kick you. Tom Turner was quoted as saying that he heard Dad had lost his job "from a very reliable source." At the bottom of the news piece it read, "See related article, page 2."

I flipped the page. Topping a separate article was a photo of my grandmother and me. It was taken just after I had wrapped her in the tablecloth. We were standing in the middle of the marching band. The headline read HAROLD THOMPSON'S MOTHER RUNS NAKED AT PARADE.

I let Dad sleep. When I called Walker back, he launched into a tirade about how the Thompsons were all embarrassing him and what if this news got back to his professors at Princeton? He'd never get a recommendation for a good job, he said. After I told him that I sincerely doubted his professors were reading *The Muskegon Chronicle*, he curtly told me that he had to go break the news to his parents and hung up. When the phone started ringing off the hook at about 7 a.m., I finally went to give Dad the paper.

Anna's was the eighth call. She sounded like she had just inhaled helium. "I cannot even go to work without being confronted with some Thompson folly. Everyone here wants to know what your father did wrong to get the boot. Every time I think it's calming down something else blows up! I can't wait to move to Florida!" She slammed the phone down hard in my ear.

Dad was shaken, but he soldiered on and went to work to put out all of the fires. After the third day, rumors were still flying and he looked tired. Mom rubbed his head every night and told him to keep his chin up.

Lucy stayed another two days. Evan, just back from captaining a boat down from the Upper Peninsula, drove her to the airport.

She was taking a commercial flight to Monterey. There was no way Mom and Dad were going to let her catch military planes for her return trip. The night before she left, she came into her room to talk to me. "Should I have this baby?" she whispered in the darkness. I patted the side of the bed and she sat down. "I don't know what to do."

"I don't know either, Lucy."

"I don't want a baby. I'm not sure if I'll ever want a baby. This family might be enough for one lifetime." I patted her hand; there was absolutely nothing I could say that would help her with this decision.

When I got up in the morning, Lucy was already packed and I only had time to give her a quick hug before she and Evan headed out the door.

"I'll be back in September," she reminded me. "Then we'll be together at Michigan State. I've already got married housing lined up for me and Chuck."

After they left, Mom and I sat outside in the backyard. "Did she tell you what she's going to do?" I asked.

Mom's cigarette smoke circled her head in the still air. "No. I got her the names of some good doctors in her area. They can help her either way." We rocked on the glider and watched Bear Lake. Some Canadian geese glided in and splashed down. "Are they here already?" Mom asked. "Looks like it's going to be an early winter."

"Nah," I said. "The squirrels aren't gathering acorns yet."

"I have to figure out what to do with Elizabeth," Mom said, more to herself than to me.

Mom had spoken to Elizabeth, who had just gotten a big job producing a commercial and now wasn't planning to come home until later that summer. "She says that she wants to be near me for advice while she's pregnant." I could tell Mom didn't buy that. I could also tell that she didn't know yet about Elizabeth's money problems, and I didn't enlighten her. "Why are neither of those girls happy about being pregnant?" Mom mused. "I loved being pregnant." We watched the geese wander up to the Longs' lawn and make themselves at home.

I was due at the BLT soon, so Mom drove me down and told me Evan would be by to pick me up at closing time. As I was shutting the car door, I paused. "Hang in there, Mom."

She looked up and smiled. "Sometimes that's all you can do."

Twenty-four

August 1986

*E*van was flipping pizza dough in the air. He wasn't particularly good at it and the wad fell on the floor. He just picked it up and laughed. "Five-second rule!" he said. "Hey, Joe?" he called to the cameraman. "Anybody clean this floor recently?"

The cameraman mumbled something from off-screen and Evan responded cheerfully, "Good enough for me. People shouldn't get all hung up on minor things like that. Builds the immune system. I think that's why kids eat dirt."

"Are you feeding your kids dirt now?" Grandma asked Dad. "Things have sunk pretty low, huh, son?"

She was right about one thing: that summer had basically sucked. Since the newspaper incident almost three weeks before, Walker had refused to come over. "You guys are like a lightning rod in a storm," he had said, "or a trailer park during a tornado. Something is bound to happen."

Even I couldn't argue that he wasn't right. That summer might have been somewhat exceptional in terms of events, but it wasn't *all* that exceptional. I couldn't even go see Walker because I was either working or watching Grandma. I stuffed a piece of Sara Lee coffee cake in my mouth and watched Evan checking the coals on the grill.

"I encourage you to start looking at things in a different way." He brushed some olive oil onto the pizza dough and then more on the grill. "For instance, today I'm making pizza on the grill. I bet you never even thought about doing that. Sometimes the obvious is hidden because you are so used to looking at things in just one way." He flipped the dough onto the grill and ladled tomato sauce on top. Then he got a pot from the stove and brought it out to the smoker attached to the grill. He threw in the soaked wood chips from the pot. "The smoke will give the pizza an unusual flavor too. So there it is, a new way to look at things."

He slammed the door of the smoker and sat down on the picnic table. Picking up a mug, he slurped his tea in the way people do when it's really hot. "Sometimes you have to look at your life from a new angle too. Because people might be telling you one thing when in fact they mean something else entirely. So you have to see through what they are telling you to find the truth."

"That boy isn't making any sense," Grandma announced.

"Shhh, this is how I find out what's happening in Evan's life," Mom said. Our eyes were all fastened to the TV on the kitchen counter.

"Here's an example," Evan said. "As you all know, I was captaining a boat down from the U.P. last week. I'm headed south on Lake Michigan, and I'm smack-dab in the middle of the lake, fifty miles from either the Michigan or the Wisconsin shore. It's twilight, one of those beautiful nights when you just want to get your downriggers out to snag a couple of coho salmon. Then I see it. Right there, not two hundred yards off starboard. Milwaukee. I can see the buildings and the streetlights and the cars. I'm wondering if I'm hallucinating."

Evan took another sip of tea and added fresh basil and chunked heirloom tomatoes to his pizza. He gestured to us with a lemon in his hand. "Then I realize the entire crew can see Milwaukee, too. The engineer comes up to me in the pilothouse and whispers, 'Do you see that?' We both checked the radar and our charts to make sure we weren't off course. Nope, we were in the middle of the lake. I didn't know what to do. If I called the Coast Guard, they'd think we were all crazy. But I didn't want to keep moving in case it was real and we hit a building. So we stopped. Twelve of us watched the lights of Milwaukee, which were supposed to be hundreds of miles away. Then the sun went down. No more Milwaukee." Evan pulled the pizza off the grill and squirted lemon onto it.

Finally, Joe the cameraman asked, "What the hell was it? Was it really Milwaukee?"

"Yes and no. It turns out that there is an unusual phenomenon of refracted light over water that can make an image literally appear miles away from where it really is. So yes, it was Milwaukee. But no, it wasn't really there."

Evan sliced the pizza in the manner favored by our family—with scissors. He took a bite and smiled. "Milwaukee looked like it was right there, when the facts said it wasn't. Too many people forget the facts in their life and want to believe the mirage that's presented to them."

"That's pretty existential for this early in the morning." Dad yawned.

Joe seemed to be having the same thoughts. "What does a mirage have to do with pizza?" he asked from off-camera.

"Nothing much," Evan said through a mouthful. "But you do have to be willing to take a new look at something to figure out if you're seeing it from the right angle."

Dad, Grandma, and I sat around the kitchen table in baffled silence. Finally I asked Mom, "Does this have something to do with Florida?"

"Could be," Mom said as she separated bacon by the stove.

"Why does Anna want to go?" I asked.

"Because we live here, not there."

Now I got it. Anna told Evan she wanted to be near her parents, but that wasn't the truth. Evan knew it was a Milwaukee.

I thought about the other Milwaukees going on right now: Elizabeth coming home soon and telling everyone that it was because she wanted to be close to Mom during the pregnancy. But no one besides me knew why Elizabeth was really coming home. She had also told me that Ron had stopped paying for health insurance months ago. The baby was going to be born here, which would be cheaper than if it were born in Los Angeles. But Elizabeth would blow into town like she was Jackie O., complete with pearls and big sunglasses.

Then there was Lucy. She kept trying to hang on to a marriage that had been a Milwaukee from the beginning. She ignored the fact that Chuck had been and might still be in love with someone else, that his IQ was barely body temperature, and that she didn't want this baby or any other baby.

I thought about myself, too. I pretended that everything was white-picket-fence fine in our family. I tried to persuade Walker that we were all normal while I kept everyone's secrets. I told

Walker what he wanted to hear instead of hoping he would accept my family as it was. I was torn between jumping into the exhilarating dog pile that was the real world of my siblings and pretending that we put up our storm windows in September and extended our pinkies with the best of them at the country club. My family was like the Mud Bowl at the University of Michigan. It was an annual football game that looked like a ton of fun from the sidelines, but you just weren't sure you wanted to get that messy.

Evan's show was ending. The theme music played and he cleaned up the dishes as the credits rolled. Then the phone on the set rang. Evan used it for viewers to call in with questions, and the caller's voice was broadcast over the air.

Evan picked it up. *"Michigan Bass and Buck Show."*

"I cannot believe you would air our marital problems on TV!" Anna's voice rang throughout the studio and over our television set.

We had all been standing up to get on with our day but we quickly planted our butts firmly back down.

"I know exactly what you're talking about with all of this Milwaukee business! You think that moving to Florida isn't about *my* family, it's about *your* family!"

Evan looked at the camera and motioned to Joe to turn it off. He didn't.

"I was right!" Mom exclaimed.

The credits stopped running. *The Michigan Bass and Buck Show,* for the first time in history, was going to stay on the air past 9 a.m. If Evan had his wits about him, he would have just hung up the phone. But he didn't, and Anna didn't let him get a word in edgewise.

"At least my parents don't let their relatives run around naked or demand my wedding dress on my wedding night or try to buy a World War II submarine for a tourist attraction!" Anna's voice rang out.

Mom looked at Dad, who looked away guiltily.

"Why can't your family lead nice, quiet lives like the rest of us? Why does every little thing have to be a drama?" Anna was really on a roll. She must have been saving up all this for a long time. I knew how she felt.

Evan finally interrupted. "Anna, you're on the air."

Silence followed, then a small gasp, then, "But the show's over."

"Negative. The station kept us on the air."

A dial tone came over the airwaves. Evan hung up and the phone promptly rang again. It was a viewer calling to offer his opinion.

"I like the pizza idea. The Milwaukee bit confused me though. But I gotta tell you, Evan, I don't blame your wife. Remember when you and your dad decided to get certified for scuba diving? But you wanted to do it in January, for some goddamn reason, and you had to cut a hole in the ice? And then the Worthingtons' ice boat hit the hole and fell through and sank?"

"That could've happened to anyone," Evan said. "The boat could've just as easily hit a hole cut by an ice fisherman."

"But it didn't, did it?" the caller continued. Evan hung up the phone again, and it rang again.

This time a woman's voice said, "Your family is the kindest, nicest family I know. Without you guys we'd never have any fun in this town. Or have anything to talk about. And everybody knows Anna's family has a stick up their—"

Evan cut her off, too. This continued for a while as various townspeople debated the pros and cons of family (deal with it), Florida (too humid), and marriage (again, deal with it). Nine thirty rolled around too soon for us, but Evan had been surreptitiously glancing at his watch. The theme music came back on and Evan skedaddled off the set with the phone still ringing.

He showed up at our house fifteen minutes later.

"That wife of yours is a bitch," Grandma said.

"No, she's not, Grandma. She has a point. Maybe we should move to Florida," Evan said dejectedly.

I answered the phone on the second ring. I heard Anna's frosty tones. "Is your brother there?"

"Yes, just a minute."

"Just pass a message along. Tell him to stay there!" I pulled the receiver away to save my eardrum as she slammed down the phone. I wished she would stop doing that.

I turned to Evan. "I don't think you have to worry about Florida anymore."

Mom and Dad were about to have four of their kids back at home. "Has anyone spoken to Sammie lately?" Mom asked.

"Yeah. She got a dog. A big Husky," I said.

"Well, thank God one of you is okay."

"I'm okay, too," I said. I was wounded. I prided myself on being the normal one. "I'm the only person who's still supposed to be at home in the summer!"

Dad and Evan took their coffee down to the gazebo for some noninterrupted nonconversation.

"Is the nursing home almost finished with the remodeling?" Grandma asked. "This household is getting to be too much for me."

I sat back and regarded my grandmother, who had created the last couple of blowups. No one could say we didn't come by it honestly. I handed her a deck of cards because I knew it would shut her up.

Mom zipped upstairs to get the laundry and then took it back down to the basement. She thought best when she was doing the wash. I called Elizabeth to get her involved in the bedroom arrangements. When I told her we would have her, Evan, Lucy, Chuck, Grandma, and me all home at the same time, she cheered up enormously. This was what she lived for: herding large numbers of people in a specific direction. She got off the phone with a promise to work out a plan. Ten minutes later she called back and informed me that I would have to stay at Evan's house, that our house just couldn't accommodate everybody.

"Have you not been listening to me?" I was exasperated. "We are not in favor with Anna right now. None of us can stay there, including Evan."

"Good point. I'll call you back." She was giddy with the excitement of a problem to be solved. No matter what she figured out, I knew I was going to be back on the couch. I was always the one on the couch, or in a chair, or the occasional bathtub. I knew this from our road trips with Dad.

Dad loved to drive and would pile all of us into the station wagon and just go. He never really had a plan; he just wanted to get out and see the world. We kids all fought to have the very back seat, the one that faced out the rear window. Later in life I would wonder at the wisdom of this seat. The kids would be the first ones to go if there were a rear-end collision. But seeing as how we never used seat belts back then either, I guess Mom and Dad had the ultimate faith that nothing would happen to us.

Every night we would stop at a Holiday Inn, with its big green arrow sign. Then, being the smallest, I would spend a luxurious night sleeping either in the bathtub or on two chairs pushed together. This wouldn't have been so bad except that modernity had struck America. The chairs had square metal arms and very little in the way of padding. I preferred the bathtub. So the fact that I would be the one without a bed had been established since I was out of the cradle. That's just the way it was.

I heard the front doorbell ring and knew there was no way that I was going to answer it. Buddy was on the prowl somewhere, and I didn't want another confrontation with super-cop Marv Carson.

"Hel-*lo*," a voice sing-songed from the hall. It was Grandma. I peeked around the door and saw her ushering Father Whippet in. I had been studiously avoiding him since that day in his office, and I wasn't going to be cornered now. I ran to the basement and pulled wrinkled jeans and a BLT shirt from the dryer. I changed fast, put on some old tennis shoes of Lucy's I found, and pounded up the basement stairs and out to the gazebo.

"Warning: Father Whippet is in the house," I panted. Then I saw that he wasn't in the house; he was sitting right there with Dad and Evan. Rats.

I tried to recover quickly. "I mean, I wanted to let you know Father Whippet was visiting."

Father Whippet grimaced at me, his excuse for a smile. "I was explaining that your grandmother called me and asked me over. She felt your father needed comfort during this difficult time."

I paused. Which difficult time was he referring to?

"Harold"—Father Whippet turned to Dad—"we have job counseling available at the church." He eyed Dad's rumpled clothes and unshaven face. "You can't let yourself get depressed, hanging around the house and letting everything go to pot."

Dad was trying to be polite. "It's Saturday, John. I'm not hanging around the house. I live here when I'm not at work. And these are my gardening clothes."

Father Whippet patted Dad's knee like he was a small child. At that point high-pitched squeals came from the bird feeder. A gray squirrel had managed to get his head into the feeder by hanging over the top of its roof. But then his fat rear quarters had flipped over and landed on the perch, which triggered the Plexiglas shield to come down smack on his shoulders. The more he struggled, the more firmly stuck he was.

"Aw, for Christ's sake." Dad ignored Father Whippet's horrified look at his taking the Lord's name in vain and hauled himself to his feet. Dad rambled over to the feeder with Father Whippet flapping behind. "Be careful! This is one of God's creatures!"

Dad analyzed the situation with a coffee mug and cigarette in one hand and the other hand on his hip. We watched Dad try to lift the squirrel's butt up off the perch. He couldn't get it with only one hand so he passed his mug and cigarette to Father Whippet. The squirrel was twisting every which way, and Dad was trying to soothe it. "All right, little guy. I'm gonna get you out of there." He managed to pull the squirrel free. It bolted over Dad's shoulder, down his back, and off toward the nearest tree, where it raced up to a high branch and chattered at us furiously from above.

"Why don't we just feed the birds *and* the squirrels?" I asked Evan. "Mr. Long feeds the ducks."

"That's so they'll be used to him when duck season opens in the fall."

I stared at him. "Do you mean to say that Mr. Long—sensitive Mr. Long next door—is luring ducks to their death?"

"Yep."

"You're not allowed to fire a rifle within city limits," I protested.

"You can if nobody sees you."

"What about the noise?" I countered. "Everyone would call the cops."

"During duck season?" he asked.

He had me there. From late October through early November, far-off rifle shots regularly woke up everyone in town.

"Fath-*er* Whip-*pet. Yoo hoo!*" Grandma was calling from the sliding doors.

"What's she doing?" Evan asked.

"Beats me." We sat back to watch the show. She attempted to prance into the yard but had to settle for shuffling. She had on a clean housecoat, but I noticed she had one pink curler dangling from her hair.

She took Father Whippet by the arm. "Would you like to have coffee with me? I have some things I'd like to discuss with you. I hear you're very attentive to older women." While she batted her eyes at him and led him away, Father Whippet looked over his shoulder directly at me. At that moment, I knew that he knew that I knew. I just didn't know exactly what.

Twenty-five

August 1986

*L*ate August is a magical time in western Michigan. The nights are filled with fireflies and meteor showers and dances at the White Lake Yacht Club. The days slide by while you're watching Sea Scout sailboat races or swimming at the country club pool or windsurfing through Muskegon Channel. For me, it meant that I would soon be done with Grandma and the Bear Lake Tavern. Soon Walker would return to Princeton. I didn't go back to college until mid-September, when MSU started its fall semester.

I wiped down the ketchup bottles fast to hurry and escape the Blit. The lunch crowd had died down and I figured Tommy wouldn't mind if I left a half hour early. Lucy, Chuck, and Elizabeth were due in to Muskegon at the end of the week. In anticipation of their arrival, I had promised Mom I would help her clean up the house after Roxie, the maid, had left. Mom didn't like the way Roxie cleaned, or didn't clean, as the case may be. But every time she attempted to fire her, Roxie would laugh and say, "Oh now, you don't mean that, Mrs. T."

I wanted to get the cleaning done fast because Walker had asked me out that night. He said it was going to be something special. He seemed to be getting over all the hoopla we had endured over the summer. I filled out my time card and was leaving the Blit when Tommy said casually, "Hey, Jeannie. Time to get out the Squirrel Board."

Not the Squirrel Board. I closed my eyes. "No way, Tommy. It's too early for the Squirrel Board. We need to wait another couple of weeks."

"I felt a crisp in the air last night," Tommy said firmly. "I can't disappoint my customers."

I trudged to the metal shed across the parking lot. It was full of spiderwebs and dirt and dried-out paint cans on makeshift shelves made out of lumber and cinder blocks. A few times during the summer, during various fits of angst, I had contemplated cleaning it out. But I'd thought better of it after Tommy suggested that, if I had so much energy, I could scrape the eaves on the building too. I found the Squirrel Board way in the back behind a broken neon Budweiser sign. I yanked and tugged and managed to get it out into the parking lot. Dragging it in the door, I yelled, "Where do you want it, Tommy?"

He stared at me from his place at the bar, where he was counting receipts. "How about the same place it's been for about a hundred years?"

I rolled my eyes and cursed him under my breath. I struggled to get it up onto the waiting hooks. Tommy tossed me some chalk and I drew a line vertically down the middle dividing the chalkboard into two halves. On the left side, I wrote BLACK SQUIRRELS, and on the right side I wrote GRAY SQUIRRELS.

Tommy came over. "Guess I might as well be first," he said.

He took the chalk from me and wrote his name on the black squirrel side. He wrote, "December 7 at 4:10 a.m." Then he put a ten-dollar bill in the big empty pickle jar he saved for this occasion.

I have no idea when this tradition began but it was a long time ago. Our town is one of the few on earth that boasts black squirrels along with regular gray squirrels. Squirrels are noted for predicting an early or late winter based on when they start gathering acorns. But townspeople noticed that black squirrels and gray squirrels each started gathering acorns at different times. Sometimes the blacks started gathering first, other times the grays. People began to have arguments over which color of squirrel was predicting the onset of winter correctly.

A not-so-elaborate—or accurate—betting game emerged. If your gut instincts told you that winter was going to come early, you'd back the squirrels that were gathering nuts early in the fall. You'd pick your "team," meaning the Blacks or the Grays. Then you would write down when you thought the first snowfall would occur. The person closest to the actual date and time won the jar and bragging rights for their squirrel team for a year. Three years running, the person who won had backed the gray squirrels. Last year, the winner took home $2,420. I took my tip money from my apron pocket, deposited ten dollars in the jar, and wrote, "Jeannie Thompson, November 30, 12:00 p.m." on the gray squirrel side.

"That's a lousy time," Tommy called after my back. "First snows never start at noon." I waved him off and kept walking. This was a familiar conversation. Every year, the fall months would be filled with arguments of statistics about past first snowfalls. But right now I didn't want to talk about it. It was sunny and eighty degrees out.

After I changed the sheets on all the beds and cleaned the bathroom, I noticed that Elizabeth's schedule for bedrooms was now posted on the refrigerator. Lucy and Chuck would be staying here until they left for school in a few weeks. My name was not next to "couch," Evan's was. It got worse. It said:

> Lucy and Chuck: guest room
> Grandma: pink room
> Elizabeth: dessert room
> Mom and Dad: Mom and Dad's room
> Evan: couch
> Jeannie: basement

"Mom!" I was horrified. "There's not even a bed in the basement!" Our basement wasn't finished. It was gray and musty with exposed pipes. Books and boxes and Christmas ornaments were piled everywhere, with only a narrow path to the washer and dryer. I had organized it many times but had given up after it kept going right back to its original mess in no time at all.

"You can switch with Elizabeth," she said helpfully.

"You know I can't ask a pregnant woman to sleep on a basement floor!" I replied.

Mom hustled off to find Dad's sleeping bag from his stint in the army during the Korean War. She figured that she could make a bed for me out of that. As she rummaged through a closet, I heard her say, "I think there's enough room for you under the ironing board."

Grandma was flipping her cards down on the table. I looked over her shoulder and saw that the dreaded ace of spades was upside down again. "Didn't you say that means death?" I tapped the card.

Grandma nodded without looking up and continued flipping until the cards were laid out in neat rows. The ace of spades was surrounded again by the jack of diamonds, the queen of hearts, and the queen of diamonds.

"Grandma, that's what came up right before we thought Lucy was dead. What's the probability of that?" I asked.

"It's inevitable," she said without looking at me. She was giving me the chills on a very hot day.

"Do you mean that card formation will keep coming up because someone is supposed to die?"

"Yes."

"But it's not what turned up the last time you did a reading."

"It depends on who you're reading for."

"Who are you reading these for now?"

Grandma looked up at me. "Your mother." I backed away from her and ran out into the yard. I tilted my face to the late afternoon sun and thought, She doesn't mean any harm. She is an old woman who doesn't mean what she says. I lowered my head and looked at the house. I didn't believe a word of what I was telling myself. And I felt bad about it.

Dad would be coming home from work soon. Evan should be docking any minute now. Once a week he captained a research vessel for scientists who studied water currents. Mom was trying to figure out what to make for dinner and worrying about what to feed two pregnant women in the coming weeks. "Everything," I teased her.

I hated when she worried so much. Sometimes, when she was getting into full-scale worry mode, I'd dance her around the kitchen. I'd twirl her in and out, carefully avoiding the refrigerator and the cabinets and Buddy lying on the floor. Once I'd tripped over the open door of the dishwasher and dropped her flat on her bottom when I was trying to dip her. We both laughed, tangled up on the floor. "Oh, Jeannie!" my mom would say, with tears of laughter rolling down her face. That usually snapped her out of herself.

With us, she didn't put up with much self-pity or self-doubt. After listening to and advising on our various complaints (boyfriend broke up with me, got fired from my job, hair turned green in the chlorine), she would eventually announce, "Pull up your bootstraps!"

Now I grabbed her for a quick spin at the stove until she laughed. Then she balanced her cigarette on the side of the counter while she studied the contents of the refrigerator.

"I want that spaghetti you made a while ago," Grandma said.

Mom said, "Well, all right, I guess that would be easy." She went to the basement to get a few jars of her homemade tomato sauce. Since Walker was taking me out to dinner, I wasn't worried about having to face the icky sauce. I was thinking about what to wear on my date when I heard Mom's voice from below. "Jeannie?" her voice quavered. I went down the steps and saw Mom standing in the middle of the room. "Do you smell something?" she whispered.

I pulled my T-shirt up over my nose to block the smell. "Omigod, Mom, what is it?"

"Gas," she said.

I could hear a hissing noise and I frantically moved boxes away from the wall until I found where the gas was seeping in. It was behind the dryer. The gas line had been wrenched apart, and gas was filling the basement. I grabbed a towel and tried to shove it into the broken line but I could still hear it hissing deep inside the wall. "Is your cigarette out?" My voice was squeaky.

Mom was moving a heavy bookcase trying to see if there was

another access to the interior of the wall. "I left it on the kitchen counter upstairs. Thank God." She grunted with the strain of the bookcase.

"Do you know where the gas shutoff is?" I asked her.

"No. Your father always handles things like that."

"I'll go call the fire department. You should get out of here now." Then I turned and saw the tiny pilot flame. "Mom! The water heater!" I yelped.

Her eyes widened. "Get your grandmother and run outside. Now!"

I didn't go. I ran around the basement looking for something to douse that flame with before our house became a fireball. I threw the washer open and, sure enough, there were damp clothes inside. I grabbed the first thing handy and sprawled on my belly. I shoved the damp cloth as far under the heater as I could, praying it reached and extinguished the source of certain destruction. I pulled the fabric out carefully and studied the space between the heater and the floor. The flame was out. I laid my head on the concrete floor and sighed.

"Hey, are you guys down there?" Evan shouted. I heard his feet hitting the top steps. Mom ran headlong up the steps and pushed Evan out of the stairwell. When I got upstairs they were picking themselves up off the floor. Evan had a cigarette in his hand. "What the hell?" he sputtered.

"Out, now, out!" Mom gasped. She grabbed Grandma and moved her bodily to the back door.

"Evan, open the windows and doors!" I cranked open every pane of glass I could find. Evan didn't ask what was happening but started helping me. I grabbed the phone and dialed 9-1-1. When the operator answered, I yelled, "Gas leak! We have a gas leak!"

There was a pause and then the operator said quizzically, "Jeannie?"

"Yes! It's Jeannie! Get somebody over here who knows where the hell the gas shutoff is!"

"End of Fourth Street, right?"

"Right!"

The operator said she'd have someone over in a minute and hung up. Evan and I left the house and joined Mom and Grandma in the front yard. We watched the house for signs of imminent explosion. Dad pulled into the driveway. When he saw us all in the front yard, he hurried over to Mom. "What happened?"

"It's a gas leak, Harold. I have no idea how long that hose was pouring gas into the house. We all could have been killed." Mom was regaining her composure.

"Ah shit, not again." Dad sighed. Mom, Evan, and I stared at Dad. Grandma turned her head away conspicuously. I heard sirens growing louder. Why they were using sirens I had no idea. The firehouse was only three blocks away. The fire truck came around the corner, closely followed by the paramedic truck and North Muskegon's lone cop car. The volunteer firemen and Marv Carson trooped into our house. I watched the blue and red lights flashing across our neighbors' houses. They were all coming out now to see what the excitement was about. A crowd gathered at a safe distance across the street. Walker jogged across the lawn to me.

"Is everybody all right?" We all nodded yes. He took my hand. "So what happened now?"

"A gas leak," I said. I looked at my grandmother and decided not to bring up my suspicions.

"I had to park over on Third Street. They've got your entire block cordoned off," Walker said. I wasn't really listening to him because I was wondering what Marv Carson was carrying out of the house. As he lugged his burden down the front steps, I ran toward him.

"Hey, you can't go near there yet!" a fireman yelled at me. I didn't stop until I was standing in front of Marv at the bottom of the steps. His head was down and the brim of his hat obscured his eyes.

"Officer Carson?" It was a question, and he knew what it meant. When he raised his head I saw his eyes were glistening.

"Ah, Jeannie. Ah, shit. I'm so sorry."

I stroked the brown fur. "Is he . . . can we . . ." I didn't finish. I knew the answer. Marv walked heavily to a corner of the yard and laid Buddy's body on the grass. He took care that Buddy's feet were not under his body and that his neck wasn't lolling. I sat next to my dog and pulled his head onto my lap. My family gathered around.

I looked up at my dad. I opened my mouth to tell his sad blue eyes it would all be okay. Instead, a wail came out. "Daaad!" He reached down and scooped me up like I was a five-year-old. He hugged me hard and only the toes of my tennis shoes scraped the grass as I hung on to his shoulders. I knew Walker and every neighbor were watching my family and I didn't care. I couldn't stop crying.

Twenty-six

April 2006

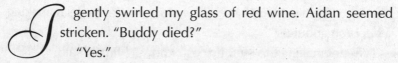 gently swirled my glass of red wine. Aidan seemed stricken. "Buddy died?"

"Yes."

"It wasn't a mistake, like with Lucy?"

"No." I stared at the fire in my little brick fireplace and readjusted the phone next to my ear. I had been speaking to Aidan for more than an hour now, telling my story.

He sounded like he had lost his best friend. "What happened? Why didn't Buddy get out?"

I thought back to that long-ago night. Once we were allowed back inside, we had talked at the kitchen table late into the evening. Every time Dad and Evan wanted to smoke Mom shooed them outside, just in case the gas had lingered. Grandma was sleeping. Buddy had been wrapped in my favorite quilt and was laid out carefully on the garage floor. I had protested that I wanted him in the house but Mom said that probably wasn't the best idea.

I answered Aidan's question. "Marv found him in the basement. He sometimes slept there on the cool concrete floor. The paramedic said that he probably passed out and never woke up."

"But you and your mom didn't see him when you were down there." That fact had tormented me for months after Buddy's death. If we had seen his body in the corner, maybe we could have revived him, but we hadn't. The difference between life and death can be as simple as a glance into a corner at the right time.

"Did your Grandma jimmy with the gas hose?" Aidan asked.

"Yes."

"That's pretty difficult to do," Aidan mused.

"Apparently she had practice," I said.

Aidan's voice was now anxious. "Practice?"

"Yeah, well, there's more to the story."

"Christ, Jeannie, you're getting to be like Scheherazade. I'm starting to feel like you just keep inventing stories to delay making a decision about us."

"I'm not making this stuff up, you know," I finally said.

"I know, I know. It's just . . . just . . . oh, I don't know."

At this point I was anxious myself. Lucy's plane had landed at 7 p.m. It was now eight thirty and she would be here any second. I pulled back the living room curtains to see if there was a cab coming down the street. "I love you, Aidan. Let's talk about all of this in person. We've been on the phone a long time now and I need to review some stuff for work."

"Yeah." Aidan sounded reluctant. "I'd better be going too. I have to get a really early start tomorrow. We're looking at new locations outside of Vancouver."

After we hung up I sat in front of the fire feeling like a complete shit. I couldn't even understand myself. What was wrong with committing to a man whom I loved? The truth was I hadn't been right about my first husband, Walker, so how could I trust myself to make such a big decision again? Walker thought he could simply ignore my family by never seeing them. But that took too big of a toll on me.

I was so deep in thought that the doorbell jolted me. Running to the door, I swung it open. "Lucy!" I swept her up into a hug.

After I released her I saw that while travel worn, Lucy looked great, as always. Her dark hair was pinned up carelessly and she wore jeans, a sweater set, and a Burberry raincoat that she certainly wouldn't need here in Los Angeles.

She rolled her suitcase inside and smiled at me. "Good to see you, Jeannie." She continued toward the guest room.

"Where are you going?" I followed her.

"It's 11:45 my time." She yawned. "I love you but it is way past my bedtime and I'm going to bed." With a final one-arm hug she disappeared into the guest room, which was just off the living room. Moments later I heard water running in the guest bathroom. I smiled to myself. Good old Lucy.

The next morning, Monday, I took several hours off from work to have some time with my sister. A long walk took us down to Venice Beach, where we found a restaurant on the boardwalk to have some breakfast. We scored a table outside in the sunshine. It faced the boardwalk with the wide beach and the Pacific Ocean lying just beyond.

"I haven't been down here in years." I marveled at the people slowly cruising by on bikes or Rollerblades. How do these people have the time to be outside on a Monday morning? I wondered.

"Years?" Lucy put her chin in her hands. "You only live about twelve blocks away."

"I don't get out much. I'm at the office most of the time." I turned my attention to the menu.

"So I hear."

Uh-oh. Alert, alert. Was Lucy going to start bashing me right away for not making time for the family? I thought she probably was, but mercifully the waitress showed up just then to take our orders. Lucy either dropped the subject or forgot about it because we spent our time talking about her caseload and my slate of movies. We both had to deal with completely impossible, insane people, and we giggled at each other's stories.

My phone rang halfway through Lucy's pantomime of a client falling out of a window and into some bushes. I checked caller ID and saw it was an Oxford Pictures phone number.

"I gotta take this but I'll be quick," I promised Lucy. I answered and it was our print production guy.

"Hey, Jeannie, I've got the artwork ready for your approval for the *TechnoCat* poster."

"Yeah, um, that's great. I'll be in later on this afternoon," I said.

"It's on press right now. We have a tight schedule, as you know. If we don't start printing it within an hour, we won't be done in time to make FedEx to get the posters out to New York. Then it won't be up in theaters tomorrow like you promised Rachael."

One thing I knew right then was that I had better damn well not leave Lucy in order to go into work. I always, without fail, approved final artwork before going to press. But I had worked with this print production guy for years. He had an amazing eye for color, and if he said it was good to go, then it was good to go. Which is what I asked him. "Yep, it looks awesome," he responded cheerfully.

"Then go ahead and print it." I tapped END on my phone and settled in for another coffee and more conversation with Lucy.

Eventually, we made it back to my house. We went to our separate bedrooms to shed our sweats and get into work clothes. When Lucy showed up in the living room I saw that she had changed into a conservative gray suit with a white ruffled shirt buttoned up to the neck. She looked so East Coast that I almost laughed. "Things sure are different in Connecticut. Out here even lawyers show up in the expensive, crumpled, creative look."

"I guess that explains what you have on," she said a tad archly.

"What's wrong with this?" I looked down at my high-heeled black boots, black tights, black skirt that was a bit short, and pink and black floral shirt.

"You could button up one more button, for starters."

I started to retort; then I looked down again. She did have a point. I buttoned up. Aidan had a funny saying he learned in Australia about older women who dress too young for their age. He called it mutton dressed as lamb. I wasn't mutton, to be sure. But I wasn't exactly a lamb anymore, either. I tugged my skirt down a bit, too.

I gave Lucy a ride over to the law firm where she was taking depositions. Then I left her with an extra house key after she assured me she could get a cab back to my place later that night.

Caitlin cornered me before I even opened my office door. "Katsu and Stripe are in the conference room."

"Doing what?" I was incredulous. Rachael had been very firm with Stripe that I was to be leading this effort.

"Adding scenes to the special shoot. I stayed in there as long as possible to take notes but I couldn't leave the phones unanswered."

Steaming mad, I stormed into my office and threw my purse on the couch. I was supposed to keep the budget under control. It was my ass on the line if I didn't. And here they were adding more expensive scenes behind my back.

Caitlin followed me. "That's not all." She handed me that day's *Hollywood Reporter* opened to the eighth page. There was Katsu's photo along with a brief story that Katsu would be handling the advertising for Ms. F.U.'s next film. The article then went on to say that Katsu was "brilliant" and "rising fast" at Oxford Pictures.

Brilliant? He hadn't even done anything yet. I sank slowly into my chair. I had never seen an article like this. Marketing people didn't normally get a mention in the trades just because they were working on this picture or that one. It was unheard of. Something politically big was going on here at Oxford Pictures.

Rachael picked that moment to walk into my office. "Katsu and Stripe are trying to add more scenes to the *TechnoCat* trailer," she said without preliminary. "Make that go away, Jeannie."

I stared at her. While the studio rulebook had some blurry lines, I knew it wasn't my job to outright deny a director what he wanted; that was *her* job. Obviously if a few weeks from now the finger of blame needed to be pointed, she was making sure it would be pointed at me and away from her.

"We can't be over budget. I'm under pressure on every one of our movies. No overages. Period." She stood over my desk and idly rolled my two pens from side to side. "There is no room for fuck-ups on this one." Rachael headed for the door and then decided to soften the blow. "We really need your magic here, Jeannie."

After she shut the door, I reached for the two pens. One had almost rolled off the edge of the desk. Very precisely I aligned them back in their proper places.

I knew I should go confront Katsu and Stripe. Instead I slowly reached for the phone. I needed information and I knew only one person who might have it. But dealing with him was like dealing with a dozing rattlesnake. You never knew when you might get bitten. He was the consigliere in the small world of ad agencies that specialized in film trailers. At seventy-five, he was perpetually tanned, sported expensive suits tailored especially for him in London, and wore leather slippers with no socks. Oddly, he carried a silver-tipped cane that he didn't appear to need. A pinkie ring and a Ferrari completed the picture. Since 1964 he'd hobnobbed regularly with top directors, producers, studio chairmen, and movie stars—all the while carefully planting seeds that could make or break a career. Ruben Hoffman, owner of the top entertainment ad agency in Los Angeles, would most certainly be clued in to any deal making at Oxford Pictures.

I worked with his editors and producers quite often but rarely dealt with the Big Man. So I was surprised when he took my call immediately. "Jeannie, love! How are you?" he boomed.

I quickly dispensed with small talk and told him I needed his advice. I could practically hear him rubbing his hands together. He loved being consulted. Leaving out no detail, I recounted Katsu's treachery and my frustration that it seemed like he was out to destroy me.

"You're being a little paranoid," Ruben answered slowly. My stomach turned. I had just shown my insecurity and weakness to someone who might use it against me. "However, that's not to say you are wrong," Ruben continued. "You need to think in a different way. For instance, what if you are not the person whom they are after?"

This puzzled me but he kept going. "You, my dear girl, are small potatoes."

Gee, thanks, I thought. But I knew he was right.

"But if you look bad, who else looks bad along with you?" Ruben asked.

I felt like a simpleton. Devious thinking is not my forte. Stammering, I told him I had no idea. He sighed heavily, saying that I couldn't seem to connect the dots. "Rachael. Rachael looks bad."

"Why would anyone want to make Rachael look bad?"

"To destabilize the marketing department. Someone who wants to put someone else in the position of president of marketing. A whisper here, a whisper there, and pretty soon Rachael is out of a job."

"But Katsu just can't be capable of that." I was starting to catch on to what he was saying. "He isn't powerful enough."

"No, he's not," Ruben answered. "Someone is pulling Katsu's strings. Who lately has shown an interest in our young friend?"

For a moment I came up short. Then I breathed, "Stripe."

Ruben sounded like he was congratulating a particularly slow student on getting something right. "And why would Stripe do that?" He answered his own question. "Because he has aspirations beyond *TechnoCat*. He wants to eventually be chairman of a film studio. First he gets his own loyal team into the marketing department, then he starts to disrupt the production department, and voilà, Oxford is a mess and he comes in to save the day."

"Where do I stand in all of this?" I had my head down now on my desk.

"Oh, you're just collateral damage," he said cheerfully. "Keep your wits about you and you might just keep your job."

I thanked him for his help, and as I was saying good-bye, Ruben casually said, "I hear that new film you're going to be working on, *Cosmic Cruisers*, will be a blockbuster."

I had no doubt that I now owed him the ad work on *Cosmic Cruisers*. And I now felt like I needed a shower. Exhausted, I didn't even try to attend the meeting with Katsu and Stripe. I left work early at 7 p.m. and straggled home. Lucy was already there and had poured herself a glass of wine and lit the gas fireplace.

"I'd cook . . . but do you care if I just get something delivered?" I flopped onto the couch.

"No problem." She waved her hand while studying important-looking legalese documents. I ordered some Italian. When it arrived, Lucy and I ate together and discussed our day. Mine wouldn't have made much sense to her, so I let her do most of the talking. She seemed to be hesitating about something though and I prodded her.

"I'd like to see Sammie and Elizabeth while I'm here."

"Sure, of course." I nodded.

"So I invited them over here to your house tomorrow afternoon. You said you thought you could take some more time off."

"Luuucccyyy." I drew the word out as I threw my head back against the chair. An emotional confrontation was absolutely the last thing I needed right now.

Lucy pushed her food around on her plate. "It's been a long day for both of us. Why don't we just talk about this in the morning?"

Glad for any delay, I said yes. We both went to bed. I assume Lucy fell asleep immediately as usual. Also as usual, I woke up at 2:30 in the morning and couldn't get my brain to shut down. At 6 a.m. I finally went to the kitchen to make some coffee and surf the Internet for news. Running water in the shower alerted me that Lucy was now awake as well. When the doorbell rang I looked up, startled. Who in the world would be here at this time of day? Scuffling in my slippers and robe through the living room, I pulled the curtains aside slightly to see who was on my porch. It was Aidan.

Oh my God. Aidan. And Lucy. Together in my house. No, no, no, this was not going to happen. They were *not* going to meet. I opened the front door without removing the chain.

"Hi, babe! I got done early in Vancouver and took a red-eye flight to surprise you." He was all smiles.

"Uh, hi," I said hesitantly. Instinctively I looked over my shoulder. Reassuringly, I could still hear the shower running. Lucy wouldn't come out soon.

Aidan paused and regarded me. "Are you going to let me in?" He pointed to the chain.

"It's not such a good time right now." My eyes darted over my shoulder again.

Behind me, I heard a door slam. Aidan heard it too. He took a step back on the porch. "Jeannie, is someone else here?"

I hung my head and nodded. He was going to be so freaking angry with me that I hadn't told him my sister was coming into town. Looking up I saw his face had crumpled.

"I . . . I can't believe this. I can't believe you would do this to me. To *us*. Why didn't you tell me?" Aidan's voice was rising. Then abruptly he stopped and spun on his heel. Halfway down the steps I heard him say, "Have a good life, Jeannie."

Lucy called out behind me, "Hey, Jeannie, do you have a blow dryer?"

Watching Aidan's car pull away, I slowly shut the door. "Sure," I said faintly.

I got Lucy the blow dryer, then sat, stunned, at the kitchen table. Lucy came out brushing her now-dry hair and trying to pull on a shoe at the same time. "I'm late," she said. "I'll just grab breakfast at the . . ." She caught sight of my face. "My God, Jeannie, what's wrong?"

Violently, I shook my head. I didn't think I could speak. But Lucy sat quietly at the kitchen table with me, minutes ticking by, until I finally found my voice. I poured out the whole story, ending with the confrontation with Aidan this morning.

Lucy eyed me. "So you told Aidan that someone was here at 6:30 in the morning?"

I twirled my coffee cup between my hands and didn't meet her gaze.

"Did you happen to mention it was me, your sister?" Lucy inquired.

I shook my head no. I mean, who else would it have been? Lucy waited for me to catch on. Then alarmed, I shot my eyes to hers. Oh God. Aidan thought I had another man over last night.

Twenty-seven

August 1986

*D*ad and Evan studied the broken hose. They couldn't figure out how Grandma had managed it. Dad finally told us that this had happened before, right before Grandma ran away to Florida. His own father had come home from work, smoking a cigarette as usual, to find their kitchen filled with gas. In that case it was from the stove. The damage had been contained to the kitchen when the gas went boom. Dad's father had sustained only minor burns. No one else was in the house at the time.

The next day Mom and Dad sat down with Grandma. I joined them for moral support. What they gleaned was that she was ready to go back to her nursing home and she figured if the house were uninhabitable, we'd have to ship her back. I eyed Mom across the table. Grandma had asked for spaghetti, knowing Mom had to go downstairs to get the sauce. She knew Mom often had a lit cigarette in her hand. Maybe Grandma thought she could get rid of Mom and get sent back to her nursing home in one fell swoop.

Any other family would have shipped Grandma off so fast that her gray pin curls would have spun. Not Mom and Dad. They understood that Grandma was sick and not truly responsible for many of her actions. In the end, though, they called the nursing home, and they agreed to take Grandma back early. That's what Grandma wanted and she was happy with the outcome. It didn't seem to bother her that she had killed our dog to achieve her objective. But her brain wasn't firing on all cylinders.

Dad asked Father Whippet to come up and perform the burial service. Buddy was to be buried under the pine tree by the dock stairs. The last person I wanted there was Father Whippet, but I didn't want to add one more log to the bonfire of chaos by telling Dad about the good Father. We prayed and then laid Buddy in the hole wrapped in my quilt.

Back in the living room, Father Whippet tried to lay a guilt trip on my parents. "Events like this occur when the Lord is angry over our actions."

My mother's coffee cup literally trembled in its saucer. I had never seen that look on her face before. He continued, "Pearl spoke to me about how you forced her to stay here."

It was like lightning had struck a tree, peeled away the bark, and laid it raw. Mom stood up, crossed the room, and took Father Whippet's cup from his hand. He did not understand that this was her signal for him to leave. When he didn't, she tore into him. "In case you hadn't noticed, Pearl is very ill. We did not force her into our home. When she needed somewhere to go, we welcomed her with open arms. That's not called force, John; it's called love! And if you think that is so wrong, well, you can just shove it up your ass!"

"Rose!" Dad and Father Whippet gasped at the same time. Then Father Whippet beat it out of the living room and shut the front door behind him. Mom felt behind her for the couch and sat down heavily. Dad sat next to her and put his arms around her shoulders.

"What he must think of me!" she said. My mother never used vulgarity. Ever. And for her first go-around she had told off our minister.

"Now, now, Rose. What you said was right," Dad crooned.

"What will my kids think of me? What kind of example am I setting for them?"

"Yeah, Mom, some role model you are." I laughed. "We'll probably be kicked out of church. Hey, Dad, can Episcopalians be excommunicated, or is that only for Catholics? And you know, Mom"—I stroked her hair fondly—"now that we may not have church in our lives, I really feel compelled to go out and drink a fifth of Jack Daniel's, find a crack house, and maybe knock over a 7-Eleven. You know, because church was the only example I've ever had in my life."

Mom wiped her eyes with Kleenex. "Jeannie, don't be irreverent!" Then she started to giggle and we had ourselves the best laugh we'd had in days.

$\mathcal{P}$ART III

The Breakup and the Breakdown
2006

The Murder, the Babies,
and the Sex Scandal
1986

Twenty-eight

September 1986

*I*t's getting to be that time of year. When you start your truck in the morning twenty minutes before you leave so it will be warm when you hit the road. When the leaves are turning yellow, orange, and red. When bow hunters anxiously wait for the results of the early license lottery for doe-hunting season." Evan was puttering around the kitchen making frittatas. He gestured to the camera with an egg. "And the salmon. Henry Williamson wrote one of the definitive books on the subject. It's called *Salar the Salmon*. 'Salar,' for those of us who didn't have Latin in school—okay, that's all of us—means 'leaper.' This is the time of year when these heroic fish swim against ferocious currents, up and over waterfalls, rocks, logs, and fish ladders to return to the waters of their birth. They do this for one reason only: to reproduce."

Evan poured olive oil into a pan and chopped a red pepper before continuing. "No one knows why the salmon need to return

to the site of their first breath to spawn. Pacific salmon will leave
the ocean and swim back up the rivers from whence they came.
These fish might swim literally hundreds of miles to make it to the
one place they know instinctively as the one and only location
to give birth. Then, ironically, after these salmon give everything
for their children to be born, they die. Is this a kind of spiritual
rebirth?" Evan smiled. "Or is it just that they don't want to raise
the kids?"

Mom sputtered her coffee out as she laughed. I buttered toast
and watched my brother. "And don't forget," he continued, "once
those salmon turn red they're usually no good to eat."

Chuck turned to me. "Why?"

"Because their meat is mushy. It's because they're dying," I
said through a mouthful of toast, wondering if he was going to
put something decent on over his boxers. Elizabeth leaned back
and rubbed her belly. She did that a lot even though she was only
three months along and her belly was flatter than mine. Elizabeth,
Lucy, and Chuck had arrived two weeks earlier.

I knew Mom was gearing up to extract the truth out of Elizabeth. Every time she talked to her eldest daughter about the situation, Elizabeth would only say, "I'm just exhausted. I don't think
I can pull it together to work and I want to be close to someone
who has been through this five times." I knew what Mom was
thinking, that if Elizabeth was telling the truth, then she was being
a ninny. Mom had worked straight up until her ninth month with
all of us. And if she wasn't telling the truth, then there was a
bigger story there. Like, where was Ron? Elizabeth hadn't even
mentioned her husband since she got home. So Mom was keeping her counsel until she had analyzed the situation and knew
from which angle to attack.

Lucy, on the other hand, slept all of the time. She only got up to eat and go to the bathroom. Mom was actually more concerned about Lucy than about Elizabeth. But all of us were worried about Evan. Anna slammed down the phone every time he called her. I had run into her at Keefe's Pharmacy a few days earlier and she pretended not to see me, which is pretty hard to do in a store that small. I caught up with her in the parking lot.

"What do you want, Jeannie?"

Was I supposed to apologize for my family? Or tell her that Evan missed her and sat in the gazebo by himself every night? "Are you moving to Florida?" I finally got out.

She brushed her dark hair from her eyes and leaned against her car door. "Yes. I'm going at the end of the month. You can tell your brother."

This was not the answer I had been expecting. "But why?" I asked in shock.

"I love Evan," she said without looking at me, "but I just can't fit in. I never should have married him. It's awful to be married to a man who has four sisters who don't like you." She got into her car and pulled away.

Another Milwaukee. All of us, even Evan, had assumed that Anna was upset by the weird things that happened to the family. But it wasn't really that at all. She didn't feel loved by us. And that, in my opinion, was much, much worse.

I did the only thing I could think of: I called Sammie. She listened to me as I poured out the story.

"I have to think on this one now," she replied. "Don't tell anybody else yet." I felt better when I hung up the phone but now, several days later, I was wondering when she was going to finish thinking.

Evan came in the back door. "How'd you like the show today?"

"It was good," Dad said. "Subtle and interesting. Come on, Evan. It's the big moment." As the two of them disappeared into the backyard I heard Dad say, "I'm December fourth, 2:45 a.m., Black."

Lucy was awake now and lying on the couch. "Does being pregnant really make you this tired?" I inquired. "Because so far, it doesn't look very pleasant." Lucy didn't answer me. The phone rang and I grabbed it.

"Hello?"

It was Sammie. "Pick me up at the Muskegon airport tomorrow night at 7 p.m. Bring Lucy and Elizabeth. Don't tell them what's happening with Anna until the car ride to the airport."

"Should I bring my miniature camera and spy handbook?" I joked.

"A camera is a pretty good idea, actually," Sammie mused.

"Are you going to tell me what the plan is?"

"Nope. Just be there." Sammie hung up.

Dad ran into the house. "Everyone! Outside! Quick!" When language like that was used in our house, everyone obeyed. Mom, Elizabeth, Lucy, Chuck, and I ran outside, where Evan and Dad were grinning like fools. Dad nodded at Evan, who flipped a switch. "Voilà!" Dad cried. The sprinklers came to life, chugging their way around in a slow circle making a "ch, ch, ch" noise. We all stood on the porch and clapped wildly. This had been years in the making. Dad smiled and then took a deep bow toward us.

Dad and Evan strutted to the gazebo, where they congratulated each other over cigarettes. I was on lunch duty at the Blit so I couldn't stay for the celebration. Mom was making lime Jell-O with shredded carrots and mini-marshmallows, which I definitely could live without. I was walking to work when I saw the pink notices stapled to telephone poles.

> WARNING: The Department of Natural Resources (DNR) will be treating Bear Lake with weed killer on September 9. DO NOT swim in Bear Lake or use the water on lawns or plants September 9–12!

I ripped down one of the notices and stuck it in my purse to show to Dad. When I arrived at the Blit that day, the lunch crowd was normal since summer was over. School had started and most college kids were gone. Walker was leaving in the morning. I had traded my night shift for the day shift so we could have a last night together.

The Squirrel Board had filled up in a hurry, and now people were taping little scraps of paper to the board to make their bets. As I sailed by with a perch sandwich, Teeni, our neighbor, called out to me. "Honey, why did you bet November thirtieth? We've never had a first snow on November thirtieth."

I called over my shoulder, "Nineteen sixty-two. Check your stats."

Teeni was leaning on the bar and sipping a Bloody Mary. She flipped through the Squirrel Board logbook. "Huh, you're right. I never win anything. I guess I'm not very lucky." She glanced out at the parking lot, straightened her Talbot's catalogue smock top, and patted her auburn-dyed hair. Father Whippet entered the bar. "But I have been *getting* lucky, if you know what I mean."

Father Whippet headed straight for Teeni. He pulled her from the bar and over to a table.

"Tommy," I hissed across the bar. "Will you take their order?"

He looked at me over his bifocals. "I do believe that's what I hired *you* for." He went back to the sports page. Father Whippet was startled to see me standing at his table with my pad and pen at the ready. He must've thought I had gone back to school already.

"I'm here to counsel Katrina," he said and patted her hand. Teeni stroked his hand with her forefinger in return. He hurriedly pulled it away. It was all I could do not to retch.

"Do you know what you want?" I hadn't bothered bringing menus because the locals already had everything memorized.

"I know what *I* want," Teeni said to Father Whippet meaningfully. I rolled my eyes. Teeni had been married for forty and some odd years. Her husband was a boring, high-level executive at Generated Power, and he only talked about pistons and stock prices, but still.

"If it's on the menu, I can help you out." I couldn't help the sarcasm. "Otherwise there might be other establishments that can accommodate you better."

"The Thompson family certainly has gotten rude lately," Father Whippet said.

I figured now that I had learned to use my mouth I might as well go for broke. "We're just saying what we have always thought. Communication, as you pointed out in your last sermon, is very healthy."

"I'll have the Junior BLT burger, rare."

"Does your wife know you're, ah, having lunch today?" I asked as I wrote down his order. Father Whippet tried to throw his napkin down in a snit but since it was paper it just floated to the floor.

"That's it! Katrina, you'll just have to receive counseling another day—perhaps when Miss Thompson has a little less to say."

I watched his Adam's apple bob above his white collar as he swallowed hard. Then he turned on his heel and stormed out the door.

Teeni wilted at the table. "Bring me another Bloody Mary, honey. But hold the Bloody and hold the Mary. Make the rest of it a double."

I was surprised at how good I felt finally saying exactly what I thought. That night I fairly danced around while I got ready for my date with Walker. I even had the bathroom to myself for once. I wore my best jeans, yellow short-sleeve shirt with the little polo player on it, and Sammie's yellow sandals. I was all smiles when I answered the door for him. All six-foot-two of him looked and smelled good. "You ready?" He smiled back at me.

"All set." I grabbed my purse and followed him down the walk.

"Feel the temperature?" He held out his hand like he was weighing the air. "It warmed up nicely today. I'm taking you somewhere I've never taken anyone: the last bend on the Little Manistee River."

As I climbed into the car I prayed that maybe he had a romantic Indian summer picnic planned. We bumped along a two-track with branches scraping the roof of the car. Finally we came to a clearing next to the river. "Here?" I asked hopefully, looking for the candles and champagne.

"Oh no."

He went to the back of the car and lowered the tailgate; then he handed me what I least wanted to see. "I brought you my little brother's waders."

"Gosh, thanks." Walker completely missed the tone in my voice. I abandoned Sammie's sandals and struggled into the waders, pulling the suspenders up over my shoulders and tightening them as much as I could. The waders still came up past my chest. My bare feet felt mucky inside of the too-large rubber boots. I was ticked off at Walker that I had spent any time on my makeup and clothes. He got out his fishing rod and tied on a fly.

"See here?" He showed me the fly. "It's called a Royal Humpy." It was black and hairy with a red dot in the middle. "The trout love them." Darkness was falling and Walker turned on his headlamp. He got into the river first, then held my hand while I slid down the bank. He walked with sure steps through the slow-moving water. I held his hand and fumbled along behind him. After a while my eyes adjusted to the darkness and I could see the outline of the trees along the bank. My foot hit a submerged branch every once in a while but I was getting the hang of it.

"Hold on, we're almost there," Walker whispered. Almost where? I thought. The middle of nowhere? But I had relaxed and the night was beautiful. Stars were overhead and lending some light. Even though I hadn't said anything, Walker said, "Shhh," then turned out his headlamp. We stood still, letting our eyes adjust to the darkness. Then I saw them: flickers of light ahead of us, flitting in the trees, above the river, in the grass. There were thousands, perhaps millions of fireflies. It was like the secret place where fairies frolic in the forest. We waded into the glowing lights. Then Walker turned to me and tilted my head up. He kissed me and I pressed into him.

"Jeannie, will you marry me?"

I was so startled I couldn't help myself. "Why?"

He laughed. "For all the normal reasons people get married."

I was so unprepared for this, I didn't know what to say. I didn't even ask him if he loved me. Instead I stuttered, "Wh-What about my family?"

Walker folded me in his arms and pulled me as close as two people can get in fishing waders. "Honey, it'll be fine. After I graduate I'm sure I'll get a job in some big city. We'll still see your family at Christmas." From where my head rested on his upper arm, I stared at the black water encircling us. Walker then gently held me out at arm's length and regarded me. I couldn't stand the look on his face. He was waiting, hopeful. I wanted it to feel right but it didn't. But I didn't want to disappoint him.

Just then a fish jumped and Walker couldn't help himself. He turned on his headlamp to study the size of the ripples. That's when I saw it: the sign I didn't know I had been waiting for. His lamplight caught the stone arch of an old bridge, and there, etched into the side in formal lettering, was my grandmother's last name: HARMON. The Harmon Bridge. I turned to Walker.

"Yes."

Ten years later, after the divorce, I explained to Mom why I had said yes in the first place. I told her about my initial misgivings in the river but then I had seen it, The Sign From Above, the bridge with her family name on it. Mom ducked her head and her shoulders started heaving. I thought she was crying, until she lifted her head. Her eyes were brimming with tears but it was because she was laughing so hard. I didn't see what was so funny.

"Oh, my little sunshine," she gasped and patted my knee. "Didn't you know that my mother was the most divorced woman in Jones County, Texas? It was a sign, all right—a sign to run the other way!"

After a beat, I started laughing, too. We howled until we cried right there on the glider, to the point where every neighbor probably wondered what was so damn humorous.

The evening after Walker and I got engaged, Elizabeth, Lucy, and I headed for the airport. I hadn't told anyone about the engagement yet. I was still getting used to the idea. Instead we talked about the situation with Anna.

Elizabeth said, "We've never done anything bad to her."

"We've never done anything nice either," Lucy said.

Sammie's plane arrived and she climbed in the car after throwing her suitcase in the trunk. At our expectant faces she simply said, "Meijer's. We need supplies." She filled us in on her plan as we drove. We got to Meijer's and bought firewood, lighter fluid, and matches. When it was good and dark, we snuck in to Evan and Anna's enormous backyard. We lugged the wood to the edge of Bear Lake. Then we searched in the dark for fallen tree branches and piled those on, too. I poured the lighter fluid on the pile while Sammie unzipped her suitcase and pulled out what looked to be a very large piece of canvas. She threw it on the grass, then dug back in her suitcase and produced five candles. Then she unrolled the canvas. It was so dark I could barely make out her or what was written on her "artwork."

"What's it say?" I asked.

"Be quiet," Elizabeth hissed, "or it won't work." Sammie tapped my shoulder, the signal for me to light the fire. I threw match after match on it until the bonfire blossomed into the sky.

"How are we going to get her to wake up so she sees all this?" I asked.

Sammie's response was to pick up rocks from the edge of the lake and hand them to Lucy. "You're the best shot."

Lucy started heaving rocks at the second-floor window we knew to be Evan and Anna's bedroom. They bounced off the glass, but no lights went on. Then we saw a shape at another window, the one next to their bedroom. Anna was sleeping in the guest room. She opened the window and peered out at the bonfire in her yard.

We were facing the house with Bear Lake to our back and the bonfire between the house and us. "Now!" Sammie commanded. Each of us four girls grabbed an edge of the canvas and held it up so Anna could read it. It said, WE LOVE YOU, ANNA. WILL YOU BE OUR SISTER? The bonfire lit our faces and the written message. The flames shot up a good eight feet. It was really about the most impressive bonfire any of us had ever made, I thought with satisfaction.

Anna stood there with her hands on the window ledge for a good long time, and then she disappeared. We dropped the sign and waited.

"Think she's coming?" Lucy asked as we all exchanged worried looks.

Then the door opened, and Anna ran across the lawn.

"Hit the button!" Sammie yelled. I bent over and hit PLAY on the boom box. Anna stopped in front of the four of us. We looked at her expectantly and she looked back at us. Then the music started, loud enough to wake up the county. "*We are fam-i-ly! I've got all my sisters with me!*" Sammie handed us all candles and Elizabeth, Lucy, Sammie, and I lit our candles from the bonfire. Anna stood apart from us holding her candle. We circled her and we lit her candle with the four of ours.

"*We are fam-i-ly. I've got all my sisters with me. Get up everybody and sing!*" We obeyed. The firelight danced off our bobbing faces and flashing feet and hips. When the music ended, we collapsed in a gasping, laughing heap in the grass.

Anna turned her face toward Sammie. "You came all the way back for me?"

"Yep."

"You *are* all crazy—you know that, right?" But Anna's voice had a smile. "But I like that about you. I like being a part of your family. And I love Evan." She sighed happily. "If he'll have me back, I can't wait to start to make our own family."

"So no Florida?" I rolled over and asked.

"Nope. I just want to have a baby, like Elizabeth and Lucy."

Lucy's voice came out of the shadows. "I'm not pregnant any-more."

We sat straight up.

"I lost it before I got home." Lucy's voice was barely audible. I reached across the grass for her hand and squeezed it. "I didn't tell anyone because I'm tired of feeling like one big apology. I wish I could scrub off every bad thing that's happened to me and make myself all shiny and new."

Anna put her arms around Lucy. I put my head in my hands and thought about why my twenty-one-year-old sister, who had just graduated first in her class, felt like she was all used up. Anna jumped up. "Into the car," she instructed, "all of you."

It wasn't a night to ask what was going on. The four of us just did what she said. She drove to the bridge over the Bear Lake channel and parked. We all got out and looked at Anna for guid-ance. She pulled her shirt over her head and then dropped her sweatpants. "It's time for a baptism, or, as Evan would put it, a spiritual rebirth. A new start."

Lucy giggled for the first time since she got home. Then she pulled off her clothes, too.

"No way," Elizabeth pronounced.

"Yes way!" Sammie threw off every single stitch. I, more se-dately, stripped to my bra and underwear.

"I'm pregnant, you know," Elizabeth said, stalling.

"You dove in to the country club pool last week!" I said.

Reluctantly, Elizabeth followed us as we clambered up onto the wide stone railing and looked down at the dark water ten feet below us. Without speaking, we joined hands.

Anna counted, "One, two, three!"

We launched ourselves into the night. After a delirious drop, the water closed over us. The shock of the cold took my breath away. I counted heads. We were all here and Lucy was laughing and sputtering and splashing Elizabeth. When the spotlight hit us, we all looked up at the bridge. Marv Carson called out, "I should have guessed it was you guys." The radio in his patrol car crackled and he went to respond to it. The five of us treaded water. We couldn't get out to retrieve our clothes while Marv was there. His face reappeared at the bridge railing. "Hey, Anna? You interested in the fact that the big, old oak tree in your yard is on fire?"

Anna gasped.

"Welcome to the family, Anna," Sammie said happily.

Twenty-nine

May 2006

*L*ucy begged me to take the afternoon off work to see Sammie and Elizabeth with her. Sitting behind my desk listening to her on my phone headset, I held my hand out level in front of my face. It didn't appear to be trembling. I took that as a good sign that my outsides weren't reflecting my insides. Steadfastly I refused Lucy. "I cannot take one more emotional drama today, Lucy." Aidan hadn't answered my phone calls or emails begging him to call me. His assistant kept telling me he "wasn't available."

My sister remained silent on the other end of the line. As a lawyer, she was probably trying to come up with an alternate line of reasoning.

"They are both completely pissed off at me. I can't have a big emotional makeup session with them today," I said.

"They are angry with you because you always miss family gatherings," Lucy finally said tartly, "which is exactly what you are doing yet again today. You know I have to leave tomorrow. It's not like we'll have more time to see each other all together later."

"Lucy, I just can't," I murmured.

"Fine. If I mean that little to you, then I'll just pack up my stuff and go stay tonight on Sammie's couch."

I didn't get a chance to respond because she hung up the phone on me. With my thumb and forefinger I rubbed at the bridge of my nose, where I felt a headache forming. I had hit the perfect trifecta: all three of my sisters were furious with me at the same time.

My computer pinged at me announcing an instant message. Caitlin was letting me know that Jeffanie from *Jet Fuel* were on the line. Pushing my sisters out of my mind, I answered the phone.

Jeff Cross's voice came over my headset. "Stephanie and I decided we're not coming for the photo shoot after all."

"May I ask why not?" I said a bit too sharply. The *Jet Fuel* shoot was in four days. Without Jeff Cross chances were good that the rest of the cast would also back out. The posters were already four months late. And now Jeff was canceling.

"We don't fly commercial," Jeff said. Ah, I thought, they want a private plane. Oxford had a private plane, but it was strictly reserved for the top-level studio executives. If the studio gave it to one star, then every other star would demand the private plane. The cost was prohibitive to say the least. But maybe, just maybe, I could make another miracle happen.

"I might be able to get the Oxford jet," I said.

"No. Not the Oxford jet," Jeff answered. "We want the same plane the president rides in."

"The president of the studio?" I was bewildered.

"The President of the United States."

I sat back in my chair. "You want Air Force One?" I asked incredulously. This was definitely a new one.

"Danny told me he got that plane when he had to fly to do publicity for his last film." Danny DiNoda, as every moviegoer knew, was the star of enormous hits. He had generated literally billions and billions of dollars at the box office. Mentally, I cursed the studio that had set a precedent by getting a plane that had served as Air Force One for their star. "And when Katsu called me this morning he said he thought it was a great idea."

"Katsu called you?" Furious, I could barely keep my tone polite.

"Yeah. He seems like a great guy. He said he wanted to help you out on *Jet Fuel* because you have an overwhelming number of movies to work on."

Katsu used the word *overwhelming*? Un-freaking-believable! It was a classic vinegar-wrapped-in-sugar kind of statement. He was pretending that he wanted to "help" me while also subtly indicating that I was no longer capable. The word "overwhelming" meant that a situation had become unmanageable for a person. It indicated weakness. Katsu had used that word very intentionally.

I forgot Jeff Cross was even on the line until he said, "Katsu told me and Stephanie that if you couldn't figure out how to get the president's plane, he could probably pull it off. That's what he said, anyhow."

I'm sure he did.

"Wow. I guess I can check on it," I said carefully. As Katsu was well aware, there was no way I was going to be able to get that plane. Neither could he, for that matter. "Is there anything else you would like?" The sarcasm in my voice was lost on Jeff Cross.

"Yeah," he said. "Stephanie and I want one thousand tea candles set up in our suite—purple tea candles. And the suite has to be redone entirely in white. White carpets, white drapes, white bedding, white furniture, white bathroom fixtures. You get the idea."

After I hung up, I figured I'd better get all the facts before taking this "upstairs" to the powers that be. I called a friend at the rival studio. True enough, they had secured one of the planes that had served as Air Force One for their billion-dollar box office star.

Surely, that had to have been before 9/11, didn't it? I asked. I was hopeful it would all be a moot point in this day and age. No, my friend had replied, it was only last year. A lot of different planes could be used as Air Force One. Baffled at government security, I thanked my friend and hung up. I had to take off my shoes to get through airport screening but any random person with enough money could hire out Air Force One? Amazing.

My friend had given me contact information for the plane. After checking to see whether Aidan had called or emailed (he hadn't), I got to work. Two hours later, after umpteen phone calls and transfers from one department to the next, I got my answer. One of the planes was available. The cost to use it would fund a small nation for a year. I called the Four Seasons. Getting this answer was less problematic. Sure, they said, they could redo everything in white within two days. With all the stars who stayed there, they were as used to strange requests as I was. But even I gasped at the price they quoted me.

In between the *Jet Fuel* problems, I was working the phones like a madman trying to get the *TechnoCat* trailer shoot organized.

After I compiled all the budget numbers relating to Air Force One and the Four Seasons, I took everything to Rachael. Silently she reviewed the demands along with the numbers. After questioning me closely about how hard I had tried to dissuade Jeffanie from the president's plane, she decided we needed to take this to the chairman of the studio. Not only was the budget astronomical but there were many political considerations as well. Rachael had the power to give the approvals but I knew she wasn't going to have this one on her head alone.

We took a golf cart across the studio lot to Vincent's office. The chairman and the production people were in a different building from the marketing people. It was a good two or three city blocks, filled with soundstages, between the buildings. When we entered his cavernous office, he could tell from the looks on our faces that this wasn't good.

Somberly, we looked at all the options. None were that appealing. Denying Jeffanie would jeopardize the current negotiations to get Jeff Cross for the sequel to *Jet Fuel*. On top of that, Oxford Music was near completing a contract to sign the platinum-selling Stephanie Langer to its label. It had already been a delicate negotiation. Finally, after discussing the pros, the cons, and the political fallout of setting such a precedent, a decision was made. We would do everything that was asked except, Vincent announced, the tea candles.

"Why not the tea candles?" I was startled. By far this was the most insignificant cost.

"Just to piss them off." He laughed. "But honestly, why does anyone need a thousand tea candles?" Vincent poured himself some Perrier. "They're just seeing how far they can push us. Plus, I don't trust them with fire. They're nuts."

I practically bit his head off. "Don't make my job any harder. They're looking for any reason to back out of this." I caught myself as Vincent sat back and frowned at me. Oh God, I had just spoken rudely to the chairman. Worse, I had not been calm. To my thinking, you *must* be calm and controlled in a studio. Clearing my throat I continued in an even, moderate voice. "It's better for the studio to just give them the candles. There is too much at stake." Not to mention better for me, as I was sure Katsu would go straight to Jeffanie to tell them I had failed to get them the thousand tea candles.

Vincent considered and finally nodded his head. "Oh all right, Jeannie. You get your way. But we're going to squeeze this for publicity," he said firmly. "Every photographer within a hundred miles of New York and Los Angeles will be alerted as to when Jeffanie are traveling." As I stood up to leave I heard him mutter, "I'll make their lives hell with the paparazzi. Serves the bastards right."

Since Rachael wanted to discuss other matters with Vincent, I left her the golf cart and began walking back across the lot. Darkness had fallen. I walked past the silent soundstages where silver screen history had been made for decades. Past the little house that used to contain classrooms for child actors in the nineteen forties and fifties. Past the recording studio where one-hundred-piece orchestras recorded the music for the films. The long trek gave me time to think about my situation with Aidan.

I could just write an email telling him that it was Lucy in my house and not some mysterious Dream Date. But that felt oddly impersonal, as did trying to explain the whole situation to his voice mail. He was still going to be angry once he found out one of my sisters had been in the house and I hadn't introduced them. Which unfortunately reminded me that my three sisters were probably trashing my good name at this very moment. Then I checked my watch. No, they had already finished trashing me and were probably all tucked in for the night by now. My thoughts drifted from families to marriage. Why couldn't Aidan just leave it all alone? Everything had been fine just the way it was until he proposed.

My marriage to Walker had been an emotional disaster. But, I questioned myself, Aidan and Walker were as different from each other as black and white, weren't they? Walker had forced me to vacation every Christmas for six years at his family's ski condo

in Aspen instead of going to North Muskegon. Every time I suggested we spend the holiday with my family Walker brought up
the year that my mom poured alcohol over a fruitcake and, holding it merrily aloft, set it ablaze. Unfortunately this had frightened
Ake, the dog, who knocked my mom and the fruitcake into the
Christmas tree, setting that on fire, too.

Mom was fine. But by the time the fire trucks left we were minus
part of our roof and most of the TV room. The local news station
played the footage of the blaze over and over, along with rehash-
ing older news stories about my family. Walker was horrified we
had created such a commotion in our town yet again. Surely Aidan
wouldn't hold something like that against me, would he?

I looked up as I crossed the courtyard, with its mature euca-
lyptus trees. The old-fashioned streetlights lining the golf cart path
lit up the branches. Nobody seemed to be around. Looking over
my shoulder, I determined that I was, in fact, alone. Mindful of
my skirt and high heels, I sat down on the grass next to the cart
path. Then I lay all the way down so I could study the way the
lights shone through the leaves of the trees above me. It looked
the same way it did when I was a kid, lying in the intersection of a
quiet street. Every color of green rustled in the warm wind against
the black sky. I knew I loved Aidan. But he just didn't know what
he was getting into. If he didn't accept my family the way I did,
shouldn't I protect him from all of that? And myself? The grass
poked me through my white shirt and against my legs but I still
lay there.

"You all right?" A voice on the cart path startled me upright.
It was a security guard making rounds. He leaned out of his golf
cart to peer at me suspiciously.

"Yes, yes, I'm fine." Awkwardly, I got to my feet while trying to keep my skirt down. Next I picked up my notebooks lying on the grass.

"Bit of a weird place to take a nap." The security guard still eyed me warily. "I thought you were dead."

"I just . . . I just . . ." I didn't know how to explain what I had been doing. I finally settled for, "I'm not dead."

"You never know around here," he said as he started to drive off. "You wouldn't believe the stuff I've seen." Oh, yes, I would, I thought to myself as I brushed myself off. I walked fast to get back to my office. Once there, I planned to grab my purse and head straight for Aidan's. We were going to talk this out once and for all. I had to make him understand that a girl shouldn't have to choose between the love of a man and the love of her family.

Entering the empty lobby of my building I said hello to the night security guard at the desk. We were old friends by now. Usually we were the only ones in the building at midnight long after the cleaning crew had left. Tonight, though, a workman was also in the lobby. He was putting the latest poster for *TechnoCat* into one of the frames that held the posters of all of the current Oxford Pictures releases. He finished and shut the glass door to the case as I was crossing the wide terrazzo floor.

Mid-step, I froze. There, larger than life, was the little "doohickey" sticking up on the side of Esperanza's head. The doohickey she had said reminded her of her third grade photo, which had made her cry for years. The doohickey I had *promised* I would fix. The glaring flaw was right now being posted in theaters around the country—hell, around the world—as I stood and stared at it.

I had sent the wrong artwork to print.

Thirty

November 1986

I crossed another phone number off the Xeroxed list and listlessly picked up the phone again. It was a beige rotary phone and I used a pencil to dial so I wouldn't have to touch its germy face. It was my own fault. I never should have answered the ad in the student paper.

"Good evening, ma'am," I started.

"Is this a sales call?" The female voice was pure vinegar.

What a bitch, I thought, but I continued, sugar sweet. "No, ma'am. I'm calling for the Lansing-area Sew-Bee's charity." We were instructed to say that, even though it really was a sales call. I didn't want to give her time to hang up as I rushed on. I find most people are at least polite enough to listen to three or four sentences before they slam down the phone. "We have a coupon book for you with over one thousand dollars in savings at your area establishments!" The exclamation point was written on the script that was provided to us callers. I rarely sounded that enthusiastic, but my boss was standing over me observing. A dial tone was the answer to the exciting news I had imparted. I smiled up at my boss. "Now, ma'am," I continued to the dial tone, "you can get a three-dollar coupon to the Smart and Sassy dry cleaner on Grand Avenue and that's only one of these great values!" My boss moved away to monitor the next caller. I hung up the phone and stretched.

I was sitting with twelve other women at long folding tables in the Ramada Inn conference room. The walls were beige, the floor was beige, and the phones were beige. The only thing with any color was my boss's shirt, an ugly polyester thing with swirling, swishing colors. He sat in front while he ate McDonald's fries. He wiped one back and forth in the ketchup that he'd squeezed from the little packet onto the wrapper from his Big Mac.

God, how much longer did I have to stay here? Lucy had landed a job as hostess at the restaurant in the Kellogg Center on campus. I envied her. Chuck would be at the house by the time we got there. He'd be sprawled on the couch that had provided years, if not decades, of flopping enjoyment to other students, watching *Wheel of Fortune* and drinking a Moosehead. It was the only thing I'd seen him excited about since we'd arrived at Michigan State—a Canadian beer.

I dialed the next number on the list. I was supposed to have had my very own place for the very first time in my life. My roommate and I had rented the top half of a house on Virginia Street, on the edge of campus. She was doing the fall semester overseas and wasn't going to be back until January. I would actually be alone. But when Lucy, Chuck, and I had arrived with our shared U-Haul, we had discovered that there was a mix-up with married housing. Lucy and Chuck were out of luck. Chuck hadn't sent in the deposit check.

"You told me you mailed it!" Lucy fumed while we sat in the

parking lot of married housing just off Hagadorn Road. Other students teemed around us, shouting and laughing, playing Frisbee or carrying milk crates of personal belongings into the dorms. Somebody blared the MSU fight song from an open window. *"Go right through for MSU. Watch the points keep growing. Spartan teams are bound to win . . ."* The song echoed through the streets. When it got to the part that goes, *"They're fighting with a vim!"* I thought, as I did every time, What the hell kind of word is "vim"? Why couldn't we have a cool fight song like the University of Michigan? *"Hail to the victors, valiant! Hail to the conquering heroes! . . ."* Now *that* was a fight song.

"What did you do with the deposit?" Lucy demanded. Chuck shrugged and put another pinch of tobacco chew between his cheek and gum. So they wound up living with me. They paid rent to my grateful, absent roommate and everyone was happy except me. But I never would have told them that. That might have made them feel bad.

When the clock finally said 9:00 p.m. I raced out past the full-sized, black plaster Angus cow at the hotel entrance and hurried to the Kellogg Center. Lucy was waiting for me out front. She threw her backpack into the backseat. Mom and Dad had bought us a sixteen-year-old Oldsmobile sedan so we could get around. Sometimes we had to start it by touching a screwdriver to the battery. We didn't know why that worked but it did. If you've ever trudged through two-foot snowdrifts, you'd know that you don't care what kind of car you're driving as long as it moves and has heat. Lucy and Chuck had the little red Ford they'd driven from Monterey, but Chuck needed it to get to his job at the Mr. Taco.

"Are you ready for your test?" I asked her.

She blew on her hands, rubbed them together, and then held

them up to the semi-useless heater vent. "Not even close. I put in thirty hours at work this week."

Lucy studied religiously every night. She had been getting straight A's while pulling a full load of classes and working almost full time. She refused to take money from Mom and Dad for rent or school, and I knew it was tight for her and Chuck. I had to pay for my books, food, and entertainment by myself, but Mom and Dad handled the rest. I often told Lucy she was making me look bad.

Chuck didn't even look up from the television when we came in. He just shouted, "Shut the door! It's fucking freezing out there. I don't know how people can live in this weather."

Lucy kissed him on top of his head. "How was work?"

"Shitty." He tipped the beer bottle up and sucked. He reeked of taco meat and cigarette smoke.

Lucy went to the kitchen, which was separated from the living room by a counter, and put a frozen pizza in the oven. "Does your boss still want you to wear that foam thing?" she called over the counter. Chuck's only response was to start flipping channels via the remote.

I sat on the stool at the counter. "What foam thing?"

"You know, like one of those costumes that people wear. They go out on the street corner and wave at passing cars dressed like a giant hot dog or, in this case, a giant taco. It's supposed to bring customers into the store."

"Why? Because seeing a guy dressed in foam is so appetizing?"

Lucy shrugged and bent over her books. I picked up the mail lying on the counter. Flipping through it I saw that the phone bill had arrived and slipped it into my pocket. I had noticed that a strange long distance number had showed up on the last two bills. Last month when we got the bill, I called information and found out that the area code was for Illinois. I called the number, and when a woman answered, I asked formally, "To whom am I speaking?"

She replied, "Carla," and not knowing what else to say, I had abruptly hung up the phone.

I didn't know if this was the girl whom Chuck had been seeing when Lucy married him or a new one. No time seemed like a good time to confront Chuck, so I'd been stashing the bills away for the past couple of months. I couldn't afford to pay them by myself. So I figured that when the phone company turned off the phone that would be a good time to have the discussion.

The next morning I made my every-third-day phone call to Walker. Since he didn't work—the pressure of Princeton, he told me, meant that he had to concentrate every second on school—I picked up the tab for the phone bills. I never asked what he did with the money his parents sent him from home. He sounded drowsy, as usual.

"Sorry I'm so out of it. I was up late last night studying with Cynthia."

Cynthia was a sharp-nosed, dark-haired debutante who most likely had grown up learning her ABC's and numbers by managing her stock portfolio. I had met her on my last trip out to see Walker. We had entered a bar on Nassau Street and she had been draped around a booth drinking a Kir Royale with her perfect, ultra-cool friends. I was wearing jeans and she was wearing thousand-dollar black pants. It would have been hard to be skinnier than this whippet, but, I consoled myself, at least I had breasts. Walker had whispered to me that her father was the CEO of a Fortune 500 company. He had been on the cover of *Newsweek* a few weeks before.

"How is she?" I asked.

"Jeannie. Enough." I held the phone tightly. Enough of what? I hadn't said anything. I hadn't even had an undertone to my voice.

"You brought her up," I snipped.

The rest of the call was not pleasant either, so I cut it short by reminding Walker that I had an early morning class. Leaving the car for Lucy I headed out to the Kresge Art Center for my four-hour History of Art class.

I cut across campus to get there. Michigan State has arguably one of the prettiest campuses in the United States. The Red Cedar River meanders through it. Most of the architecture is classic red-brick-and-pillar set among broad lawns and woods. It had, however, been a shock freshman year to suddenly be in a classroom that had more students in it than had been in my entire elementary, junior high, and high school rolled into one. I dug my mittened hands into the pockets of my pea coat. Damn, it was cold. It was almost December and the temperature was already in the twenties in the morning.

No snow yet, though. Dad had called me to tell me there was a false alarm at the BLT in regard to the Squirrel Board. Several people thought they saw snowflakes, but it turned out to only be ash from someone illegally burning garbage. Tempers flared since the pot was up to $2,810.

At least, I thought, Evan and Anna had plenty of firewood for the winter. Their 150-year-old oak tree had to be taken down after we had unwittingly set it on fire. My sisters and I had bought a weeping willow to replace the oak. We had stuck it in the gigantic hole, stepped back, and stared at it. It looked like that tree Charlie Brown brings home at Christmas.

Evan spent his next two cooking shows on the subject of the ephemeral nature of, well, nature. How something has always been there, and you think it will always be there, and then *poof*.

Gone. At first, the callers were deeply sympathetic. They knew the close relationship a man can have with his yard. But then they turned on him, told him to pull up his bootstraps and start talking about how to properly freeze venison. After all, they currently had bucks hanging upside down from their own beloved trees and the deer had all just about drained of blood. It was time for the butchering and the subsequent storage of meats in the Deep-freezes kept in their garages.

I arrived at class, actually participated in some of the discussions, and left the room feeling proud of myself. Lucy met me at the student union with the car. We usually had lunch there before I dropped Lucy off at the Kellogg Center and went to work.

"How'd the test go?" I asked as I stuffed a French fry in my mouth.

"I'm pretty sure I aced it." She grinned.

"Excellent!" I sat back. "Maybe we should go to Dooley's tonight to celebrate. It's dollar beer night."

She reached out to swipe some of my French fries while we talked a while about our classes. Then Lucy stood up and grabbed her coat off the back of the chair. "Come on, I can't be late for work."

I dropped her off and drove to the Ramada Inn. The workday started with the Bossman asking who wanted to do his laundry instead of dialing the phones. My hand shot up, but not fast enough. I lost out to a middle-aged woman who simpered like Ed McMahon had just come to her door in the prizemobile. It's a sorry state of affairs when sorting the dirty underwear and sweaty polyester shirts of a stranger is preferable to dialing number after number. I picked up my sheet of phone numbers and began. By the fourth hour I had sold three coupon books, which was pretty good. I had laid my head on my outstretched arm and held the receiver to my free ear. " . . . and you also receive a coupon for ten percent off a one-night stay at the Daisy Motel in Gatlinburg, Tennessee."

"Why would I be going to Gatlinburg?" the voice asked.

I dialed the next number without picking up my head. I was more than halfway through my script when my victim interrupted me. "Could you repeat that?"

"Sure." I yawned. "You can get a two-for-one dinner of mouth-watering Penis Chicken at Penis Barbecue."

A chuckle came over the phone. "Honey, I'm not sure if I should call the cops or ask you for a date. But I think you mean Penni's Barbecue. It's that joint on the highway."

My hand came up to my mouth as I stared at the script. There was a typo: one of the *n*s was missing, so it read *Peni's*—or, as I was pronouncing it, "penis." I hung up the phone. How many people had I read this script to? Two thousand? Three thousand? Did they think I was selling them something entirely different from a coupon book? Bossman saw me and came marching down the narrow aisle.

"Why are you just sitting there? Dial!"

I stared at the gold chain resting in its nest of black chest hair. "Jeannie, I've never told you this, but you are my number one seller. So come on, let's look alive." He walked away. I was perplexed. How could I be his number one seller? Then I realized. Penis Chicken. For the first time in my life I recognized the power of marketing to an unsuspecting consumer.

After work I met Lucy and Chuck at Dooley's. They were a few beers up on me and were nuzzling each other so I headed to the bar to escape them. I was trying to get the bartender's attention when a waitress slid up next to me. "You with them?" she asked, jerking her head at Lucy and Chuck's booth.

"Yeah," I said. "Why?"

"Who's the girl?"

"My sister."

The waitress slammed her round tray on the bar and signaled the bartender. She turned to me. "No. Who's. The. Girl?" she repeated, getting right in my face. Now I got it.

"She's his wife."

"That figures." She jerked the beers onto her tray. "That just fucking figures." She started to leave, but I pulled on her arm. She had no choice but to turn back to me or lose the load on her tray.

"Why do you care?" I asked.

"Because he's been seeing my roommate. They work together at Mr. Taco. This is so going to piss her off."

Piss *her* off? I thought. I let the waitress go and went to sit with Lucy and Chuck. The waitress studiously avoided our table all night. Several times, Lucy tried to flag her down but she just sailed by. Chuck said it was easier just to get beer from the bar anyway. He darted up there every time the waitress entered the danger zone. This meant anywhere within three tables of us. Lucy could tell something was up but she didn't know what it was. Fortunately, the music was so loud we couldn't do much talking anyway.

After we got home there were raised voices coming from their bedroom, and then it sounded like a lamp shattering against our adjoining wall. I tossed my blankets back and went to my wall to listen. Instead there was a knock on my door.

"Jeannie," Lucy called, "can I spend the night in your room?"

I let her in. She went straight to my double bed, flopped down, and faced the wall. I shut the door and made sure it was locked.

Chuck was already gone when we woke up the next morning.

"Lucy," I said at breakfast, "is there anything you want to talk about?"

She fiddled with a fork.

I sat down and waited.

"It's hard for him, you know? He's in a place where he doesn't know anybody and he can't stand the weather. At least I have a reason to be here."

"Lucy, are you sure this is the right thing for you?" I tried to tread carefully but she threw the fork at the wall.

"Leave me alone!" she shrieked. Then she fled to her room and slammed the door. I knew then that it was time to call in the Special Forces. I needed Mom. I picked up the phone, but there was no dial tone. Our phone had been turned off. Shit, shit, and goddamn it.

I worked on Saturdays, and I was already late. I didn't have time to take care of Lucy. When I finally shrugged out of my parka at the Ramada Inn, I was twenty minutes late. One of the other girls told me Bossman was out on a fast food run, so I relaxed. I looked to my left and right, but no one was paying attention to me. I was about to break a cardinal rule and make a personal phone call.

"Mom?"

"Hello there. I've been wondering what you were up to. You never call home," Mom said. I knew she was waiting for me to talk more so she could tell which daughter it was without asking.

"It's Jeannie, Mom."

"I know that!" Mom lied smoothly. "Now tell me all about school." She was back on her game.

"Mom, I'm at work and I can't talk long. I'm not even supposed to be calling you." I had to keep going before she made vain attempts to keep me on the phone anyway.

"Here, say hello to your father." Mom then yelled for Dad to come to the phone. I looked anxiously at the door and smiled wanly at my seatmate. It was the same woman who had brown-nosed the boss by doing his laundry.

"Hello, sweetheart. How's Michigan State treating you?"

"Uh, good, Dad," I said. I couldn't talk to my dad about Lucy's problem. This was Mom's territory. Bossman ambled through the door and scanned the room for loafers. His antenna went up when he saw me hunched over. Now he was coming down the aisle toward me. Desperately, I launched into the script. "And you can get twenty percent off a dinner at Red Lobster!" Bossman paused by my side. I looked up at him innocently.

"Well, that's real good, sweetheart. My, twenty percent off." My father clearly felt like he had been dropped into a mysterious conversation I had started with my mother.

My seatmate was making motions next to me and mouthing over my head, "She's on a personal call!" Bitch.

Bossman poked me maliciously with a pencil. "Read the part you told me about. The part that always gets 'em sold." Then he punched speakerphone so that the entire room could hear my conversation.

I closed my eyes tight. "And you can get a special coupon to, um"—I coughed—"Penis Chicken."

"What did you say, honey? I can't hear you for some reason." Dad's voice sounded like he was stretching the cord across the kitchen so he could watch his TV show at the same time. Bossman motioned for me to repeat the line. Frantically, I looked around the beige room for help, but all eyes were now upon me and they weren't sympathetic.

"I said you can get a special coupon to Penis Chicken." I closed my eyes before I read their slogan. "There's no place my mouth would rather be than at Penis!"

There was a long pause on the other side of the line. Then I heard Dad yell to Mom, "Rose, I think she wants to talk to *you*."

Bossman took the phone from my trembling hand and hung it up. "You're fired."

"That was my first personal phone call!" I protested.

"That I know about," he said sternly. He turned to the others. "Let Jeannie here be an example to you. Make a personal phone call, get fired."

I rose and took my purse and coat off the back of the metal folding chair. I tried to hold my head up as I walked out, criminal though I was. At the door I asked, "Can I get my check for last week?" My voice quavered.

"Sue me," Bossman sneered.

I stopped outside in the Ramada Inn hallway and stared down at the ugly carpet. Fired. I had been fired. And I didn't get to ask Mom's advice about Lucy. And I had said the word "penis" to my father. Not just once but several times.

I sagged out of the Ramada Inn, got in the car, and drove over to the Kellogg Center. Lucy would cheer me up. She would confirm that I was lousy at this particular lousy job but that I could aspire to mediocrity at another crummy job. When I got there, Lucy was waiting outside. How could she have heard about my being fired already? She pulled open the car door and slid in.

"Thank God they gave you my message. Your boss was acting really weird. I wasn't sure he would tell you," Lucy said.

"What message?"

"Chuck's in jail."

I was speechless. We drove across town in a silence that was broken only by Lucy reading directions she had written down on a napkin. When we arrived at the police station, we gave our names and told the desk clerk whom we were there to see. "Wait there," she said, and pointed to a row of molded plastic chairs that were bolted to the floor.

We sat for several uncomfortable minutes under the fluorescent lights. I studied the notices for bail bondsmen and drug rehabilitation facilities. They both featured the smiling faces of happy couples. "So why is he here?" I asked Lucy.

"I don't know and I don't want to talk about it." She stared straight ahead.

"What did he say when he called you?"

She turned to me. "I just told you I don't want to talk about it. Why do you always keep talking when I tell you I don't want to?"

"Because you really do want to talk when you say you don't want to talk. I'm helping you out."

Lucy couldn't help smiling. "You're a brat."

I smiled back. "If it makes you feel any better, I got fired today."

"What for?" She looked mildly interested, but I turned my head away in a grand gesture. "I don't want to talk about it."

Lucy laughed and I knew I had her. "So why is Chuck in jail?"

"He got in a fight with the manager at Mr. Taco. Why did you get fired?"

"Because I made a personal call."

An imposing cop strode up to us. "Is one of you the wife of Chuck Tanner?" Lucy nodded and the cop sat down next to me in the awkward three-across formation. He talked past me to Lucy. I tried to lean as far back as possible to stay out of their way.

"Ma'am, your husband is incarcerated tonight on very serious charges." He paused, waiting, I guess, for some reaction. When there was none, he continued. "The manager of Mr. Taco would be within his rights to file attempted murder charges against Mr.

Tanner." At this, both Lucy and I sat straight up. She shoved me back so she could see the cop.

"Attempted *murder*? What happened?" Now it was the cop's turn to lean back and away from Lucy's rising voice.

"Mr. Tanner allegedly picked up the manager of Mr. Taco and threw him through the plate-glass window. The manager probably would not have survived except . . ." The cop stopped and looked up at a commotion at the front doors. A giant foam taco was storming through the police station reception area.

"Where is that little cocksucker?" the taco screamed. Then he spotted Lucy. "Your husband is an A-Number-One Looney Tune! He should be put away, and I'll make sure he is!"

Lucy shrank back from the onslaught. "All I wanted him to do was wear this fucking costume! Is that so hard?" Foam stuffing was falling all over the floor and he kicked at it viciously. "But he was too cool to wear it in front of his Little Miss Hot Pants." At this, he jerked a finger toward a plump, pimple-faced girl who trailed behind him. Her uniform wasn't doing her any favors—the material was straining hard at her thighs. She was sobbing.

Lucy stood up and straightened her skirt. Then she strode past the taco to the girl. "You," she said, "you need to go home and have a hot bath. Forget you ever met Chuck."

"But I looovve him," the girl blubbered.

"No, you don't," Lucy said firmly. She took the girl by the shoulders. "I'm doing you a huge favor. Go home and do not contact Chuck again." Lucy looked into the girl's eyes, not unkindly. "Can you do that?"

The girl raised her eyes to Lucy like a trusting puppy. Then her chin went up and down. "Yes, I can do that."

"Are you okay to drive?" Lucy asked.

"I think so."

"All right, then. Off you go." Lucy propelled her gently toward the door. When the girl disappeared, Lucy turned back to the matter at hand. She took in a deep breath as she regarded the man in the taco suit. It was clear that the plate-glass window had shredded the costume but that the costume had also cushioned the manager from the flying glass and the impact of his landing. The cop confirmed this. He also told us that the manager was here to file charges against Chuck. Finding out the bail amount would take several hours, but we were welcome to wait, the cop said. With that he took off and Lucy and I sat back down in the bolted chairs. The taco leaned against a painted cinder block wall with his arms crossed.

"Do you want to sit down?" I inquired. Nothing. "What's your name?" I kept going. The taco shuffled his feet and then turned his back on us.

"It's Mr. Sanders." Lucy sighed.

"Why don't you work at a chicken place with a name like that?" I joked, before I could stop myself.

"Like I haven't ever heard that one before. Fine. Make fun of me. I'm twenty-nine years old, I'm a college graduate, I'm a manager of a lousy food franchise, and now I'm standing here dressed like an idiot in a police station. And why? Because I didn't score high enough on my LSAT." Mr. Sanders wasn't angry anymore. He just hung his head. Lucy walked over to him.

"Do you have anything on underneath that thing?"

"I wouldn't still be wearing it if I did."

"Chuck has his sweatpants and stuff in the car," Lucy said. She and Mr. Sanders left to go to the parking lot and returned shortly with a gym bag. Mr. Sanders took it and went into the men's bathroom.

Lucy sat with me. "Mr. Sanders told me that he's willing to let the whole thing go." I looked up hopefully. Maybe we could get out of here soon. But Lucy continued. "Unfortunately, it's out of his hands. The Mr. Taco corporate headquarters is pressing charges for assault. I also had to give Mr. Sanders a check for the damage to the costume and the window. It was the last three hundred dollars in our checking account. I'm not sure how I'm going to bail Chuck out." Lucy put her head in her hands and slumped over in the plastic chair.

A guy dressed in sweats and a T-shirt approached us. "I'll get the clothes back to you," he said to Lucy. He started to walk away but then turned back to her. "I might be out of line saying this to you, but be careful. That isn't the first time Chuck has done something violent. He tried to deck a customer last week." Shaking his head, he made his way out through the glass double doors.

Much later, Lucy and I jerked awake in our chairs at the sound of a buzzer. "The bail has been set," the receptionist called over the desk to us. "It's ten thousand dollars."

Lucy gasped.

"Relax. You only have to come up with ten percent of it."

"I don't have a thousand dollars." Lucy panicked. "I can't leave him in jail! Bad things happen to people in jail!" She was working herself up to hysteria now and I couldn't blame her. The stories about what happened to inmates were not pretty.

I did have a thousand dollars. Mom and Dad had sent it to me last week to pay for the winter trimester. The payment wasn't due for another week or so, and right now my sister needed money.

"I can write a check."

"No personal checks!" the receptionist said. "You gotta go to the bail bondsman and get a certified check. And there's only one that takes personal checks without collateral." She gave an address that was clear on the other side of town.

Jesus. We weren't going to get home until nighttime at this rate. But we did it. We drove across town, got the certified check, drove back, gave it to the receptionist, and, finally, Chuck was brought out to the lobby. Nobody said a word on the way home. Only later, when Chuck had gone to bed and Lucy and I were having a late-night Tab, did I think to ask her about the girl.

"How did you know Chuck was seeing that girl?"

"If it wasn't her, it would have been someone else." Then she went to join Chuck. I was sound asleep when someone pounded on the front door. I bolted straight up, my heart pounding in fright. After throwing on a robe and running down the stairs, I peered through the eyehole. It was a policeman. Had Chuck done some other heinous thing? Cautiously I opened the door, leaving the chain on. "Are you Ms. Thompson?"

"Yes," I squeaked.

"Do you have a brother, Evan Thompson?"

"Yes," I said, my heart racing.

"He called the station when he couldn't get through on your phone." I looked at him blearily, waiting for the bad news I knew was coming. "He wanted you to know that your father has had a heart attack. You don't have much time to get home."

Thirty-one

May 2006

The next three days were a nightmare. Aidan would not return a voicemail, email, or text message. I had even broken down and left a voicemail telling him that it was my sister Lucy at my house and not another man. Still, nothing.

The poster for *TechnoCat* had to be recalled, reprinted, and reshipped—none of which was cheap. The reaming I got from Rachael was nothing compared to what Esperanza put me through. Rachael forcefully told me that she was angry about the money, but even worse, that I had made our department look "scattered" and "stupid" at a "critical time." Further, she questioned my judgment, implying that it seemed my head had been elsewhere for months now. Her last words were that the *TechnoCat* shoot had better be "fucking perfect." Rachael didn't swear much so I more than got the point.

Esperanza had turned my next hour and a half into a sobbing therapy session. She cried that no one liked her (I knew I didn't). Her childhood had been a disaster: her parents forced her to take piano lessons instead of modeling lessons. And on and on, all while I tried to make soothing noises on my end of the phone.

As much as I had dreaded the flight to Prague for the *TechnoCat* shoot, I was secretly relieved to have hours and hours to myself with no way to talk to anyone else.

Almost as soon as I landed though, my phone rang.

"Jeannie, we have a problem," Caitlin said as I balanced my cell phone between my cheek and shoulder. I was trying to grab my bag off the baggage carousel at the same time.

"What now?" I had just flown seventeen hours and I was wiped out. Since even I couldn't be in two places at once, I had left Caitlin in charge of the *Jet Fuel* photo shoot.

"Jeffanie won't get on the plane. They're standing on the tarmac right now," Caitlin said. "They said that there's no Xbox to play video games on board." Dropping my bag I switched the cell phone to my other ear. Maybe I hadn't heard correctly.

"Jeffanie said that Danny had an Xbox on board his Air Force One plane. So they won't get on the plane unless an Xbox is on board. They're having their luggage transferred back to their limo now."

I sat down on top of my bag and put my forehead in my free hand. "Caitlin?"

"Yeah?"

"Get them an Xbox."

"What do I do if they won't stick around long enough for me to get an Xbox installed?"

"Have them escorted back to the airline lounge and make sure they are entertained. Find them belly dancers. Sword swallowers. Whatever it takes," I said. Then I added as an afterthought, "And start giving them liquor. Now."

"Got it." The trusty Caitlin hung up.

I had barely enough time to get to the hotel and shower before I had to take Stripe and the production team for the special shoot out to dinner. I was beyond tired, but protocol demanded such things. The others had arrived several days before to do the pre-production so they weren't jet-lagged. I met them at the Balfy Palace. It was formerly an elegant old mansion. Now part of it was converted to a restaurant. The dining room was located in what used to be the ballroom. The ceilings were high, the chandeliers were extravagant, and the walls were painted robin's-egg blue with gilt trim. The food was terrible, but so much wine was flowing that I doubted anyone else noticed.

Afterward, we wandered across the Charles Bridge to a tiny hole-in-the-wall bar called the Blue Light. Pleading jet lag, I left after the first drink. But, as I learned later, Stripe stayed for another tequila, then another, then six more—which matched the number of stitches he needed when he slid off his stool and hit the sharp corner of the bar. I was summoned from my nice, warm bed to pace up and down the gray hallway of a Communist-era hospital. It was now 5 a.m., and we were supposed to start shooting at 7.

"How are we going to prop him up on set?" I asked the producer who was waiting with me in the hall. "We can't shoot without him."

"Maybe the first A.D. or the D.P. can shoot it," he suggested. I shook my head. We had been publicizing this trailer as a one-of-a-kind from the personal vision of Stripe. We had even built, at enormous cost, a set depicting twenty-third-century buildings on the streets of Prague. I couldn't let the first assistant director or the director of photography shoot it. The publicity backlash would be too damaging. Finally, Stripe staggered out into the hallway with a gigantic bandage on his forehead held in place by a lot of white medical tape. We hustled him into a waiting car and got him to the set. The first shot was miraculously under control by nine. It was the only shot of the day to go off without a hitch.

Now it was 4 a.m., nineteen hours after we started. I had drunk fourteen cups of coffee to stay warm, eaten M&M's, granola bars, cheese and crackers, pizza, and then more M&M's off the craft services table, out of stress. Mostly I stood around, hunched up against the unseasonable cold, with the unit photographer, Action Jackson. His name was actually Jackson Jenkins. But at the age of fifty-five he was still wiry thin, and nervous energy vibrated off him, hence the name Action. His job was to shoot the still photography on a film set in case our publicity department wanted to use it.

"This one is a little different from the last one," Action observed while bouncing on the balls of his feet.

"Yeah, about eighty degrees different," I answered. We had last worked together on a film that was shooting in Hawaii. I fell silent as I watched the clock, and therefore money, tick by. Usually my job was pretty much done by the time we actually made it to set. I was just there to handle talent tantrums or to make sure nothing went seriously awry.

So far, a lot of things were going seriously awry. First it had started raining. Then the crane that had shown up for the overhead shot—the shot that Katsu and Stripe had added despite all pleading—was not the one originally promised. The new one was too heavy to be hoisted on top of the set, which meant that the set needed to be reinforced or we had to get a different crane, and on and on. Which meant time was slipping away. Which meant we were going way over budget. My stomach twisted as I wondered how to break this to the studio. Rachael had been more than clear about avoiding cost overruns and coming back with a "brilliant" trailer—neither of which was happening right now. I nervously considered the age-old question: "Can we save it in post-production?"

"Jeannie, I need you over here."

I squinted through the glare of the spotlights that were currently illuminating the deserted street in Prague. I knew it was the producer by the color of his down coat, the hood of which was cinched tightly around his face. In the middle of the night, in pouring rain, everyone looked pretty much the same.

"Is it the crane again?" I asked miserably.

He replied, "No. I thought you'd better see this last shot."

As I began to follow him my cell phone started ringing. I searched through pocket after pocket trying to locate it. When I did, I managed to open it without taking off my mittens.

"Hello," I croaked.

"Jeannie?" I instantly smiled when I heard Aidan's voice. He sounded so close I wished he were right there with me instead of six thousand miles away.

"Caitlin said you were in Prague when I called the office." He sounded hesitant. "How's the shoot going?"

"Awful, actually. But I'm so happy you called. I know I've been acting so strange, but—"

Aidan cut me off. "Look, Jeannie. I love you but this is not going to work. We need to end this."

Now I stopped and headed in the other direction. I figured that the producer would realize at some point that I was no longer in tow.

"What are you talking about, Aidan?"

"I want to get married and you don't. It's really as simple as that. So the best thing for me is to break this off."

I took off the mitten so I could get the cell phone closer to my ear. "Aidan, I—"

He interrupted me. "Jeannie, I love you. But you have way too many reasons why we can't get married. I need to move on." Then, as with all great moments, when something is really, truly important, the cell phone service cut out. I stared down at it willing it to ring back. When it did, I rushed to answer.

"Jeannie, we have a problem," Caitlin said.

"Can it wait? I need to keep this line free."

"Jeffanie set their hotel room on fire," Caitlin went on as if I hadn't spoken. "The curtains went up in flames from all those tea candles and it went from there."

"Was anyone hurt?" My throat tightened.

"No, nothing like that. Apparently, Jeffanie went out to dinner and left the candles burning. The room is completely torched, but the sprinkler system put it out pretty fast. The Four Seasons is plenty pissed off, and the cost to fix everything is going to be incredible."

"Does the studio know?"

"That's why I'm calling. I wanted to warn you that Vincent and Rachael are on the warpath. They want to know why you would have thought that one thousand tea candles in a room with lunatics like Jeffanie would have been safe."

Slowly, I hung up the phone. We had discussed all of this and they had given their approval. But, I realized, I was the one who had pushed for the tea candles. And I had unreasonably pushed because I was afraid that Katsu would crow that I couldn't deliver.

Now, the studio could legitimately say this was my fault.

I stood dazed, letting the phone dangle in my hand until the producer found me again. "Jeannie, come on! We really need you." Numbly, I followed him. We arrived at the video village. This is where the director, producers, and script supervisor can watch the video monitor and see what is being shot.

The producer asked for playback for me. I watched the shot of the gun firing in a close-up.

"Omigod." My stomach flipped over. I turned to Stripe. "What are we going to do?"

He shrugged.

"You have been filming this man all day long and you mean to say you didn't notice he only has four fingers?"

"So what?" The director was scratching his stitches by rubbing lightly on top of the massive bandage.

"He is a body double for the third-biggest male star in America. And the third-biggest male star in America happens to have all five fingers! Plus"—I gestured wildly at the video monitor—"the point of this entire concept is that he grabs the gun, then pulls the trigger! Not only that, it's a *close-up* of his finger pulling the trigger! Tell me: which finger is missing?!"

Stripe ignored me. He turned his back on me and pretended I did not exist. Me, the one who had promised the studio I would deliver a great trailer. Me, the one who had just lost the love of her life. "Which finger is missing?" I repeated, stabbing his puffy down coat repeatedly with my forefinger. I got silence from Stripe. He kept his head turned away and began a conversation with the script supervisor about the unpredictable weather in Prague.

Freezing rain pelted around the tent, my heart ached, my feet hurt, and my butt was on the line for a million-dollar production that was about to be useless. Shoving my way between Stripe and the script supervisor, I reached up, grabbed a wad of medical tape, and ripped the jumbo-sized bandage away from his stitches.

"Ouch!" The director grabbed his forehead and doubled over in his chair. *"Ouch! You fucking bitch!"*

"One particular finger is needed to pull the trigger! And what finger is missing? *His trigger finger!"* I screamed at him. My throat started to close up then. I never yelled. I never ever, ever yelled. That was a no-no. Then I burst into tears. That was another big no-no.

Silence fell over the video village. Finally the producer cleared his throat and said, "We can find another body double. It's a close-up on just the hand and the gun. No one will be able to tell that it's not the same guy firing the gun."

I nodded while heaving some kind of blubbering, snorfling assent, then stumbled around the corner of the set. Tears blurring my eyes, I moved out of the range of the lights and into the dark of the night. Standing in the mud among discarded planks of lumber and pieces of rope, I bent over and threw up. When I was finished retching, I sagged against a metal pole and watched the rain wash my puke away. It was then that I noticed I had not missed my coat. It was covered in long, chunky strands all the way down the front.

The last shot was completed thirty-two hours after we started. We had gone into twenty hours of overtime. It was 3:30 p.m. by the time I got back to the hotel and threw my muddy clothes in my bag. Then I checked out and took a cab to the airport. I found a 6:20 p.m. flight on British Airways to Los Angeles and I slumped aboard, heaving my bag into the overhead bin without help from any of the male passengers. After transferring at Heathrow, I ordered a cocktail from the stewardess but fell asleep before it arrived and didn't wake up until we landed, twelve hours later. After making it through customs I took a cab straight to Aidan's house. I fought that icky, dirty jet lag feeling and dabbed some blush and lipstick on.

Using my key I entered his house. "Aidan?" I called out. When I heard no response I checked from room to room. The house felt oddly empty. On a hunch I opened his closet door. Half of his closet had been cleared out. In the storage closet several of his suitcases were missing.

Aidan was gone.

Thirty-two

December 1986

*L*ucy and I drove the two hours to Muskegon in silence. Chuck didn't come with us because he wasn't supposed to leave the city limits until his mess was straightened out with the courts. I watched the bare trees fly by as we drove west on I-96. It was a grim, gray morning, which fit our mood. We had stopped once at a gas station to use the pay phone. Lucy had called General Hospital but Dad wasn't there. That left Northern Hospital and that's where we were going. I didn't dare think about any other option. He just had to be at Northern and not at one of the funeral homes on Getty Street. As I hit the Holt city limits, I slowed down. I could hear Dad's voice reminding me that the cops had a speed trap there. When we finally reached the hospital, I parked in a red zone and Lucy and I ran through the doors.

"Harold Thompson? Where is he?" Lucy blurted to the lady at the desk.

She shuffled through some papers for an agonizingly long

minute. Then she said, "He's still in surgery." Still in surgery? I thought. It had been hours since we had gotten word that he had been taken to the hospital. The lady continued speaking. "I know your mom is in the waiting room." She pointed down the mint green hall. We ran to the waiting room and Mom was immediately on her feet hugging us hard. I peppered her with questions but Evan pulled me away.

"Let's go outside," he said gently. We went into the hall and left Mom with Anna. Evan spoke firmly to Lucy and me. Elizabeth stood in all her big belly-ness next to him. "The county board brought up firing Dad at a meeting last night. It was about that dumpsite on Muskegon Lake that Dad has been trying to get moved. It was pretty brutal. Channel Thirteen was covering it and everything. Dad got home and started having chest pains, so Mom, Anna, and I brought him in to the emergency room. The doctors discovered a blockage in his heart. So the surgeon did an angioplasty. They ran a tube up an artery in his leg and tried to push the blockage against the walls of the artery to open it up."

We waited breathlessly for the rest.

"But the angioplasty triggered a massive heart attack. Dad is having a quadruple heart bypass right now."

Elizabeth put her arm around me. "Now we're all going to be cheerful and hopeful. Mom is under enormous stress. So no moping or crying. She's worried enough about Dad without worrying about us, too." Lucy and I nodded.

"Did the doctors say what his chances are?" I asked quietly.

Elizabeth and Evan looked at each other. "They said his chances are fifty-fifty," Evan finally replied. That's what Sammie heard as she came racing down the hallway pulling a suitcase behind her. She had come straight to the hospital from the airport.

"His chances are only fifty-fifty?" Her voice was several octaves above normal and had a hysterical edge. She dropped her suitcase and ran toward us. "Evan, do something! Find another doctor! Another hospital! Do something!"

Elizabeth spun Sammie around so she was facing her. "Shut up! Mom doesn't know!" Sammie stared at her as Elizabeth commanded, "Take a deep breath and calm down!" Sammie did as she was told.

A doctor strode toward us and Evan went to meet him, with Elizabeth, Sammie, Lucy, and I trailing behind. Evan wanted to hear the news before Mom. He shook hands with the doctor. "Hi, John."

"Evan, sorry we have to see each other under these circumstances," the doctor responded. I vaguely recognized the doctor as one of my brother's high school classmates.

"He made it through the bypass," the doctor said. "Now we just have to wait to see how your father responds."

"When can we see him?" Evan asked.

"He's in recovery now and he'll be groggy for quite a while." The doctor hesitated before adding, "Do you have a family priest?"

Elizabeth answered crisply, not acknowledging what this question meant. "Yes, Father Whippet."

"I'd suggest you call him here as soon as possible," the doctor said as his beeper went off and he excused himself.

I wrapped my arms around Elizabeth. She put her chin up in the manner of my mother. "I'm going to go tell Mom he's safely out of surgery." I nodded at her. "And you are going to go get Father Whippet," she continued.

"I can just call him, Elizabeth," I said. "That way I can be here if, you know."

"No, I want you to go because I want you to take Sammie with you. She doesn't handle trauma well and I don't want Mom to be more upset. The drive will give Sammie a chance to calm down."

I nodded again. She was right. Elizabeth turned to speak quietly to Sammie, then disappeared into the waiting room. Sammie stomped over to me and I tried to hug her but she shook me off. Tears streamed down her cheeks as she stormed toward a bicycle rack in front of the hospital and untied a large white dog that promptly planted both paws on my chest.

"What the hell is this?" I asked, backing up under his weight.

"That's Snowflake."

"Get him off of me."

Sammie hauled Snowflake down and we walked to the car. "I had to bring him home," she said. "I couldn't find anyone to take care of him on such short notice." Sammie pushed him into the backseat.

Sammie railed the entire way to the church about the inadequacy of medical care in Muskegon and why hadn't Mom and Evan seen fit to have flown him to a better hospital, at least one in Grand Rapids, for God's sake? I didn't bother trying to tell her that the medical care in Muskegon was actually pretty good. I finally pulled up at the church. Sammie said, "I can't stand that sanctimonious old bastard and I'm not going in there." So I climbed the steps alone, walked down the hall, and, without knocking, opened the door to Father Whippet's office.

"Oh for God's sake!" I gasped while covering my mouth with my hands. Father Whippet had Roly Poly pinned against his desk with her skirt hiked up over her hips. I caught a glimpse of a tan Playtex slip. Dropping my hands, I demanded, "Can't you do this somewhere more private? Don't you ever think some parishioner might walk in here in a time of need?" Roly Poly shoved Father

Whippet away, giving me an unwanted view of his erection. It died quickly, but still. Yuck.

Father Whippet yelled at me angrily as he stuffed his offending member into his pants and fumbled with his zipper. "I've had about enough of you!" He advanced on me and I backed away. "You're spying on me! I know people spy on me. They have cameras on me all the time!" He kept coming toward me. Christ Almighty, I was going to get decked by a man of the cloth. I'd like to say that what I did next was only in self-defense, but the events of the previous few days seemed to have incited a rage in me. I grabbed a heavy book off the end table and swung it hard. It clocked him on the head and he went down like a stone. Roly Poly and I stood over him, staring at his chest to see if he was breathing. He was. Then Roly Poly picked up the book. "I guess this is appropriate," she said wonderingly. It was a Bible.

"He's a nutcase, you know," I stammered.

"I know." She looked at his still form fondly.

"When he wakes up, tell him that my dad might need last rites. He's at Northern Hospital." Then I turned and ran. I heard Roly Poly shout after me, "Oh, honey, I'm so sorry! Give my best wishes to your mom, and I'll pray for your dad!"

When I opened the car door, Sammie was more composed. "Is he coming?" she asked.

"Yeah, but he needs a few minutes." I threw the car into drive and headed back to the hospital. When we arrived, Elizabeth and Lucy came out before we even parked. I rolled down my window anxiously. "What's happened?"

"Nothing," Elizabeth said and got in the car. "Mom just thought it would be better if only she, Evan, and Anna stayed. She said we girls were making her nervous."

Lucy got in the other side and slammed the door. I pulled away from the hospital and started for home. They didn't even ask why there was a large, smelly dog in the car. Lucy just shoved Snowflake to the middle of the backseat and said, "It's not us making her nervous. She doesn't handle true trauma well. That's where Sammie gets it from."

"What do you mean, I don't handle trauma well?" Sammie snapped her head away from the window to look at Lucy.

"You always fall apart," Elizabeth said.

"That is a total lie!" Sammie stormed.

"Why are you saying mean things about Mom, Lucy?" I blurted. "She's under pressure."

"She's under pressure because she puts herself there," Lucy said while picking ferociously at a cuticle.

"That is such a cruel, bitchy thing to say! Dad is really sick! He might die!" Elizabeth retorted.

"And if he does, she'll somehow figure out how to blame herself for it. She'll spend the next twenty years mentally flogging herself for not getting Dad to a doctor for his annual checkup." Lucy's voice was rising.

"Lucy, why don't you just shut up? Nobody needs to hear any of this right now," I said as I clenched my hands on the steering wheel.

"Nobody in this family says what they really think, or what's really real, except me!" Lucy roared. I slammed the car to a halt in the middle of the street. All four car doors flew open and all four of us stormed out. We each took up a defensive position by our door.

"Nobody says what's real except you? Is that what you just said?" I shouted at her over the car roof. "Then why don't you just say what's real in your own life, Lucy? You married a guy that you didn't want to marry because you didn't want to tell Mom and Dad that you didn't want to get married. And you don't even realize that they don't like the guy and they wish you never married him! And why don't you tell Elizabeth and Sammie how he nearly killed his boss at work!"

"Don't you tell *me* what's real!" Lucy screamed right back. "You're engaged to a guy who barely gives a shit about you. Is that how much you think of yourself? Ooooh, he goes to Princeton! Ooooh, he can win the regatta! So big fucking what! And you hardly try at school because God forbid you should not measure up! Better not to know, right?"

"I think that's about enough, you two," Elizabeth snarled from her side of the car door. "Get back in the car."

I turned on her. "You! You say that's enough? Not hardly, Miss I-Don't-Have-Any-Money-Because-My-Loser-Husband-Stole-It-All! Miss I'm-Having-My-Baby-at-Home-Because-I-Don't-Have-Health-Insurance-But-I'm-Telling-Mom-It's-So-I-Can-Be-Close-to-Her! Do you really think Mom and Dad don't know something is wrong? Why can't you tell the truth? Is that so hard? Do you think we'd care any less about you?"

"Goddamn it!" Sammie screamed over the car roof. "I can't take this. This isn't about us, it's about Dad! You're all being selfish bitches!"

"Stop being so goddamn above it all, Sammie!" Elizabeth yelled as her hair whipped around her face in the cold wind. "You look down your nose on all of us because you're an *artist*!" Elizabeth fairly ripped the word out. "You're so much deeper than all of us. You're so much cooler than all of us. You are so much *better* than all of us! I may not have any money now but at least I've *made* some in my lifetime!"

"Shut up, shut up, shut up!" Lucy had her hands over her ears. "I hate you all!" she screamed.

I felt a desperate need to be as far away from my sisters as possible. Reaching into the car, I grabbed the car keys. Then I arched back and threw them as far as they would go into the woods off the side of the road. They wouldn't be able to follow me.

I broke into a run and I didn't stop for a long time. I saw the playground ahead of me and collapsed against the chain-link fence. I sank down among the dead leaves that were stuck in its crevices at the bottom. I buried my head in my arms and gulped air until I thought I was going to throw up. I said every prayer that I could remember for my dad to be safe. I apologized to God for every bad thing I had just said to my sisters and for every bad thing I had ever done. I swore to be a better person. When I finally threw my head back to plead to the sky, I saw that it was snowing.

Sammie and Lucy found me a few hours later. They knelt beside me and took my hands and rubbed them to warm them up. Then they helped me to my feet and into the car.

Elizabeth breathed a sigh of relief when we all came into the living room. Her swollen, red feet were propped up on the table. She held out to me the hand that wasn't caressing her belly. I took it and sank down next to her on the couch. "Is Dad okay?"

Sammie stroked my hair from above. "He's out of the woods. The doctor said so far so good."

"Thank God." I closed my eyes against the tears. "How's Mom?"

"She's doing better now. You know her; she toughs it out. She's staying with him tonight."

Throughout the years, on the rare occasion when one of us was in the hospital—Elizabeth with her tonsils, Evan with his broken collarbone, me with mononucleosis—Mom had sat up all night in a hospital armchair right there at our bedsides. She said that there was nothing worse than waking up in a strange place in the middle of the night without a loved one there to comfort you. Even though it was against hospital policy, no nurse or doctor had ever taken her on. One look from her and they were out the door.

I looked around at my exhausted sisters with a sudden clutching of my heart. "I'm sorry. I shouldn't have said all of those horrible things."

"No, what you shouldn't have done"—Elizabeth stroked my hair—"is make a woman who is seven months pregnant walk three miles in twenty-degree weather."

My hands flew to my mouth. How could I have been so stupid and selfish?

"Lizzie, don't torment her," Sammie said. "We didn't walk at all. We found the car keys pretty much right away."

"Thanks to me," Elizabeth said and poked Sammie to ease her off to a more comfortable position. "Sammie and Lucy were all set to race into that field and start mucking around. But I made Sammie stand where you had been. Then she threw a rock from there, and bingo, it landed right next to the car keys. You and Sammie both throw like girls."

"I'm still sorry, you know, for everything," I said into the cushion. My sisters had obviously made their peace with each other before I got home.

Lucy shrugged. "As Mom says, sometimes you gotta shake things out. I think it was a good thing we got everything off our chests." It must be real love when you could say terrible things to each other and then accept it and move past it. After all, who is going to tell you the truth if not your family?

The phone rang and nobody moved. We were all afraid it could be Evan with bad news. Lucy finally got up on the third ring and answered it in the kitchen. When we heard her laugh, we relaxed. She came back into the living room and crowed, "I won the Squirrel Board!" She did a little dance around the table. "That was Tommy. It's the first time in BLT history that someone hit it smack-dab on the minute. Normally the celebration and crowning would be tonight, but Tommy is postponing it until tomorrow because of Dad."

"He knew about Dad already?" Sammie said.

I thought about how fast bad—and good—news flies through our town.

Evan and Anna came in carrying casserole dishes and stomping the snow off their feet. "Didn't you see these piled up on the porch?" Evan griped good-naturedly as he pulled off his boots. "Half the town must have left food for us."

"Did Dad wake up yet?" Elizabeth asked anxiously.

"Yep. He squeezed Mom's hand and smiled at us. He managed to get out a few words before he fell asleep again."

"What did he say?" I prodded.

"He asked if it was his turn in the bathroom yet."

We all laughed in relief and joy.

"Did Father Whippet ever show up?" I asked.

"Yeah, but by the time he got there Dad didn't need last rites anymore. Father Whippet seemed kind of pissed off at that." He yawned. "Anna and I gotta go. I have to prep for my show."

After he left, I told my sisters, "I threw a Bible at Father Whippet and hit him in the head this morning."

No one even asked me why. "Too bad it didn't knock any sense into him," Sammie said.

We didn't discuss the grenades we had all thrown at each other. On some level, each one of us recognized the truth in each accusation. They were all things that stirred in the deep recesses of our subconscious. But the secret truths we think are safely tucked away are usually apparent to everyone else. It wasn't that Walker was mean to me. He wasn't. I knew he worried I would come off like a midwestern hick when I showed up at Princeton. But I figured he was worried *for* me, not *because* of me. I told myself of course he loves me. Why else would he want to get married?

Sammie yawned. "I'm going to bed." We followed her upstairs. There, we jostled at the bathroom sink trying to brush our teeth and wash our faces. For the first time in a while, everything seemed right again.

Thirty-three

December 1986

I want to thank everyone who called my family yesterday with good wishes for my dad. I just talked to my
mom, and he's doing much better. She says he's up this
morning and watching the show from his hospital bed. Hi, Dad.
Good to have you back among the conscious." Evan had big vats
boiling away on the stove. "Today, we're making homemade
summer sausage. As the name suggests, we should be making
this in the summer. But I just got a great recipe courtesy of Mr.
Frank Bukowski from way up in Iron Mountain. Seems he caught
our show last time he was down here visiting his nephew.

"Frank says he separates out the shoulder, loin, ribs, and all the
good stuff. You can put that in the freezer. You're not gonna need
it. Now take the rest and remove the bone and cartilage. Toss
that in the garbage or to your dog. What you have left is what
you make the sausage with: you know, the stomach, the hooves,
and the intestines for the casing. Frank writes that in his seventy
years of cooking"—Evan grabbed tongs and lifted out a steaming,

droopy-looking flesh-bag—"the most important thing he learned is patience." He dropped the disgusting mess back into the vat, crossed to the fireplace, and stirred the logs.

"Damn, it's getting cold. The ice on Muskegon Lake is almost two inches thick now. Ice fishing shanties are popping up everywhere out there." Evan shuffled back to the stove and I saw he had on his fuzzy moccasin house slippers.

"It's like he doesn't even bother getting dressed for this show," I said to Elizabeth, who was up early with me. She gestured impatiently to me and I resumed rubbing her feet, which she had plopped in my lap.

Evan pulled something that looked like a cloven foot out of another vat and examined it, then tossed it back in. "Frank says you've got to have patience with sausage. Otherwise it won't turn out the way you want it to. That's the way it is with most things in life. You have to think things through. Plan ahead. Take these guys I heard about in Wisconsin. They drove a brand-new Toyota truck out on the ice, dragging their fishing shanty. Their big plan was to blow a fishing hole in the ice with a stick of dynamite instead of taking the time to ice-pick one out by hand. One of the guys gets out of the truck, lights the dynamite, and throws it as far as he can. Next thing you know, his yellow Labrador jumps out of the bed of the truck and races after it. The guys are screaming at the dog to stop. But the dog grabs the stick of dynamite and starts back to the truck. The guys are still yelling, and now the dog thinks he's in trouble, so he crawls under the truck, and *ka-blam*, everything blows. The dog goes sky-high and the truck drops through a nice, big hole in the ice and sinks." Evan paused and took a sip of tea. "I think Frank is right about patience. And I say that even though he *is* from the U.P. You have to think things through, or they may not wind up the way you intended. That, and let it be a lesson not to buy a foreign-made car."

Evan unfurled some paper and tacked it to a board. "We have a little time to wait while the ingredients boil, so I'm going to give a lesson in Japanese brush-painting."

Evan dipped his brush in black ink and made a careful stroke on the paper. The phone rang on the set and the caller came over the speaker box. "So what happened? Was the truck insured? Were the guys killed, too?"

Evan continued painting as he answered. "Apparently the truck was insured but not for being blown up by dynamite. The devil is in the details, hmm? Oh, and the guys weren't hurt."

"Those men should have been killed instead of that poor, innocent dog," the caller insisted.

"Maybe. But that's never the way it goes, is it?" Evan murmured. "Hey, can you guys hold your calls for a sec? This painting takes concentration."

I leaned on my elbows and watched Evan form a flower. He was surprisingly good at it. When he drew his brush away from the paper, the phone rang again.

"You done?" the caller asked. "Is it okay to ask a question now?"

"Yep." Evan wiped off his brush.

"Aren't there some things you just can't plan for? Some things you never thought could happen in a million years?"

"I suppose you have a point there."

"Things like your sister Lucy winning the Squirrel Board?"

"Just like that."

"See you at the BLT tonight?"

"Yep."

"Oh, my dad says cow intestines are better for packing the sausage meat in than pig intestines. Are those cow intestines you're boiling there?"

"No, they're pig intestines."

"Okay, then. Bye."

"Bye."

Later that morning, the five of us went to see Dad. The doctor warned us that we could only stay a few minutes. We approached the bed quietly. Dad looked pale and small and helpless. His eyes were closed. I think it was only at that moment that reality hit us. Dad had really come close to dying. I had never seen him look so weak. My throat tightened and I saw that Evan's eyes were shining with tears behind his glasses. Lucy stroked his hand, careful of the IV drip. His eyes fluttered open and he managed a half smile.

"I'll do anything to get my kids to come home, huh?" he croaked. Anxious laughter and more silence followed. We took turns holding his hand and kissing his forehead. Evan whispered to him, "December tenth, 3:42 p.m., Black. Guess who won? Lucy." Then the nurse came in to usher us out.

Dad smiled.

The Bear Lake Tavern was jammed that night. We had to park along Ruddiman Drive because the lot was overflowing. Slipping and sliding across the bridge, we made our way toward the bright lights and laughter.

"I'm the Queen! I'm the Queen!" Lucy skipped and sang next to us.

"Couldn't they have saved a special parking place for the Queen, then?" Sammie groused. Elizabeth had stayed home to nurse her feet, and Anna stayed with her to keep her company. A car went by, honking loudly. We saw a bumper-hitcher at the back. Bumper-hitching is a singularly dangerous and singularly fun activity. The road conditions have to be just right: icy. Then an intrepid soul crouches at the back of a car and hangs on to the bumper for dear life while he is dragged, squatting, on the soles of his boots down the road. This particular bumper-hitcher let go of the car at the curve and flew into a snow bank, howling with laughter. "It's Squirrel Board night! Wahoo!"

As we entered, Evan shouted, "The Queen is here!" Cheers went up from the masses—it was the King or Queen's responsibility to buy the first round of drinks. Tommy signaled for Lucy to ascend the throne. As usual, that meant sitting on top of the bar. Lucy waved like she was the Queen of England: elbow, elbow, wrist, wrist. Tommy held up his hands for everyone to settle down. He was the sports announcer at all of our high school football and basketball games and had developed a sports personality somewhere between Red Barber and Harry Caray.

"Laadies and geentlemen, your attention please. Tonight marks several milestones. For the first time in history, a Squirrel Board contestant has hit the First Snow at the exact date and time." Tommy was interrupted by more shouts as the throng hoisted their beer mugs. He paused until they quieted down. "And the astounding sum of $2,810 is the largest Squirrel Board pot of all time!" There were more whoops before Tommy continued, "And lastly but certainly not leastly, for the first time since 1968 we have a Queen!" This brought cheers from the women and some boos from the men. "I think this proves that females truly are the stronger, smarter sex!" He laughed. "My wife told me I had to say that."

"Before I crown our Queen," Tommy continued, "I ask for your thoughts and prayers for Harold Thompson. He can't be here tonight because he's knocking back a couple of cold IVs at the hospital. Rose is with him and says he's doing better. So, please, a round of applause for our Queen's father!" The Blit exploded in clapping hands and stomping feet.

"Now, the moment you have been waiting for. Twelve! Ten! Black! Three! Forty-two! Your Queen, Luuuuucy Thompson!!!" Then Tommy solemnly took the black construction-paper crown that had been decorated with Elmer's glue and silver glitter and placed it on Lucy's head. It was a little too big and she had to hold it with one hand so it didn't fall over her face. Then she stood up on the bar and waved her other arm wildly. That signaled the round of free drinks to be served and the crowd went nuts. Lucy disappeared into a wave of well-wishers and celebrity hangers-on. I clapped madly for her.

It was then that I realized I was mashed up against Teeni. I tried to get away from her so I could see the formal signing of the Squirrel Board logbook by Lucy, but it was too packed. Teeni half turned and saw me. "I ga' here early to ge' a good place," she slurred. Quite a bit early, I thought, enough time to get loaded already. "Say, wha' you got against John?" She staggered against me. At least the crowd was holding her up.

"Who's John?" I got jostled and sloshed my beer down my shirt.

"Whippet, ya know? Johnny. He says you won' leave him be."

"I just keep walking in on him at, say, inopportune times." I saw Teeni's brain working out the word "inopportune." Anything over two syllables right now was going to be a challenge.

"He won' see me an'more," she said about two inches from my face. I moved sideways to get away from her. She grabbed my shirt and pulled me back. "You tell an'one else about us?" she asked with her hundred-proof breath.

"No," I lied.

That's when she threw her vodka tonic in my face and lunged at me. We both went down in a heap, taking a few people with us. She was on top of me, and she clearly had a weight advantage.

"Girl fight!" some guy cried with delight. We weren't fighting. Teeni seemed to have passed out cold on top of me. Evan fought his way through the circle around us and hauled me out from under her. Tommy and two other men picked Teeni up like a sack of potatoes and took her off to the kitchen to pour coffee into her.

Evan grabbed a bar towel and handed it to me. It reeked of grease and stale beer as I wiped the liquor from my face. Evan looked more amused than sympathetic at my embarrassment, so I elbowed my way through the crowd until I could see Lucy. She was laughing in a carefree way I hadn't seen in years. She was also leading a game of Quarters. You play it by bouncing a quarter into a shot glass full of beer. If it goes in, you pick someone to drink the shot. If it doesn't, then you drink it. Not a whole lot of skill is required, which is why it's a drinking game.

I finally found my coat on the floor, where it was being trampled. Leaving the lights and the laughter behind me, I walked home in the quiet hush of the falling snow and the squeak it uttered under my boots. I was shivering when I finally walked up the steps at home. I shed my coat and boots and found Elizabeth reading in the family room.

"How'd the crowning go?"

"Lucy was glowing. I don't think she's had that much fun in a while. Did Mom call?"

"Yeah, they think he'll be able to come home in about a week. And, more good news, Ron will be here tomorrow." Elizabeth was beaming.

"Did you guys make up?"

"I called him after we girls had our, uh, discussion. Turns out he's been missing me terribly. He's saved up enough money for me to have the baby in Los Angeles." Elizabeth looked so happy that I didn't burst her bubble with a rude comment. "We'll all be here together for Christmas and then we'll go home."

For Elizabeth's sake I tried to look happy. I knew Sammie was staying on in North Muskegon because it was so close to Christmas anyway. Lucy and I were going to head back to Michigan State in the morning if the snow stopped. I told Elizabeth that I was sorry we'd have to leave before Ron's arrival. Then I beat it upstairs to snag a bed before anyone else got there first.

Thirty-four

December 1986

*L*ucy paid me back the thousand dollars from the Squirrel money. She also asked me not to say anything to Chuck about her winnings. He had found a new job at Mr. Lube. When he told me that, I asked why there was never a Mrs. Taco or a Mrs. Lube. Or why menial jobs always had a company name that started with "Mr."

I swear, it didn't even occur to me that this might hurt his feelings. After all, I had just been fired from a job where dialing a phone had apparently been too tough for me. He glared at me and stomped away. He now hadn't spoken to me for several days and it was wearing on Lucy as well as on me. Because I felt guilty, I wound up making Chuck dinner and going out to buy him Kodiak chewing tobacco when I noticed he was running low. He still didn't utter a word in my direction.

During *Wheel of Fortune*, the doorbell rang. When I answered it, our downstairs neighbor was at the door, fuming. Apparently Chuck had parked in his parking space *again*. After I offered to move his car, Chuck wordlessly flipped me the keys. I went outside without my coat. The snow had piled up on the windshield and the driver's-side door had iced shut. I crawled in the passenger side to find the scraper. Meanwhile the guy from downstairs was idling in his own car waiting to pull into his space. I hurriedly scraped the windshield with the plastic straight edge, then flipped it around to wipe off the loose snow with the plastic bristles. I was scraping at the ice on the door handle when Chuck yelled out the window above the parking lot.

"Hey, you're going to scrape the paint!"

"No, I'm not. This is the way you do it," I yelled back. I said under my breath, "You moron from California, what would you know?"

The door of the duplex flew open and Chuck raced across the parking lot, nearly losing his balance on the ice. His full weight hit me and pushed me up against the car. "You stupid bitch!" He wrenched the window scraper from my hand and hit me on the side of the head with it. Then he hit me again. The jagged plastic edge winged my cheek. It didn't really hurt, but I had never been hit before in my life. And I was scared that he wasn't going to stop.

"Lucy! Help!" I screamed in real terror. Chuck kept me pinned against the car with one arm and raised his other arm to backhand me across the mouth. I shut my eyes but the strike never came.

I heard Lucy scream, "Not my sister, you bastard! Don't hit my sister!" I opened my eyes and saw that she had jumped on Chuck's back, holding his arm as best she could. I got out of hitting range as Chuck flipped Lucy off him onto the snow and gravel. He brought his boot back to kick her, but again he was stopped—this time by our downstairs neighbor, who had jumped out of his idling car when he saw what was happening. The neighbor, an art history classmate of mine, pulled Chuck away.

Chuck tried to get around him but the guy stepped in front of him and said, "Let's not get the cops involved, man. Let's keep it cool here."

Chuck flipped Lucy the finger. Then, picking up the car keys from where I had dropped them, he jumped in the car. He screeched out of the lot, fishtailing on the ice the whole way. Lucy pulled me to her and said, "Did he hurt you, Jeannie?" She pushed me away to inspect me. She licked her finger and dabbed at the blood on my cheek, then rested her forehead on mine. As she helped me up the stairs, she called to our neighbor, "We can't thank you enough."

"Are you two all right? Do you need anything?" he asked.

"Just keep an eye out tonight, would you?" Lucy asked meaningfully.

"You got it," he said and disappeared into his own part of the house.

We locked every door and window, then put chairs under the doorknobs for good measure. Our neighbor brought up a pool cue that we lodged in the sliding door track. As we ran around the house securing it, Lucy sobbed. The night passed with Lucy and me flinching at every sound the old house made. At about four o'clock in the morning, I whispered to her back, "Did Chuck cause your miscarriage, Lucy?"

She didn't answer for so long that I thought she was asleep. Then she simply whispered, "Go to sleep, Jeannie."

The next day was my last big test in Art History. It counted for fifty percent of our grade. I normally just crammed the night before a test. Which in this case had been impossible. I arrived an hour late and motioned to the teacher, who was running the slide projector. "I'm sorry I'm missing this test." I was shifting from foot to foot because I had to pee, which is my normal tendency when

I'm lying. "My dad just had a heart attack and I'm very upset and I need to drive home right away. He's in very bad condition."

His gray eyebrows shot upward. "I thought that's why you were gone two weeks ago."

"Um, well, yeah." I was grasping at straws. "He had a relapse last night so I've really got to drive home."

"Miss Thompson, let me tell you something: you're just not dedicated. Some days you are my most stellar student. You have ideas that are quite astute. Other days you don't even bother to show up or you aren't prepared. Now even if you ace the final, at this point you are only looking at a C or even a D. I don't appreciate my students' not taking their studies seriously. Perhaps you should strongly consider transferring to another major. Now, I have students who are waiting for their next slide." He turned on his heel, brushing me with his tweed coat. I stood in the hall feeling like the biggest loser of all time.

I wasn't in the mood to be in our tragic house so I walked to the student union. I lay down on a vinyl couch in the women's lounge and stared at the perforated tile ceiling. I heard a chair scrape.

"Hi," Lucy said.

"Hi."

"You okay?"

"Yeah. But I think I just got kicked out of my major," I said.

"It happens." Lucy shrugged. Then she showed me a notice from Campus Legal Aid that said, "Cheap, Fast, and Confidential. 517-555-3379." I gave Lucy money for the pay phone and watched her cross the room to make the call. Then I went with her to the Administration Building and up to their fourth-floor office. She spoke briefly to a woman at a desk and returned with several forms to fill out. We found two seats among the metal chairs lining the hallway. To a man, everyone waiting there was a woman. After two hours, Lucy was finally called in to an inner office. I waited outside. When Lucy reappeared, she said, "I filled out all of the paperwork to get the divorce procedure started. I just need his signature too."

"Lucy, don't do this because of last night. He didn't really hurt me."

She whirled on me. "I'm not doing this because of you! I'm doing this because of me. Sadly, I could only get motivated to do it when I saw that he might hurt someone I love." Then she stomped down the hall.

Later that day, we discussed the logistics of getting Chuck to sign the papers and getting him out of the house. It was a Friday, and since Lucy was working all weekend, she decided she was going to wait until Monday to talk to Chuck. It would also be Christmas Eve and Lucy and I were leaving anyhow to go home to Muskegon. That way we wouldn't have to be around him for very long after he heard about the pending divorce.

Thirty-five

December 1986

Lucy drove Chuck to work at Mr. Lube, having pleaded that she needed their car because I needed the one Mom and Dad had provided. Chuck was going to get a ride home from a coworker later that day. Then Lucy and I drove to U-Haul. We rented a trailer and hitched it to the back of Lucy and Chuck's Ford EXP. Then we spent the rest of the day loading the trailer. We dragged the bed frame and mattress down the stairs. I packed the stereo while Lucy wrestled with the bureau and the desk. Lucy handled the locksmith, who changed the locks while I sorted through clothes, albums, and stuff from the bathroom, piling it into boxes I had gotten from the grocery store. Finally we were done. We sat on the front stoop to wait. It was four o'clock and night was already descending. Lucy and I took turns going into the house to get warm. She was inside when I saw the headlights turn in to the parking lot at about five thirty.

The car stopped and Chuck emerged. He gave a brief wave to the driver, who drove off.

I knocked frantically on the front door and Lucy emerged quickly, locking the door behind her. The porch light overhead was on and I was holding a heavy Sears flashlight that Dad had given me. I flashed it in Chuck's eyes as he walked up. I also planned to use the flashlight as a weapon if need be.

"What the fuck do you think you're doing?" He had a hand up to shield his eyes. Lucy strode up to him with a clipboard. "Chuck, there's something I didn't tell you. I won the Squirrel Board."

"The fucking what?"

"Never mind. The thing is, I have a check here for you. It's for $610. You just have to sign right here to get it." Lucy thrust the clipboard at the dazed Chuck and handed him a pen. I kept the light in his eyes as well as I could.

"Can you turn off that fucking light?" he yelled at me. "You're blinding me."

"Oh, sorry," I said, holding the flashlight steady. "I just want you to be able to see where to sign."

"Six hundred dollars, huh? Cool." Chuck took the clipboard and signed where Lucy indicated. Lucy took the clipboard back, then pulled a check out of her pocket and handed it to him.

"Here you go, all yours. And so is that." Lucy pointed to the U-Haul.

Chuck looked at the U-Haul, then back at Lucy.

"You just signed the paperwork so the divorce procedure can get started," Lucy said.

"So that's it?" Chuck asked.

"Yeah, that's it."

Chuck stood with his hands hanging at his side. He didn't seem to know what to do next. I had expected more drama. I had worked myself up all afternoon for a brawl, the cops coming, and the works. But none of that happened. Lucy hugged him and he hugged her for a long time. Then she told him to drive home, back to California. He got in the car. Then without a wave he pulled out of the parking lot, braked once halfway down the block, and then continued on and out of our sight.

"Merry Christmas Eve, Jeannie." Lucy hugged me and pushed her face into my earmuffs.

"Merry Christmas Eve, Lucy."

The highways were clear the whole way home. I drove fast, except near the Holt city limits, and we were crossing the Causeway when Lucy said, "I suppose he's making good time. The highways are good."

"Yeah." I glanced over at her in the dark and patted her knee. "I'm sure he's fine." It was then that I saw her crying. "I spent two hundred dollars on that round of drinks, then eight hundred dollars on the legal aid person, then the money for the U-Haul, and I gave Chuck the last of the Squirrel money. Now I'm broke again."

I pulled over on the shoulder of the road. "That's not why you're crying, Lucy," I said gently. "It's going to be all right. I promise." We sat in the dark for a while. "Hey, Lucy. Look up." I reached over and pulled up her chin, directing her gaze outside. "See that?"

The local VFW had been at work again. Every pine tree lining the Causeway was decorated with Christmas lights. The colored lights reflected across the windswept ice of the pond. Snow had begun to fall. "It's Christmas, Lucy. I bet Mom has eggnog with fresh grated nutmeg. And I bet that the carolers are out. We'll go to midnight service and they'll turn off the lights during 'Silent Night' so only the candles are lighting the church." I reached over and hugged her. Then I carefully pulled back onto the Causeway, made my way past the Four Corners, and drove down Ruddiman. I turned on Fourth Street and headed to our house, to the water. Maybe every road in North Muskegon wasn't a dead end. Maybe the water that waited at the end of every road was there to soften our falls.

Thirty-six

December 1986

When Lucy and I arrived home, Lucy holed up with Mom and Dad at the kitchen table. She explained what had happened, omitting some of the juicier details. Dad said he was happy with whatever Lucy was happy with and went back to the TV. He was looking almost normal now, though he was pretty weak. The doctors said he couldn't smoke anymore and that he had to take walks every night. This was good news for Snowflake, the dog.

He had taken an instant liking to Dad. He padded after Dad everywhere he went, including the bathroom. Dad took to calling the dog Ake, because he said he was an ache in the behind.

From my vantage point on the couch, I could tell Dad was relieved that Lucy had left Chuck. I think he knew what had been happening between the two of them.

Eventually, Mom, Dad, Elizabeth, Ron, Sammie, Lucy, and I left for midnight Christmas service. Evan and Anna were meeting us there. But when we walked up to the church it was dark and the doors were locked. There was a note taped to the door that said the service had been postponed. "How do you postpone Christmas Eve?" Sammie asked. "Postponed until when? Next year?" The note blew away in a gust of freezing wind.

"You have to go get it, Jeannie," Mom fretted.

"Why?"

"So people will know there is no service tonight."

I looked up at the darkened and locked church and thought that if the congregation couldn't figure it out, then they really had problems. But I dutifully chased after the paper and then made my best attempt to get the wet Scotch tape to stick to the door. Other churchgoers joined us and we huddled on the snowy sidewalk discussing the situation. It became apparent that the only thing to do was go home. I climbed into the backseat of Evan and Anna's car since I could sleep on an actual bed at their house.

"What do you suppose happened tonight? Do you think Father Whippet is okay?" I mused to them. Evan passed the town square with the prominently lit scene of the shepherds gathered around the baby Jesus in his manger before he spoke.

"I'm sure Father Whippet had a good reason to cancel the service. I just think there's some . . . difficult things happening in his life right now."

I leaned forward and put my elbows on the back of their seat. "He's having an affair, isn't he?"

Evan looked steadily at the road. Anna patted his hand and said, "You might as well tell her; she obviously already knows something."

"I promised the Catholic priest at our wedding that I would never tell anyone," Evan said.

"What does this have to do with your wedding?" I was startled. "Was he having sex with Roly Poly at your wedding?"

"Roly Poly?" Evan and Anna said together. They even both turned their heads at the same time to stare at me.

"Not Roly Poly? Then Teeni—he was having sex with Teeni?"

Anna and Evan stared in the backseat until Anna swatted Evan and told him to watch the road.

"Actually, it was . . ." Anna considered. "Actually it doesn't matter. But yes, he was having sex with someone. Evan and the priest walked in on them in one of the back church offices. That's why Evan was late to the altar. After seeing that, he didn't want Father Whippet to be a part of our ceremony. He and your dad talked it over before they decided they had to go ahead and just let Father Whippet help conduct the service."

I sat back. Who knew our little town could have so many secrets?

"Is Father Whippet having affairs with Teeni and Roly Poly, too?" Evan said wonderingly. When I replied yes, he demanded to know if I had told anyone. If the news was out, then he didn't want anyone to think that he had been the one to tell. He said that he had been sworn to secrecy by the Catholic priest. Since Evan wasn't a Catholic, I wasn't sure why he thought it mattered, but Evan took promises very seriously. Evan didn't seem convinced when I told him I hadn't said anything. He fell silent and focused on driving through the snowy night. When we arrived at Evan and Anna's house, I gratefully crawled into bed. It had been a long, long day. I fell asleep almost immediately.

Ring, ring. Ring, ring. Why the hell is the phone ringing at 5 a.m. on Christmas morning? I wondered as I rolled over and pulled a pillow over my head. It rang about fifteen times before thankfully it stopped. After a minute, it started ringing again. I sat up. I was closest to the phone since I was in the Jimi Hendrix room. On the tenth ring, I got up and answered it.

"Hello?"

"Is Evan Thompson at home?"

"Who is this, please?" Even at that hour, I was pretty good with my manners.

"This is Bishop Smyton from the Episcopal Diocese. It's urgent that I speak to Mr. Thompson."

I tiptoed to Evan and Anna's room and knocked on the door softly. There was no response. I knocked louder. Evan ripped open the door in his boxers. "Do you know what time it is?"

"Yeah, I do. But Bishop Smyton from the Episcopal Diocese doesn't." I motioned toward the phone. This must have something to do with last night, I figured. Evan grabbed the phone as I went back into my room.

But my curiosity outweighed my need for sleep so I got dressed and padded down the stairs. Evan was hurriedly microwaving tea. He had a parka on over a pair of jeans and his red flannel shirt. I plugged in the Christmas tree lights because it was, after all, Christmas.

"What did the bishop want?"

Evan was trying to drink the hot tea too fast and winced. "He said that there's an emergency down at the church. I have to go there right now."

"Why you?" I yawned.

"He wouldn't say. But he told me to pack a bag."

I noticed the small duffel bag at Evan's feet. Anna shuffled in, wrapping the tie to her robe around her. Evan kissed her good-bye without breaking stride and was out the door. Anna quizzed me but I didn't know any more than Evan had told me.

We decided to go to Mom and Dad's house to be with every-one on Christmas morning, but only Mom was up. She was busy making her famous cheese and egg casserole. I noticed she didn't have a cigarette in her hand and asked about it.

"I've quit and I don't want to talk about it," Mom snapped. As an afterthought she added, "Merry Christmas."

As Anna told Mom about the early morning phone call our own phone rang. Anna answered it.

"Evan called from a gas station to say he forgot his duffel bag. I've got to take it up to St. Peter's for him," Anna said.

"I'll do it," I said. I wanted to know what was going on up at St. Peter's. Anna was all too happy to turn the delivery duty over to me. Who wouldn't be? It was six o'clock in the morning and eight degrees outside. I drove over to their house, picked up the bag, and headed for the church. The front doors were still locked. Weren't they doing a Christmas morning service either? I went around to the side door and went in. Father Whippet's office was locked, too. Finally, I went down to the basement. I could hear raised voices from the big, open room where they sometimes set up folding tables for bingo or lunch receptions after funerals. Entering, I squinted at the fluorescent lights reflecting off the green-and-white-checked linoleum floor.

Roly Poly, Teeni, Shirley, and several other women from the congregation were there, sitting on the steps of the choir's portable risers. Father Whippet was sitting with them. My brother was, oddly, smoking in church. He stood across the room next to a man dressed in red robes who, I figured by process of elimination, was Bishop Smyton. Mr. Roly Poly was there, too, along with several men I recognized as the husbands of the women on the risers. Mrs. Whippet was sitting off by herself.

"There she is! The bitch that told everyone and ruined everything!" Teeni pointed at me. All heads swiveled around and I blinked.

A woman I recognized as Mrs. Mearston patted Teeni's knee. "There's no need for profanity, dear."

I would have responded with a witty remark but the rifle in Teeni's lap put me off. Evan gestured me over with a jerk of his head. I walked slowly over to the group of men, careful not to make any sudden movements.

"I didn't tell anyone anything!" I hissed to Evan. "I swear!"

"That's not what she's mad about anyway." Evan took another puff. Bishop Smyton held out his hand and Evan passed the cigarette over. I expected the bishop to stub it out, but instead he took a very long drag, then handed it back.

"What's going on?" I asked.

Shirley piped up. "I didn't realize so many people would be coming. I'm going to put some coffee on." She stepped from her perch on the risers and went over to where the large metal coffee makers were stored. She lugged one by its black plastic handles over to the sink to fill it. Teeni brandished the rifle. "Shirley, damn it, get back over here. We have to have a show of solidarity."

"This will only take a minute." She measured out the coffee and said in a stage whisper, "After all, the *bishop* is here."

"Is Father Whippet a hostage?" I leaned into Evan.

"Sort of. They are demanding that the bishop let Father Whippet keep having sex with them or Teeni is going to kill him."

I looked nervously over my shoulder at the women. Roly Poly was shifting her large bottom back and forth on the hard step of the riser, obviously trying to get some circulation going. She was also knitting a pink bootie for her new granddaughter. Mrs. Mearston leaned over to compliment her on it.

"How long have they been here?" I asked.

"Since last night. The bishop paid Father Whippet a surprise visit because of an anonymous phone call spilling the beans on Father Whippet." Evan paused here and looked at me meaningfully.

"It wasn't me!" I protested.

Evan didn't look convinced, but he continued. "Bishop Smyton came to the church yesterday evening and found some sort of papers on Father Whippet's desk, like sex rituals or something. He told Father Whippet that he was going to have to resign or go to a church psychiatric hospital in Kansas. He doesn't want to go to the hospital but if he resigns he'll lose his pension. Shirley overheard them and called all the other women, and, well, here we are. Apparently, Father Whippet has been . . . servicing all of these women."

Sex with *all* of them? I thought. What in the world could possibly be the attraction to the good Father? Mr. Roly Poly skittered toward the group of women on his Florsheim-clad feet. "Eunice, let's go home. We've been here all night. The grandkids are probably already up and waiting for us. I don't want to miss them opening the Lincoln Log set we bought them."

Eunice looked torn, but Teeni whispered in her ear. Eunice straightened her spine and said stiffly, "George, I have loved you for forty years, but we haven't had sex in the last ten. I still love you and I don't intend to leave you, but John makes me feel alive."

"But it cost us $39.95, Eunice!"

"You see!" Eunice turned to the other women. "He never listens to me. For forty years I have been trying to have a two-way conversation with this man but he doesn't listen. He just waits for me to stop talking so that he can say what's on *his* mind." The other women nodded their heads. They knew exactly what Mrs. Roly Poly was talking about.

Evan hissed at me, "Go home."

"No way." I wasn't missing this—especially since Teeni was no longer threatening me with the rifle. Right now she was pointing it at Father Whippet.

"Enough fooling around," Teeni said, waving the rifle around again. "Either we all leave here peaceably and go on like before, or the Linen Guild is going to have a helluva time cleaning up this floor."

"Why don't you call the police?" I murmured to the bishop.

"It's a church matter," he said matter-of-factly. "We have pro-cedures for this kind of thing." How often did "this kind of thing" happen? I wondered.

Bishop Smyton approached the risers with his hands up in a placating manner. "Why doesn't everyone just step down and we'll talk this problem over? I know you gals think you have a solution, but it's not going to work."

There was a stunned silence from the group. Shirley said it first. "He called us 'gals.' We *hate* being called 'gals.' It's derogatory."

"Does anyone have any Valium?" Mrs. Whippet asked sud-denly from her faraway chair.

The women began digging in their purses. Shirley looked up. "Five milligrams or ten?"

Mrs. Whippet said, "I think I need ten."

Shirley got a glass of water and brought it with the Valium to Mrs. Whippet.

"Why do you need an overnight bag?" I asked Evan.

"I'm supposed to escort Father Whippet on the plane to Kansas. They even said I had to be handcuffed to him."

"Why you?"

"Because I'm the youngest adult male member of the church. They think I'm the strongest in case Father Whippet tries to over-power me."

"Guess they don't know that you're a pacifist, huh?"

"Guess not."

Teeni's husband burst into the room. "Teeni! Honey! I've been so worried; I didn't know where you were!" His gray hair was completely askew. His slippers and the legs of his pajama bottoms were wet from the snow.

Teeni eyed him, keeping a tight hold on the rifle that she had now swung toward her husband. "Don, I left you a note on the kitchen counter plain as day. You were too busy to notice because you were watching the Alabama-SMU game."

"I fell asleep in the La-Z-Boy. I didn't realize you were missing until this morning!" Don protested.

Teeni still had him in the sights of her gun. Don weighed his options, then joined the men's side. He told Evan in a low voice, "There's no ammunition in that gun."

Bishop Smyton said, "Are you sure?"

"Sure. Last time I used that gun I was hunting. Saw a huge buck in the woods, thirty, maybe forty yards away."

Mr. Roly Poly looked interested. "How many points?"

"That rack must've had sixteen points on it. Like I said, it was a huge buck. Anyhow, I used every shell I had firing at it."

"Did you bag it?" Evan asked.

"Nah." Don shook his head. "Good thing, too. I probably would've had a heart attack dragging it back to the car. But the point is, that gun is empty." The men glanced knowingly over at the women. The jig was up. Bishop Smyton strode over to the risers. "Hand over the gun, Teeni. We know it isn't loaded."

Her response was to fire an ear-splitting blast up through the ceiling. We all covered our ears and cowered. Plaster rained down on us. "Don Patterson! Do you really think I don't know where the sporting goods store is?" Teeni demanded.

"I think she hit the altar," Evan said, peering upward.

Shirley stood up to shake dust from her Christmas sweater.

"Darn it, Teeni! I just got this sweater and look at it." Embroidered on the front of the red sweater was Santa in his sleigh being drawn by reindeer.

"That is really attractive," Mrs. Roly Poly observed. "Is that from Talbot's? I think the dust will come out fine if you use the cold rinse cycle."

Father Whippet finally brought the situation to an end. He rose calmly, took the gun from Teeni, and held it just out of Evan's reach. "I'll go to the treatment center as long as I can return to my church."

Bishop Smyton nodded in assent. Father Whippet nodded his head solemnly back, then stepped forward and handed Evan the gun. The bishop hustled in and quickly put one handcuff on Father Whippet's wrist and the other on Evan's. Evan handed the gun to Don, who promptly opened it and shook out the rest of the shells. "I'll be damned," he said shaking his head.

The women got up and made their way to the door. Mrs. Roly Poly took her husband's arm. "My, that was a long night."

"Eunice, I think we have some things to talk about at home," Mr. Roly Poly said sternly.

Eunice looked delighted. "Yes, I guess we do."

Don climbed the risers to Teeni. He held his hand out to her. "Honey, we'll work this out. We've been through a lot of tough times together. We'll get through this, too." Teeni picked up her head and I could see her eyes were fogging her bifocals. She stood up and flung herself into his arms, sobbing. "There, there," he said while patting her back and guiding her to the door.

Shirley looked around the room. "This place is a mess." She turned to the bishop. "Are you going to do the eight o'clock service? Because if you are, I've got to get this cleaned up, get the candy canes for the little ones, and make more coffee."

Bishop Smyton rubbed his head. "Yes, I'll conduct the service."

Hearing this, Teeni paused on the way out. "Then you should know there's no communion wine left."

Only a few of us were left. I helped Mrs. Whippet up the stairs and out to her car. She stopped with her hand on the open car door. Looking up, where snow was swirling around the finger-pointing statue that was damning us all to hell, she said, "I had to, do you understand? I couldn't let it go on."

I nodded my head and watched her pull away from the curb. The red taillights blinked from behind their blanket of piled-up snow. Wrapping my arms around me for extra warmth, I waited to leave until Evan and Father Whippet were safely in the car headed for the airport. I couldn't wait to get home and regale my family with the details. I pulled up to find a police car parked in front of our house. Marv Carson was just getting out. He waited for me on the snowy walk.

"Is this about the gunshot at the church?" I asked breathlessly.

"What gunshot at the church?" Marv looked puzzled, which was how he usually looked when someone in my family spoke to him.

He followed me to the kitchen. Mom, Dad, Anna, Elizabeth, Sammie, Lucy, and even Ron jumped up. They had obviously been waiting for news. The addition of Marv threw them, but Mom said, "Merry Christmas," and asked him if he wanted coffee.

"No, thank you, Mrs. Thompson." He took off his hat and started somberly, "I'm afraid I have some bad news. Maybe you all should sit back down. I just had a call from the Lansing-area police. It regards a certain person named Chuck Tanner." He looked at Lucy. "As I recall, that's the gentleman you married this past summer?"

Lucy nodded mutely. She was shaking. Mom went to stand over Lucy like a mother hawk.

"They got a call from the Maywood, Illinois, police this morning. Mr. Tanner apparently had a court ticket in his pocket so they traced him back to Lansing. The Lansing police went to your house"—he nodded at Lucy—"and the neighbors told them that Chuck was from Muskegon. So they called us." Marv stopped and we all waited.

"For heaven's sake, Marv, what happened?" Mom demanded.

"Chuck has been murdered, ma'am."

No one spoke. No one moved. We all just stared at the policeman until finally Dad said, "Marv, let's take this out to the living room." They left the kitchen together.

Lucy sat stunned, looking at the door they had just exited. "Illinois? I guess he made it all the way to his ex-girlfriend's house," she finally said simply. Mom took her by the hand and gently led her into the TV room. There she made her lie down on the couch. Mom pulled over a chair and sat next to Lucy stroking her forehead while she cried. Later, when Lucy was sleeping heavily from a shot Dr. Shurgard had given her, Dad told us what Marv had told him.

Chuck had driven to see his ex-girlfriend, Carla. They had apparently spent a few torrid hours in bed. She had neglected however to tell Chuck that she had a boyfriend who, she thought, was safely in jail. Unfortunately for Chuck, the boyfriend's mother had bailed him out. Very early in the morning, the boyfriend entered Carla's trailer and found them in bed together. He grabbed a steak knife from the kitchen and stabbed Chuck six times and Carla once. Chuck put up quite a fight. The boyfriend was in the hospital with a broken nose and five cracked ribs. Carla called 9-1-1 before passing out, but by the time the police and the ambulance arrived, Chuck was dead. Carla was going to be okay.

The thing I remember most clearly about that Christmas is being curled up in a ball against my mother and Lucy on the couch. I asked Mom over and over again why such things happened. Was it our fault that Chuck was dead? Should we have foreseen that such a thing could occur?

"Of course not, honey," she soothed me. "You can only do what you think is right at the time."

Lucy and I weren't sure that we believed her. Lucy thought she had changed Chuck's destiny and this was the result. I understood. As a family we had the best of intentions but it seemed like nothing turned out the way it was supposed to. Last summer, Chuck could have waited for Carla to arrive to save him from being shipped out. Or he could have just gone to Germany. If he had, he might still be alive. But the poor guy had been pulled into all of our lives because Lucy had decided it was her job to help him.

Mom pulled Lucy closer while she patted my head, which lay in her lap. "Chuck had a choice, honey."

I knew Lucy was thinking about the wedding that past summer. Chuck really hadn't had a choice. I didn't recall anyone asking him about what he wanted to do.

"I don't know, Mom. Maybe you've got it all wrong. Maybe we're not supposed to get so involved in each other's lives. I don't know one other family that seems so intertwined with each other," I said into the side of her leg.

Mom didn't say anything for a while. We watched the overcast sky turn into the dark of night. Sammie, I think, was the one to light the Christmas tree but no one had opened any presents. Through our picture window I watched the falling snow blow in sudden circles when a gust of wind hit it.

When Mom finally spoke, I had nearly fallen asleep there on the couch.

"One thing I do know for certain is that no matter how much you kids complain about each other, you all drop everything to be there when someone in the family is in trouble. I think a family is measured by how it shows its love. Some people think that love is like a pie, that the more people you have to serve, the smaller everyone's piece is. But that's not the way it is. The more love you give, the more you create. My parents and your father's parents poured their love into us. We poured that love into you. Elizabeth will pour that love into her baby and so on. Everyone has human weaknesses, and problems, but those will come and go during life. Love goes on nonstop forever."

Evan told us later what had occurred at the Muskegon airport. He and Father Whippet waited an hour for their flight to Chicago, connecting to Kansas. Father Whippet announced he had to pee. Well, as Evan put it, there was no way his hand was going to be attached to Father Whippet's hand during this particular act. So Evan unlocked the handcuffs with the key thoughtfully provided by Bishop Smyton and went outside to have a smoke. He stood watching the crows circle the snow-covered mown corn stalks through the chain-link fence.

It was a heavy gray sky, certain to dump more snow before the day's end. The last he saw of Father Whippet was him leaping across those fields, his black cloak flapping against the white snow, toward the trees on the other side. Evan smoked and watched the good Father gain on the woods. Then he stubbed out the butt with his boot and turned for home.

Thirty-seven

June 2006

*N*ear the end of my marriage to Walker I started having the dreams. Sometimes I was driving down empty L.A. freeways at night, so fast that I could feel the wind in my hair and see only blackness that the headlights couldn't pierce. I felt free and light. Then fear and doubt began to grip me. I knew the brakes weren't working so I could not take one of the exits. I visualized the car flipping over and over in midair. I would wake up in the soup of my own sweat. Walker would grumble and move away from my thrashings.

I had the same dream night after night. I finally decided it was a sign from the heavens above that I had to get my act together with the marriage. The next day I came home from work early to make dinner for Walker. It was a futile gesture, and he recognized it when he arrived. I hadn't made—or been home for—a dinner in more than a year. Walker ignored me while he hugged and kissed the dog lavishly. Then they played outside for nearly an hour while dinner got cold on the table. We hadn't had sex more than ten times in eight years. We hadn't really spoken in months. We had been through marriage counseling, during which the therapist made charts for us to track how often we hugged each other weekly. We got points off if we hadn't hugged three times. We were about forty points in the hole at that point.

I sat at the kitchen table and watched Walker speak lovingly to his dog and smooch his face. It was Walker's fault that he thought he could change me into his personal vision of a good wife. It was my fault that I worked long hours to avoid being home. But in the end, it wasn't Walker's fault or mine. It just wasn't working. I packed a bag the next morning and left a note. I never went back.

Now it was Aidan who had disappeared. I had called him over and over again: at home and on his cell phone. His office told me that Aidan had taken a leave of absence. I asked where he had gone only to be told that Aidan did not want to be disturbed. "By me?" I heard myself beseeching his assistant.

"I'm sorry, Jeannie. He left very strict instructions. He doesn't want to be disturbed by *anyone*." Then his assistant lowered her voice. "Totally on the QT? He's in Australia with the Veronica Robison film."

"So he can't call in or out or something from Australia?" I asked hopefully.

Probably feeling she had said too much, she shut me down with a polite, "If I hear from him, I'll tell him you called."

"But wait!" I knew I was overstepping my bounds with Aidan's poor assistant, but I couldn't help it. "Can I talk to Montana, then?"

"She's in Australia, too."

After I hung up, I put my head down and, for the first time ever, cried at my desk.

Thirty-eight

June 2006

I hadn't heard from Aidan in over a month. *TechnoCat* would open in two weeks. The new trailer had been an unmitigated disaster. The first day after my return from Prague, Rachael called me into her office and shut the door. "Can you explain yourself?" she said coldly. She threw a copy of *Star* magazine at me. I stared at the open page. It was a photo of me ripping Stripe's bandage off his bloody stitches. Stripe was wincing and I was glowering. The headline read, OUCH! IS *TECHNOCAT* A RIP-OFF? The smaller type read, STUDIO PANIC! OXFORD PICTURES ADVERTISING EXECUTIVE LOSES IT WITH *TECHNOCAT* DIRECTOR.

"I should fire you on the spot," Rachael raged while I was squished like a small child into her overpadded couch. "The hotel room fire at the Four Seasons should have been enough to can you . . . but this! This!" she sputtered, gesturing at the offending magazine. "If you hadn't opened *Heaven Is in the Wind* and *Sheer Panic* to such good numbers, you would be out."

I thought, Ten years of opening all the other impossible movies and working one-hundred-hour weeks doesn't count? But I didn't say anything.

"I don't care what you have to do but you are going to open this damn movie," Rachael continued. Then, having delivered the slap, she softened. "I know you have it in you. You have saved so many movies it's hard to remember them all."

I had found myself back out in the hallway lined with classic movie posters, Rachael's message ringing in my head loud and clear: open this movie or else.

I sagged against the wall trying to collect my thoughts. I straightened up fast when someone passed by, then sagged again when they were out of sight. You never wanted anyone to think you were in trouble at a studio. Much later it dawned on me to wonder, Just who had taken that photo of me on set? And then who had managed to feed it to the magazines? I figured out the answer to the first question. Undoubtedly the photo had been taken by the only photographer around, Action Jackson. I called him to confirm my thinking.

"Yep, that was mine," Action said cheerfully. "Helluva shot, don't you think?"

"You sold it to the tabloids!" I protested.

"What do you think I do for a living when I'm not working on a film?"

"You can't sell a photo to the tabloids!" I protested. "You were hired by the studio. Those pictures belong to the studio!"

"You're right. But this turned out to be kind of an unusual situation, you might say." He was still cheerful. "Tabloids wouldn't have bought it if it was just you in the photo though. You aren't worth five bucks to them. But for some reason they want anything to do with Stripe."

It sounded almost reasonable when you thought about it from his point of view. Business was business.

Even though I was preoccupied with worrying about Aidan, I tried to think of a new angle to open *TechnoCat*. I was working until 2 or 3 a.m. every morning. When I did get home, I couldn't sleep. I was waiting for a phone call from Aidan. Every time the phone rang my heart would leap and then fall when it wasn't him.

Katsu in the meantime had gone mysteriously quiet. He wasn't trying to snake my place at the conference table anymore and had mostly stayed out of my way. After the hideous photo in *Star* of me ripping off Stripe's bandage, a sudden barrage of articles began appearing in magazines about Stripe. One said he was an alcoholic and an adulterer. Another interviewed Esperanza, who trashed the director from one end to the other, adding the announcement that he was a terrible lover. A TV show implied that his production company was heavily in debt to a suspicious foreign interest and that Stripe had disappeared.

I knew Stripe hadn't disappeared because he called me daily to bitch about the TV spots we were cutting for *TechnoCat*. Nothing, and I mean nothing, satisfied him. He became so unreasonable that I finally had to go to Rachael to discuss the matter.

"He's under some stress," Rachael said calmly. "Just try and work around him." How was I supposed to do that when I had to consult with him on every matter concerning his film? I wondered.

"Rachael"—I hesitated because I was getting into unknown territory—"what's with all this negative publicity on Stripe? It's going to hurt the movie opening."

"As they say in the movie biz, Jeannie, any publicity is good publicity." She was, at that very moment, flipping through a tabloid on her desk.

"But why is it happening?" I thought I knew the answer but figured I'd ask anyway.

"I guess someone wants to put him in his place." I thought I almost saw her smile. "Someone who can afford a really good publicist."

On the way out of her office I was reminded that one major film studio had actually fired a top-level executive while she was enduring fifteen hours of labor. They sent a note into the delivery room while her legs were in the stirrups. Now, they could have easily fired her a week before or a week after the birth. But they made sure to kick her when she was at her most vulnerable.

The Mafia could learn something from studio tactics.

None of which helped me with my current problems. In the next week, I lost nine pounds, which normally would have delighted me. But I couldn't eat without hearing from Aidan. Caitlin brought me soup, as if I had the flu. I tried to eat it because she had made an effort to go get it for me, but when she left my office I dumped it into the garbage.

One morning, I was staring out of my office window. There were two doves that nuzzled each other nearly every morning in a tree covered with thorns. Why in the world would they pick that damn tree to nest in? I wondered. It looked really uncomfortable, and there were other trees available. I went over to the window to watch them more closely. It wasn't a perfect situation but they were definitely making the best they could of it.

Caitlin came into my office. "Jeannie, you've got Vincent on the line. He sounds worried."

"Can I call him back?" I was still gazing out the window.

Caitlin stared at me. "No, Jeannie. You don't refuse a call from the chairman of the studio unless you have been in a car accident and they are loading you into an ambulance." She picked up the headset and jammed it on my head. "And maybe not even then." With that, Caitlin hit the line and put him through.

"Jeannie, we have a problem," Vincent began. "The early reviews of *TechnoCat* are lousy. We need to do something really ingenious."

"I know."

There was a pause. Vincent had never called me directly before. Clearly this was Very Important and I was not responding appropriately. I knew I should have been enthusiastically telling Vincent how we were going to come up with something so amazing that no filmgoer in his right mind could resist it.

"Jeannie, are you listening?" Vincent sounded mildly pissed off.

"Yeah." I was watching the two doves carefully making their way through the thorny tree. "Vincent?"

"You have an idea?" He sounded relieved.

"No, Vincent. I'm going home."

"Are you not feeling well? I'll have a limo take you right home and have some chicken soup from Gottfried's delivered. We need you healthy."

"No, I'm going home to Michigan."

"When?" he asked coldly.

"Right now."

"You can't! You have to solve this *TechnoCat* problem. And Rachael told me you're supposed to make a presentation to Taco Bell tomorrow. They're worried about their cross-promotion with this film! And I really talked you up to a director I'm trying to get over here. He's the next Spielberg! You're supposed to meet him on Friday!"

"It can wait. Or have somebody else do it. Who would do it if I dropped dead? You'd have to find somebody then."

"I can't believe you would be this irresponsible. I'm going to take this up with Rachael immediately."

"Vincent," I said, "I've worked eighty- and ninety- and one-hundred-hour weeks for years. I have never let this studio down. I have been here through Christmases and New Years, even earthquakes. I have gone three days at a time without having time to shower. And right now *I'm going home!*" I disconnected the line and threw my headset across the room. Caitlin, who was still standing next to me, asked in a small voice, "What do you want me to do?"

"Get me a reservation on any plane that'll get me to Muskegon." I grabbed my purse and stormed out the door. I got into my car and headed straight for LAX. By the time I got there, Caitlin had gotten me on the one o'clock United flight to Chicago, then on to Grand Rapids. A rental car would be waiting there for me for the hour drive home to Muskegon. It wasn't a great car, but it was the only one she could get. Caitlin then asked me if I was coming back.

"I don't know, Caitlin," I said and hung up with her. Then I dialed the familiar number. I nearly cried when her voice answered. "Mom? I'm on my way home."

Thirty-nine

June 2006

When I landed in Grand Rapids and picked up my rental car, I couldn't get the car door to open. Tired and wrung out, I trudged back to the counter, where a teenage boy offered to come out and see what was wrong. He took the key from my hand and inserted it into the door handle—*et voilà*. I looked at the keys when he handed them back to me. There was no remote unlock on the key ring that I had been futilely pressing. Had I forgotten how to unlock a car door manually? I heard myself from twenty years ago saying, "Someone has been in L.A. too long."

"*Well, she was an American girl, raised on promises . . .*" I sang along with Tom Petty as I drove west on Interstate 96. "*She couldn't help thinkin' that there was a little more to life . . . somewhere else . . .*" Reassuringly, the songs on the radio hadn't changed. The local stations could still be counted on for Bob Seger, Led Zeppelin, and Rush. I rolled down the windows and the moist green smell of trees and weeds and wildflowers rushed at me. I would tell Mom, tonight anyway, that my tear-streaked face was from the dust in my contact lenses.

I peered down the road, which was lit only by my headlights. I couldn't remember the last time I had been on a highway where my car was literally the only one on the road. The speed limit was a civilized seventy miles per hour. I inched the car up to eighty-five, figuring I was getting even for all that time spent doing five miles per hour on L.A. freeways. At 12:40 in the morning, I had crossed the Causeway, turned at the Four Corners, driven down Ruddiman, and turned right onto Fourth Street. I parked in the driveway, then walked around the side of the garage and up the walkway to where the porch light was burning. I bumped the door sharply with my hip and it opened. Ake 3 thumped his tail on the floor, without bothering to bark in case I was a burglar. Mom and Dad got up from their posts at the kitchen table, and I was enfolded in hugs.

We did the traditional "Are you hungry? I made sloppy joes" ritual from Mom, to which I always replied, "No, I'm not hungry," and then she always set them on a plate anyway, and I always ate them.

Dad gave me a hug, then went on to bed. That left me alone with eagle-eyed Mom. I expected her to sit down at the kitchen counter, pat the stool next to her, and say, "Let's shake this thing out." My eyes started watering just at the thought of somebody being *nice* to me. Instead, she held me at arm's length and re-garded me closely.

"So how do I look?" I asked miserably.

"You look beautiful," Mom said soothingly.

"Nice lie," I managed to laugh through my sniffles. "How do I look really?"

"Awful," she pronounced. "You're too skinny, you have big bags under your eyes, your hair is stringy, and you need to have your roots touched up."

I grinned at her through my tears. "I love you, too, Mom." She smiled back at me and touched her forehead to mine. "Welcome home, sunshine."

Forty

June 2006

When I woke up I could tell by the angle of the sun filtering through the trees that it was early evening. I had slept for seventeen hours. I stretched in bed, taking in the chocolate éclair wallpaper and Lucy's cheerleading photos and pom poms hanging over the mirror. I didn't want to get up. It was so real here. I hadn't heard my cell phone ring once. Finally, I threw back the sheets and looked through Lucy's closet, where I found a pair of my jeans from eleventh grade. I held them up to me in front of the mirror. Then I tried to wiggle into them, but I couldn't get them past my thighs. I found a pair of Dad's sweats and rolled them over at the top, then swiped one of his white Hanes T-shirts. I wandered downstairs and out through the sliding doors to the backyard. Nobody seemed to be around. I walked across the grass and found Dad sitting in the gazebo by Bear Lake. I went down the steps and flopped next to him.

He gave me a squeeze. "Hi, honey. Feeling better?"

"Sort of. Yes. No. Not really."

He gazed steadily out at the lake. "I suppose that's progress." We both watched a blue heron stroll through the shallow water. The heron paused, head held high, and then darted his beak into the water, but he didn't come up with anything food-worthy. I stretched and yawned. "I can't believe how long I slept."

"You must have needed it. But what are all of those infernal bells and whistles you had going off in your backpack? I rooted around in there for ten minutes and turned off all the gadgetry."

I sighed, blowing my bangs out of my eyes. "When did you turn them off?"

"At ten o'clock this morning. You had had nineteen calls and it looked like thirty-eight new emails."

Out of habit, I jumped up and started back up the stairs. Dad called after me, "Honey, think about why you came home. That stuff can wait." I looked over my shoulder. For all of the years I felt nothing could take priority over my work, I suddenly knew why I had come home, and I knew Dad was right. It could wait. I sat back down with him and we watched the heron take a slow stride and flap its long wings until it soared above the trees. "I love him, Dad." I pulled my knees up into my chin. He put his arm around my shoulders and squeezed.

"What are you going to do about it?"

"I don't know. He won't take my calls." I pushed my chin deeper into my knees. The sun was tucking itself behind the trees across the lake. A bluegill jumped. I studied the ripples and calculated it was a whopping six inches long. I closed my eyes and felt the air on my face. "Perfect temperature. The Caddis Hatch must be in full swing. Fly-fisherman heaven right now, huh?"

Dad just nodded. I found all the sameness reassuring. "The grass looks good."

"Yeah, I find hand-watering to be kind of relaxing. But Meijer's has a new sprinkler system I'm going to check out tomorrow."

"Will you get me some cream horns when you're out there?" I realized then how hungry I was.

"Sure." We sat outside until it got dark and the mosquitoes discovered us. When we went back into the house, Mom had dinner ready. I almost fell asleep at the table and I crawled back into bed as soon as I could. Maybe I could sleep until it all got better. Except I couldn't sleep. I tossed and turned for a couple of hours, then went downstairs, stood at the counter, and ate a carton of butter pecan ice cream with frost growing on it and a box of stale Triscuits. Jesus, did my parents not go grocery shopping anymore? I tilted the box up to catch the last couple of salty crumbs in my mouth. I watched an infomercial for better abs while Ake 3 whined at me. I was disturbing his sleep schedule. He was probably going to pack his doggie bags and check in to the nearest motel. "At least you're not sleeping under the ironing board," I informed him. "Consider yourself lucky."

I went back to bed until 8 a.m., when I heard Mom and Dad puttering around. I came down again and dropped into a kitchen chair. Mom handed me coffee and patted my unbrushed, unwashed hair. Dad flipped on the TV and sat down next to me as we listened to the opening strains of *The Michigan Bass and Buck Show*. My eyes were gummed together because I hadn't bothered taking out my contacts in more than forty-eight hours. I rubbed them, then tuned in to the show. It was Evan's backyard.

"Why are they shooting at Evan's house?" I asked.

"Shhh," Mom said without taking her eyes from the screen. The camera focused on the back door of Evan's farmhouse as he emerged.

"He looks pretty good." My eyebrows went up. "When did he start shaving for the show?"

"Shhh." Mom waved me off again.

"Morning, Joe." Evan nodded at the cameraman. The picture of Evan went up and down as the camera nodded back. "We're doing something a little different today," Evan said as he walked down the broad sweep of lawn to the edge of the lake. "We're cooking outside over a campfire." He stopped next to his fire pit, which was rimmed with rocks and had a pretty good flame going. "This is about how to cook with unregulated heat. It might be too hot or it might be too cold. It's all about balance." He motioned with his hand and Evan's youngest child, six-year-old Joy, ran into the picture and shyly hugged his leg. Evan squatted down and handed her a stick. "Sweetheart, you put the marshmallows on this pointy end and start roasting. I'll get the graham crackers and Hershey bars." The camera followed Evan to a tree, where he picked up his mug of tea off the ground, sipped it, and then grabbed a paper bag.

"He's making s'mores?" I turned to Mom and Dad. "Everyone knows how to make s'mores." Mom shushed me again and we continued watching. The camera went back to Joy, who had set her marshmallow on fire. She blew on it frantically but it was too late. The marshmallow was charred black. Joy stared at it and burst into tears. Evan patted her head and called beyond the camera, "Hey, Anna, we got a geyser here."

Anna's voice came from off camera, "Joy, come here, honey. We'll fix the marshmallow." Joy, still bawling, ran offscreen. Evan smiled after her, then turned his attention back to the camera. Then a phone rang. Evan put an earpiece in his ear and punched a button on the phone on his belt.

"Good morning, caller. What's up?" Evan said as he stoked the fire.

"Wow, that's pretty tech." I sat back in my chair. "He finally got rid of that rotary phone."

"No offense, Evan, but every damn person knows how to make s'mores," the caller griped.

"Tommy Noyce, that you?" Evan looked delighted.

"Yep."

"How'd the perch fishing go last night?"

"Got a mess of 'em off the channel wall. I was hoping you were going to talk about lobster diavolo today."

"I'm illustrating a point," Evan said. "So just sit tight." He held up two graham crackers. "You've got two crackers. Each one is kind of fragile, so you have to have something to strengthen them and hold them together." He motioned off-camera. "I'm going to need another assistant for this." A man in jeans and a T-shirt walked into the frame and shook hands with Evan. I sat up straight as Evan said, "Everyone, this is—"

"Aidan!" I said in unison with Evan's TV voice. Mom and Dad smiled at me. I turned on them accusingly. "How long has Aidan been here?"

"Honey"—Mom laughed—"listen to the show."

I couldn't stay in my seat. I bounced around the kitchen but kept my eyes glued to the set. Evan handed Aidan two more marshmallows. He deftly impaled them and then twirled them above the fire. Aidan smiled and waved at the camera, clearly at home. His faded T-shirt said, BLT BREW CREW. "Pretty good technique there, Aidan," Evan observed. He turned to the camera again. "See, if you let things get too hot, everything goes up in smoke, but if you aren't close enough to the fire, everything goes cold." He held up the graham crackers again. "In order to stick together, you gotta be all warm and gooey. Add some sweetness"—he stuck a Hershey bar on top of the marshmallows Aidan had deposited on the crackers—"and it's the perfect balance."

I flew out the back door in Dad's sweats and T-shirt, unbrushed hair and teeth, and no shoes. Halfway across the lawn I turned around and flew back in. "Keys! Keys!" Dad underhanded me the rental car keys. I snagged them and ran back outside in one motion. The whole way over to Evan's house I tried to rub the mascara out from underneath my eyes while keeping the pedal to the metal. I roared past the Blit and turned up Bear Lake Road. It was then I passed the cop car, which pulled out and turned on its sirens. I angled the rearview mirror to see it better. Shit! If there was ever a time not to be pulled over, this would be it. That cop was just going to have to understand. I kept my foot pressed firmly on the gas pedal. I screamed up to Evan's house and almost forgot to put the car in park as I jumped out, leaving the car door swinging. I bolted around the corner of the house and covered the lawn faster than I thought possible to Evan, Aidan, and Joe the cameraman. I saw Aidan smiling at me as I got closer. I leapt into his arms, wrapped my legs around his waist, and hugged him tight. He swayed back and forth with me, then pulled away to look at my face. "Jeannie, will you marry me?"

"Yes!" I shrieked like I was at a Beatles concert.

We kissed long and hard. Smiling into my eyes, Aidan said, "Then the first thing I'd like to say as your future spouse is that you have dog breath."

Evan, Anna, and Joe were clapping and smiling. Joe wiped away a tear. When Aidan finally put me down I saw that Elizabeth and her two kids, Sammie, her husband, son, and daughter, and Lucy, her husband of eighteen years, and her daughter were all there, too, and they were all laughing and crying. They had all come for me. Even when they were mad at me they had still come.

Aidan's various parents, stepparents, and half-siblings streamed out of Evan's back door, beaming at us. Mom and Dad arrived just then, along with Marv Carson. He sighed wearily as he surveyed the whole scene. Then he came up to me. "Hi, Jeannie, welcome home. You're under arrest for evading a law enforcement officer." He took handcuffs off his belt. "Turn around."

"You've got to be kidding me. Okay, so I was doing forty in a twenty-five. I'm sorry."

"Rules are rules, Jeannie."

I turned around for Marv to cuff me. Aidan stepped up to the cop. "Marv? Can I call you Marv?"

"I prefer Officer Carson," Marv said stiffly. Then he relented. "But okay, Marv."

"See that white tent over there?" Aidan squinted over to the far side of the lawn. "There's a surprise wedding planned for Jeannie and me right now."

In my cuffs I turned and yelled over my shoulder, "Mom! Again?"

"Not me this time, Jeannie. This is all Aidan's doing," she said.

"Not going to happen. I'm running her in right now," Marv stated firmly.

Then the phone rang. Evan hit SPEAKER so we could all hear. "Yes, caller, you're on the air."

"Marv, damn it, you're just going to have to let this one go. Didn't you see how happy Jeannie was when she jumped up in that young man's arms?"

Marv turned accusingly to Evan. "We've been on the air this whole time?" Evan smiled and punched in the next caller.

"Marv Carson, I'll pull my donation to the policeman's fund if you arrest Jeannie. Why, first she gets divorced, and now you're trying to ruin the rest of her life? I mean, take a look at her. This might be her last chance."

I cringed at that. Evan looked over at Marv. "I have six calls holding. What are you going to do?"

Marv unlocked the cuffs. "Okay. But only if I get to stay for the wedding."

I turned to Aidan. "You planned all this? Your disappearance, the surprise wedding, everything?"

"I'm not sure how much planning was really involved. I just kind of winged it. After I finished up in Australia I flew here. I've been in good ol' North Muskegon for weeks now. It's about time you showed up."

"But"—I hesitated—"weren't you there in Australia with Montana?"

He squinted his eyes at me. "She's my business partner. That's all. You know I love you, Jeannie. We all love you. I mean, look around." He gestured to both of our entire families, who were trying to politely pretend they weren't interested in what we were saying.

The knot that had gripped my stomach for the past several weeks began to unclench. I smiled up at him. "But how did you get here? I mean, how did this all happen?"

"I took matters into my own hands and called each and every person in your entire family to ask for advice. Your parents said we needed to meet so they could look me over, so I flew here."

"How did you find everybody?"

"Ever heard of Google?" Aidan grinned down at me and squished me closer.

"As soon as your mom got the call from you saying you were coming home, your entire family and my entire family got on planes and came, too."

"And the wedding is . . . now?" I looked down at my sweatpants and T-shirt in dismay. Elizabeth, Sammie, and Lucy grabbed me and pulled me toward the house.

Aidan yelled after us, "Yeah, right now! Elizabeth, you've got the schedule, right?"

"Right!"

My sisters marched me upstairs to Evan and Anna's bathroom. Along the way I tried to apologize to them but they waved me off. "Time for that later, Jeannie. We have more important things to do right now," Sammie said cheerfully.

The water was already running and I hopped in. Elizabeth rapped out instructions. "Five minutes, shower. Five minutes, hair. Five minutes, makeup. Five minutes, dress." Ah sweet Jesus, I thought. What the heck was the hurry on my wedding day? Which is what I said.

"Because we go back on the air in twenty-three minutes," Elizabeth barked. "Now, scrub!"

"I'm getting married on *The Michigan Bass and Buck Show*?" I asked as Lucy pulled me out of the shower. Sammie threw a towel over my head and started drying. As soon as she was done, Lucy grabbed a brush and yanked at my wet hair. Sammie had her makeup out and was in front of me doing her "look up, look down, now look up again" routine. Standing behind me, Lucy blow-dried my hair, then turned me over to Elizabeth, who deftly swept it up into a French twist. Lucy ran out of the bathroom and returned with a white dress.

"Is that Anna's old wedding dress?" I joked.

"No, Aidan chose it." Lucy looked puzzled. "Why?"

I realized that she was far beyond where she had been twenty years before. So were we all. I smiled. "No reason."

"Suck your cheeks in," Sammie commanded. I did and she applied blush.

"Who's the minister?" I asked in between pummelings.

"It's Evan." Elizabeth motioned for me to step into the dress.

"He got ordained just for this wedding. He found an ad in the back of *Rolling Stone*. He and Aidan have been getting along like a house on fire, by the way."

"Speaking of which"—Sammie dusted me with powder—"is Jack Williams still mad at them for shooting bottle rockets and setting his boathouse on fire?"

"What?!" I turned to Sammie.

"Eh, Jack had insurance. Evan and Aidan paid the deductible."

Elizabeth had a stopwatch going. "We have three minutes to get down to the lawn." With one minute left, we all stopped and stared into the mirror. I was beautiful. The silk dress had tiny spaghetti straps and was devoid of any frills. It was snug to the waist and then fell open to a beautiful wide skirt. A simple headpiece held a short veil that accented the French twist. My wide blue eyes stared back at me and I realized that for the first time in a very long time they looked happy.

"Twenty seconds, and ten, nine, eight . . ." Elizabeth counted down to "on air." I stood on the back porch facing Bear Lake. Magically, a white carpet of rose petals had appeared. They led all the way down the lawn to the open tent. Mom was now in a pink mother-of-the-bride dress and Dad was in his tux. I could see Aidan and Evan standing at the end of the rose-petal carpet. Dad stayed with me while the rest of my family trooped down to join them and Aidan's family. The music from *The Michigan Bass and Buck Show* started up and I whispered to Dad, "Is this my wedding march music?"

"Don't be silly. That wouldn't be appropriate." He gave me a wry smile. We turned our attention to Evan.

"Welcome back to *The Michigan Bass and Buck Show*," Evan said. "For the first time in history, we are hosting a wedding. This is the groom, Aidan." The camera zoomed in on Aidan who smiled and waved. "And that's the bride, Jeannie." Joe, the cameraman, turned around to do a slow zoom in on me. "Now that we're all introduced, let's begin this solemn ceremony."

Evan nodded to Joy, who hit PLAY on a boom box. As I listened to the opening strains, I burst out laughing. It was ABBA's "Take a Chance on Me." They sang, *"Honey, I'm still free, take a chance on me . . ."*

Dad squeezed my hand. "Now *that's* appropriate." I practically danced down the "aisle." Evan performed the ceremony and ended with, "By the powers vested in me by *Rolling Stone* and *The Michigan Bass and Buck Show*, I now pronounce you husband and wife."

Aidan picked me up off my feet and swung me around while we kissed. Everyone clapped, and I saw Marv wipe a tear from his cheek. But when our families stopped cheering we heard cheers and hollers echoing from across the lake and across the town.

As people began trooping in for an impromptu reception, we learned that the Bear Lake Tavern breakfast crowd had been held in rapt attention by my near arrest and through the entire wedding. Tommy even popped open champagne for his customers. June at the June Wedding had watched the wedding ceremony while three brides-to-be clutched each other and cried at how perfect it was. Alan down at Alan's Beauty Shoppe had brought all business to a halt so everyone could watch. He took time out from the show only once, when he realized he was over-perming someone and had nearly burned off her hair.

Soon, it seemed like the entire town was descending on Evan's backyard. People danced and laughed and ate the fried perch sandwiches that Tommy Noyce brought from the Blit. Tom the handyman showed up with a keg of Stroh's beer. Evan dragged his stereo speakers out on the porch and Mom and Dad danced to "String of Pearls," then "Chattanooga Choo-Choo." Charlotte and Sam danced next to them, while Jim and Janet held hands and beamed at the whole scene. Aidan's half-brother and -sister and my various nieces and nephews chased each other across the lawn, and my brother, sisters, sister-in-law, brothers-in-law, and husband were companionably laughing and talking together. I watched them from where I leaned against the massive willow tree my sisters and I had planted twenty years earlier. We had all been together during the easy times and the not-so-easy times, and it was comforting to know that now, with Aidan at my side, it would all go on nonstop forever.

Forty-one

*A*idan and I honeymooned in North Muskegon. We stayed at my brother's house because my parents' house was filled to capacity with Aidan's assortment of parents, half-siblings, and some of my older nieces and nephews.

My sisters, their husbands, and more kids all crammed into the rooms left at Evan and Anna's. I felt kind of sorry that my youngest nephew had to sleep on the floor in the living room, until he told me he preferred it. He said he could actually be alone for a minute or two there. Aidan and I did, in honor of our nuptials, get the one room with its own bathroom. Every day the huge gang of us piled into cars and hit the beach at Lake Michigan or went blueberry picking on Mrs. Blaine's farm or took the little Butterfly sailboat for a spin on Bear Lake.

The car radio let me know that *TechnoCat* opened at the box office with not-so-stellar numbers and in second place to *Station Break* over the Fourth of July weekend. But neither Aidan nor I checked a text message, voice mail, or email. Electronic devices were firmly off-limits, we had decided. We were sitting at the kitchen table eating ice cream one evening when my parents' phone rang. It was Rachael, who had finally managed to track me down. It didn't sound like she was pleased that my six-year-old niece had answered the phone.

"Where are you?" she demanded once I wrestled the phone away from Joy and sat back at the table.

I licked my spoon before replying, "In Michigan."

"When are you coming back?"

With a glance at Aidan I replied, "I'm not sure if I am coming back." Her tone changed so fast I wondered if a different person had gotten on the line. She began pleading with me.

"You have to come back. Katsu is a disaster. He alienated Fiona Underwood and she took her next project to Paramount. Vincent can't stand him and rejects anything that he presents. Jeannie, we need you. What can we do to get you back here?" Rachael cried. I was so taken aback I forgot to be pleased that she was begging.

"I . . . can I call you back, Rachael?"

"You'll think about it?"

"Yes, I'll think about it." Carefully I put the phone back on the cradle. I filled Aidan in on the call and we decided it might work with some conditions attached. Then I called Rachael back. A week later Aidan and I headed back to Los Angeles. I would be returning to work at Oxford Pictures. During my conversation with Rachael I put in boundaries for the first time. I asked that my workload be reduced to just eight movies a year. We decided that Caitlin was more than ready to move up and handle a couple of movies on her own. We also agreed that there would be no phone calls after 7 p.m. or on weekends unless it was really, truly an emergency. I didn't ask about Katsu. But his office was cleared out when I got back. He had been moved over to a different division of Oxford.

I sold my house and moved into Aidan's house and we went on much as we had before. Except now we could spend evenings and weekends mostly uninterrupted. We still cooked and gardened but now we were working together on an exciting new project—one that was due in about nine months.

Peter Tanger

Dana Precious

DANA PRECIOUS grew up in North Muskegon, Michigan, and lives in Los Angeles with her husband and son.